CJ Washburn Mysteries

Deserving of Death (Book 1)

Sailing into Death (Book 2)

Angel of Death (Book 3)

Never Surrender to Death (Book 4)

Parker DuPont Mysteries

Driven by Death (Book 1)

Remembering Death (Book 2)

Secrets in Death (Book 3)

Lost in Death (Book 4)

Time-Travel

Before Anne After (Book 1)

Time Will Tell (Book 2)

Sabre-Toothed Cat Suspense

Smilodon (Book 1)

Sabre City (Book 2)

The Last Sabre (Book 3)

Other Suspense

Saving Ebony

Lost & Forgotten

Angels in the Mist

Novella

Hot Roast Beef with Mustard

Short Story Anthology

No Swimming

Connect with James Paddock Online

www.JamesPaddockNovels.com

This is a work of fiction. Names, characters, places and incidents either are the product of the author's imagination or are used fictitiously, and any resemblance to any actual persons, living or dead, events, or locals is entirely coincidental.

DESERVING OF DEATH

Cover art by James Paddock

Printed in the United States of America.

CreateSpace Independent Publishing Platform
ISBN: 978-1-4928-2008-6 (Soft cover)

Amazon Kindle
ASIN: B00EXBQO02 (ebook)

Recommendation

Deserving of Death is book 1 in the CJ Washburn, PI series. We recommend books 2 and 3 to continue the story of CJ and Stella.

Sailing into Death - Alexandria's father walked out of her and her mother's lives five years ago. Now Alexandria has been murdered. Her killer is dead; case closed. Her father deserves to be told, but first, he must be found. Leave no stone unturned, CJ is told. Find him no matter what. From Tucson, Arizona to Fishers, Indiana to St. Petersburg, Florida, he follows the leads only to find himself handcuffed to a table in a St. Petersburg Police Department interview room in front of Detective Parker DuPont. The charge: Murder. In fly Special Agent Joshua Washburn, CJ's son, and Stella Summers, his fiancé and partner. With the FBI, HLS, Interpol and who knows what else involved, can CJ and Stella figure out what it all has to do with Alexandria's father being born in the middle of the Battle of the Bogside in Derry, Northern Ireland in 1969? And what's the United Irish Republican Army doing in Florida?

Angel of Death - CJ and Stella are to be married in eight days. Yes, finally, they are doing the deed. They've been declining new, involved cases (Stella is now a licensed P.I.) in preparation for the honeymoon to New Zealand, but the call from Parker DuPont in St. Petersburg, Florida has them on a private jet and then settled into a luxury stateroom aboard the French super yacht, *Angel of Paradise*. They have their own steward who calls them monsieur and mademoiselle. Their client, and yacht owner, billionaire Édouard Philippe Monnier, is paying three times the going rate to prove that his son, one of two 23 year-old identical twins, did not commit suicide, as the medical examiner has determined.

Did Jesper Monnier die at his own hand or was it the young man who the twins hustled on the pool table in Atlantic City, or a jealous boyfriend, or a disgruntled employee of the huge superyacht? Or was it someone else altogether?

And who is FBI Special Agent Jessie Milwood, who CJ's son is bringing to the wedding? He's never said anything about a girlfriend.

Thank you to all my loyal readers,

most especially
Penny

For Chat
Happy Reading

DESERVING OF DEATH

A CJ Washburn Mystery

James Paddock

Chapter 1

It was the best of days; it was the worst of nights. The words kept replaying in CJ's head, though different from whatever novel inspired them; what novel and how they were different he couldn't remember and he wished they'd get out of his head. There certainly had been some good days since hiring Stella Summers and in the last few years there had been some great nights. But at this particular time, this particular night, things weren't so great. He was in his office, lights dimmed, alone with Jack D., wondering how he had gotten himself so worked up. Where the hell was Stella anyway? Was she dead like the other victims, stuffed in a dumpster as though nothing more than last week's hot chili tacos? Or did she head up into the mountains, Summerhaven or Madera Canyon, like she was always talking about, to clear her head and realign her psyche? What the hell does realigning ones psyche mean anyway?

He took a sip of the amber liquid.

If she simply took off, that was okay. Well, maybe not okay because....

He sipped again.

Of course it wasn't okay. If she needed to clear her head, why wouldn't she want to clear it with him? He'd be glad to go into the mountains with her. She did say she wanted them to spend more quality time together. She even gave him her key. What the hell did that mean and what is quality time to a woman anyway? Does she even know? Does any woman know?

It's all about feelings, or so he's been told by every woman he has ever been with, including his first and only wife after whom he'd sworn off marriage seven years back. How the hell does a man get a hold of feelings? It's not something he can wrap his hands around.

He looked at the glass, held it in the air, swirled the liquid, emptied it with one gulp and licked his lips.

A man can deal with something he can touch, feel the grain, the weight, the strength... the taste. How can a man touch a feeling? He held the glass in the air again, stared through it and then at it.

It's like the air in this glass, he thought. I'm holding it, but am I really? I'm holding the glass but the air inside is invisible. It could be pure oxygen or laced with poison. How would I know until I've let it fill my lungs? How would I know about feelings of any kind until it's too late?

He put the glass to his lips again and realized it was empty. He considered refilling it but wanted to keep his head clear, in case. He let his hand fall to the side. The glass slipped away, bounced once on the rug and then rolled under the old sofa.

So where the hell is she?

His gaze fell to the cell phone where it rested on the edge of his desk, as though the act of wishing it would play its merry little ringtone would make it so, the ringtone he hated because it was stupid, the ringtone he loved because it was *her* ringtone. *Beautiful Woman* would have been perfect, but no, she liked the *Gummy Bear* song. One day she snatched the phone out of his hand and in a flurry of flying thumbs had downloaded the stupid song and assigned it to her number.

He wished it would play the *Gummy Bear* song right now... RIGHT NOW!

And suddenly, the phone came to life. It wasn't *Gummy Bear*, though; instead it was the default ring for any caller who was *not* Stella. He snatched at it, nearly tilting his chair over as he strained to keep from dumping his feet off the other corner of the desk. He settled and touched the *Answer* button.

"CJ."

He heard nothing but dead silence.

"Hello!"

Still nothing. He pressed the phone to one ear and covered the other, dropped his feet to the floor and leaned forward.

"Hello?"

There came what sounded like a shuffle followed by a soft slap as though a paperback book was dropped and then a click. He looked at the phone.

Call Ended, it displayed.

Duration: 19 seconds.

Caller Unknown.

After a time he took a breath, tossed the phone back on the desk and stood. He paced to the door, then back to his desk. He snatched up the phone and paced again, the fear he had been suppressing for the last hour rebuilding with each step, each turn. Without stopping he pressed "2" to speed-dial Stella's cell phone. When her voicemail kicked in he ended the call. He'd already left three messages in the last dozen or so times he had attempted calling her.

What was it he'd heard during the dead call? Was the shuffle actually Stella crawling out of sight while trying to sneak a call on the perp's phone? And the other sound, the paperback slap; what was that? Her hand reaching, slapping down for a grip? And then the shuffle; her pulling herself along? Why didn't she say anything? Couldn't? Gagged? Afraid of being overheard? Why did she hang up? Afraid of being caught? Accidental? Why has she not tried to call again?

He looked up at the ceiling.

Or was the call as simple as a wrong number, the caller embarrassed to say anything?

Something tightened in his chest. He pounded on his breastbone, blew out air, sucked in, blew out again, coughed hard with each exhale.

"Not now!"

He'd never had a heart attack, but Stella made him read about how to stave one off because he was at *that age*. He was only 44. What did she mean by *that age*? The pressure didn't go away, but there was no pain and he otherwise felt fine.

He jumped with a sudden start as the phone vibrated in his hand

and began playing the *Gummy Bear* song. He looked at the name, Stella, displayed on the caller ID, unable to believe that she chose to call at that very second. He punched the *Answer* button and put it to his ear.

"Stella?"

Silence.

"Stella?"

"Clinton. Sorry I didn't pick up when you called. I'm still a bit tied up and won't be..."

"What happened? You just disappeared."

"I know. I'm sorry. Can't talk right now, but tomorrow I'll call. Sorry. Okay?"

CJ looked up at the ceiling again and then closed his eyes. "I don't understand. Where are you? When tomorrow?"

"Sorry. Got to go. Bye."

"Stella!" He looked at the phone. The words, *Call Ended*, glared back at him again. He touched "2" until her number started dialing and then put the phone to his ear. It rang once... twice. "Damn!" He waited through the uninterrupted ringing until her voicemail greeting cut in, then waited for the tone.

"Stella. What do you mean you can't talk? You can always talk, even when you shouldn't. When tomorrow? What's going on? I'm worried about you. Call me."

He allowed several cycles of breathing and who knows how many racing heartbeats before he finished with the words he'd had been avoiding their entire relationship.

"I love you."

He looked at the phone for a long time before he pressed the *End Call* button, fearing when he did that the end would be all too literal. When the screen went black he lowered his weight onto his chair, the air escaping the cushions in rhythm with that escaping his lungs.

Chapter 2

It was several minutes before CJ's mind came back around to Stella's call and then he tried to convince himself that she was trying to pass him a message, that she was being cryptic because, hell, that's just the way Stella was. She never said anything straight forward, always had to present her ideas in such a way that he had to, one, understand that there was something between her lines, and two, figure out what the hell it was.

He put three fingers to his forehead and thought about her words. First, she talked slow and he was surprised he hadn't picked up on that right off. Slow talking was not part of Stella's persona. Second, she let him interrupt her. She's uninterruptible. He tapped the three fingers against his forehead. Third.... There's got to be a third. So what if she talked slow and allowed him to interrupt. It's 1:00 in the morning. She's probably tired, a long day of whatever she was doing. But.... He shook his head, grabbed the phone and jumped to his feet. He put it to his ear and tried to replay from memory the conversation exactly as it came out of her mouth.

"Clint," she'd said. "Sorry I didn't pick up when you called."

She never says she's sorry, even when she is.

"I'm still a bit *tied up....*" What did that mean? Was she being figurative or literal? *Tied up!* He started pacing again. *Tied up!* He shook his head. They only do that in mysteries or police shows. No way that she meant it literally, thinking that he'd really get it. But he did get it, didn't he, or would if that's what she meant.

He suddenly realized he was going on like she always accused him; making a mountain out of a fire ant hill. Her little joke that never made sense. Where did he get the idea she might be in trouble anyway? There were two women found, a month apart, wrapped in old quilts and left in a dumpster; one on the Eastside, the other south of the interstate. They were believed to be call girls, undoubtedly were, while Stella was anything but. However, she was investigating the murders even though he had told her to leave them alone. *He* was the PI. She was his secretary slash assistant. Besides, they had no related client and it was for the police to solve.

One doesn't *tell* Stella anything.

She wasn't licensed, wasn't trained, didn't carry a piece or at least not one that he knew of and he certainly would know, wouldn't he, if it was strapped to her body somewhere. Maybe in her purse? She did carry mace. *That* he did know, because he'd bought it for her just last month. It wasn't the only birthday gift he'd given her. He smiled at the vision of her appearing in the little lacy thing and then him taking it off of her.

He snapped his mind back to the phone call. She'd said she couldn't talk, that she'd call tomorrow and then, "Sorry" again. That was twice, or was it three times in a thirty second phone call? Was that on purpose? It wasn't that she'd never say she was sorry, but would reserve it for only those times when she was truly, to the bottom of her heart–her words–sorry. He closed his eyes and tried to remember the entire conversation, word-for-word. She used it at the beginning. "Clint, sorry. I'm tied up." Then he said something like, "What happened?" She said, sorry, again and that she couldn't talk, she'd call tomorrow and then, sorry, a third time. Then he asked when she'd call. She said, "Sorry. Got to go. Bye."

That was four times! She talked slow so he'd hear it and said she was sorry four times. That was calculated, each sorry like a poke in the arm saying, "Read-between-my-lines."

And then, suddenly, he saw it, saw her very first word. He was staring at the window overlooking the parking lot, but the focus was on the reflection in the glass, his own shocked, slack-jawed expression. She had not opened with "Clint." She'd said, "Clinton." She didn't like initials for a name, preferred the full given name. He had stood his ground and they compromised on Clint because he detested Clinton, went by CJ with everyone but her. She had used Clinton to get his attention right off and then said, sorry, four times.

After patting himself on the back for figuring it out, he paced back and forth a half dozen times, wondering what he should do about it. His conclusion was that there wasn't anything he could do except go home, but going home was too much like giving up. He holstered his cell phone, grabbed up his keys and went out the door.

Stella's apartment was as dark as it had been when he had gone by two hours before. He let himself in, then called her name as he strode straight into her bedroom and flipped on the light. The made bed was crumpled in one spot. He froze for several seconds before recognizing it as *his* crumple, not Stella's. The crumple was where he'd sat earlier. He let out a disappointed breath.

He turned around and went to her desk in the living room, found her address book, opened it to her sister's name and then wondered what the point would be to call Sara in the middle of the night. She wouldn't know anything and he'd just be getting her unnecessarily worried. Besides, Sara didn't much like him, he had the feeling, even though they'd never met. He entered her number in his cell phone contact list because it just seemed like a good idea. Then he paged through the address book, finding nothing more that would be of any help.

He closed the book and sat at the desk. Her laptop was closed. He considered opening it and powering it on, but what would be the point? He knew how to do little more than email and web surfing.

Email! Maybe she sent him an email. He'd never thought to check. Sometimes she'd do that when she didn't want to get tied up on the phone. Also to annoy him, he was sure, because he hated email. He opened the computer, touched the start button and then pulled his hand back. This was her private space and he felt very weird violating it, had already felt weird going through her address book. If it was a case he was working on, that would be one thing, but this was Stella.

He closed the computer. He could go home and check his email, or back to his office. Going home still felt like giving up. Going back to the office would accomplish nothing. He spun around in the chair but didn't get up. He didn't know where else to go to look for her. Besides, now that he was in her apartment, he didn't want to leave. If he didn't hear from her by 8:00 in the morning, noon latest, he'd think of something else. She'd probably come bounding in the door any minute now and all his fears would turn out to be rather silly.

He rose with great effort, went into her bedroom and sat on the crumpled spot on her bed. He took off his shoes and stretched out, setting the cell phone on the bed within easy reach, and closed his eyes.

Chapter 3

CJ awoke to a vibration. He was lying flat on his stomach in the middle of Stella's bed, daylight streaming through her curtains. He rolled off the offending device and gritted his teeth at the incessant ringtone. He picked up the phone, squinted at the name, Dan, thumbed the button and said, "What!"

"Good morning to you, too, CJ. You hung-over?"

"No. What time is it?"

"Time to say thank you. I'm throwing you a bone."

"Hold on a minute." CJ dropped the phone onto the bed and went into the bathroom to throw water on his face. When he returned he was toweling his hair and neck. He picked up the phone. "Okay. I'm ready to talk now."

"Where the hell did you go?"

"Had to wake up. It's not even 8:00 yet. You already on the job?"

"These call-girl murders have us doing overtime. Just got a call on a third one found this morning. Same as the other two. We may have a serial."

CJ could have sworn he felt his heart stop. "Do you have ID?" he managed to say with a dry tongue.

"No. Not yet. First responders just got there. I'm heading out. That's why I'm sending you this bone, ah, recommending you to a couple from Missouri here looking for their daughter. We're being spread rather thin and if there is any private investigator I'd turn them over to, it'd be you."

"Where?"

"Where? They're right here. I'm sending them over to your office."

"No!" CJ ran his fingers through his hair. "I mean, where was the third girl found? How do you know it's not the couple's daughter?"

"The initial report is the dumpster girl is white. The parents here are black as they come. She was found behind a shopping center over on 22nd, between Craycroft and Swan."

"I'll meet you there," CJ said, ended the call before Dan had a chance to argue, and all but jumped back into his shoes.

A block from the scene CJ had to park and walk. 22nd Street westbound was blocked by two Tucson City police cars, officers directing traffic north up a side street. Only one of the eastbound lanes was open. The entire thing took on the flavor of a three-ring circus without a ring leader and with the audience trying to participate. CJ saw an opportunity to slip around a rig towing a trailer stacked with roofing tiles. Just when he thought he was clear a female cop stepped in front of him.

"Sir. I have to ask you to turn around and vacate the area."

CJ had been there, done that for too many years. He knew their job and the crap they had to go through. "Sorry. I'm CJ Washburn. Detective Dan Payne is expecting me."

"CJ... Washburn," she repeated back to him.

"Yes." He nodded his head thinking that maybe she had heard of him. He had served better than ten years on the force and she looked familiar, but she was too young to have been on the force when he was.

"Your business?"

"Ah... consultant."

"Do you have some ID, Mr. Washburn?"

He pulled out his wallet as though it was burning a hole in his pocket. He noticed that his hands were shaking when she took the driver's license from his outstretched fingers. She looked at the name and his picture, compared it with his face.

"You don't look like the CJ Washburn I remember."

He looked at her name tag; Bowers, it said. "It's been a few years, and I've had a rough night. Can you contact Dan for me, please?"

"Certainly. Stand right here." She turned away and keyed her mike. Over the diesel rumbling behind him, he couldn't hear what she was saying. He shuffled his feet and waited. After a few minutes she returned and pointed. "See that fire apparatus about 100 yards out?"

CJ nodded his head.

"Follow where it's pointing. You'll find him behind that building, with the M.E. You know the drill. Don't touch anything."

"Thank you," he said and turned to head off.

"Washburn."

CJ stopped and turned around to face the young officer.

"I remember what you did for my dad. Thanks."

CJ nodded at her and set off at a jog, not knowing at all what she meant.

He found Detective Payne in earnest conversation with another suit, about 30 feet from where a half dozen people, most of whom CJ knew or at least recognized, were preparing to lift the body out of a dumpster. CJ kept his distance while trying to catch Dan's eye.

And then the body was out and on the cart, what looked to be an old blanket still wrapped around it. CJ wanted to run up and pull the blanket aside, needed to know right now who it was. Why the hell did he fall asleep? He should have been out looking for her, should have kept doing something.

"What the hell is with you, CJ?"

CJ didn't realize Dan had walked up to him. He looked at his friend, "I ah... who is it?" He looked back at the blanket-covered body. "Do you have an ID yet?"

"No. You look like you slept in your clothes."

"Stella didn't come home last night. I...."

"Stella? Oh hell, CJ, it's not Stella, if that's what you're thinking. And what do you mean she didn't come home last night?"

"Haven't seen her since lunch yesterday, got a strange phone call from her last night. Spent the night at her apartment. She never showed."

"What do you mean, strange?"

Without taking his eyes off the activity in front of them, he opened his mouth to explain Stella's cryptic words, the fact that she called him

Clinton and that she said she was sorry four times. He closed his mouth without uttering a word. It sounded stupid, even inside his own head. "You sure that can't be Stella?"

"I got a look. The victim has to be in her 50's, and she's Hispanic, not white like the 911 caller said. I don't know who she is, but I certainly know who she isn't."

CJ turned his head to look directly at the detective. "That doesn't match the profile. The other two were call-girls, Caucasian."

"Exactly. Other than female, no relation. The others were wrapped in quilts. This one's in a blanket."

"An opportunity kill?"

Dan nodded. "Someone with refried beans for brains thinking he can get rid of the old lady and it'd be blamed on the call-girl killer. As soon as we have an ID it shouldn't be hard to come up with a suspect or two."

"Any leads on the call-girls?"

"Nothing. I don't know whether to be glad this wasn't another one, or not. On one hand we'd immediately get Fed help. On the other we'd have a real life serial killer, an unknown to Tucson. So, back to Stella. What about this cryptic phone call?"

CJ Shrugged. "Probably nothing. My overactive imagination. She called in the middle of the night, didn't explain where she was, said she'd call today. That's basically it."

"You're not husband and wife so it isn't like she has to check in with you, be accountable to you. Hell, you're not even living together... or are you?"

"No."

"Doesn't she have family in New Mexico, or Texas? Maybe she went there. Have you called them?"

"Albuquerque. I was going to but it was 2:00 in the morning. I will if I don't hear from her by noon."

"Good plan. Now go get yourself cleaned up. I've got a job for you, if you want it." He pulled a folded sheet of note paper from his pocket and handed it to CJ. "Couple from Missouri. Their daughter, U of A student, has fallen off their radar. They came to find her, arrived two days ago. No sign of her. They saw the news about the two murders and got all worked up. Since you were obviously not at your office this morning, I sent them back to their motel to wait on your call. They don't appear to be super well off, but enough that they should be able to afford your fee. My impression is she ran off with a guy. They're frantic because they can't even find that she had any friends. Any she had, I'm afraid, have likely gone home for the summer. It's going to take some digging, and luck, it appears."

CJ stuck the note in his pocket and made his way back toward his car. He paused to say thanks to Officer Bowers again, but she was in earnest debate with the driver of the roofing tiles truck. He remembered his days as a cop and how non-routine a routine day could be, what he both liked and hated about it. And then he thought about how he had quit being a cop to save his marriage. All it did was put off the inevitable. In the end he'd walked away from his career, and his wife still walked away from him. He looked back across the parking lot, past the fire apparatus, to where he knew the action was going on, and felt a twinge in his center.

He *could* go back.

And then he remembered who Officer Bowers was. She used to be Lisa McDermott, daughter of Sgt. Dave McDermott. CJ had served briefly in the same unit with him just before 9/11. Everything changed after that and they wound up in different parts of the city. His daughter was a teenager back then.

He thought again of her comment about remembering what he'd done for her father, something he'd totally forgotten. It was one of his first cases after hanging his PI shingle on the door of an overpriced location south of 22nd on Alvernon, before moving to his current location and hiring Stella as his secretary. McDermott had responded to a noisy college party, alone. The party goers were none too happy about his intrusion. One of the young ladies, if one could call her a lady, filed a sexual harassment charge against him, claiming that he tried to rape her. When it appeared that the powers to be were going to take her word over his, McDermott's wife hired CJ to investigate. What he turned up was that a bunch of the party goers got together, dreamed up the charges and then talked the young girl into filing the complaint. Dave McDermott was exonerated; however, he never totally recovered from the ordeal, not wanting anything more to do with a police force that wouldn't have his back, as CJ remembered him saying. He took early retirement. And now his daughter's name was Bowers; married and a cop. She followed in her daddy's footsteps and joined the force that he resented.

CJ wondered what her father thought of that. Was he proud, scared or pissed? Probably all three.

Back at the car CJ pulled out his phone, hoping to see a missed call that he didn't hear come in. There was nothing. He considered, again, calling Stella's sister. After some thought he decided to wait a little longer. He dialed the number of the couple from Missouri. The call was answered by an anxious female voice before he even heard a ring.

"Mrs. Lindendale?"

"Yes. Is this Washburn?"

"Yes it is, ma'am. Please call me CJ."

"Fine. Can you meet right now?"

"Yes, ma'am. Wherever is convenient for you."

"We're at the Radisson. It's on.... George! What street is this?"

"It's on Speedway, ma'am. I know where it is. I can be there in fifteen minutes. It has a nice restaurant. I'll meet you there."

"I don't want to eat," she said.

"No, ma'am. This time of morning we should be able to find a quiet table and you can give me your details."

After the call CJ sat for a few minutes chiding himself for not saying an hour so he could swing by his apartment and get a shower and change of clothes. But Mrs. Lindendale would be focused on only one thing, her daughter. The fact that he had been in this same shirt for the third day and needed a shave would probably blow right by her and by her husband as well.

CJ found the Lindendale couple sequestered at one end of the patio. Although there were other couples, it was easy to pick them out because they'd already found him. Their eyes, hopeful, tired, followed his approach. He introduced himself, shook their hands and sat. He saw they had coffee, felt the sudden desire and then pushed straight to the reason he was there.

"Tell me your story. Bring me up to speed."

When CJ poised to take notes, Brenda Lindendale handed him a folded sheet of paper. "It's all right here," she said. "Professors, landlord, phone numbers, everything I figured you'd need to get started."

He opened it, did a quick scan and then nodded to Mrs. Lindendale. "Tell me what you've done so far."

By the time Mrs. Lindendale had recounted everything they had been through for the previous few days, CJ was sipping on a strong, black coffee, thanks to an attentive waitress. Mr. Lindendale had said very little, rather normal for a husband, CJ figured, when the wife was riled up. What CJ learned was that the daughter, Lizzi, was a third-year student at the University of Arizona, College of Optical Science. She was very independent, choosing to live off campus in an apartment by herself. She had a car, but normally walked or rode her bicycle a mile or so to the campus. Her car was currently parked outside her apartment, her bicycle inside. The landlord had granted them access. She was last seen, as far as the Lindendales could determine, on Thursday of last week. Today was Friday, day eight.

When Mrs. Lindendale appeared to be finished, CJ scanned through the notes again and then said, "There's nothing here about a boyfriend and you didn't say anything about a relationship. I gather she doesn't have one." He had noticed that the only name listed as friend was a male lab partner in the previous semester.

"No. She didn't have a boyfriend," she said. CJ didn't miss the change in her posture when she made the declaration. "As far as we can tell, she didn't have any friends."

CJ nodded and then looked at Mr. Lindendale, who looked away and then over at his wife. He put his hand on hers and after a few seconds she gave a slight nod.

"Our daughter, Lizzi, is gay, Mr. Washburn. She doesn't currently have a...." He paused, apparently looking for the right word.

"Partner," his wife said.

"Partner," he repeated. "She has been alone now since December."

CJ looked down at the note. "Her previous partner isn't listed here."

"No," Mrs. Lindendale said. "She transferred to some school in Florida, we believe."

"Do you know what the reason for the breakup was?" CJ asked.

She shook her head.

"I'll need her name and anything else you know about her."

"She's not in the picture anymore. What would she know?"

"Probably nothing, but if it winds up being an avenue I need to explore, it's better I have the information up front instead of you paying me my hourly fee to dig it up."

With that Mrs. Lindendale opened her phone and after scanning through her contact list, added a name and phone number to the notes. "That's all I have. Anything else?" she said, slapping the phone closed and pushing the paper back at him.

"How long will you be here?" CJ asked.

"As long as it takes," she replied.

"We...." Mr. Lindendale glanced at his wife and then over to CJ. "We both have jobs to get back to."

"George has a job to get back to," Mrs. Lindendale corrected. "I couldn't give a rat's ass about my job. My daughter comes first!"

Properly put in his place, Mr. Lindendale bowed his head and closed his eyes.

"Anything else I can tell you?" she asked, her voice softening a little after taking a deep breath.

CJ started to stand and then paused to ask one more thing. "Was her sexual preference common knowledge or did she keep it quiet?"

"What are you implying, Mr. Washburn? Do you think she might have been targeted?"

He put his hand up. "Please. It's just a question. Violence against gays is usually directed at males, seldom against females. If anything, they might be shunned. I do need to know how she presented herself, how others saw her."

She appeared to grind her teeth as she considered the question. "No. We don't know how she presented herself, and as you can see, she didn't have any friends. To be truthful, we never talked with her about her… love life. Not like she was ever going to give us a grandchild." She pushed her chair back and stood. "I think we're done. If you don't call me by the end of the day, I'll call you. Now if you'll please excuse me." With that, she picked up her purse and walked away.

Her husband watched her until she turned from sight. CJ watched him.

"You have my information," CJ said. "Not counting this meeting I'll spend one to two hours researching and talking to people. If from that I feel I can be of help, I'll present an invoice for that time at $165 per hour. Once funds have been paid I will continue until your daughter is found, you tell me to quit, or I determine that further effort would be wasted. If in that first hour or two I decide that I can't help you, I'll invoice you for a flat one hour. I will then keep the case open for thirty days in case new information comes available, at which time I will contact you."

"That sounds very fair." The husband stood and presented his hand, which CJ accepted. "Thank you. We'll be waiting for your call."

CJ sat back down and, while finishing his coffee, wondered and worried about Stella. He'd wait until noon, little over an hour and then call her sister. Meanwhile, he'd go home and shower and then begin organizing his thoughts on the Lindendale case.

Chapter 4

CJ unlocked his apartment door, pushed it open, flipped on the light, stepped to the side and waited until the door hit the stop, a habit he developed early in his career as a cop when entering questionable premises. If there was someone hiding behind the door, he'd know immediately. Also, as he moved into the threshold, he'd be able to scan the entire apartment before setting his foot in. He'd never considered his home questionable until six years before when he opened his door and was knocked down by some guy trying to make a very fast exit. Caught off guard and in the dark, CJ, the ex-cop, was embarrassed that he'd gotten nothing for a description other than very big and very fast. He also never determined what the guy was after and if he got away with anything. Why CJ called 911, he didn't know. He was sure he was a joke around the department.

None of the history behind his obsession crossed his mind as he followed his routine and then closed the door behind him. The apartment was just as he'd left it... cluttered; not exactly the way he liked it, but it was the way he was. Stella nagged at him about it. All he could do was agree with her but he just didn't know how to keep it neat. She had taken to coming in and cleaning, attempting at the same time to organize the clutter. Two days later it would be right back where it was, only with a little less dust.

He sat down in front of the computer where it resided on the old dining room table, pushed aside an empty beer bottle and punched the power button. While he waited for it to boot up he thought about the Lindendales and realized he needed to get cleaned up before pursuing that, and he needed to get started on it right away. Mrs. Lindendale will be wanting an initial report from him by that evening. He needed to make phone calls, visit Lizzi Lindendale's apartment, and interview people. First, he needed a shower.

He pushed the chair back and started stripping on the way to his bedroom.

When CJ turned off the shower, *Gummy Bear* was playing from where he'd dropped the phone next to the computer. Without grabbing a towel he raced through the bedroom and snatched up the phone just as it quit. He hit speed dial to call her back but got her voicemail.

"Damn!" He wanted to throw the phone across the room, but instead carefully set it back down on the table and then sat down to wait. "Be patient, she's leaving a voicemail," he said to the ceiling, then looked at the computer. He rested his hand on the mouse and clicked the email shortcut Stella had made for him. He looked at the phone, knowing it would chirp as soon as Stella had finished leaving the voicemail.

The email program opened and started checking for new mail.

The phone chirped and he snatched it up. He debated between listening to the message or calling Stella straight off. He punched and held "2" until it indicated it was trying to connect. He scanned the incoming emails. There were three from Stella. He opened the oldest one, time stamped 2:13 the afternoon before.

> *Clint,*
>
> *I tried calling but you didn't pick up. I got a call from Sara. Things are looking bad. I'm heading up there. Will call tonight, might be late.*
>
> *Stella*

"Hello?"

"Stella? Are you okay?"

"Yes. Why shouldn't I be? Did you get my messages?"

"What messages?" CJ clicked on the next email.

"What messages!? I left a voicemail yesterday on your cell phone and have sent a bunch of emails. I left you another voicemail just now. I also talked to you last night. What have you been doing?"

"I...."

"You didn't even look at your email, did you?"

"I just got home."

"Just got home? It's 11:00 in the morning. You mean since yesterday? You didn't go home last night? Where the hell have you been? Did you catch a new case?"

"Yes.... no. I was at your place."

"My place? Why?"

"You disappeared and I...."

"I didn't disappear. I called and left a voicemail, which obviously you didn't listen to, left a slew of emails, which you didn't read, and come to think of it put a note on the whole cooked chicken I picked up for you and put in your fridge. Obviously, you haven't seen that either."

"Oh." CJ walked into the kitchen and looked in the refrigerator. The chicken with note attached glared back at him. A container of potato salad sat next to it.

"What did you eat last night?"

He considered the question for a few seconds. "I don't recall."

"How in the hell did you survive without a woman for so long?"

He wanted to ask if that was a rhetorical question and then thought better of it. "You called me Clinton."

"I what?"

"You called me Clinton last night when you called."

"I called you Clinton? What does that have to do with anything?"

"You never call me Clinton."

"Well, I'm sorry. Won't happen again."

"And you said you were sorry a bunch of times."

"And *that* certainly won't happen again either."

CJ considered mentioning how she said she was tied up, but thought better of that as well. After a long uncomfortable silence he said, "How is Sara?"

"She's my sister but sometimes I'd like to choke the life out of her. She's as much at fault in this divorce as her crazy husband. I hate to say it but I think they're made for each other. If it wasn't for my nephew, I'd just wash my hands of it all."

"So, what's your plan?"

"At this point, give her some space to patch it up with her husband or go forward with the divorce. I've got to go. Lucas is coming out of the bathroom so we'll be getting back on the road."

"Lucas?"

"It's all in my emails and my last voicemail? My nephew is spending a couple of weeks with me while his parents work things out. Got to go. We'll be there in a few hours. Bye."

CJ closed the refrigerator door and returned to his computer. He read the emails about how Stella was running up to Albuquerque to bring her nephew back, that she should be back the next day, that there was chicken and potato salad in his refrigerator and that she'd call when she had a chance.

He was feeling very stupid.

In the middle of getting dressed CJ's eye caught the smiling faces of his two children, Trish and Josh—the six-year-old photo stared back at him from the top of his bureau—and he thought about how hard on them their parents' divorce was. They were adults now but his son moved back east—New York, then Boston, then parts unknown—shortly after the photo was taken. He'd dropped out of the University of Arizona, refusing to acknowledge that he had parents, while his sister, who still communicated on occasion, was attending the University of Idaho. Why Idaho, CJ had no idea, but at least it was on this side of the country, and he had her phone number. He tried to remember the last time he talked to her. Her birthday, January 25th. Not since. Here it was July and she didn't come home for summer break. Something about a summer job, her mother had told him. She talked to her mother, but she didn't talk to him.

That brought him around to thinking about George and Brenda Lindendale and how they knew almost immediately when their daughter went missing. Trish could be gone for months before he'd know anything was wrong. What kind of father was he? At least her mother kept in contact, though not much more than once a month, she'd said. She was too busy with her new husband and three step-children to keep up with her own daughter. At least she had an excuse, lame as it was. He had no excuse at all.

He wondered what Lucas was like. He was 9 or 10 years old, if CJ remembered correctly. Stella had mentioned him a couple of times. He supposed that sleepovers at Stella's, or vice-versa, would be on hold. That he didn't like. He didn't like that at all.

And then he chided himself for that thought. First he went nuts over her disappearance, and now he was becoming jealous of a 10-year-old. Maybe a little time apart would be good. Maybe, after this case, he'd fly up to Idaho and visit Trish.

Feeling better about himself, CJ made a pot of coffee, sliced three generous chunks off the chicken, dished up some of the potato salad and then sat down with his notes and the list Mrs. Lindendale gave him. When he finished eating he started making phone calls.

Chapter 5

CJ stood in front of a badly-in-need-of-paint ranch-style adobe home in a dilapidated neighborhood northeast of the university. He checked the address against his notes and then walked up the cracked and sun-beaten sidewalk. Not finding a doorbell, he knocked. He looked back at his car, parked at the curb, and thought about how hot it was going to be when he returned to it, and about the already overworked air conditioner. The high for the day, according to the radio, was supposed to inch toward 110 degrees. It already felt that hot and it was just noon.

The door opened and an older Hispanic woman's face peered out.

"Ms. Ortega?" CJ said.

"*Si.*"

"I'm CJ Washburn, private investigator." He held up his identification. "We spoke on the phone."

"*Si.*"

"Could I see Elizabeth Lindendale's apartment? You said you'd already spoken to her parents."

"*Si. ¡Adelante!*" She pulled the door open and stepped aside. "Come in."

He waited while she turned down the volume on a Spanish television program and then retrieved a key from a desk drawer. "Follow me," she said, heading down a hall. She turned left into another short hall that widened into a laundry room, stopping at a plain door. She poked the key into the lock and pushed the door open. "She have private entrance. No *usan esta puerta.*" She looked up at him and saw his confusion. "She no use this door. You no speak Spanish?"

"No. Sorry."

She shrugged and went in. "She not home over week. She no tell me she leaving."

"Does she normally?" CJ asked.

"She tell me, *si*. No gone much."

"How long has she lived here?"

The old woman held up one finger. "One year next month. Already renew lease for one more year. You wish look round? I go."

"Another question, first."

"*Si*."

"Did she have visitors very often?"

She shook her head. "No. Not often. One boy she study with few months. No hacer el amor.... No make love together."

"You sure?"

She looked right at him. "*Si*. I sure. No boyfriend."

"How about girlfriends?" he asked. "Did she pal around with anyone?"

"She have friend until Christmas. No see since. No other friends. Just boy for study with."

He looked about the room. "Thank you, Ms. Ortega."

She nodded and left the apartment.

When she was gone CJ began a slow walk around the little apartment. The first obvious note was the cleanliness. Not even Stella's apartment was this neat. Was it because she was on a planned absence and thus cleaned up before she left, or was she always this tidy?

He opened the refrigerator, a small, inexpensive model with the freezer at the top in which were two trays of ice-cubes, a partial carton of ice-cream, chocolate revel, a bag of frozen mixed vegetables and a box of frozen hamburger patties. He opened the patties. There were two missing. The layer of frost in the freezer was very thin, as though it had recently been defrosted. The lower section of the refrigerator sported an unopened quart of milk, a six pack of diet Pepsi, one missing, two unopened bottles of water, a half jar of strawberry jam, and the usual condiments, plus a stack of individually wrapped cheese slices. No leftovers. No rotting vegetables. No guilty pleasure snacks. Basically, nothing.

He closed the door and started going through kitchen cupboards. It was more of the same. Sparse and tidy. He did find an unopened box of Honey Nut Cheerios to go with the milk, peanut butter and a half loaf of bread to go with the jam, and hamburger buns to go with the patties. Two were missing. Her meals were efficient and sparse.

The living area, separated from the kitchen by a short counter, revealed nothing more than did the kitchen. A love seat-size sofa was angled away from the wall, facing a 30 inch flat screen TV, also angled from the adjacent wall. In between was a large entryway into the bedroom. CJ stood in the entryway and noted that she could watch the TV from either the sofa or her bed. Convenient, efficient.

The bedroom closet was, again, neat and organized. There was a small selection of various color blouses and slacks, two dresses and something that to him looked like a formal gown. A half dozen empty hangers were shoved to one end. Under the empty hangers stood a narrow, free-standing shelving unit holding folded blue jeans and t-shirts. On the floor on the other side was a shoe rack that would hold about eight pairs. There was a pair of slippers and a pair each of light brown sandals, black sandals and black high-heeled pumps. Four spots were empty.

He thought about his own daughter and wondered what her closet looked like. He was certain it would be the opposite. Neatness was never one of Trish's traits. Or had she changed since growing up? He hadn't been fully involved in her life since she was fourteen.

Bringing his attention back to the bedroom, he noted the small dresser. Feeling already like he was violating a young woman's personal space, he started to bypass it. However, if he was nothing else, he was thorough. He opened the drawers one at a time and moved things around. Nothing more than he expected.

He turned back to the bed and got down on his knees. From under the bed he pulled out a plastic storage box. It had a few sweaters, a light jacket, a heavy ski parka, boots, gloves, and other assorted winter gear, if one were to go hiking in the mountains, or participate in any of a number of winter sports, or maybe to walk a mile to class on a cold winter day.

He pushed the box back under the bed.

The bathroom, which connected back to the main living area, was as expected, very neat and clean, sparkling even. Not even drugs, outside of aspirin and Tylenol.

On the left, as he returned to the living area, was a coat closet with a broom, a small upright vacuum and a variety of cleaning products. A couple of hats sat on a shelf. Angled between the closet and the door to the outside—Lizzi's main entrance—was a bicycle. He stepped around it, unlocked and opened the door. Sitting just outside was a five or six year old silver Toyota Corolla. He walked around it and noticed the Missouri plates. He tried the doors, which were locked and then peered in the windows. Nothing lying out except what looked like a charging cord for her cell phone. The car was as clean as her house.

Back in the living area, on the wall between the kitchen and the door into the main house, sat a medium sized desk and a swivel chair. He sat in the chair and looked at the laptop computer, open but dark. Under a desk lamp sat a ceramic cup with a couple of pens, a pencil and scissors. Next to the cup lay her car key and remote on a University of Arizona Wildcats key fob. He turned on the lamp and opened a drawer. Finally, he thought to himself, a junk drawer. He was beginning to think this girl was perfect or never actually lived here. Finding nothing more than he expected—sticky notepads, glue sticks, binder clips, paper clips, pens, pencils, rubber bands, a penknife, two flashlights, batteries of various sizes, three travel-size tissue packs, and something that looked like some kind of feminine hygiene thing—he closed it and opened the file drawer. It was packed tight with what appeared to be school files. He noted labels that looked like class names and numbers, others he couldn't make sense of, and some he did, many of which started with the word, Whipple. This, he knew, referred to the Fred Lawrence Whipple Observatory. The files were labeled: *Whipple - Light Pollution, Whipple - MMT, Whipple - Tillinghast, Whipple - PAIRITEL,*

Whipple - Gamma-Ray Reflector, Whipple - VERITAS, Whipple - HAT, Whipple - MEarth, Whipple - Visitors Center, Whipple - Smithsonian.

He closed the drawer.

A small HP printer sat on the side opposite the lamp, a stack of paper next to it. To the right of the desk sat a freestanding bookshelf. It was packed with textbooks, school-related materials and a few framed pictures; Lizzi with parents and maybe her brother, Lizzi with friend, friend by herself. There were no fiction titles of any kind. He recalled that the only book on the nightstand next to her bed was a textbook.

CJ pushed away from the desk, spun the chair to face into the apartment and thought about what he'd discovered. Elizabeth Lindendale was a very neat and organized young lady. After a bit he got up and returned to the bedroom closet. On the shelf above everything else stood a light blue suitcase. There was no matching carryon. He returned to the desk chair.

She more than likely had a carryon to match the suitcase. If she had left for a planned get-a-way for a few days, or even a week or two, she might not need the large suitcase. There was no backpack so with that and a carryon, she would probably have everything she needed. He turned and looked at the desk. There was a cord, plugged in, the end waiting for something to connect to. Her phone, of course. The computer was already plugged in, as was the printer. If she was planning a long get-a-way, she'd have taken one of the phone chargers with her, this one or the one in her car, or else she simply forgot them.

So, she left with a carryon and her backpack, which he assumed she had because every college student owns one, and possibly a purse. She left her car, specifically leaving her keys behind. Only other key she'd need if going with someone else would be her apartment key. Her parents said all they'd gotten when they called her was her voicemail. Phone turned off, or dead? In eight days it is likely dead. He walked back into the main house.

"Ms. Ortega?" he called.

"*Si*." She appeared out of nowhere it seemed.

"You said she didn't go away often. When she did, how long was she gone and where did she go?"

"Oh, few days. Up at that telescope. She work there sometimes."

"Observatory?"

"*Si*. Observatory. It call Whipper, I think."

"Whipple," CJ corrected. "Whipple Observatory."

"*Si. Si*. That it. Only place she go all year."

"Thank you." He looked at the apartment one more time and then said, "I think I've seen all there is to see. If I have any other questions, I'll give you a call."

Chapter 6

CJ knocked and then entered the door labeled, "*Professor Steven Jarvosky, PhD, MS, BA, Assistant Research Professor, Deep Space Optics*." CJ expected an older, slack-jawed man with half moon spectacles. Instead, he was greeted by a clean-cut young man, thick black hair, trimmed short, open collar shirt, penetrating eyes. CJ didn't know whether to call him doctor, professor, Mr. Jarvosky, or Steven. He stepped forward and extended his hand. "Professor. I'm CJ Washburn. We spoke on the phone a bit ago."

"Yes sir. Have a seat." He pointed to the only other chair in the very cramped office. "Steven, please. You're not one of my students."

"Thanks, Steven."

Steven leaned back in his chair. "You mentioned Elizabeth Lindendale. I looked her up. A third year student. She's had two of my classes in the last two years, the last being this previous semester. You said that she was missing. I haven't seen her since the semester ended. It's summer break, you see, and," he pointed a finger at his computer screen, "I don't show her as registered for any summer classes. I don't know what else I could tell you. I would imagine she's off on holiday somewhere."

CJ nodded. "On holiday? European term."

The young man smiled. "Yes. I spent much of my youth in London. Claim Colorado otherwise."

"Love the mountains of Colorado," CJ said. "Holiday is pretty much what I'm thinking, too. According to her parents she kept in regular contact with them. Now they can't find her."

"How long has it been since they talked with her?"

"Eight days."

Steven made a face and shrugged. "I have students that disappear longer than that in the middle of a semester. She probably decided to go off with a friend and didn't want to answer parental questions."

"Did you notice if she had a boyfriend, or anyone she was close to?"

"I hardly remember her face... a name on my computer monitor is as much as I can tell you."

CJ looked past the professor to a poster on his wall. Behind the words "Petal to Heaven" and "14,110 Feet" and "Pike's Peak" was a photo of a lone bike rider on a mountain road, racing into a blanket of fog.

CJ pointed toward the poster. "You've ridden to the top of Pike's Peak?"

The professor turned to look at the poster. "Not yet. It's on my bucket list. That's why I keep the poster there, to remind me of one of my goals."

"You have other goals?"

"Many. Shouldn't we all?"

CJ stood. "Yes, we should." He extended his hand again and as the professor took it, said, "Thank you for your time. Good luck on reaching the Colorado summit."

"Thank you. Next summer, I think. Good luck on your search. I'm sure Lizzi is off on holiday with a friend, but I understand her parent's concern."

When the door closed behind him, CJ took several steps and then turned and looked at the name plate, thinking about Professor Jarvosky's last words. He looked at his notes and thought through the entire conversation he'd just had with the professor. He was certain that at no time did he mention Elizabeth Lindendale's nickname. Was it coincidental that Steven Jarvosky guessed that she was called Lizzi, or was it part of her official university records and Steven had simply made note of it from his computer screen while they talked?

CJ knocked on the door again and then, without waiting, opened it and rushed in. The professor had no more time than to turn about in his chair. "One more thing, do you still have her records up on your computer?"

Steve looked back at his screen. "Well, yes I do."

CJ proceeded around to the professor's side of the desk. "Can you see whether she has registered for fall classes?"

Flustered, Steven tried to spin around, fumbling with his mouse. By that time CJ was peering down at the screen, scanning as quick as he could through the displayed data; her name, Missouri address, Tucson address, College of Optical Science, advisor: Clair Wingdom, major: Optical Science, stuff that made no sense to CJ's layman mind and then the window went away to show only the computer desktop with a dozen or so icons. The desktop background was a collage of photos; family and friends obviously.

"No. I'm afraid she hasn't registered yet for the fall semester, Mr. Washburn. If you have any other questions I'd recommend you visit the Dean of Students."

Hearing the dismissal in the professor's voice, CJ backed halfway out and then paused in the doorway. "Did Ms. Lindendale do any work or study up at Whipple Observatory?"

Professor Jarvosky seemed to be surprised by the question. He opened his mouth to respond, closed it for a second, then said, "I really couldn't tell you. Like I said, take your questions to the Dean of Students."

"Thank you," CJ said and then closed the door behind him. In the hall he opened his notes and wrote under the heading Professor Jarvosky:

Knows Lizzi better than he lets on.

He looked up at the ceiling and again thought through the conversation. He looked back down at his notes and added another note under the professor's name.

Said she was probably off on holiday with a friend. Never alluded that it might be a boyfriend, even when I suggested such. He knows she is gay.

As he walked out of the building, CJ tried to figure out why the professor lied to him. It would have been no big deal to admit that he remembered Elizabeth Lindendale and even knew her nickname. She attended his classes several days a week for two semesters, after all. The fact that he said he didn't remember her was suspicious in itself.

Chapter 7

CJ checked the time as he stepped out into the hot sun. It was almost 1:30. Stella should be home by now. Despite his initial inclination to run by and check for sure, he decided it would be better to hold off. Maybe she would be less likely to make fun of him if he waited until this evening. And what about this evening? Should he go by or not? Lucas would be there and things could become rather awkward; his aunt kissy-facing with a guy she wasn't married to.

He was parked in the university parking garage. He started his car and then remained parked, out of the sun, while the AC struggled back to life. He looked over his notes. There really was little else to do outside of visit a couple of other professors of whom, earlier, he was only able to leave voicemails. Until they called back all he had left was the ex-girlfriend in Florida and he didn't know if he was ready to reach that far just yet.

Browsing back to the beginning, he looked over the notes Mrs. Lindendale provided and then his own after the meeting with her and her husband. He flipped between his walk around Lizzi's apartment and the visit to Professor Jarvosky. Then it occurred to him that there was something that he'd missed, or something that he'd seen and overlooked. He closed his eyes and tried to recall the photo on Lizzi's bookshelf, the one of her and a friend. He looked at the name he wrote down after convincing Mrs. Lindendale that the ex-girlfriend may be important. It was Kelsie. She didn't know the last name, had never cared enough to find out anything about the woman with whom her daughter was in love, though she did have her phone number. Was the photo of Lizzi with a friend that of her and Kelsie? And was the friend the same face he saw in the collage of faces on the professor's desktop? The longer he sat there with his eyes closed, flipping between his memories of the two different images, the more certain he was that the two were the same. Whether they were Kelsie or not made little difference at this point. The fact was, it was one hell of a coincidence, or, more than likely, the professor lied not knowing Lizzie personally.

He locked the car and headed back to Professor Jarvosky's office.

As CJ debated between knocking or simply barging into the office he had left only twenty minutes before, the door opened and Steven Jarvosky stood before him, frozen in mid-step.

Between the shocked look and recovery, he managed to say, "Mr. Washburn." He squared his shoulders. "I suppose, like Columbo, you have just one more question."

"Yes, I do, professor." Looking directly into his eyes, he said, "Who is Kelsie?"

Steven tilted his head and furrowed his brow. "Kelsie? I don't know a Kelsie." He pushed the door closed, checked that it was locked and then added, "If there is nothing more, I do have someplace to be."

As the professor walked away, CJ said, "I don't mean one of your students, Professor. I'm referring to your niece, or is it your sister? Where in Florida did she transfer to, and why?"

Steven Jarvosky spun around, looked up and down the hall and then returned to his office door. He unlocked and opened it, then motioned CJ to enter. When the door was closed and they were both seated, the professor said, "She's my half-sister. How in the hell did you figure it out?"

"I'm an investigator, Mr. Jarvosky. It's what I do and sometimes I even do it well. May I assume, since she is a half-sister, that Kelsie's last name is not Jarvosky."

Steven shook his head. "Mom and Dad divorced when I was nine. Mom remarried a couple of years later and had Kelsie. Her name is Progue."

"And you kept your father's name."

"Yes."

"Where is Kelsie now?"

"She transferred to Florida State."

"I don't mean what school she's attending; I mean, where is she right now, today, this minute?"

Steven's jaw tightened. After grinding his teeth for a few seconds he said, "I made a promise that I wouldn't divulge where they are."

"They?" CJ's eyebrows went up in fake surprise about something he was already beginning to guess at.

"Kelsie and Lizzi," Steven said.

"They're having a reunion of sorts, patching up their relationship?"

"You might say that, yes. And I've probably said a lot more than I should have."

CJ nodded as he considered his next question. "You maintain a lot of loyalty toward your sister."

"My mother and step-father turned their backs on her. I saw no big deal in the fact that she was gay."

"Why did they breakup back in December?" CJ asked.

"My step-father refused to pay for any tuition if Kelsie kept up her, quote, lifestyle. She and Lizzi got in a fight over it so Kelsie thought the best thing to do was leave Tucson, transfer to a school far away and try to convince her father that she became heterosexual. She even took on a boyfriend in Florida."

"That didn't work out very well, I gather."

"No. Greg, her father, paid the semester and then it all fell apart around spring break."

"So, now," CJ said, "Kelsie's father has kicked her off the feedbag and she is back here trying to patch things up with Lizzi. Where are they?"

"I'm afraid, Mr. Washburn, that I have to draw the line there. I'm all Kelsie has now. I'm not going to violate her trust."

"What do you think I should tell Lizzi's parents? They're very distraught over her disappearance. They saw the news about the women being left in dumpsters, so you can imagine, I'm sure."

"Yes, I can. Believe me, I was worried at first with where they were going and then this came up. I'm now glad they aren't here."

CJ smiled. "If I was a good investigator I'd be able to deduct from that statement that they went to Mexico."

"You're obviously a top notch investigator, Mr. Washburn. I'm sure you'd figured it out eventually that they both applied for passports."

"Then this was planned for a while?"

"Yes."

"Have you talked to your sister since they left?"

"Yes."

"Then you have a way to get a hold of them?"

"Yes."

"Here's what you do. Call her and tell her that some asshole investigator is on their tail and if they don't want to be found to have Lizzi call her mother and ensure her that she is not dead."

Steven blew out a lungful of air. "I can do that. Thank you."

"No." CJ stood and presented his hand. "Thank you." As they shook he added, "Do it right after I leave. Her mother is waiting for my report this afternoon. I'd like it that she receive that call from her daughter first."

As CJ walked through the front entrance of the hotel, he double-checked the room number Mrs. Lindendale had given him and then went straight to the elevator. When the elevator door opened he stepped aside for a man with a cane, then entered and punched the button for the fourth floor. He thought about how easy this case had gone and wondered again if he should go by Stella's apartment, or go home. Or maybe I should just walk in circles, he thought. He hated it when he got like this and he couldn't make a decision.

After leaving Professor Jarvosky he had gone by his office to create an official case file—Stella would have his ass if he didn't—and an invoice for three hours in an official "Desert Investigative Services" envelope with the client's name printed on the outside. Before Stella came to work for him, things weren't quite as professional. She had improved his life in so many different ways.

He stepped off the elevator and wondered where it was all going. Was there going to be a time when she'd want more from their relationship, more than just sleeping with the boss?

He stopped at the door, checked the number again and then knocked.

Mr. Lindendale opened the door and a big smile blossomed on his face. He grabbed CJ's hand and started shaking it. "Thank you, Mr. Washburn."

CJ spotted Mrs. Lindendale looking out the window, her cell phone pressed to her ear. "It's what you hired me for," he said and then pointed to the wife. "She talking with your daughter right now?"

"Yes," Mr. Lindendale said.

"Then I guess this case is closed." CJ opened his folder and handed the envelope to Mr. Lindendale. "This is my bill."

George Lindendale opened it, considered the amount for only a few seconds and then fetched a checkbook from a briefcase on the bed. As he wrote out the check, CJ was able to pick up on some of the mother's conversation with her daughter.

"Like I already said, your father and I are going to have to think about it."

CJ wondered what they were going to be thinking about. Hanging around until the girls return from Mexico? Extending an invitation to the newly reunited couple to their Missouri home for Christmas? Accepting a Thanksgiving invitation from the happy couple? Accepting that their daughter was homosexual and they'd never get a grandchild? All of it?

CJ's thoughts had drifted to his own daughter when George handed him the check. He took the 2-part invoice back, wrote that it was paid, with date and check number, returned one copy, shook George's hand again and left. On the way down the elevator CJ thought about the fact that that was probably the easiest $500 he'd made in some time. He'd have to serve a lot of court subpoenas to make that much. And this was much more satisfying.

CJ stood outside Stella's apartment door trying to decide whether to knock or just go in. Her car was in its usual spot, so he knew she was home. He looked at his sweaty hands—nervous or just hot?—and knocked. The door opened and he found himself looking down at a young boy.

"You must be Lucas," CJ said.

"Let him in, Lucas," Stella called from within. "That's Mr. Washburn, my boss. He's okay."

Mr. Washburn? Her boss? Why not her boyfriend? Suddenly feeling even more awkward, CJ stepped in and let Lucas close the door.

The young boy turned from the door and said, "Hi. I'm Lucas," and extended his hand.

CJ took it and said, "Good to meet you. I'm CJ."

"I thought Aunt Stella said your name was Clint."

"She does call me Clint, sometimes. I mostly go by CJ. You can call me anything you like."

"You call him Mr. Washburn," Stella said from the kitchen.

"Okay." His duty done, Lucas trotted over to the sofa and picked up a handheld device. Some kind of game thing, CJ assumed.

CJ turned toward sounds in the kitchen and found Stella at the sink. He leaned against the counter next to her and crossed his arms. "Your boss? I thought I would be introduced as your lover, sex slave."

She gave him the evil eye. "Hush! And keep your voice down. Lucas has enough turmoil in his life already. Until he gets to know you, you're Mr. Washburn, my boss. I'm sorry, but that's the way it'll be for a while."

CJ stared at the refrigerator for a time without saying anything.

"Are you going to be okay with that?" she asked.

"I guess I have to be, don't I?" CJ tried to understand, but couldn't overcome the building indigestion-like pressure growing in his chest. "Caught a case this morning. Missing girl. Found her. Closed case."

"Excellent! Did you do a case file?"

"Yes. Did the invoice, received payment, have yet to make the deposit?"

"Oh." She rinsed a glass and put it in the drainer. "Guess you don't need me around then."

CJ could tell she was trying to be humorous, trying to thin out the heavy air. He wasn't having it. "No. Guess not." He pushed away from the counter and walked to the kitchen door. "Have to get going. See you tomorrow unless you need to take more time off. If so, that's fine." With that he walked through the living room, past Lucas who was engaged in his video game, and out the door, ignoring Stella trying to call him back.

Chapter 8

On the way back to his office, CJ received a call from the county clerk of court. They had three subpoenas that needed to be served. He put on his *process server* hat, figuratively, and detoured downtown for the paperwork, then continued to his office to finish closing out the Lindendale case. When that was done he sat down with the subpoenas to consider which to do first. He wished Stella was here because she knew how to get online to determine where best to catch up with the individuals.

The farthest away was a woman who lived and worked in Nogales. From his office it was an hour and a half drive, almost to the Mexican border. Of the three she appeared the easiest as her home and work were the same. Chances of catching her on the first try was high. Sure didn't need Stella to figure that one out. The other two were men living in South Tucson. By the time he would get back from Nogales it would be after the end of the work day so there would be a fair chance of catching them at their homes. These three might be a slam-dunk.

With his plan in mind and addresses ready to enter into his GPS, he sat down with his cell phone. He punched the speed dial for Trish and stared out the window at the ugly building next door. After four rings he knew she wasn't going to pick up. He debated on whether to leave a message.

"Obviously I'm not answering. You know my excuses so just pick one. If it's really important, text me. If you want to leave a message I might call you ba..."

He hung up. When did they teach their kids to be rude? Neither he, nor her mother, treated callers that way, not even sales or political calls; although he had to admit it would feel good to tell them where to stick it.

He flipped the phone closed, stored it in its pouch and headed out the door.

By the time CJ arrived back in South Tucson, it was after 7:30. The woman's business in Nogales was closed when he'd arrived and she wasn't home, so he'd waited. When finally she returned, and as she and a young man Lucas' age were pulling bags of groceries from the back seat of her car, he served the subpoena. She said something in Spanish and then he was on his way.

The second subpoena was as though the guy was waiting for him. He was sitting on his front porch when CJ pulled up, met him halfway up the walkway.

The third, not so lucky. His GPS took him to a rundown trailer guarded by a snarling black lab on a heavy chain. The trailer was dark and no vehicles sat out front. CJ considered waiting, but from the scatter of what appeared in the waning light to be beer bottles around the platform that passed for a porch, he surmised that the individual was at a bar somewhere and would likely be late. Besides, he'd rather serve the subpoena in the daylight on someone who was sober.

On the way home, CJ stopped for gas. Standing at the pump, watching the numbers to the right of the dollar sign get bigger and bigger, he wondered if he should stop by and see Stella. He was still a bit peeved by the way she dumped him to the backseat with Lucas there. And then he thought about Trish again and considered trying to call her once more. He'd tried a second time on the way to Nogales but in the middle of connecting he'd lost service.

When he was through and had shoved the receipt into his folder, he pulled up to the gas station exit. Left to Stella's, right to home. For nearly a minute he debated back and forth, then turned right.

Chapter 9

CJ awoke in a sweat. As he tried to remember the dream, images of trees and dark water faded until he could no longer recall anything. He looked at the clock. 2:18. He hadn't even been asleep an hour; had finally gone to bed when the bottle of Jack Daniels was empty. He lay for ten more minutes then got up, went into the kitchen and opened the refrigerator. There were two beers and no sodas. He was thirsty for something besides water and there was no way he was drinking a beer at 2:30 in the morning, even if he thought it would get rid of his headache. Jack Daniels maybe, but there wasn't any left.

He pulled on a T-shirt, which still smelled of where he had spilt the whiskey, and a pair of shorts, slipped into his sandals, grabbed his wallet, keys and phone, and headed out the door.

Out of habit, again from his days as a police officer, CJ backed into a spot in front of the convenience store a half mile from his house. After he completed his purchases, he sat in his car with the windows down, sipping on a Dr. Pepper and munching on chocolate chip cookies, thinking about those days too many years back when he wore the uniform. How many nights did he do just this, drinking sodas or coffee while sharing history and solving world problems, he and his partner bored out of their skulls, hoping they'd get a call on a domestic disturbance just to be doing something? And how many nights did they wish all the crazies would go to bed so they could get a break long enough to grab a mid-shift sandwich?

And what about Stella? He pulled another cookie from the pack. The right thing to do was go apologize, even though he knew she was half the issue. He should be more understanding, but then so should she. If he apologized, then maybe she would too and then they could work something out.

Maybe he should wait for her to apologize first. It wasn't his fault that she had her nephew staying with her.

CJ half noted a dark-colored van cruise by significantly slower than the speed limit—half noted, meaning he was aware of it—but didn't record any detail, something he would have done automatically a decade back. He drank some soda and shoved the remainder of the cookie into his mouth. He extracted another cookie.

If he didn't call her, would she call him? He looked at his phone to be sure he hadn't missed a call during the short time he was asleep. He hadn't. He put his head back, hoping it'd help ease his headache, and closed his eyes. He swallowed the last bite of cookie and wished for a breeze. It had to still be 90 degrees. He drifted for a time, slipped into a light doze and then awoke with a start to something like a car door slamming in the distance. While his senses struggled to come fully alert he considered whether the sound was a gunshot, decided that it wasn't. He could see a fair distance to the east but not far to the west. To the south, directly in front of him and across the street, stood a restaurant, it and the parking lot fully dark. He was still the only one in the convenience store parking lot, other than the store clerk's car parked to the side. He glanced in his mirror and could see the clerk watching something on a small portable TV. All was quiet.

And then he wondered what the hell he was doing anyway. He wasn't a cop anymore. What had his life come to that he was sitting in a convenience store parking lot in the middle of the night? He should be spooned against Stella. It was going to be a while before that happened again, if at all. He considered another cookie then took a sip of the soda instead.

Suddenly there came a red glow at the southwest corner of the restaurant. It lasted no more than a second. CJ watched the area, expecting lights from a vehicle, thinking that the red glow came from taillights as someone applied the brake just before starting their car or shifting it into drive. Because his eyes were focused on the southwest corner, and because he had little night vision in the brightly lighted store parking lot, CJ almost missed the movement at the southeast corner, where the restaurant parking lot spilled out onto the side street. A dark colored vehicle without lights, large enough to be a van or SUV, pulled onto the street and turned south, virtually becoming invisible within seconds.

CJ considered what he'd seen for far too long, he'd later conclude, before starting his car and maneuvering across the four lanes to the side street. He drove for five or six blocks, checking cross streets before turning back. He pulled in behind the restaurant, his suspicions running hackles up and down his arms, and parked with his headlights pointed at the dumpster. With flashlight in hand he approached the dumpster, pushed the lid open and pointed his flashlight down into it. A quilt with a flowered pattern glowed back at him.

"Shit!" he said, shoved the flashlight into his pocket and, after pushing the lid all the way open, hefted himself up and into the container. The smell of leftover lasagna, vinegar and oil, wine, rotten vegetables and rancid something rose up around him. He pulled the flashlight from his pocket and immediately dropped it. In the thirty seconds it took him to find and recover it he managed to catch a foot and topple across the quilt bundle.

"Son of a bitch!"

He straightened up, wiped a hand on his T-shirt and, while attempting to breathe only through his mouth, searched for an edge to the quilt. Almost to the point of frantic, he finally located a corner, yanked it aside and found exactly what he'd feared; the partially nude body of a young woman. He checked her pulse in several places to ascertain she was dead and then, as he turned around to climb out without contaminating any more evidence, he slipped and fell on his back. Something smelling of cheap wine filled one ear. As quickly and carefully as he could, he righted himself again and climbed out of the container. As he walked away from the stench, wiping the sweat from around his eyes so he could see, he dialed 911 on his cell phone.

While CJ waited for the first responders he dialed Detective Payne. Just when he thought it was going to go to voicemail, the detective's growly voice broke in. "Payne."

"Good morning, Dan. Thought I'd return the favor with an early morning wakeup call."

"What the hell, CJ? It's three fu... Hold on."

There were a lot of muffled noises and voices, Dan's wife, CJ hoped and then silence for a time.

"Okay," Dan finally said. "What the hell is with a call at 3:17 in the morning?"

"I thought you'd like to hear that I found your third victim, the one that will raise your case to that of a serial killer."

"You what? Where?"

CJ told him and Dan said he'd be there in a half hour.

As he holstered his phone, a silent, fully lit patrol car screamed into the lot from the main street, followed within seconds by another from the side street. CJ remained where he stood, illuminated by all the headlights, hands where the officers could see them as they approached.

CJ knew the drill. He also knew that he looked like hell after rolling around in the dumpster, and he felt like hell.

Chapter 10

Satisfied that he wasn't a threat, or the perp–Officer Bentley knew CJ from when CJ was a cop, knew he was a private investigator–the officers took CJ's description of the vehicle and then directed him to move his car and to not go anywhere until the detective arrived. And so he sat against the trunk with what was left of his soda. He'd lost his appetite for any more cookies. He was sure he'd smell like cheap wine and rotten lettuce for the next week.

Detective Payne pulled in with his blue lights flashing, got out and went straight to the dumpster to confirm what everyone knew and then to confer with the officers, of which there were now a half dozen. A few minutes later the coroner arrived followed by a news truck.

And the circus begins, CJ thought, glad and sad that he was not in the middle of it, relegated into the category of witness.

He sipped at his soda and considered going across the street for coffee. He looked toward the convenience store where a number of very early morning commuters rubber-necked the activity around the restaurant. If he waited much longer it would be a crowd over there. He pushed off the car and started in that direction.

"CJ!"

CJ turned to his name being called.

"Where the hell you going?" Detective Payne said.

CJ considered the tone of voice, then brushed it off and pointed. "Coffee. Want one?"

Dan appeared to think about that for a moment before saying, "Black."

CJ ignored the stares as he drew coffee into two large cups. Two men parted for him when he approached the counter.

"What's going on over there?" one of them said.

"Is that the coroner?" the clerk said.

CJ handed over a five dollar bill. "Sorry. Can't say anything."

"Weren't you here earlier?" the clerk said. "You sat in the parking lot for a long time. Are you undercover?"

CJ accepted his change and shook his head. "Sorry." He pointed to the news truck on the street. "You'll have to watch it on the news." With that he picked up the coffees and walked out. He took a wide birth around the blond with a camera pointed at her face. He could tell she was watching for someone to talk to and that she was sizing him up. He ducked under the crime scene tape and nodded to Officer Bowers.

"You get around CJ," she said, a lot more friendly than the morning before. "The detective's going to start liking you for these."

"Funny, Lisa. How's your old man doing?"

"Quite well. He's getting tired of retirement, thinking about going back to work doing something easy and less mentally taxing than being a cop, like becoming a private dick."

CJ laughed. "That's two in a row. You should get a standup gig. Tell him it's not all it's cracked up to be."

"I will, though it might be too late." She turned away to wave a rubbernecker along.

Detective Payne saw CJ approaching and broke away from a conversation with the coroner. He took one of the coffees. "The uniforms put out a BOLO based on what you told them. Wasn't much there. Tell me what you saw."

CJ described the van that drove by, or more like drifted by, and what he saw maybe ten minutes later, pointing out that he had no idea if the two were the same vehicle.

"And in between you fell asleep," the detective scoffed.

"I'm not on the force anymore, Dan. I'm a private citizen doing what private citizens do."

"And what were you doing here at 3:00 in the morning?"

"If you'll notice, this convenience store is near my apartment. I couldn't sleep, decided to come out for a soda."

"Really! Just soda, CJ?"

"What do you mean by that, Detective?"

"I don't know. You tell me. Kind of convenient, wouldn't you say? I'm picking up an odor that's anything but carbonated beverages."

CJ stepped back. "What you're smelling is garbage from when I climbed into the dumpster to find out if she was alive. Am I a suspect?"

"I smell alcohol." The detective's nostrils flared. "Not beer. More like whisky. This restaurant doesn't serve Jack Daniels?"

"Oh, hell, Dan. You know I drink Jack Daniels."

"That I do. What's that on your hand?"

CJ glanced at his hand. He'd seen the dried blood when he was getting coffee. "Cut myself on something in the dumpster, I guess."

Dan waved over a uniformed officer. "Officer Bentley, do a breath analysis on Mr. Washburn. Even if his BAC isn't over point-o-eight, take him into custody. Take his clothing for testing and order up a tox screen. Don't let him clean up until swabs have been taken from him. Also, impound his car."

Officer Bentley put his hand on CJ's bicep and CJ jerked away, knocking the officer back a step.

"What the hell are you doing, Dan? I..." Before he could say anything else he was on the ground, his face dancing against the pavement, a knee in his groin.

Dan squatted down next to him and said, "Sorry, CJ. It's for your own good."

"Fuck you, Detective!"

"Yep," Detective Payne said, then straightened up and spoke to the officer sitting on CJ's back. "Cuff him then send someone to his apartment for a change of clothes and to lock it down until a team can go over it. He's a PI, Desert Investigative Services. His office is going to have to be gone through as well. Also, he's an ex-cop, so don't rough him up too badly." With that he returned to his crime scene.

Chapter 11

The lights hurt CJ's eyes and all he wanted to do was turn them off and go back to sleep until he remembered the events of the night before, or actually earlier in the morning. He groaned and put his arm over his eyes. All he could think about was his headache and about getting his once good friend, Dan Payne, out in the desert on a dark night.

He was on his back, on the floor in an interview room, a pair of hiking boots for a pillow because that was what some idiot chose to bring him from his apartment; that and an old shirt and blue jeans. That was it; not even clean underwear or socks, and he had to give up everything he'd been wearing. The entire thing was insane and humiliating. But they hadn't locked him up. After they took his blood and saliva, dug under his finger nails, and scraped samples from a variety of blood and food particles, and a few non-food particles, adhering to his skin, they gave him the interview room and closed the door. Probably to contain the smell, he figured.

After a time he rolled off the boots and sat with his back against the wall. He wondered what happened to his coffee. He remembered holding it with one hand and then trying to fend off Officer Bentley with the other and then he was on his face. He touched his face. It hurt like hell, was starting to scab in some places, still raw in others.

When his butt started hurting he struggled to his feet and walked over to sit in the chair, carrying his boots with him. He'd no sooner placed his head on his arms when the door opened and Detective Payne entered.

"About time you woke up, CJ."

CJ wanted to glare at him but his head and face hurt too much. It was either two separate pains or one big pain. Or one big Payne! CJ thought.

"I think I've got a concussion," CJ said.

"Fine," the detective said. "You could try suing us but we could prove resisting arrest and assaulting a police officer."

This time CJ managed a good glare.

"I called Stella. She's on her way to pick you up."

"You don't have to do me any favors."

"You can be pissed if you like, CJ, but I did what I had to do considering you trampled all over my crime scene, compromised evidence, spread your own blood all over the victim, and who knows what all else. And your alcohol level tested in at 0.12. I had to come down hard and fast before someone decided to accuse me of favoritism. The press was already on this and asking questions, you were seen hanging around before the body was dropped and there was only your word that there was a suspicious dark color vehicle."

CJ only blinked at him.

"I know you didn't have anything to do with it but I had to eliminate you from anyone else's suspect list, and I had to do it before the Feds show up."

"I didn't have any choice but to get in the dumpster, Dan. I didn't even want to take the time to dial 911 first because if there was someone in there and she was still alive, every second counted."

"But you did take the time to race up and down the street looking for your phantom vehicle. Why didn't you go straight to the dumpster first for the same reason you just stated?"

CJ considered that for a few seconds. "I don't know."

"Because you were drunk and you shouldn't have even been out on the road. That part I'm trying to slide under the table in lieu of bigger fish to fry here. You all but passed out on top of her. I should be glad you didn't throw up on her as well."

CJ pulled his fingers through his hair, found something that shouldn't have been in there, looked at it and then flipped it aside. "I'm sorry, Dan. Have you found anything that points to the killer?"

Dan shook his head. "Nothing yet, but all we've managed to do so far is separate you from the scene."

Dan's phone chirped. He put it to his ear. "Payne... Thanks."

"Your girlfriend is here. Put on your boots and get out of here."

CJ pushed his feet into the boots and didn't bother tying them. "When can I have my car back?"

"I'll call you about that and your apartment later today, or maybe tomorrow."

"Tomorrow!"

Dan shrugged and opened the door. "We're understaffed and overworked. Except for budget cuts it never changes. Your phone and personal effects are at the desk. You know where that is, right?"

"Yeah," CJ growled as he walked out.

"And take a bath," Dan said after him.

When CJ walked out Stella was sitting next to Lucas reading a magazine, her legs crossed. She looked up, dropped the magazine and came to him. "You okay, Clint? What happened? Detective Payne wouldn't tell me anything."

CJ eyed Lucas and then said, "Let's just get out of here and then I can fill you in."

"Sure. Sure." She turned toward the door. "Come on Lucas."

Lucas jumped and ran ahead of her, catching the door from someone coming in. As CJ and Stella passed through he said, "You smell funny."

"Lucas!" Stella said.

"Don't worry about it," CJ said. "He's right. I need a shower."

"I'll drop you by your apartment. Where's your car?"

He drew in a deep breath. "That's going to be a problem. They impounded my car."

"Oh," she said.

"And my apartment."

"Why did they pound your car?" Lucas asked.

"Impound, Lucas," Stella said. "Means the police took his car."

"Will they give it back?"

"Eventually."

"How do they impound an apartment?"

"They didn't impound his apartment. Mr. Washburn was just being funny. What he meant is they won't let him in his apartment until they are through searching it."

"What are they searching for?" Lucas looked up at CJ.

"That's the same question I have," Stella said and pushed the unlock button on her key fob. "Let's worry about any more questions later. Why don't we stop and pick up some lunch on the way home. Since Mr. Washburn can't get into his apartment I'm going to let him shower at my place."

Lucas got in the back seat. When they were all in the car and pulling out of the parking lot, Stella said, "When do you get back into your apartment?"

"Maybe tomorrow," CJ said.

"Oh."

Chapter 12

When CJ awoke it was after 7:00 in the morning. He'd eaten takeout with Stella and Lucas after showering in Stella's bathroom and cleaning up his face. He'd then put on the same clothes because she didn't want Lucas to know that he had clothes there. With fresh clothes concealed in a trash bag tucked under his arm they'd delivered him to a motel on Broadway.

"If you need anything else, Mr. Washburn, just give me a call," Stella had said just before driving away with her new best friend in the passenger seat next to her.

Like hell, he'd call her.

With no place to go and nothing to do he'd watched TV until he thought his head was going to explode, only going out for a fast food dinner because that was all that was within reasonable walking distance. He'd considered calling Trish, but didn't know if he could take being rejected, or in her case, ignored, twice in the same day. He'd fallen asleep with the TV on, waking an hour later long enough to turn it and the light out and going back to sleep.

He rolled off the bed, stumbled a little and then went straight to the shower. When he was done he stood at the sink staring at his scabs, realizing he had no razor, toothbrush or comb. He already hadn't shaved in two days. Maybe the beard would hide the worst of his face.

He finger-combed his hair, got dressed and headed down to partake in the hotel's breakfast. He was starving, and still had a headache. He was counting on coffee helping.

Sitting at a table by himself, irritated by a couple of male siblings squabbling several tables away while their parents filled plates, CJ sipped on his coffee and chewed on a pastry. He was trying to watch the morning news on a TV monitor over the boys' heads, had to strain to hear the commentary.

"And here is the scene again from early yesterday morning when a fourth dumpster victim was discovered by a former Tucson police officer. As you know, it took a bazaar turn when the officer, or I should say ex-officer, wound up in a scuffle with police and then was subdued and handcuffed."

CJ froze in mid-bite as he saw himself in the video pushing at the uniformed police officer and then being knocked to the ground and handcuffed.

"His car, which was at the scene, was impounded. When our reporting team attempted to visit his place of residence they found a police seal."

"What do we have here, Chelsea? Is it possible that a former Tucson police officer is responsible for these gruesome murders?"

"That's the big question isn't it Reuwben. We have learned that the former police officer, one Clinton Joshua Washburn, currently a Tucson private investigator, was released under his own cognizant. I can't imagine the police would release an actual suspect."

"Do they have any other leads at all?"

"None that we know of, but they are keeping the investigation very tight."

CJ put his pastry down and looked around the breakfast room. No one appeared to recognize him as being the same as the crazed individual the news team was just talking about. As a matter of fact no one took notice of him at all when he dumped his entire breakfast, including coffee, into the trash, picked up his bag of clothes and walked out.

Once outside and walking east along Broadway, CJ punched up Dan's number. When Dan answered he said, "When can I have my car and life back?"

"Where are you?" Dan said.

CJ told him.

"Stay put. I'll be there in five minutes and run you over to the impound lot. Your apartment should be released in about an hour. The team is there right now."

CJ sat down at a bus stop and waited, a layer of sweat already building on his skin. How hot was it going to get today? Anything over 100 was just too damned hot. He'd about had it with everything concerning Southern Arizona, Tucson especially. The heat; the crime; the people. Everything.

A bus pulled up, discharged a half dozen passengers who scattered as though they were all late for work and then was gone, exhaust billowing in CJ's face. He closed his eyes and held his breath until it cleared and then thought about what he was going to do. He had one more subpoena to serve. After that he had no more obligations, not one single open case. Of course that also meant he had no income, but he did have money invested from half of an inheritance when his mother died seven years back, the other half of which was putting Trish through school and had allowed Josh to disappear. He could tap into that, get away for a while, maybe disappear himself.

There was a honk and then Dan's unmarked pulled up. When CJ was in and Dan had pulled back into traffic CJ said, "I'm really sorry I screwed up the crime scene. I don't know where my head was."

"Your head was having a party with Mr. Daniels. In the long run I don't think there was any harm done. We're dancing with the Feds now and I think we've gotten you removed from their sights. You may be hearing from them, of course, as they go back over ground we've already covered, but strictly as a witness, not a suspect."

"I saw the news."

"Yeah. That was unfortunate. What were the chances there'd be a camera pointing at you right at that moment? You can't even scratch your ass anymore that someone doesn't get it on video. At least no one's going to accuse me of giving favoritism to my friends or ex-cops."

But to hell with my reputation, CJ thought. He bit his lip and watched businesses pass by.

At the impound lot Dan said, "I'll call you when the apartment is released. Hang loose until then. Keep a low profile for a while. When we catch this lunatic everybody will forget about you." Just then Dan's phone chirped. When he hung it up he said, "Your office is cleared."

CJ watched Dan drive away, not sure if he was abandoned or set free, not sure if he appreciated Dan for being a friend or hated him for being a cop, not sure where the hell he stood with Stella.

CJ Washburn wasn't sure of one damn thing.

He signed the paperwork, drove his car until he found a gas station and then parked to look at the mess that had been made. Is this the way cops always treated suspect's property, or was it just him, the ex-cop, the one who abandoned his fellow soldiers in blue? Sure, he still had friends on the force, but there were many who were indifferent and a few who flat out didn't like him because he rolled over into the private sector, the ones who had no respect for P.I.s. The rest didn't know him at all.

He gathered together everything that belonged in the glove box and stuffed it back in. The rest, outside of his P.I. folder, was his own trash that the officers just pushed around and made a little messier. He gathered that into two piles, one to keep and one to throw, left the keep on the backseat and carried the rest to a nearby trashcan. Back in his car he opened the P.I. folder. It appeared to be as he left it, the one subpoena remaining to be served. He considered his appearance, decided it wasn't as bad as it could be, looked through his notes for the individual's work address and then headed out.

He'd do this last thing for the county and then that was it. He could be accused of a lot of things, but not doing his job was not one of them. Already on 6th Avenue, he continued south into South Tucson, found the body shop, the individual's place of employment, and walked right into the open bay doors. There were three men making a big racket on a monster truck.

"Enrique Santiago!"

None of them heard him. He was in no mood to pitter-patter around. He spotted a short piece of two-by-four, picked it up and slammed it against a slab of sheet metal leaning against a workbench. All three men looked up. CJ suddenly wished he had his piece, which was, he hoped, still locked in his desk in his office.

"Enrique Santiago!" CJ said again with much bravado.

"What?" one of the men said.

CJ approached him and said, "Are you Enrique Santiago?"

The man nodded his head. "Yes."

CJ handed him the subpoena. "You've been served." With that he turned and walked out. As CJ accelerated out of the parking lot, Enrique was standing just outside the bay doors, looking down at the subpoena and appearing very confused. "Welcome to the legal system, Enrique," CJ said to his rearview mirror.

Chapter 13

Unlike his car, CJ's office was only a partial wreck. The normally locked desk drawer, where he kept his Glock, along with its permit, was standing open. The gun was gone. Of course it would be gone. Ballistics had to be run on it even though all three of the victims were strangled, not shot.

He was surprised the computer was still there. He pushed Stella's desk drawers shut and pressed the computer power button. While it booted up he went looking for a drink. He kept his *Jack Daniels* in the bottom drawer of the filing cabinet. The drawer, surprisingly, was closed, and even more surprisingly, the half full bottle was still in it.

As he studied the bottle, however, he realized that getting drunk again was probably not one of his better ideas, but just having a finger or two.... He closed the drawer and went to his mini-refrigerator.

Two beers and two sodas looked back at him. He debated about it for a time and then snatched out a soda. He opened it and sat down at the computer. It was still booting. He thought a little more about the beer and took a long slug on the *Dr. Pepper.* The carbonation did feel good and in some weird way made his face hurt a little less.

When the computer appeared to be ready, he opened *Internet Explorer.* Stella had it set so that *Google* was the default home page. He wished she was here now to help him, but then she was part of the reason he was doing this. He couldn't remember the name of the website he wanted so he put "maps" in the search box. The second thing that showed up was *mapquest.com*. He clicked on that and when the page was open carefully entered his origination, Tucson, AZ and the destination, Moscow, ID.

The results displayed fast. Just under 1400 miles, routing through Las Vegas. Good place to spend a night... or two.

He wondered when Dan was going to call to let him know his apartment had been cleared. They'd had more than enough time to toss three apartments the size of his. He leaned back in Stella's chair, sipped on the soda and looked at where the wall met the ceiling until his eyes drifted closed.

When CJ's eyes snapped open he was pouring soda in his lap. He jumped up and the chair flew back. "Son of a bitch!" He fetched a towel from the bathroom and cleaned himself up as best as he could. He looked at his watch. He'd only drifted off for ten minutes or so. Where the hell was Dan?

He grabbed his keys and locked the office door behind him.

As he pulled into his apartment complex parking lot he spotted a uniformed police officer coming out with someone in civilian clothes he recognized, one of those who didn't particularly like him. Bryan something. CJ parked to the side and waited. He didn't want any kind of confrontation or another question and answer session. They tossed a small duffle into the back of a police van and then loaded up and left, paying him no attention.

He pulled around and parked where the van had been and went in. He paused at his apartment door for a few seconds and then unlocked it. He eased it open far enough to flip on the light and then gave it a shove and stepped aside. The door stopped halfway. CJ's hand went to his hip where his Glock would normally be. Swearing under his breath, he scanned what he could see of the apartment, saw no motion, no shadows, looked through the crack and found that it was his footstool stopping the door.

He let out a breath and stepped in, pushing the door closed behind him. He wanted to utter all kinds of expletives, at the top of his lungs, but what would be the point. He didn't do this kind of thing when he was a police officer and he doubted trashing a suspect's home was a standard today. These were simply a couple of scumbags with badges who had a beef against him for some reason. This was personal.

CJ spent the next two hours putting his apartment back together; vacuuming, cleaning the kitchen and bathroom, getting it not quite to Stella's standard, but not bad as far as he was concerned. Then he pulled out the remainder of the chicken Stella had left for him, grabbed his last beer and sat down to eat and think.

Was there something driving Dan to have him arrested and searched besides his claim to get him immediately off the suspect list? Granted, if the roles were reversed he might have taken the same action.

Or would he have?

CJ placed himself in Detective Payne's shoes and attempted to see the scene behind the restaurant from his perspective. The person who called 911 had the victim's hair and skin cells on his hands, had left his own blood on the victim, had been seen hanging around the drop area, had been drinking—CJ didn't want to admit that he might have been flat out drunk—and had absolutely no verifiable alibi for the estimated time of death. There was also no other witness to the dark-colored van he said he'd seen.

He thought about the news video. It was obvious that he'd pushed Officer Bentley. If he had been in Bentley's shoes he'd have had the inebriated perp—okay, so he might admit he'd had a few—on the ground and handcuffed, no questions asked. That's what a police officer was trained to do. Was the force excessive?

CJ felt the scabbing on his face and chewed on the chicken.

He could have subdued him without dropping him, maybe. He thought about the fact that he was two inches taller than Bentley, and trained to fight, and that Bentley knew that.

Okay, so maybe it was mostly justified.

He emptied his beer and set the can on its side next to the chicken carcass. He wanted another beer, or better yet, a tumbler or two of Jack Daniels. He was glad that he was out of both or he'd be on his way to shit-faced. The last thing he needed to do right now was go down that road. He rose as though hefting another fifty pounds and carried his plate to the trash, scraped it clean and dropped it in the sink.

He stood with hands in his pockets for a time, staring out the window at the parking lot, then turned on the TV. Unable to focus on any of the 200 plus channels, he wandered around the apartment, eventually coming to stop in front of the photo of his children. He wished he knew where Josh was. What was he doing with his life? Why did he run away?

He studied Trish's smiling face and wondered how her life was going, considered trying to call her again. Instead he put his phone on charge and pulled his duffle bag out of the closet. There was nothing keeping him in Tucson right now: No cases to run down, no subpoenas to serve, no girlfriends to entertain and Dan didn't say a thing about not leaving town. He realized, also, that the decision had already been made when he researched it on *MapQuest* at the office.

He started transferring items of clothing from drawers and closet to the duffle.

Duffle bag staged next to the door, he sat down in front of the TV and thought about how it would be good to get out of the heat, literally and figuratively, for a while, and how good it would be to see Trish. And then he fell asleep in his easy chair.

Chapter 14

CJ was showered, dressed and on the road just at the leading edge of dawn, rolling into Las Vegas in the noon hour. He parked in the Monte Carlo Casino parking garage and spent the afternoon walking from casino to casino playing primarily slot machine blackjack. Just before leaving he stopped back in the Monte Carlo and played the last $10 of the $50 he started with, figuring he'd go when he lost it. He picked a $1 slot machine and put the $10 dollar bill in and sat down. The first four tries got him nothing and then the fifth rang a couple of bells and started ringing up credits. Now feeling good he played a little more and won a little more. When finally he cashed out he was $383 over the $50 he started with.

He celebrated with an early dinner then drove on to Caliente to spend the night. Before turning in he spent some time again trying to get his trunk open, not understanding why neither the button on his fob nor the release from inside the car worked and then why his key would go in and not turn. He hadn't worried too much about it that morning since all he packed was the duffle bag, which he threw into the back seat. Now it was bugging him. How could both the electrical and mechanical fail together? After a time, he gave up and went to bed. He'd have it looked at in Idaho while he was visiting with Trish.

Up again at dawn, CJ pushed forward, stopping only for gas and fast food, arriving on the outskirts of Moscow, Idaho right at 8:00 p.m., surprised that it was still daylight. In Tucson it would be dark already. He followed the GPS through the town, coming almost out the west side before he found the Palouse Inn just off Pullman Road.

He got out and stretched, pleased with how he held up with nearly

14 straight hours behind the wheel. He thought about calling Trish, then decided he'd get checked in and grab some dinner first. Besides, she'd probably not answer her phone anyway. He'd put her address in the GPS and surprise her at her front door. He couldn't wait to see her face.

He went inside, presented his credit card and driver's license, signed and initialed where asked and then drove around to park near the stairs up to the second floor, thinking about the odd look on the desk-clerk's face. It was a look of shock, CJ thought as he ran it back through his mind and then as quickly, the look was gone. Something about it bugged him. Maybe by some weird coincidence this guy knew Trish and had put the two names together. Or did it have something to do with his credit card? The clerk would have said something in either case, surely.

He shook the thoughts away as he lifted the duffle from the back seat, noting the McDonald's right next door. His stomach growled. He carried the duffle up to his room, dropped it on the bed and went right back out. CJ could already taste the Big Mac.

The line was short. In less than five minutes he was pushing backwards out the restaurant door, a bag with a Big Mac and fries in one hand and large drink in the other. He navigated between cars in the parking lot and then entered the trees separating McDonald's from the hotel property, hearing a wail of sirens in the distance; multiple emergency vehicles, CJ figured. Just as he started to step out of the trees where he had a view of the hotel parking lot, a Sheriff's patrol unit roared in, silent, lights flashing. The sirens he'd been hearing suddenly went silent and in seconds another deputy and two Moscow police units screamed into the parking lot from different directions. And then there were uniformed officers out of their vehicles pointing their police issued weapons at... his car!

CJ took a step back, looked around and then eased deeper into the trees. He knew that the right thing to do would be to present himself and ask what the hell was going on; however, what his head was saying was the right thing and what his gut was saying was the right thing were not in agreement. Before he was going to make some rash move he had to know what the game was all about. He figured with the dark shadows beneath and behind the foliage in which he was secluded and with the fact that it was now well into dusk, he had as good a cover as he was going to get. It was open ground to get to anywhere else.

As CJ watched, two officers entered the office, ran out no more than thirty seconds later and pointed up to the second floor. He watched, in shock, as they stormed up the stairs, two at a time, gathered at CJ's door, nodded to each other, weapons drawn, then without knocking scanned the key card and rushed in as though ready to engage a gun fight. Down at his car he looked on in horror as a deputy pulled a tool from his patrol unit and proceeded to pry at the trunk. In only seconds there came a loud pop and the trunk flew open. They looked down inside and all CJ could see were their heads shaking while one spoke into his shoulder mike.

He didn't like the looks on their faces. Whatever was in the trunk was bad, and CJ did not put it there, hadn't even been in the trunk since getting the car back from impound.

He needed a better vantage point. He looked up into the tree under which he'd been standing and then at the meal in his hands. And then he started thinking like a cop. At any moment they were going to start searching the area for him. If he put the food on the ground a sharp-eyed deputy might spot it. One thing would lead to another. He looked back through the foliage toward McDonald's. On the edge of the parking lot, on the grass not twenty feet away, stood a trash can. He edged out, dropped everything into it then returned, grabbed a branch and pulled himself up into the tree. It was an easy climb, the tree full of thick limbs with just enough space for a body to squeeze through. Once as far up as he thought safe he positioned himself to see out. While he had been busy dumping the meal and climbing the tree, the officers had pulled something partway out of his trunk. CJ blinked several times, trying to clear his focus and get an idea what it was.

Then a familiar image flashed in his mind's eye and there came a terrible twist in his stomach. He slipped and caught himself, pulled his bulk upright and looked again. It was a quilt, different from, yet similar to the one on which he'd fallen in the dumpster nearly four days before, and there was no doubt in his mind that wrapped inside the quilt was the body of another Tucson woman.

Chapter 15

Except for lighting from McDonald's and the hotel, and a rising full moon, it was completely dark when the deputies and Moscow officers finished and drove away. His car had been hauled off on a flatbed, his duffle thrown in the back of a police van, and the body handled with forensic care and sent away for further study. But they weren't completely gone. A patrol car cruised by every fifteen to thirty minutes. Sometimes, like right now, it parked nearby for a time. They were watching for his return, CJ assumed. Why in the hell would a perp come back after everything was taken away? What would they think he'd return for?

Small town hick cops.

It was after 2:00 a.m., CJ guessed because he couldn't see his watch. Every contact point on his body as well as all major and minor muscle groups hurt like hell and for the last half hour he hadn't been able to move at all. A police cruiser was parked right next to the trash can where he'd dumped his dinner, the dinner he wished he'd eaten. He was not averse to retrieving it if they'd just leave.

Getting to the *Big Mac* was the smallest of all his problems, however. What in the hell was he going to do? It was pointless to contact Trish. They would certainly have someone parked outside her apartment, maybe even inside. She was probably completely freaked out, on the phone with her mother. He would be stupid to go there, but they had to assume he might be that stupid.

The first thing he was going to do once he could get out of the tree and to somewhere safe and hidden, was call Dan. Right now he didn't even want to turn his phone on. He sure didn't need to light up his position. He'd turned it off when he left Tucson because he didn't want to have to answer Stella's questions. Actually, he had to admit to himself, he didn't want to know if she didn't call. With his phone turned off he could go on in ignorant bliss that she was frantically worried about him, wanting to apologize for stiff-arming him in front of her nephew, wanting to beg him to come back. What the hell was she thinking right now?

Talk about stupid! He should have realized something was up when he couldn't get his trunk to open. If he had investigated it before he left and discovered the body himself... that certainly wouldn't have come off very well either. Who was going to believe him that the body was planted by the killer to turn the heat off of himself? But they'd have only circumstantial evidence, certainly less than with the dumpster because there'd be no blood, prints, hair or fluids that could be tied to him. It would certainly not be as bad as transporting a dead body through three states in the trunk of his car. And what kind of serial killer had this kind of forethought and planning, the wherewithal to pull something like this off? They were normally so focused on their obsession that they couldn't think outside themselves.

He thought about the suits who had arrived just before dark and began envisioning his face on the FBI's most wanted list as well as on the morning briefing of every law enforcement agency between here and Tucson; hell, between the Canadian and Mexican borders. And of course, with them around, just turning on his phone would light up their tracking devices.

All of a sudden the police car keeping him in place sped out of the parking lot and turned left toward city center, lights blazing, engine roaring. CJ wasted no time getting to the ground. He hobbled over to the trash can, felt into the dark space until his hand landed on a closed up bag with weight. He checked inside to ensure it was in fact a complete sandwich and fries, and not someone's half consumed discard. It was his. With dinner tucked under his arm he moved west from concealment to concealment, passing behind Schuck's Auto

Supply and then a Zip Trip gas station that was way too lit up. He crossed into the Best Western parking lot, stayed close to cars, half crouched, until he came to the corner of Farm Road and Pullman Road. Ahead of him was the Palouse Mall parking lot. If it was open he might have gone into the Old Navy for a change of clothing and a jacket. Shorts and a T-shirt weren't hacking it in the chill night air. At least he had decent shoes.

The empty parking lot provided no concealment. To the right up Farm Road didn't look much better. Left would take him across Pullman Highway and into a less lighted area. That would be his direction, but first he needed to call Dan. He crouched completely out of sight amongst a group of bushes on the corner then pulled out his phone and turned it on. He punched up Dan's number and hit the call button.

"CJ! What the hell is going on?" Dan answered as though he had been holding it in his hand waiting for CJ's call. Maybe he had been.

"I was about to ask you the same thing, Detective. You impound my car and when I get it back there's a dead body in it."

"That's bullshit and you know it. Where the hell are you?"

"Can't tell you that. I'm being railroaded. Until you figure that out and catch the real killer, I'm off the grid."

"Dammit, CJ," Dan said.

"Just shut up and listen. Two mornings ago when I left Tucson my trunk was jammed closed. Key wouldn't turn. Neither the inside release or remote would work. I didn't put the pieces together at the time or even knew there were pieces to be put together. Means that in the middle of that night someone put the victim in there and then disabled the mechanism. He didn't want me discovering the body, would rather you or someone from the Tucson police make the discovery. He never counted on the fact that'd I leave town with the body so I guess that's a bonus for him. I never noticed any evidence of a break-in so he knew what he was doing. Make sure someone looks for prints and any other forensics that don't belong to me."

"Turn yourself in, CJ."

"I'm being setup, Dan. You know it and I know it." CJ ended

the call and powered his phone down and then sprinted across the highway, dropping to a comfortable jog down the middle of the road. When he came to a split he bore left as there were too many lights straight ahead. Trees on the right made him feel a tad more secure as they'd give him cover if any vehicles appeared. None did, however. A huge parking lot appeared on the left and then a domed stadium. He came to where a road came in from the right and from what he could tell in the moonlight, appeared to climb. Staying on the road he was on would take him back toward town center, he guessed, or into the university, both of which he didn't want. He turned right and started up the grade.

At the top of the hill he stopped to catch his breath and let his heart rate slow. He looked back across from where he'd come and could see a number of flashing blue lights west of the McDonalds, exactly where he was when he made the call to Dan. He opened his phone and removed the battery. Having it turn on by accident would be like putting a beacon on his head.

He walked for a time eating his sandwich and fries and then walked and jogged until the pavement ended. From then on he had to be real careful because even in the moonlight it would be easy on the dirt and gravel road to make a misstep and twist an ankle. He had to get off the road for cars only twice. It was the second one where there was no ditch to hide in, so he stumbled into a farmer's field and fell into whatever was growing there, no more than a foot tall. He peeked though the plants in time to see a five-pointed star on the side of the car as it went by, a deputy racing for town.

Soon after he'd turned left at another split, taking what appeared to be the road less traveled. For a half hour he remained on that road until it T'd at another road. Sand Road, the sign read. He looked left and right and then back a hundred yards to a trailer and several buildings he had passed. He went back to investigate. There were no cars so he made the assumption that there were no people, that the trailer was some kind of workday office.

He knocked and listened, prepared to bolt if there was so much as a grunt or a thump. When there was nothing he pulled a credit card from his wallet and went to work on the trailer door. Apparently there wasn't much worry about security in the boonies of Idaho because in fifteen seconds he was in.

He stood still for a time, hand on the door, listening for any sounds that would indicate that the trailer was occupied. Once fully satisfied that it was not he debated with himself about turning on the lights. After a time he decided that it wasn't worth the risk, no matter how small. As the low-setting moon was at the wrong angle, there was no hope of getting light from it, so he stumbled around the dark space, running into several chairs before he discovered a desk. The stench in the room told CJ that the regular occupants were smokers. Although he was feeling through the drawers for a flashlight, he figured his chance of coming upon a lighter were pretty good. After pawing though papers and clipboards, pens and pencils, and things he couldn't identify, he landed upon what he assumed was a carton of cigarettes in a left-hand drawer. Lying next to that were three lighters. He pulled one out and lit it.

With that he went through all the drawers finding no flashlight and nothing else useful. Then, holding the lighter in front of him, he walked about the small space. At the end opposite the desk was a sofa with a hat rack standing next to it. He resisted the urge to lay down for a nap, going, instead, to the hat rack. On that were a couple of ball-caps, a jacket made of blue jean material, and a heavy parka. He took the jacket and a ball-cap. The ball-cap was dark red with the words *Semper Fi* in black. He debated taking the other one instead, but it was bright orange. In the end he put on the jacket and left both hats. Chances were the hats might be missed right away, but not the jacket until the daytime weather turned cooler.

Behind the desk sat a small refrigerator almost identical to the one in CJ's office. Inside CJ found nine cans of diet Pepsi and three more cartons of cigarettes. He debated over the Pepsi, then took one and moved the others to disguise the fact that one was missing. What he didn't want was for someone to notice that they'd had an intruder and call the police. He didn't need the authorities to even suspect in what direction he'd gone.

He started to put the lighter away and then thought to take one more look around the room. It was then that he spotted two things, the phone on the desk and the map pinned to the wall next to the door. As he approached the map he wondered who he could call. Certainly not Dan. Caller ID would nail him to this trailer. Stella? Would Dan or the FBI be monitoring her phone? Certainly she knows by now that something's up because Dan or someone would have asked her if she'd heard from him.

So he definitely couldn't call Stella. And even if he could, what would he say? What would be the point?

He studied the map for a time, figuring out that Sand Road went toward Pullman, Washington to the right and meandered back toward Moscow to the left. He didn't feel as though either option was very smart. But then was there a smart option anywhere?

Yes, there was. Get back to Tucson. Running from the law in Idaho was going to accomplish nothing, and doing unlawful things like breaking into trailers and stealing stuff wasn't going to help at all.

What the hell is he thinking? He's about to go down for multiple homicides and he's worried about a little break and enter.

First things first. Get back to Tucson, therefore, procure a car. He had more than enough cash for gas and food having pulled $500 in cash before leaving and then winning at the casino. Credit cards were useless except for opening doors with cheap locks.

He sat in the desk chair for a time pushing ideas around in his head. They all just wound up in the same bog. If he was going to procure a car, he'd have to get into a town. Moscow was out so at this point it'd have to be Pullman. He got up and stepped out onto the trailer platform. The moon was setting and it appeared there was a glow in the eastern sky. He'd run out of time getting to anywhere before daylight.

He sat on the porch step and put his head in his hands, considered turning his cell phone on and seeing how long it would take someone to show up. It was one way to get back to Tucson, though extradition might take a few days. But then he'd be stuck in jail, unable to do anything except insist that he was innocent.

He thought about Stella, wished he was spooned with her under her blankets and that the alarm clock would fail to go off. He remembered how crazy he'd gotten when she'd seemed to have gone missing and then started feeling very guilty for doing it right back at her. She'd have no clue what happened to him, would likely be going as crazy as he did. Unlike her, he didn't leave any notes or voicemails, or chicken in the refrigerator.

Now he really felt like a dope.

But of course, she now knew where he had gone. Dan certainly has talked to her. What was she thinking of him? Did she think he was guilty? Would she stand up for him? He remembered the brief call she'd made to him when she said sorry so many times and then his return call to her voicemail where he'd told her he loved her. He looked over at the setting moon, now almost all gone, and wished he had told her that long before. Now it was too late.

He wondered if she had listened to that voicemail.

Automobile lights suddenly appeared up the road from the direction he'd come. He stepped inside the trailer, closed the door and watched out the window. The vehicle, a small pickup truck it appeared, passed on by. CJ couldn't see the intersection, but from the sound it turned right and accelerated toward Pullman.

CJ's mind went back to Stella. He considered calling her just to hear her voice, then stepping outside in the open to wait for the sheriff to show up. He could stay on the phone with her until they put him in handcuffs. At least then he'd have an opportunity to tell her directly how he felt about her. There'd be no doubt.

He touched the pouch in which his phone resided and then drew it out. He considered it for a few seconds and then pressed the power button.

He waited.

Nothing happened.

He touched it again and waited. Still nothing. The phone was dead?

He holstered it and felt his way around the desk until his hand touched the phone. He picked it up and with slow deliberate care, punched in Stella's number, pausing on the last digit. After a half dozen heartbeats, he pushed and waited.

After one ring he got a recording. "Your call cannot be completed as dialed. Please include the area code."

CJ laughed at himself, hung up and then redialed, this time using the 520 area code. Again he paused on the last digit. A stray, but important, thought kept flipping through his mind and it had to do with Stella's sister. He was certain that calling Stella on her cell phone would be equivalent to calling the FBI and telling them where to pick him up. However, what if he could get to Stella through her sister, Sara? He remembered looking up Sara's number when Stella had gone missing and wondered why he'd never made the call. It'd have been so simple and would have solved everything.

His mind suddenly became clear. He hit the disconnect and then started dialing the number he'd looked up in Stella's address book. For some crazy reason he could actually remember it. He dialed the complete number without pausing and then waited through three rings. He thought about the time and was prepared to be very apologetic.

"Hello!" It was a man's voice, Sara's husband of course.

CJ struggled for a few seconds to remember his name. "Bill?"

"Yes."

"This is CJ Washburn, a friend of Stella's. I'm really sorry to..."

"Hold on."

The line went silent and CJ tried to guess what the hell was going on. Was he fetching Sara, calling the FBI on another line, or did he just plain hang up not wanting to get involved with an accused serial killer.

The silence hung on and on until suddenly, "Clint!"

"Stella?" CJ couldn't believe his ears.

"Where are you? We're coming to get you."

"I'm in Idaho."

"I know that. Where in Idaho, exactly?"

"I don't understand. What do you mean coming to get me. How you going to do that?"

"Bill's plane."

And then CJ remembered. Bill was a pilot, owned a small business flying parts and people around the country.

"We'll be there in seven hours. We just need a place to pick you up. We've got to get you back down here so you can help fix this. You're being framed."

The relief that passed through CJ left him almost wanting to cry. His biggest fear was that Stella wouldn't believe him, that she'd turn her back on him. "I'm sorry I left without telling you first," he said.

"Damn it, Clint. That's not important now. Do you know how to tell us where you are?"

CJ pulled the lighter out of the desk drawer and stepped over to the map, pulling the phone cord behind him. "Yes." He flicked the lighter and studied the map again. "I'm at the intersection of Brown Road and Sand Road, south of Moscow."

She repeated that to someone there and said to CJ, "Hang on. Bill's looking it up on Google Earth. Everything went nuts down here when you left. There was an anonymous 911 call that someone saw you loading a body into the trunk of your car."

"That's a flat out lie."

"Of course it is. Dan's chasing down his suspicions."

"Dan? He doesn't believe it?"

"Of course not. We know the body was planted, but Dan has to do what he has to do, especially with the FBI running lead on it. Anyway, they'd have gotten you when you filled with gas in Boise, but someone dropped the ball. I don't think they had their shit together yet. It was when you checked into the hotel and then eluded them that everything went nuts. Accusations and blame were flying everywhere."

"I suppose you even know what I had for dinner last night."

"Big Mac and Fries. Large drink."

CJ just blinked.

"Dan's been keeping me informed. It's only a matter of time before they find you unless we can get you out of there. It's like a contest now; FBI, county sheriff, Moscow police. Each one of them wants to wipe the pie off their face with your collar."

"So it's just you and Dan on my side."

"And Bill and Sara. Yes, that's about it. Just a second."

There were some mummers in the background. CJ looked out the window. It was the leading edge of dawn.

"Okay. We've got you. Are you in that trailer just north of the intersection?"

CJ looked up at the ceiling. How in the hell? "Yes. I don't think I can stay here too much longer."

"Go to the intersection and cross over to the south side of Sand Road. There appears to be a drainage or creek that goes off to the left. Follow that until you get into the trees, a hundred yards, maybe less. Get down and stay there."

"Okay."

After another conference with Bill, Stella said, "Bill is thinking that we'll be there somewhere in the noon hour. We'll refuel once along the way, will plan to pick you up with a light fuel load, but enough that we can be well out of the area before having to refuel again."

"Okay."

More conferencing. "You'll know we're there when we fly low right over the top of you. Bill will need to check the roads for a place to land so watch and be there fast. He's anticipating, from what he can see on Google Earth, that we'll land on Sand Road. Chances are the locals won't pay much attention if we are in and out fast."

"Okay," CJ said again. "I'll be waiting."

"Thirty seconds on the ground, Bill says."

"Thirty seconds." He let his heart beat for a few seconds. "Stella."

"I'm still here, but we've got to get going."

"I just wanted to say, I'm sorry. I..."

"I'm sorry, too, Clint. See you this afternoon. Bye."

The phone went dead and CJ tried to understand why he couldn't get the words out that he wanted to say. Maybe it was because even more now than ever, he loved her, but he didn't want it to seem like he was saying it just because of what she was doing. For certain, for himself, he wanted to make sure he was saying it for the right reason.

He restored the office to how he'd found it and then scurried over to where he could hide and wait. There wasn't a creek. It was more like an irrigation ditch with a few inches of water. He settled and hoped he wouldn't fall asleep.

Chapter 16

CJ found himself in the middle of a monsoon, wind, thunder and rain whirling and pounding around him. Suddenly he realized he was asleep and in the middle of a nightmare. He struggled to push out of it, rolled over and half fell into the ditch. He splashed to his feet, remembering where he was, making sense that the sounds from his nightmare were actually that of a plane flying low overhead.

"Stella!"

He half jumped, half sloshed across the ditch, pushed through the brush and stumbled onto the road as the plane finished its bank to get lined up to touch down. CJ looked both ways for traffic—there was none—and then over at the trailer from where he'd made the call. He could see the backend of a red truck and hoped he'd left the place the way he'd found it, no evidence that he'd been present. He also hoped they'd overlook the strange long distant charge on their phone bill.

He stood in the middle of the road until he was certain Stella and Bill had seen him and then stepped off just as the wheels touched. Thirty seconds later he was scrambling head first into the space behind Stella, and Bill was accelerating. The plane never came to a complete stop and not a word was said. By the time CJ got himself righted and settled, seatbelt buckled, they were well clear of the area and banking south.

"We're not going to have cell coverage for very long," Bill said to Stella, "so make the call now."

CJ looked between Bill and Stella, trying to guess who she was calling, assumed it was her sister. Bill was a big guy. He wasn't fat, just tall—his head nearly brushed the overhead—and broad shouldered.

Next to him Stella looked like a little girl. She punched numbers into a cell phone and waited for the connection to go through.

"We've got him," she said without any introduction. "No, no problems. Hold on. I'm handing the phone to him." With that she passed it back to CJ.

CJ took it, looked at Stella's smiling face for a minute then said, "Hello?"

"Daddy! Are you all right?"

"Trish! Yes, yes, I'm fine, thanks to some great people here. Are you okay? I was worried that the police would show up at your door and throw a scare into you."

"They did and yes they did. I don't think they ever believed me that I didn't know where you were. Why didn't you tell me you were coming?"

"I wanted to surprise you."

She grunted something sort of like a laugh, sort of not.

"I'm really sorry for all this. You don't really believe I did this, do you?"

"Of course not, Daddy."

"I was in the wrong place at the wrong time."

"It sounds like that happened a couple of times, and this guy doing the killing is taking advantage. Stella has told me everything."

CJ put his hand on Stella's shoulder. "She's been wonderful." Stella put her hand on top of his.

"Should I come home? Is there anything I can do?"

"No. Stay in Idaho. You don't need to get involved in this. I just need to get back and help find this guy."

"The FBI thinks it's you, Daddy."

CJ squeezed his eyes closed when he heard the tears in his daughter's voice.

"I've seen the movies about serial killers," she said after she'd taken a deep breath. "This guy isn't going to quit. Maybe you should turn yourself in so that the next time he strikes it'll be obvious it wasn't you."

"That means another woman has to die to set me free. I don't want that to happen. And then, what if he does quit, or moves to another part of the country, or out of the country for that matter."

"He's probably not that smart, Daddy."

"He was smart enough to turn the heat on someone else. He's probably smart enough to figure out what he has to do to keep it there."

"You can't stay on the run... a fugitive!"

"I'll figure something out." He listened to her sniffle, looked out at the mountainous horizon ahead. "You're not on your cell phone, are you?"

"Of course not. I'm using Dillon's."

"Who's Dillon?"

"My boyfriend."

"You have a boyfriend? When did this happen?" It was after he said it that CJ realized he knew about Dillon, but he hadn't heard anything more about him in a long time. He'd sort of forgotten. "Aren't you still thirteen?" he said to try to hide his momentary lapse. "Since when are you allowed to have a boyfriend?"

"Daddy!" With that she laughed. CJ loved to hear her laugh.

"You give Dillon a big kiss for me."

"I sure will, Daddy. You call me and let me know what's happening, but call on Dillon's phone. Stella has the number."

"I will."

"Stella sounds nice."

"That's because she is. I love you, Trish."

"Love you, too, Daddy."

CJ handed the phone back to Stella. She punched a number for speed dial, waited and then said, "Hey sis. We've got him and are heading back. Everything went as planned. See you tonight."

When she put the phone away, CJ reached around the seat and touched her face. "Thank you for doing this."

"It's what we do. We take care of each other. But you really need to thank Bill."

"Thank you, Bill," CJ said to him. "I'll be forever in your debt."

"You're quite welcome; however, all I'm doing is supplying quicker transportation. Stella was already on her way, stopped long enough to drop Lucas back off. She was going to drive all night to get here to try and find you before the police did."

"You were?" CJ asked her.

"Yes. Bill and Sara talked me into waiting, was sure that you'd call me for help. He fueled and serviced his plane just in case."

"I couldn't call you, assumed they'd have a watch on your phone."

"You assumed right," Bill said.

"I don't know how you thought of calling Sara," Stella said, "but I'm sure glad you did."

CJ took her hand. "Me too."

Chapter 17

CJ stayed awake until they stopped for fuel somewhere in northern Nevada. After consuming vending machine junk food and bottled water, he slept the rest of the way to Albuquerque. He awoke in a fog. Stella was shaking him and yelling in his ear.

"Is everything okay?" CJ asked as he looked around. Bill was already out of the plane chocking the wheels and attaching tie-downs.

"Yes. We need to get going."

After climbing out and while walking across the small air strip to Bill's SUV, Stella explained that the plan was to spend the night and drive to Tucson in the morning. After that, she had no plan.

"Does Dan know what's going on?"

"No," Stella said. "I don't think he suspects that I'm doing anything, probably wouldn't want to know about it if he did. He's keeping me informed but he's not asking questions."

CJ thought about Detective Payne and suspected that he knew a lot more than he was letting on. Dan was no dummy; he was quite capable of piecing things together. CJ also saw how Dan was putting his career on the line if he did suspect what Stella was up to. He decided he needed to take back all the bad things he'd been thinking about him. "Does he have any leads yet? Were there any usable forensics found in the trunk of my car?"

"If anything's been discovered, he hasn't told me. But then, your car is in Idaho, he's in Tucson and the FBI has control. He sounded very frustrated the last time I talked to him. In his words, he's a basketball player who after being benched, got a new coach who tied his hands behind his back and sent him back in."

CJ couldn't picture Dan settling for that.

He climbed in the backseat of the SUV and Stella got in next to him. She rested her head on his shoulder. "I was so scared. I was afraid they'd find you and something would go wrong and you'd get shot."

He put his arm around her.

"If you think you need to turn yourself in, I'll understand," she added.

"I'm not ready to go there yet. We've got until tomorrow to talk about it."

For a time they rode in silence. From what CJ could tell the airstrip was well outside the city, and they were going nowhere near the city. They turned off the main highway and drove along a narrow, paved road until the pavement ended and then continued for another couple of miles into the hills, throwing dust behind them. When Bill turned off of that he came up to a steel gate. He hit a button on his visor that looked much like a garage door opener and the gate started swinging in.

"If anyone wants to set foot on my property they'd better be a friend or relative, or have a warrant," Bill said to CJ's questioning look in the rearview mirror. "I know you used to be a cop, Clint, but I won't hold that against you as long as Stella will vouch for you. You hurt Stella, though, you hurt the entire family."

"Bill!" Stella said.

"Just saying how it is, Sis. On the other hand, Clint, if Stella needs help, she has the power of the entire family standing next to her and as long as you're with her...."

They came to a stop in front of a large ranch-style adobe home. Two black Labradors, each nearly as big as Bill himself, appeared out of nowhere.

"Sit tight a minute, Clint, while I let them know you're friendly. They don't take kindly to strangers." He got out and said something to them, put his hands on their heads and then waved CJ out.

CJ had never owned a dog but otherwise liked them, except when he was entering their property when he was a cop. Stella slid out behind him and they didn't seem to pay her much mind. Their eyes were on him. Of course they knew who Stella was.

"This is Duke and Duchess." Bill touched each of them, slapped them on their shoulders, and added, "They're really just big babies."

Sure they are, CJ thought. Tentatively, he approached them, scratched their ears, felt the muscle along their necks and shoulders.

Bill rubbed their heads and slapped their shoulders again. "They're okay by you now. Let's get inside. Sara likely has dinner ready and I'll bet you're hungry."

After the vending machine food, CJ was ready for anything.

Chapter 18

Dinner was fabulous; baked potato, corn-on-the-cob, huge steaks. CJ thought it was more than he could handle, but before he knew it there was nothing left on his plate but a bone and two corncobs, and Sara was pushing apple pie in front of him.

Although he could see the similarities in the sisters, there were some striking differences. Where Stella's features were round and smooth, Sara was sharp and angular. She also stood about two inches taller and carried a bit more bulk, not fat, more like ranch-hand muscle. Like Stella, however, she had all the proper female proportions. They were two fine looking women.

"Aunt Stella," Lucas said around a bite of pie. "Am I going back to Tucson with you tomorrow?"

His mother reached over and touched his hand. "No, Lucas. Maybe another time, if we can squeeze it in before school starts back up."

"Okay," he said. CJ couldn't tell if he was disappointed or relieved. "Where's Mr. Washburn going to sleep?"

"Mr. Washburn is with Aunt Stella so he's going to stay in the guestroom with her.

"Oh." Lucas thought for a minute. The sisters exchanged looks. "Does that mean they're married? Should I call him Uncle Clint?"

Stella laughed. "No, Lucas. We aren't married, but we are a couple, which means for adults it's okay to sleep together. And yes, you may call him Uncle Clint." She looked at CJ with a slight twist of her head, and smiled.

"Are you going to get married?"

CJ looked between Sara and Bill who, it appeared, were letting the conversation go wherever it was going. They were both grinning and Sara was exchanging looks with her sister.

Stella wiped her mouth with her napkin, and set it to the side of her plate. “No, Lucas. There are no plans at this time.” She gave him a big smile. “But it was sure nice of you to be interested enough to ask.”

From the mouths of babes, CJ thought.

Stella turned to CJ. “Close your mouth, sweetie. Haven’t seen any flies in here that need to be caught.”

Lucas laughed until he fell out of his chair and then everyone laughed, even CJ.

After dinner CJ sat with Bill and Lucas, watching a nature program on alligator wrangling in Florida. The women were cleaning up in the kitchen. While Lucas asked questions of his dad about alligators, CJ thought about how the perp was able to get so much personal information so quickly and have the wherewithal to act on it. He thought about his conversation with his daughter. She thought that because the perp was a serial killer, he wasn’t very smart. In actuality, serial killers had a twisted intelligence. Some had an innate ability to clean up behind themselves so as to leave no forensic evidence. Others knew how to sidetrack investigators with planted evidence. Some could manage to go completely underground for a while, then surface years later, sometimes in another city. A rare few could ingratiate themselves into the investigation as a consultant, or official of some kind. In all cases the perp had either an uncontrollable urge resulting from a major trauma in their past, usually their childhood, or was driven by a brain injury or illness. In either case it never just stopped. They never had the control to kill three or four times and then cease altogether. They might be able to pull it in check for a time but, like an alcoholic, the urge was always there. Unlike the alcoholic, however, there was no serial killer anonymous to help them through it.

Hi. My name is Charles.

Hi, Charles.

I'm a serial killer. It has been eight months since my last kill.

"Clint!"

CJ looked up at Stella and the thoughts melted away. For just a brief second one of his thoughts hung back as though demanding more attention.

"Let's turn in," she said. "Long day tomorrow and it's starting very early."

With that CJ's mind cleared of all speculation. He wanted nothing more than to curl into a spoon with Stella until they fell asleep. He was suddenly surprised with himself that he didn't want sex, actually hoped she didn't either.

CJ undressed down to his boxers and climbed into bed. He stared up at the ceiling, his mind flitting between trying to figure out the profile of the killer and thinking about Stella minutes or even seconds from climbing in next to him. It flashed back at him again that there was something about the aspects of a serial killer that he had already thought of that was important, but his mind seemed to dance around it.

Stella came out of the bathroom brushing her hair. CJ loved her hair. It reached to her shoulder blades, a mix of rich brown and deep red, and when she moved in the light just right all he wanted to do was bury his hands in it. She stood facing him in a long T-shirt. He wondered what she was wearing under it, if anything.

"What's your plan tomorrow?" she said.

His gaze went from her thighs to her eyes. She raised an eyebrow. He loved the way she could do that.

"I don't know," he said. "Since you have a rapport with Dan right now, I'd say call him first thing in the morning, see if he has anything new."

"Should I tell him that you're not in Idaho any longer? Anything?"

He shook his head. "Not right off. Let's play it by ear, see what he has. There's something that's bugging me about this whole thing and I can't seem to get my thumb on it."

"Other than the fact that you're the prime suspect?"

"Yeah. Other than that."

She set the brush aside and climbed in next to him. "I don't want to fool around tonight. I just want to be close to you."

"I don't want to do anything either," he said as he pulled her toward him.

She rested her head on his chest. "That's not what your face was saying a few minutes ago."

"I liked what I saw. Can't turn that off."

She gave a little snort, the same snort CJ knew accompanied a smile. They lay quiet for a time and then she rolled to face away. He matched her roll to spoon against her and put his arm around her to cup a breast. Within minutes they were both asleep.

Chapter 19

At 4:00 am, the alarm Stella had set on her phone went off. By the time they were downstairs Sara had coffee, eggs, toast and bacon on the table. CJ ate in silence while the sisters talked about their mother. Their father had passed away about 4 years before of stomach cancer. Just over a year ago their mom met someone, online. Six months later, with only a few days warning to her daughters, Mom left the care of her Albuquerque home with Sara and moved to Cleveland, Ohio.

"A trial run," Stella said for CJ's benefit.

"And how's it going?" CJ asked.

"We're not really sure."

"I've visited twice," Sara said. "As far as I'm concerned, the jury is still out. He's not too well off, but seems nice enough. Not like he's a serial killer or anything." Sara put a hand to her mouth. "Shit! I'm sorry. Didn't mean that."

Stella laughed and put her hand on CJ's arm. "We know that. Don't worry about it."

Just before 5:00 they were on the road, Stella driving. CJ snoozed on and off until a few minutes after 8:00 when Stella took an exit for gas. They switched drivers and Stella slept while CJ pushed hard. With an hour time change it was just past 10:30 when they approached the downtown exits of Tucson.

Stella gulped down some of her cold coffee from the fuel stop and pulled out her cell phone. "About time to call Dan."

She dialed and put the phone to her ear.

"Good morning, Detective, it's Stella. Has there been any new developments?"

CJ watched Stella's face, at first neutral, then serious and then, "Oh my God! No Dan! It wasn't Clint."

CJ mouthed, "What?" at her.

"That's impossible, Detective, because he wasn't in Idaho last night.

"I know because I know.

"Damn it, Dan! He was with me all night, has been with me since noon yesterday.

"Yeah I'll swear to that, because it's true."

CJ grabbed the phone from Stella. "What the hell is going on, Dan?" he said into it.

"Holy crap, CJ!" Dan blasted in CJ's ear. "Where the hell are you?"

"I'm sitting right next to Stella." On a hunch he pulled away from the Speedway Street exit he was about to take and re-entered the interstate traffic. "What the hell happened?"

"Christ! There's been another victim, this time in Moscow, Idaho. Same exact MO, and you're suspect number one. Turn yourself in right now and if what Stella is saying is true you'll be off the hook. You certainly can't be in two places at the same time. Please tell me you're back in Arizona. Don't know how you'd have done it, but I hope to hell you are. Where the hell are you?"

"Don't know if I want to answer that right yet."

"Don't even tell me you're still in Idaho."

"Nowhere near there. Do you have any ideas on who this guy is?"

"No, I don't. And this puts another spin on it."

"Puts a huge spin on it. This guy is smart and has some serious inside knowledge and resources." And then it occurred to CJ what he missed the night before, the one thing that hovered just out of reach. "It's a cop."

"What?"

Stella's eyes got big and her mouth dropped.

"Think about it, Dan."

"I am thinking about it. I'd put my life on the line with any officer on this force. I don't believe any one of them would just up and start killing women."

"You had your doubts about me."

"Not once, CJ. I never once thought you were the perp."

"Even after the body was found in my car?"

Dan didn't say anything but CJ could swear he could hear his teeth grind. He swerved over a lane as he passed the Grant Street exit and accelerated past a plumbing repair van barely doing the speed limit.

"I wasn't there last night and it can be proven, so I'll be off the hook, as you say, but until then I'm not about to be stuck in some holding cell."

"If you turn yourself into me within the hour, I think the FBI will be convinced this last one wasn't you."

"You're not sure, though, are you? And what about the one that was found in my car?"

"An obvious plant."

"Obvious to you, maybe, but not to the Feds." CJ swung back to the right lane and took the Miracle Mile exit. "I can see some career climbing happy agent getting his rocks off bringing down an ex-cop private investigator, and passing last night's off as a copycat."

"I think you're over-thinking this CJ. Turn yourself in and everything will fall into place."

CJ punched the gas as he turned right onto Miracle Mile, crossed to the left lane and pushed toward the Flowing Wells intersection and a red light.

"What the hell you doing?" Stella demanded.

"Yeah, what are you doing?" Dan said, obviously having heard Stella.

"I'm proving I'm not in Idaho. After that I'm playing it all by the seat of my pants." He looked over at Stella's panic-stricken face and said, "It'll be okay. I know what I'm doing."

"I don't think you have a clue what you're doing, CJ" Dan said.

"Hold on a second, Dan."

CJ eased off the gas for a second just before the light turned green, then accelerated again. Seconds later, just beyond the intersection, he swerved into the left turn lane, punched between several oncoming cars and bounced into a parking lot.

"But this is…" Stella shut her mouth.

"CJ, talk to me," Dan said.

"Just hold on a minute."

He swung the car around the edge of the parking lot until he was at the main entrance to the Westside Police Service Center. He said, "Okay, Detective, here's what I want you to do." He put the emergency brake on and climbed out of the car. "Go to the nearest window where you can see the public parking lot."

"What the hell you doing, CJ? Fine, I'll play your game."

CJ waited and watched, hoping the hell Dan wasn't a step ahead and ushering uniformed cops out the door.

"Okay. I'm there. What am I looking for?"

CJ started waving his hand in the air. "See that idiot waving at you with a phone plastered to his ear. That's me. Now you're a witness as to my whereabouts at this precise moment." He got back in the car and started it rolling toward the parking lot exit. "If I have to I can produce several witnesses as to my whereabouts from noon yesterday until this moment which will place me far from the Idaho crime scene. Going off the grid again, Dan. I'll call you."

With that CJ hung up and handed the phone to Stella. "Turn it off and take the battery out." He swung the car into Miracle Mile west-bound traffic.

Stella did what he said. "Now what?"

By this time CJ was entering I-10 east-bound, back the way they'd come. "I don't know. Maybe I should just drop you off at home. It's me they're after."

"No way."

"Why not? You're probably already in trouble for aiding and abetting. You don't need to add more to it."

"First of all, Clint, this is my car. I'm not giving it up that easy.

Second of all I'm with you on this. I'm not sitting alone at home while my man goes off and has all the fun."

"Your man?" He looked at her, his eyebrows raised.

She looked away.

"Where was *your man* when you showed up with Lucas last week? You did everything short of actually denying that you had a boyfriend."

When she turned back to face him tears were running down her cheeks. "I'm really sorry about that. The entire situation was new to me. I didn't know how to handle it, how to handle you. I wanted to be a good aunt, wanted to show my little sister I could be responsible. And then I was called to get you out of jail and I had to bring Lucas with me. Children are so impressionable at that age, aren't they?"

CJ took the Speedway exit and reached over to take her hand. "I'm sorry. Shit happens at the exact wrong time." He stopped at the light.

"Yeah."

After a long silence CJ said, "If you're sticking with me we're going to have to change our names."

"What?" She wiped at her tears and gave him her confused look. "Why?"

The light turned green and he turned left. "You're going to have to call me Clyde from now on."

She furrowed her brow. "Clyde. I don't get it. Why?"

"So I can call you Bonnie."

She knuckle-punched him in the arm and laughed.

"Hey! Careful. I'm driving here, you know."

She laughed some more, sniffled and dug a Kleenex from the glove box.

Chapter 20

"What do we do now?" Stella asked.

They'd continued east on Speedway for twenty minutes before anything more was said, each receding into their own thoughts.

"It's rather obvious that you're part of this now," CJ said, "so going to your apartment is out of the question, at least it is for me. If we separated you could return."

"No."

"You'd get a little bit of heat."

"No."

"Dan would likely pick you up but he couldn't hold you very long, would probably let you go in hopes you'd lead them to me."

"I said, no! I'm not separating from you. We're in this together."

"Then let's go to Las Vegas and get married," CJ said.

Stella whipped her head around. "What!"

"We could be up there by late afternoon, have an evening wedding, find a cash-only motel and have a wild honeymoon, be back here by tomorrow afternoon, or just stay up there for a few days walking the strip, playing a few machines."

"Are you serious?"

"Sure. That way when we're caught they won't be able to make you testify against me nor make me testify against you."

"That's not right," she said.

"What's not right? The not testifying or the getting married?"

"Stop! Stop somewhere!" She pointed to a strip mall parking lot. "Over there. I'm not going to talk about this in the middle of traffic while we're waiting for Tucson police to surround us."

"Okay." He signaled as he turned and then steered the car across the half empty parking lot to a spot between two large trucks.

"What's not right," she said before he had the car completely parked, "is doing it like this. My dream wedding is not a disgustingly cute little chapel with witnesses pulled off the street while we're running from the FBI and police in three states."

"So…" he paused for a very long time, debating whether or not to allow more of this crazy notion to spill out of his mouth. He looked her straight in the eyes. "...you think we should have a big wedding, then invite your mom and her boyfriend?"

She tilted her head and met his gaze, eye for eye. "Is *this* a proposal?"

He took a deep breath and made the final plunge. "I love you Stella Summers. Will you be my wife?"

Her mouth opened and then closed. She looked out at the bright day and then back at him. "I have been waiting three months for you to ask me and you choose *now* to pop the question?"

"You've been waiting for me to ask you?"

"Yes."

"So the answer is yes?"

"No."

"The answer is no?" he said, suddenly deflated.

"No."

He blinked at her a couple of times. "Which is it, yes or no?"

"Neither. I'm not answering until you've asked at the right time, in the right place, and if you don't know what that is then God help you."

"Okay.

"I'm thirty-nine, three years older than my sister and she has the marriage and the family, even if it is a little screwed up, but I'm not desperate enough to run off to Las Vegas with you, at least not until the day before I turn forty, which is still ten months away."

"Is that, then, a tentative yes? If I hold off until June eleventh, you'll do the chapel in Las Vegas?"

"If you're not in jail on June eleventh and you've been stupid enough to wait that long, then I guess if I'm not in jail, I'll be stupid enough to go to Las Vegas with you. Is that answer enough for you?"

He nodded. "It is. I guess, then, to keep us from having to testify against each other, we'd better figure out who the dumpster killer is."

"Back to my original question, what do we do now?"

"We've got to find a hideout, and for that I've got an idea. But I'm going to have to turn on my phone."

When CJ explained his idea to Stella, they remained out of sight between the two trucks for another half hour, until a man appeared and drove one of the trucks away. They discussed how he could get his phone turned on, find the number he wanted and then turn it off before the FBI could lock onto his location.

"What if we went somewhere that you had no signal?" Stella said. "They couldn't see you then, could they?"

"No, they couldn't. Great idea. And I know just the place. First, since we can't trust yours either, we need to get a new phone.

Chapter 21

They turned south off of Speedway onto Houghton and found a place to buy a phone with chargers for both house and car. He remained in the car while Stella did the shopping. Afterwards they continue south on Houghton out of Tucson until it intersected Sahuarita Road in Corona de Tucson. From there they drove west to Old Nogales Highway, turned south again until they intersected with Interstate 19 in Green Valley then continued south toward the Mexico border. Once out of Green Valley, CJ started relaxing. He was pretty sure the border patrol hadn't been advised to keep an outlook for him. They were frying other nasty fish. He was also fairly sure the word had not been fully disseminated that he was not in Idaho.

"How far south do we have to go?" Stella asked. "All the way to Nogales?"

"No. I believe I was somewhere between Amado and Tubac; twenty miles or so from Green Valley." He'd remembered trying to call Trish on his way to Nogales to serve the subpoena. He pointed to the phone sitting in the tray between them, connected to the charger. "Turn on the new phone. When we lose the signal on that we'll activate yours. If you also don't have a signal we should be safe to activate mine. It won't take but a minute to get the phone number and then I'll shut it down."

"And you're sure the Lindendales will do it?" she said.

"If I have to I'll offer to tear up the check, which I haven't deposited yet. I don't really want to do that because it might make them suspicious as to my reason. I'm sure they're back home in Missouri so probably haven't seen the news about me."

"What are you going to tell them to get the number?"

"I have no clue."

CJ's idea was to use Elizabeth Lindendale's apartment as a hide-a-way. To get Lizzi's okay and have her pass it to her landlady he'd have to get her phone number in Mexico. To do that he'd have to contact her parents and hope that they have a number where she could be reached.

"We just lost signal," Stella said.

CJ glanced down at the phone; saw that there were no bars. "Okay. Turn yours on."

As she started to insert the battery into her phone, he said, "Wait! We've got bars again."

They drove on, watching the phone, waiting.

"Damn!" CJ suddenly declared.

"What?"

"Border patrol checkpoint."

Stella looked up to see the checkpoint complex enveloping the northbound lanes, cars and trucks backed up waiting their turn to be cleared through.

"I thought you said border patrol wouldn't be a problem," she said.

"Random border patrol units driving around I doubt have name and photo of a Tucson murder suspect pasted to their dash, especially if that individual is believed to be in Idaho. But a permanent checkpoint might have that information, especially if Dan has already started disseminating his new knowledge as well as your car make, model and plate number."

"It's only been a couple of hours. Do you really think?"

He shook his head. "No, not really. But it still makes me nervous."

She looked over her shoulder at the checkpoint after they passed by. "Me too."

They continued south past Tubac and the Tubac exit while the signal went in and out. "I'm taking the next exit," CJ said, "and then heading up into the mountains. We'll eventually lose signal for sure."

And so he did, turning east on Palo Parado Road and then

bouncing from road to road until finally Stella said, "The signal has been completely gone for a while now. We should be good."

CJ pulled over on a wide spot and as Stella inserted the battery in her phone. They watched and waited while it powered up. After five minutes when they were sure there was no signal, they did the same with his phone. In less than two minutes he had Mrs. Lindendale's phone number and had shut down both his and Stella's phone.

He turned the car around.

At the border patrol checkpoint CJ slowed the car as per the posted speed limit and stopped behind the third car in line. They looked at each other.

The first car accelerated away and the rest moved up. A border patrol officer escorted a dog around the car in front of them.

"You don't have drugs I don't know about, do you?" CJ asked.

Stella gave him a dirty look.

"C4?"

"No, but I forgot about the nuke next to the spare tire. Think he'll smell that?"

"Not likely. We should be okay. Just relax."

"Look who's saying relax," Stella said, pointing to his hands. "You squeeze any harder you're going to break my steering wheel."

CJ looked at his white knuckles. He released his grip and flexed his fingers. The front car accelerated away and CJ moved up to the second position. He pressed the window down. The dog and handler walked around the car.

They moved up to first position and stopped next to a border patrol officer who looked in at their back seat and then at them.

"Are you citizens of the United States?"

"Yes, we are," CJ said.

"Yes," Stella said.

"Where are you coming from?" the officer asked.

"Nogales," CJ said. "Just down for the drive."

The officer looked up at something to the rear. The officer with the dog was saying something. All CJ could tell was that they were having a short conversation. He looked at Stella, wondered what would happen if he floored it, if they could outrun a border patrol chase vehicle. Of course that would be stupid, he thought. There were border patrol units everywhere between here and Tucson. They'd have the interstate blocked and the exits covered before he could get five miles.

"Sir." The officer was back at his window.

CJ turned his head to look up at him. "Yes?"

"My canine officer just informed me that you have a brake light out. Just a courtesy, sir."

"Thank you," CJ said without making it too obvious how relieved he was.

"You have a fine day."

CJ carefully pulled away from the checkpoint and accelerated up I-19.

"That was nerve-wracking," Stella said. "What now?"

"We're going to stop in Green Valley, find a secure place to park and call Mrs. Lindendale.

Chapter 22

"Hello," Brenda Lindendale said after two rings.

"Mrs. Lindendale. This is CJ Washburn in Tucson."

"How are you, Mr. Washburn?" she returned. "Funny you should call. I was just now drafting you a thank you note for finding my daughter so quickly."

CJ was enthused by the tone of her voice, and her statement. "Thank you, ma'am. That certainly isn't necessary."

"It's called manners, Mr. Washburn. To me, it is necessary. What can I do for you?"

"I need a favor. I'm trying to close out my files on your case and have yet to tie up all the loose ends. As you know, I'd gone in and searched your daughter's apartment and even though it was with your permission I'd still feel much more comfortable talking directly with Lizzi so that she at least has a voice to the person who violated her personal space."

"I thought you'd already talked to her, the reason why she called me from Mexico."

"Actually, I never did talk to her. I'd found a professor who knew how to get a hold of her. It was he who passed the message to her to call you."

"Oh. I guess I don't understand what you're asking for, then."

"I never got that phone number from the professor and at the moment I can't find him. I was hoping you had the number."

"I'm afraid I never got it, Mr. Washburn. Wish I had. I tried calling her since then on her phone but never get anything but her voicemail. She did say she was leaving her phone off because of roaming charges."

"I can certainly understand that," CJ said. "I'll catch up to her when she returns. Did she happened to say when that would be, when she'd return that is?"

"Another week, I believe," Mrs. Lindendale said.

"Very good, then. Nice talking to you."

"You too."

CJ dropped the phone into the tray between the seats and pulled his fingers through his hair. "I guess we go to plan B."

"And that is?"

"We still have to come up with one."

They sat in quiet thought for a time and then Stella said, "What if I go talk to Professor Jarvosky?"

CJ looked at her and nodded. "Might work. How would you approach it?"

"You're wanted by the police but as your assistant I need to close out your cases. I'll tell him I find it necessary to personally talk with Ms. Lindendale, especially since you entered her apartment, that I need to be sure everything is copacetic."

"Sounds perfect. I don't know what his office hours are, but at this time of day there may be a chance of catching him."

CJ drove Stella's car back onto the interstate and headed north.

Chapter 23

While Stella went in search of the professor, her speech rehearsed a half dozen times, CJ stayed with the car in the university parking garage, thinking about how he was going to go about solving the case. He'd already planted the notion of a cop in Dan's mind. Now he needed to figure out how he was going to start eliminating the huge suspect pool. It'd been too long since he'd resigned and even though he was in regular contact with the force, he knew only about a quarter of them. That was just the Tucson police. There were other neighboring police agencies like Marana, Oro Valley, South Tucson, or even the Pima County Sheriff, any of whose officers were in a position to pull off something like this. He needed Dan's help.

But what if it wasn't a cop? He wished he could say for certain that it wasn't. Police officers had a hard enough time without one of them going rogue. It wasn't unheard of, though, for an individual who had sworn to uphold and enforce the law, to develop his own twisted idea of what was right and wrong, or get frustrated with the bogged down legal system and to become the jury and executioner. As a matter of fact, history was full of such men.

Dan might be looking in that direction, now that he knew for sure that CJ was off the suspect pool. But the FBI probably still had him as their one and only suspect.

A car pulled in and parked two spaces away from where CJ sat. He dropped his seat back so that he was out of visible range and returned to his thoughts.

Is Dan taking a serious look at cops, yet? If CJ were in his shoes he'd be comparing shift schedules with times of victims' deaths.

He'd also be looking into who took sudden time off. The perp would have to have in order to get to Moscow, Idaho to arrange for another murder, unless the timing coincided with his regular days off. Either way, the suspect pool could be narrowed down to no more than a handful very fast.

CJ considered the timeline. He arrived in Moscow on Tuesday and used his credit card that night. The local police were almost instantly on top of him. That information would have become know to Tucson police within the hour, maybe within minutes. The killer would have seen it as an opportunity and would have booked a Wednesday morning flight out. He'd have gotten to Moscow with plenty of time to study the town and find a suitable victim. He'd have then made his kill, stashed the body in a convenient dumpster and then returned to Tucson Thursday, likely arriving on an afternoon flight.

CJ looked at his watch and then sat up. It was nearly 4:00. This guy could be landing at any time. They needed to get to the airport.

He got out of the car and looked in the direction from which Stella would be returning. There were two guys heading in his direction. CJ turned his back to them and leaned against the car. As they passed he rotated away and looked back from where they'd come. No Stella. He paced, had to avert his face three more times before, finally, there she was.

As she approached he noticed that she had her phone, or the new dump phone, plastered to her ear and she was smiling and chatting. This irritated him because this was not a smile and chat situation. There wasn't time for this crap. She stopped at the passenger door, saying something about how she completely understood.

CJ glared at her across the top of the car.

"I'm sure everything will work out. I know how mothers are. We've all got one. My impression is she got the scare of her life and is reevaluating her priorities."

Who the hell is she talking to? "We've got to go," CJ said.

Stella held her finger up to him. "We'll stay in contact. Again, thank you so much." She ended the call and looked at him. "What?"

"Who the hell you talking to? We've got to get to the airport."

"Airport! What for?"

"If this guy is a cop he'll be returning from Idaho today. We need to get where we can look at flight schedules and determine what time he'd be arriving."

"You don't even know who you're looking for."

"I know it's a long shot, but there's a chance I might recognize someone."

"It's a bad idea."

"Why?"

"To fly out of Moscow, Idaho, he'd probably fly from Spokane, Washington which would connect through Salt Lake, Denver, Los Angeles or Minneapolis-St. Paul. That could be anything from a few hours ago to midnight tonight, or even tomorrow. Do you want to hang around the airport that long? There'd be a higher chance that airport security would spot you than you recognizing the killer getting off the plane. Consider also that he may have flown out of Phoenix. If I was him, that's exactly what I would have done rather than leave a trail out of Tucson."

CJ just stared at her for a while and then said, "You're right. Stupid idea. I need to talk to Dan again."

"How're you going to do that?"

"I don't know. Who the hell were you talking to? We don't have time for idle chit-chat."

The car right next to CJ beeped and the tail lights flashed. They both looked up to find an older woman approaching, book bag in one hand, keys in the other. CJ and Stella got into the car and said nothing more until the woman had started her car and backed out.

"For your information, Mr. Washburn, I was talking to Elizabeth Lindendale. She and I now have a rapport because I took the time to listen to her and commiserate on her situation."

"Steven Jarvosky just gave you her number, no questions asked?"

"He didn't get a chance to ask me any questions because I never saw him, or should I say, he never saw me."

CJ was puzzled and told her so.

"As I was approaching his door, he came out and walked in the opposite direction. I caught the door before it fully closed and watched until he disappeared. To the restroom is where it appeared he went. Fortunately, for me, he left his cell phone on his desk. It was easy enough to find his sister's number, or I should say numbers. There were several. I wrote them all down and then took my best guess. I got her on the first try, explained who I was and she handed me right over to Lizzi."

CJ closed his open mouth. "What did you say to her?"

"Well… I remembered you saying that Professor Jarvosky didn't say anything about you when he contacted his sister."

"Right. I was there when he called. He just passed a message that Lizzi needed to contact her mother right away."

"Based on that I introduced myself as part of the PI team who had been working for her parents. Didn't want to bring up your name unless I had to."

CJ nodded. "Nice job."

"Thank you. I then told her that our apartment had been flooded as the result of a broken pipe and we needed a place to stay for a few days while the repairs were being made."

"She bought that?"

"Of course; especially after I sympathized with her about her mother not understanding her lifestyle and then after I sweetened the deal with offering to pay half a month's rent. By the time we get there the landlady will have a key for us."

CJ grinned. "Might have to give you a raise."

She lifted that eyebrow again. "No doubt."

Chapter 24

CJ parked the car on the street in front of Ms. Ortega's home. He pointed out Lizzi's car and the fact that it was parked on the far side, right at her entry door. They discussed Stella's approach and then she got out and walked up to the landlady's door.

In less than five minutes she was back, leaning in through the car window, displaying a single key on a worn out plastic fob. "We're in. Slipping her five twenties certainly didn't hurt. Grab my suitcase while I open up."

When CJ set the suitcase down in the small apartment, Stella was opening cabinets and drawers in the kitchen. "Nice place," she said. "Elizabeth is very tidy."

"I figured you'd like it. Did you talk to her about her car?"

"No. Couldn't figure out how our flooded apartment would require a car change. We'll just use it and leave her with a full tank of gas."

"Do you think Ms. Ortega will notice and say anything?"

She shrugged. "Don't know. Considering the big picture it's not something worth worrying about. I did notice, as you did, that she was watching a Spanish speaking program. It didn't appear to be local. She probably doesn't pay much attention to local news, may not be aware that the police are looking for you, or that there is even a killing spree going on. I'd still keep a low profile though."

"Low profile is going to have to be my middle name."

CJ grabbed the keys to Lizzi's Corolla and in a matter of minutes had Stella's Hyundai backed in to replace it. Once it was off the street, he felt much better.

Stella snatched Lizzi's car keys from CJ's hand and said, "I'm going out for food and clothes for you."

"I'll go with you."

"I don't think so. Until you're disguised, you'd better stay hidden. That's what's called low profile."

CJ blew out a lungful of air. "I guess you're right."

"Why don't you start writing down the names of any police officers to whom you think we need to pay attention. Start making lists."

"Pick up another phone," CJ said.

"We're not made of money, Clint. The cash between us has to last until this thing is over."

"You could write a check for the clothes and food."

She considered that for a minute. "Yes, I guess I could." She looked in her checkbook. I've got four checks. After that it's cash only. What do you have?"

He opened his wallet and counted. "$372.00."

She counted hers. "$225.00. I'll do everything at Wal-Mart. That'll take just one check."

After Stella left, CJ settled down with a pen and paper. He wrote down a couple of names, neither of which he truly believed could be rogue and then set it aside. The exercise seemed useless. There had to be a better way. His stomach growled and he wished they'd stopped for food before coming here. He put his feet up and closed his eyes.

When CJ awoke it was nearly 6:00 and he was worried about the fact that Stella wasn't back. How long did it take to buy food and some clothes? He turned on the TV, figured out the remotes and found one of the local stations. There was a series of ads and then a few seconds of footage of a young woman walking alone along what CJ recognized as Stone Avenue in downtown Tucson.

> *Coming up next, how dangerous has it become for a woman to walk the streets of Tucson? Candice Reed has*

some new developments on the dumpster killer. You may or may not like what you are about to hear.

After another thirty seconds of ads, Reuwben Chavez and Candice Reed appeared in the station newsroom, Reuwben holding a pencil, Candice a half-dozen or so sheets of paper.

"We're going to get right to the top story," Reuwben said, "Candice, tell us what you know about these horrific dumpster murders."

"It's a nightmarish story, Reuwben. Already we have seen four women strangled and left in various trash dumpsters throughout the city. You may recall our broadcast just four days ago in which we told about how Tucson private investigator and former police officer, Clinton Joshua Washburn, had been held in connection with those brutal murders and then was released under his own recognizance."

"Wasn't one of those murders a copycat, Candice, an opportunist killer, the police described him?"

"Yes, Reuwben, that's correct and they have the husband of that victim in custody now. We'll have an update on that sad story next."

"So, that makes three young women who have been murdered by this serial killer?"

"Actually, Reuwben, there are five that can be directly attributed to this one individual."

"Five! My God, Candice."

"Yes, five. The fourth, a Tucson resident, was discovered

in the trunk of a car in Moscow, Idaho just two nights ago. It is believed that the woman was taken from the streets here in Tucson, killed in the same manner as the other three victims, stuffed into the trunk of a car and then driven to Idaho."

"I assume that the police, or FBI in this case I imagine, know who the owner of this car is."

"Of course, Reuwben. It is registered to the man they had in custody over the weekend and then let go, Clinton Joshua Washburn. He eluded a massive search by local law enforcement in the Moscow and Latah County area of Idaho as well as Eastern Washington State. But that's not all. This morning a fifth woman was discovered in a trash dumpster in Moscow, Idaho."

"The same killer?"

"Believed to be so, Reuwben. But now we have a bizarre twist. I went out to interview the lead Tucson detective on this case, Detective Dan Payne, and got this."

CJ was frozen to the screen as Dan appeared not far from the spot in front of the criminal lab where CJ had waved at him earlier in the day. He was being approached by Candice, thrusting a microphone at him.

"Detective Payne, what can you tell us about the latest murder in Idaho?"

"I cannot comment on a crime committed in another state."

"The other woman found in a car registered to a former Tucson police officer; what can you tell us about that?"

"Again, a crime committed in another state, Ms. Reed."

"But it is believed that the murder was committed here in Tucson before being driven to Idaho. Is that correct, Detective?"

"That hasn't been determined at this time. It is possible that the woman was either abducted here, or went of her own freewill and then was killed somewhere along the way, in Arizona, Nevada or Idaho. It falls under federal jurisdiction now. Local police agencies are assisting the FBI."

"The report was that the car was registered to former police officer, Clinton Washburn. At one time he was your partner. Is that correct, Detective Payne?"

Dan attempted to walk away without responding, but Candice pursued him.

"Our understanding is that Mr. Washburn is the FBI's prime suspect?"

"I have no further comment, Ms. Reed."

The screen split between Dan's angry retreat and Candice in the studio.

"The bizarre twist, Reuwben, is that it seems that Detective Payne had a conversation with Mr. Washburn this morning outside of Tucson's new crime lab on Miracle Mile. I found this out after I spoke with him and also discovered that he has been removed from the case. The two of them were not only partners many years ago, but were best friends, and still are."

"If that's true, Candice, that Mr. Washburn was in Tucson

this morning, how could he have committed the latest killing in Idaho last night?"

"I tried to reach the FBI for comment. The best they would give me is that they are still treating Washburn as their prime suspect. On top of the APB out on him, there is another for his girlfriend, Stella Summers and her car, a 2005 Hyundai Sonata, light blue."

Mug shots of the two of them appeared on the screen.

"If you see either of them call 911 immediately. Whatever you do, do not approach or engage them."

"Thank you, Candice. Up next, how an unemployed construction laborer thought he could get rid of his wife in the guise of the dumpster killer. Also, is this record-breaking heat ever going to quit? And how about them Wildcats?"

CJ turned off the TV and tossed the remotes aside. He stood and walked to the door to look out and became momentarily excited with seeing Stella's car. Then he remembered that she took Lizzi's car. He closed the door and looked at their phones on the counter, batteries lying next to them. She'd taken the new phone but that certainly didn't do him any good. He couldn't take a chance calling her even if he did know the number.

He pushed his hands into his pockets and started pacing.

If Dan was pulled off the case, who took it over, or has the FBI decided the entire Tucson Police Department had a conflict of interest and threw everybody out? Was there anybody pursuing the angle that the perp might be a police officer?

He pulled his fingers through his hair.

Where the hell is Stella? She's been gone over an hour. She probably has no idea there's an APB out on her. Could she have tried to write a check and was spotted, didn't even get out of the store before she was arrested? He needed to get a hold of Dan.

He looked at Stella's car keys where he'd dropped them on the counter and then at the time. It wouldn't turn dark for another hour. Dan lived off Fort Lowell Road, about as east as one could go and still be in Tucson. With the news broadcast, the chances of being spotted in Stella's car jumped up a couple of notches. He'd be crazy to take the risk. Still, if she was in custody, he'd have to do something.

He went into Lizzi's bedroom and looked in her closet. There was nothing there he could use as a disguise, unless he wanted to dress like a woman. That was certainly worth considering, but the sizes were too small. He probably couldn't pull it off anyway.

He remembered the coat closet, by the door. He pushed the bicycle aside and looked up at the hats on the shelf. One was too feminine, but the other, army green with a chin cord, would work just fine. He put it on his head and looked at the bicycle. Even at night taking the car was risky, but he could take the bicycle, though it'd be a long ride to Dan's.

But he could ride to a payphone.

He stepped outside and looked up at the sky. The sun was still hanging too high. Not only was it still light, but riding a bicycle at 110 degrees would likely prove suicidal. He noticed a thermometer just outside the door. It indicated 102 degrees. Still suicidal.

He stepped back in and returned to pacing.

As he thought about it, Stella hadn't really been gone that long. If it was him he'd have been in and out of Wal-Mart in less than twenty minutes with food and clothes. But Stella was Stella. He'd give her another half hour, hour on the outside.

He turned the TV back on and mindlessly stared at the rest of the local news and then Wheel of Fortune until it ended. At 7:00 he pushed the bicycle out the door and then just stood there, realizing that Stella took the key. If he locked it he wouldn't be able to get back in, so he left it unlocked.

It took him a half hour to find a pay phone, by which time the sun was completely gone. The pay phone he found, however, was at a busy, lit like midday, McDonald's. He kept the hat pulled low and his head down as he dumped change into the phone. He dialed, leaned hard against the wall, closed his eyes and waited.

"Payne," Dan said into CJ's ear.

"Mr. Payne, this is Josh McKenzie. We spoke a time back about a piece of real-estate you were interested in. I'm just calling to let you know that the seller has reduced the price and I thought you might like to revisit it if you're still in the market."

There was a long pause and CJ was afraid he'd blown it. Then, "Josh McKenzie? I don't... McKenzie. Oh, yes. Been a while, hasn't it?"

"Yes, it has. My seller is anxious now, would like to close a deal soon."

"Well, tell you what, Mr. McKenzie. I'll have to get back to you on it. How much is he asking?"

"He's dropped it to eleven."

"I appreciate the call, Mr. McKenzie. I'll have to think on it, discuss it with the wife and all that. Eleven, you said?"

"Yes."

"Like I said, I'll get back to you."

"Certainly. Good talking to you." CJ hung up, threw a leg over the bicycle and rode out through the back of the McDonald's parking lot. Two blocks away he stopped in a dark area behind a hedge of overgrown cacti, laid the bike down and peered back between the cactus pads. There were no police vehicles or FBI in unmarked vans screaming into the area. Either Dan's phone wasn't being monitored, or they got away with it and Dan didn't blow the whistle.

Chapter 25

When CJ arrived back at Lizzi's apartment, Lizzi's car was there, but when he went to try the door, it was locked. He knocked, waited five seconds and knocked again.

"Stella, it's me," he said at the door.

From the corner of his eye he caught movement at the kitchen window, the only window Lizzi had. "Stella, open…"

The door flew open. "Where the hell have you been?" Stella reached to hug him and got tangled in the bicycle.

CJ shoved it aside and pulled her into him with one arm.

"I was about ready to call Dan, figured they'd found you."

"I..."

"You had me scared out of my mind."

CJ pushed the bicycle in while Stella pulled the door fully open and stepped out of the way. "I went out to call Dan for the same reason. I thought they'd gotten you. Both of our pictures were on the news as well as the description of your car. You'd been gone two hours."

"You called Dan?"

"Yes."

"From where?"

"Pay phone on Speedway."

"What did he say?"

"Couldn't really talk to him in case he was being monitored. He's been pulled off the case. I found that out on the news."

"Why was he pulled?"

"Because I was his partner and because we are still good friends."

She pushed the door closed, locked it and then put her arms around him again. "You had me so worried. You should have waited, or left a note."

"Sorry."

"What did you say to him? I don't get why you called if you thought he was being monitored."

"Years ago, when I was still on the force, we had invented a couple of fake names. It was a drug case we were working. I was Josh McKenzie and he was Brian Shako. When he answered I told him I was Josh McKenzie, a real estate agent he'd previously dealt with. I knew he'd recognize my voice and catch on right away. I reminded him of a piece of land he had been considering and that the price had dropped to eleven thousand."

"Okay. What does that mean?"

"It means that we are meeting tonight at 11:00 at the shack in the desert where we nabbed the drug ring. That was nine or ten years ago so there is no one who is going to figure it out, even if they were listening."

She pulled him over to the sofa where they sat and she leaned against his shoulder. "How do you know Dan isn't going to bring his buddies along?"

"He doesn't like it when the Feds poke their noses into his business. Now he's been fired from the biggest case of his life, and he's pissed. Candice Reed ran her interview with him. He had everything he could do to keep his foot out of his mouth about the FBI taking over, couldn't say FBI without making a face. Also, my hunch is he agrees with me about the perp being a cop. He doesn't know who to trust so he won't be bringing anybody."

"It doesn't feel right," she said.

"What do you mean?"

"I don't know. I just don't trust this meeting."

"I know Dan. He isn't going to rat us out now. Maybe before when he was on the case, because he has always been duty first, but now... I don't think so."

"What if somebody follows him?"

"He'll suspect he's being watched and will take evasive action."

Stella went silent for a time and then said, "I still don't like it."

Stella's bad feeling killed her appetite. CJ forced her to eat a slice of pizza anyway. He had no problem consuming enough for both of them.

At 9:30 they cleaned up everything and got into the car. Just after 10:00 they were pulling into the Casino Del Sol employee parking lot on West Valencia Road.

"Now we wait," CJ said.

"Why are we parked here? This is rather public."

"If I were on this case and suspected that there was a meeting happening nearby, I'd put some assets in the Del Sol parking lot where they could see Valencia Road. The shack, or where it used to be, is almost directly north from here, the other side of Valencia a couple tenths of a mile or so. From Valencia to Irvington it's about two miles, most of it desert. Right here in front of Del Sol is the only easy access point." He pointed out the driver's side window. "Right over there is a utility access road that passes about a hundred yards by the location. Off that is a dirt track that goes right to it. Four-wheelers use the area.

"What do you mean where the shack used to be?"

"After the drug ring was broken, the shack was torn down and hauled away to keep anyone else from making use of it. Dan and I both know where it was, however."

They sat in silence for a time, watching cars come and go from the casino parking lot, and the traffic passing by on Valencia Road.

Stella broke the silence. "I don't like the idea that men have pawed through my personal belongings."

"What do you mean?"

"You know they've searched my apartment. A bunch of FBI suit and ties thinking they have license to touch my underwear. When this is over I'm burning it all. There's no way I'm putting anything they've touched against my body."

"They're just doing their jobs."

"Whose side are you on?"

CJ smiled in the dark. He kind of liked it when she got feisty. "Can I go with you when you buy underwear?"

"Shut up."

He took her hand and they watched a light-colored sedan pull into the employee parking lot and then creep along the row of cars. They had to turn in their seats to watch.

"Could that be Dan?" Stella said.

"His wife's car is cream colored. I think that's closer to white. It would make sense for him to take her car, though. I don't know if he'd come into this parking lot, however."

The car turned around at the end of the lot, came part way back and then stopped, its headlights filling CJ and Stella's backseat. They both lowered themselves as much as they could. After a time the passenger's door opened and a man got out. As he walked toward the building the car accelerated out of the parking lot and turned east on Valencia.

The two of them straightened and turned around. It was 10:33.

In the next fifteen minutes a half-dozen cars came and went and then one slowed on Valencia. Instead of turning into the employee parking lot it turned north onto the access road CJ had pointed out. Its lights went out and it continued into the desert for fifty yards and then stopped. CJ couldn't be sure it was Dan, though it sure did look like his silver Tahoe. In the unrestricted light of the full moon, it glowed like a beacon.

"I think you should stay here," CJ said. "I'm going to go on foot."

Stella opened her mouth to argue and then closed it.

"There's no need for both of us to wind up in jail if something goes wrong."

There was a silent stretch and then Stella said, "Okay." Her voice sounded unconvinced, though.

"Here's the plan. If something does go wrong and if I manage to get away, I'll go north toward Irvington instead of this direction. When I'm able to find a phone, I'll call you. I have the new number memorized now."

"How will I know if you get away? If the area gets crazy with cops I'm not going to be able to tell what's going on."

"Just wait for my call. You don't have to wait here. As a matter of fact, after I get out you ought to drive back to the Wal-Mart, park there and wait. If everything goes well I'll have Dan drop me there. If you don't hear from me by 2:00 in the morning, assume I'm in jail."

"I want to be part of this meeting," she said.

"I want you there, too. There's just too much uncertainty here." He reached across and touched her cheek, then pulled her closer and kissed her. "I love you, Stella. This is all so we can find this guy. The FBI has nothing but circumstantial evidence so there is no way I'm going down for this. We just need to get through it."

"I…" She closed her mouth.

"What?"

"Nothing. I'll wait."

"You were going to say something else."

She shook her head. "Not important. Dan is moving on into the desert. You'd better get going."

CJ turned and watched the SUV disappear into the forest of saguaros, palo verdes and mesquites. He opened the door and got out.

Chapter 26

CJ wished Stella had bought him darker clothes. She thought that light khaki would not attract attention, that he would better blend with the environment. In the light of a full moon he felt like someone was shining a giant search light on him.

At the edge of Valencia he crouched beside a prickly bush and waited until he could not see traffic for several miles in both directions, at which time he sprinted across, onto the dirt road that Dan had taken. He dropped to an easy jog, keeping an eye for potholes, trip hazards and nocturnal creatures. What he didn't need was an attack by a pack of javelina. In the heat of the summer, after a day of sleeping in the shade, they'd be wide awake and active.

Just as he entered the cacti forest he turned and looked across Valencia, into the employee parking lot. Stella was backing the car out of the parking spot. As she pulled up to Valencia road CJ eased behind a growth of mesquite so as not to be illuminated by her headlights. Her turn signal came on and she pulled onto the road and accelerated east.

CJ turned and continued his trek after the detective, starting to feel Stella's reservations. Although she didn't voice it all that much, he could tell she was not at all happy that he was doing this. He stopped for a moment and considered turning around. He could find a phone in the casino and call Stella to come get him. He looked up at the stars and the full moon and tried to come up with an alternative approach to finding the killer. There wasn't one. He had to have a partner who had connections on the inside, and that could only be Dan.

In the light of the moon CJ was able to easily follow Dan's track. Once inside the line of desert cacti the dirt road went straight for a long distance. Dan's tracks turned where CJ expected. He followed that at a trot until he spotted the Tahoe. CJ approached cautiously, not sure if Dan was in the vehicle or watching from a secure location.

"You're losing your edge, Mr. Washburn."

CJ turned around to find Dan standing five feet behind him.

"I expected you to be here before me, camouflaged like a saguaro or something."

"I watched you drive in, glowing like a damn Chinese lantern."

Dan laughed. "I regretted the color when I drove that thing home from the dealer. Would have had to wait for a black one."

"And the wife thought it was so pretty," CJ said.

"Well, there's that, yes. What can I say?"

"You sure you weren't followed?"

"I can't believe you even had to ask that question, CJ."

"Did you check for a tracking device on your Tahoe?"

"I doubt they're thinking that clearly. They haven't even put a watch on me yet. There was no one for me to shake."

CJ didn't like that, would have expected more from the FBI, but he put the thought away. "I wouldn't assume anything. Have you put anymore thought into the fact that this might be a rogue cop?"

"You certainly had me thinking down that road and then they pulled me from the case, thanks to you."

"You didn't have to blow the whistle on me."

"CJ, your timing was impeccable. I was in conference with two FBI agents when you called. Not only did *I* see you waving at me, but so did they."

Dan lifted the hatch on his Tahoe and opened a cooler. He pulled out two beers, handed one to CJ and sat back against the vehicle. CJ twisted the beer cap and did the same.

"So, Mr. Josh McKenzie, why did you call this meeting?"

"We need to figure out how to narrow the field of cops down to this one individual."

"How do you know for sure that it's a cop?"

"Balance the timing with what has been released to the press and you'll see that it's either a cop or someone on the inside with all the information. It wasn't known that I was in Idaho until I checked into the motel in Moscow. Twenty-four hours later he's there killing so that I would become the number one suspect, not knowing that by that time I was in…"

"Where were you, CJ?"

"I can't say, but I was at a location way south. I really don't want to get those parties involved unless I have to."

"You may have to. The FBI may have seen you when I did, but the woman in Moscow was killed about 11:00 last night. You were spotted here at 10:52 this morning. The way the FBI see it you did the Moscow murder and chartered a private plane to get back here as a way to fool the police into thinking you aren't the killer. You're going to get picked up eventually and unless they've caught the real killer with a woman's neck in his hands, you're going to have to produce your witnesses, and even that is no guarantee. They may wind up becoming accessories if they're the ones who helped you get away."

CJ shook his head. "My only way out of this is find the real killer. Because he got up there so quickly after the motel scene, he has to be someone who saw all the communications that went on. It should be easy. Check all flights leaving Tucson yesterday morning and look at the last minute bookings. If that doesn't pan out check all Phoenix flights and then all charter flights."

"And if that doesn't pan out shall we check all Las Vegas flights, then San Diego flights, or how about Los Angeles?"

CJ took a swig from his beer. "I hear your point, but still, he'd be stupid to fly out of Tucson. It still has to be someone who took last minute time off."

"A lot of ground to cover and I'm not even allowed near the case."

"Who took over for you?"

"Ralph Bunko."

"You're kidding!" CJ shook his head. "He'll play by all the FBI rules."

"Exactly."

"And he doesn't much like you, does he?"

"Doesn't like you either."

"We're probably screwed."

"That's the way I see it, CJ."

They both took hits on their beers and then CJ said, "Do you have any good friends in Personnel?"

"One, who does happen to owe me a favor. But that's just Tucson police. I have no connections in any of the other law enforcement agencies."

"Then let's hope he's Tucson." CJ finished the rest of his beer and then turned his face up to the sky. "Do you hear that?"

Dan listened for a few seconds. "No, what?"

CJ set the empty bottle down, pushed from the vehicle and looked east, then as far as he could see in all directions in the sky above the desert. "It's a ways off yet, but that's a helicopter."

Dan listened again. "Has to be air force or medevac."

"Heard anything happening on your police scanner?"

Dan turned his ear to the interior of the Tahoe. "No. Haven't been hearing much of anything at all since I left home, come to think of it."

"How often this time of night does the police network go this quiet?"

"Only when there's a major operation and we go radio silent."

"I repeat my earlier question; did you check for a tracking device?" He squatted and started feeling around under the rear bumper.

"Shit, CJ. You don't think…"

CJ stood and handed a small device to Dan. The sound of the helicopter was louder, but it was not yet visible.

"They're coming in low," CJ said and picked up the beer bottle. "Thanks for this, but I think you'd better get out of here. This is the only thing I touched so I'll take it with me."

Dan over-handed his open beer as far as he could into the desert, pulled the hatch down and ran to his driver's door. "I'll toss the bug as soon as I'm a ways away from here."

"Hope you can convince them you're just out here drinking by yourself, Dan," CJ called to him as he jogged away sideways. "I'll find a way to contact you again." With that he took off running in one direction while Dan's Tahoe threw up desert sand taking off in the other.

While they were talking CJ had been analyzing the desert around them in anticipation of just this scenario. He'd dumped his original plan to head north. That direction was so sparse that even with only moon light he could see as much as a quarter mile, it seemed. The best cover was within a hundred feet of where he'd been standing, and probably the last place they'd search for him, hopefully assuming that he'd be with Dan or on the run.

As soon as Dan's Tahoe was out of sight, CJ sprinted over to the denser area, maybe an acre worth, and found a place to lie down. The problem with Southern Arizona desert is there is very little native plant life without needles. With that in mind he carefully eased himself under and amongst a grouping of bushes, hoping that the only bites he was getting were from needles, that he didn't disturb a rattlesnake or scorpion. He was none too soon getting settled when a black SUV whipped into the area where the Tahoe had been parked, slowed for a few seconds and then continued on after Dan. CJ heard a second one pass a couple of hundred yards to the west. Dan had drawn them northwest, onto a track that took him, and them, deeper into the desert.

The sound of the vehicles was suddenly drowned out by the helicopter. It slowed right overhead, pointing its searchlight everywhere but right on CJ. It made a three hundred and sixty degree circle then took off to become part of the chase. As soon as the chopper was well away, CJ stood and worked his way south, toward Valencia Road. He remembered a shallow wash that ran somewhat parallel to the road. When he found that he began trekking east, bent over in a crouch.

What bothered him now was that he could clearly see cars parked in the casino parking lot, which meant he was likely visible to anyone watching from one of those cars, especially if they had any kind of night optics. Despite the wash, the vegetation was not as thick as where he had originally hidden ten minutes before. He crouched even lower and virtually crawled along, stopping occasionally to extract cactus needles. He was beginning to know what it was like to be a

Mexican sneaking across the border and covering mile after mile of Arizona desert.

Suddenly the foliage ahead of him became illuminated. He went flat to the desert sand and crabbed sideways into a stand of prickly pear, having to bite his lip as a half dozen needles lodged into his shoulder. For a long minute the light moved back and forth, controlled by a patrol car idling slowly by, west-bound on the shoulder of Valencia Road. Just as it was nearly past, the engine roared and the light went out. When the sound of the patrol car speeding away receded, CJ looked up to find he was directly across from the main casino entrance. He stood, pulled out the more painful of the needles he could find, and pushed on, the moon shining in his face.

Chapter 27

The wash gradually angled away from Valencia Road. CJ paused at a dirt track that ran southeast to northwest¬–probably the same one on which Dan raced away–and then crossed over to arrive a minute or so later at the corner of a housing area. This worried CJ because he knew that this was not an HOA organized community. There were about two-dozen plots of land with unpaved streets and a mixture of mostly low-income trailers and houses, with and without fences, many of which had dogs, big barking dogs. He decided to stay with the wash as it wound through and around the properties.

For an hour CJ kept moving, leaving one dilapidated track of properties for another, crossing an occasional road, alerting only a few dogs. No one appeared nor did any lights come on. The only evidence of human presence was when, after a deep bark, there came an equally deep, "Shut up!"

The helicopter droned in the distance. At no time did it get near him. At one point, early on, he saw a post office a couple of hundred yards south and debated checking to see if it had an exterior phone booth. In the end he decided it wasn't worth the risk and moved on. To avoid stepping out onto Valencia Road, he kept to the skirt of a mountain—hill in any real sense, rising less than 300 feet above the desert floor, a mountain according to the locals. Without the wash he was having to bushwhack and was feeling more and more like a pin-cushion.

Just as he realized he could no longer hear the helicopter he stepped out of the desert onto a rough, paved road, hardly more than a single lane. He couldn't think of what road it was. Across the road was a sprawling construction business. A few hundred yards to his right the road intersected Valencia. A car turned toward him from that intersection. He backed into the desert and lay down as he did before. The vehicle passed by very slowly and CJ spotted the star of a Pima County sheriff deputy. Were they looking for him or on routine patrol?

After the deputy passed out of sight, CJ analyzed the business across the road. It didn't appear like the type that would have a security system. He extracted a few more cactus needles then sprinted across and into the shadows thrown by the building.

He crouched and listened while waiting for his breathing to return to normal. After several minutes, when he was sure he'd not been observed, he proceeded to analyze the entry to the building, hoping to get to a phone to call Stella. There were no security decals or other evidence of a security system. He had to get in and out without leaving evidence that a break-in had occurred. Any such reports in the area would prompt deeper investigation, in his name, he was sure. He didn't know how thorough the feds would be, but it'd only take one over-achiever to check phone records on the night of the break-in and then get a lock on their phone number and thus their location.

The door had a deadbolt. He tried the door knob and found it locked as well. From his wallet he pulled out the card he used for just this situation and slipped it between the jam and the door, in the hopes that only that lock was thrown and not the deadbolt. He felt the lock release, but the deadbolt held the door in place.

Lights appeared from the direction the deputy had disappeared. CJ hid and watched as the sheriff's car again went by, just as slow as before. When gone, he began inspecting the remainder of the building looking for any weak point through which he could make entry. After finding nothing, he crouched against the north wall and considered his options. He was starting to regret telling Stella to go all the way to Wal-Mart and that if he didn't show up by 2:00 to assume he was in jail. There was no way he could get there by that time without getting out on Valencia and jogging. He'd have to just keep moving, maybe find another business, hopefully one with lousy security.

He pushed to his feet and turned to head east from the property in hopes of finding an egress to the desert beyond. He stopped in the middle of the yard and realized that there were more buildings; two garages and a trailer, odd machines and beaten up trucks scattered about. Wires ran from a pole next to the main building to a pole next to the trailer. Likely a phone line, and trailers are a cinch to get into.

With his break-and-enter card back in his hand he approached the trailer. Thirty seconds at the door and he was in.

The interior was a junk hole compared to the one he broke into in Idaho. In the mess he could find neither a lighter nor a flashlight, but he did find a phone with a lighted keypad and a dial-tone. He punched in the number.

"Where are you?" Stella answered, barley controlled panic in her voice.

"I'm not sure," CJ said. "My guess is I'm about two miles east of the casino, a block or so north of Valencia; been making my way through patches of desert and housing."

"I saw a helicopter," she said. "Was that…"

"Yes. We think they had a GPS tracking device on Dan's Tahoe."

Her, "Oh," was followed by a long silence, then, "Where do you want me to go?"

CJ thought for some time before coming up with a plan. He told her what to do and then, after hanging up and locking the door behind him, started working his way toward Valencia Road.

He crossed back over the road he knew not the name off, for better coverage should he need to hide, and got up as close to Valencia as he could. He crouched amongst a spattering of bushes and prickly pear cacti and watched for headlights approaching from the east. Two vehicles went by going away from the casino before he spotted a set of west-bound headlights. It wasn't until the car came abreast of him and drove on before he was sure it was Stella. He eased out where he could watch the taillights and waited. It seemed like forever before the brake lights came on and she turned into the post office. A few seconds later she was back on Valencia and heading his direction. As she got closer he looked all around, saw no one and then sprinted across in front of her. She skidded to a stop and in seconds he was in.

"Go! Not too fast."

"I'm not."

"Stay the speed limit."

"I am!"

Chapter 28

CJ lay next to Stella in Lizzi's bed, staring up at the ceiling and thinking about the meeting with Dan. Nothing had been accomplished; as a matter of fact, things may have gotten worse. Dan was his only contact and he may now be more than off the case, he might be off the force.

"Are you awake?" Stella's whispered words filled the darkness.

"Yes."

She rolled toward him and he put his arm around her.

"What are we going to do?"

As hard as he tried, CJ couldn't come up with one optimistic response; there wasn't an ounce of optimism to be had.

"I don't know. Maybe it'd be better if I turned myself in; let the chips fall."

Stella sat up. "What do you mean? Everything's against you."

"They can't convict me on circumstantial evidence."

"The prisons are full of men who were convicted from less."

"That's not really true."

"The hell it isn't!" Stella pointed off into the dark. "There have been dozens who have been released in the last five years because new DNA tests exonerated them. And they've got everything on you, including DNA, everything except the s*moking gun*."

"None of the women were shot," CJ corrected.

"I was being metaphorical and you know it. A jury would see you as guilty. Hell, if I was on a jury viewing the evidence stacked against you, I'd be inclined to hang you."

"Another metaphor, I hope."

"Damn it, Clint. This is serious."

He reached out for her and pulled her back down to him. "I know. I honestly don't know where to go from here. I'd try to make contact with Dan again, but to be truthful with you, I don't know what good it'd do. With being off the case his investigative resources are limited."

"Do you think the FBI caught him last night?"

"Probably."

"What'll happen if they did?"

"At best he'll be suspended pending further investigation."

"At worst?"

"We'll be playing chess together over at the county jail."

They both went silent for a long time and then she said, "Make love to me."

"Are you sure? I…"

She put a finger on his mouth. "If you wind up in jail, likely so will I. I don't think we'll be able to play chess together, or do anything else. This might be our last time." She replaced her finger with her mouth and then pulled away. "I'll be right back."

He lay as before, staring up at the ceiling, thinking about her words, the impact of them slamming down on top of him. Their lives of freedom, at least his, were likely over. If he told them that she talked him into giving up, maybe they'd go easy on her. And if he turned himself into Dan, maybe they'd go easy on him as well.

In any case, though, she was right. This night together could possibly be their last. Would he even be able to perform?

The toilet flushed and suddenly she was back and her mouth was on his again and then she was all over him, naked and hot, and any doubts about performance vanished in the heat of his own sexual rush.

It was after 9:00 when they found each other one more time in the shower and then stood still, pressed together, until the hot water ran out. Wordlessly they dressed, made the bed, put together a modest breakfast and then turned on the TV and sat down. The local morning news was long past so they switched over to national news. After a half hour with no mention of the Tucson serial killer, they turned it off. They cleaned their breakfast dishes then looked at each other.

"What now?" Stella said.

CJ felt so defeated he couldn't respond. He looked away, not wanting to see the disappointment in her eyes, and started to say he'd call Dan, to tell her about his plan to keep the heat off the two of them as much as possible, but found his mouth so dry that he couldn't get out a single word.

She stepped into him and put her arms around him. "Is there anyone you could trust in the department, anyone who owes you a favor?" she said, her cheek pressed against his chest. "A damned janitor… anyone?"

And then CJ remembered Dave McDermott and his daughter, Officer Bowers. After more than six years she'd remembered what he'd done for her father though he'd barely recognized or remembered her.

He pushed Stella to arm's length. "Maybe." He then told her about Sgt. McDermott and the false charges leveled against him and how CJ found people who would testify that it was all a setup to take down the police officer who interrupted their party.

"So you think he still feels indebted to you?" she said.

"Yes. I doubt he could do much, though. He retired shortly afterwards. However, I ran into his daughter at a couple of the dumpster crime scenes, directing traffic. Officer Lisa Bowers."

"She's a cop?"

"Yes, and even though I didn't recognize her at first, she remembered me and made a point of thanking me for helping her father."

"If she was directing traffic, she's likely not close enough to the case to be of much help," Stella said.

"Maybe, but she's all we've got. She's worth a try. Better than a janitor."

"She could just turn you in."

"She knows about a cop being framed. She'll at least listen first."

"How do we find her?"

"Normally that might not be easy, but since I know where her father lives, let's start with him."

"Do you think he'll help?"

"Does a bear poop in the woods?"

Stella grinned at him and shook her head. CJ thought about how even the slightest bit of hope could totally shift a mood.

Chapter 29

Stella drove while CJ sat slumped low in his seat, giving directions to McDermott's home in Indian Ridge Estates off Sabino Canyon Road. When they arrived in front of the house he told her to pull the car all the way up the driveway to park next to what he assumed was McDermott's truck, a black Ford F-250 backed up to the garage door. He figured that being the middle the week, Dave's wife, Nancy, would be at work and Dave would be home alone. After a few seconds of debate they decided that she'd go up first, ring the doorbell and tell McDermott that CJ needed his help.

Stella got out and walked up the walk. She was within three feet of the doorbell when the door flew open and Dave McDermott stepped out and grabbed her arm. He said something to her and then pulled her into the house. For a few seconds CJ remained frozen in his seat. Jump and run? Climb into the driver's seat and drive away? Abandon Stella?

He blew out a lungful of carbon dioxide, rubbed his forehead, waited. The door opened again and Dave stepped out. He pointed at CJ, though CJ knew Dave couldn't see anything but a human form, wiggled his finger and then pointed at the house.

CJ considered the look on Dave's face and the fact that he couldn't read anything, then pulled the hat low and got out. He looked around at the quiet neighbors and casually walked up to the door. Dave didn't say a word until they were both in. He closed the door and grabbed CJ's hand. "I couldn't believe my eyes when I saw Ms. Summers here walking up to my front door. Just happened to be looking out."

"You recognized me?" Stella was startled.

"Damned right. You and your boyfriend's photos are all over the news, especially after the body found this morning."

"Another one?" CJ said. He tightened his jaw and dropped his head. "Damn! We missed the news, couldn't find anything."

"The young woman was discovered by a homeless guy in a dumpster near the downtown library." He pointed them both toward his living room. "Sit down."

"Same MO?" CJ asked as he and Stella sat together on a leather sofa.

"Pretty much, though no mention of whether she was a hooker."

"And I'm still suspect number one."

"According to the Feds."

"What do you think?"

"You're in my house and I haven't called the swat team. There is no way CJ Washburn would ever do anything like this. This killer is insane, plain and simple."

"Thank you for that, Dave."

"Even if I thought you did it there's no way I'd have those backstabbing blue varmints tracking their boot dirt through my house."

"I'm glad to hear you're not bitter anymore, Dave"

Dave laughed. "Actually, CJ, they're all good cops. I get a little excited over the old crap now and then. I'm really only bitter at those few individuals higher up the food chain who thought the department image was more important than that of a single cop. If you found the truth then so could have they, if they'd only tried. And now, with you, they're turning their heads again. I wouldn't be surprised if it's the same individuals who are taking the opportunity to smear your face as much as they can. You certainly made them look bad six years ago."

CJ sat back on the sofa and thought about that. "Do you think it's one of them doing this?"

"Oh, hell no. They're just opportunists. I can't imagine any cop doing something like this."

CJ glanced at Stella and then looked back at Dave. "It's not unheard of, Dave."

Dave's mouth dropped open. "You're thinking it's a cop?"

"I wish I weren't, but everything's pointing in that direction. It's either a cop or someone on the inside with near instant information at his fingertips."

"How do you figure?"

CJ went over everything that had happened since he discovered the third body, covering almost minute by minute the events in Idaho and his theory that it had to be someone having the information fast enough to book a flight there and then back. "A serial killer opportunist," he said at the end, "with a badge."

Dave had been leaning forward in his easy chair, entranced by CJ's story and Stella's occasional input for clarification sake. When CJ was done, Dave sat back in his chair and said, "Holy shit. I see where you're coming from now, CJ. It has to be someone with a very fast communications pipeline. All we should have to do is find a guy who took those two days off, or was already off. Should be able to run names through the airlines, bounce credit cards, see where he went."

"I said the same thing to Dan but he made a good point. This guy is likely smart enough to have covered his tracks, probably driving as far as Los Angeles to pick up a flight."

Dave considered that for a few moments. "No way. If I were doing this, I'd go maybe as far as Phoenix. LA is an all night drive. Maybe Las Vegas, but definitely not LA."

CJ nodded. "You're right. Never thought about the credit card thing, though. It'd all mean getting the Feds on board with the theory to be able to access all the data."

"Who took over for Dan when he was taken off the case?" Dave asked.

"Ralph Bunko."

Dave snorted. "You're screwed."

"I don't know this Detective Bunko," Stella said. "What's he got against you?"

Dave and CJ looked at each other, then Dave said, "When a young lady, I use the term lady loosely, filed a rape charge against me, it was

Bunko who was assigned to investigate. He was a brand new detective at the time. He botched it."

"I thought you just said it was some higher ups that were responsible."

"The press blew it up and the public wanted blood. The higher ups either knew that Bunko had botched it or refused to hear it, wanting instead to turn a blind eye so that they could say to the public that they took quick action, that they did not tolerate such conduct by one of their own. Bunko started the bus rolling in the wrong direction and the bosses were making ready to throw me under it, until CJ came along." He looked at CJ. "I doubt Bunko would lift a finger to help you now. When he got the case he probably started salivating, not giving a rat's ass who the real perp was. Bet you twenty that right now he's trying to figure out how he's going to finish throwing you under the same damned bus."

Stella fell back in the sofa next to CJ, discouraged.

"So, why have you come to see me? If there's something I could do to help, you know I'd do it in a heartbeat. I'm so far out of the business I've forgotten what it means to be a cop."

"I don't believe that, Dave. I ran into Lisa at several of the crime scenes, before the finger started pointing at me."

"Ah."

"I was shocked. Last time I saw her she was looking at colleges."

"My baby girl became a cop. It wasn't my choice, believe me."

"It certainly wouldn't have been my choice, either."

"You guys don't think a woman can be a cop?" Stella cut in.

"On the contrary," Dave said, "we think women make great cops. We just don't want them to be our daughters."

"Nail on the head," CJ said.

"Ah," said Stella.

"So, it's not what I can do for you, it's what Lisa can do for you. I don't see what it could be."

"I know she hasn't access to vacation and time off dates; however, there might be a chance that she has connections, knows someone in the right places."

Dave raised his eyebrows and then reached for his phone. After dialing and listening for a few seconds he said, "Hey, it's your dad. Isn't this your day off?"

Stella dropped her head on CJ's shoulder. He took her hand.

"Good," Dave continued. "I need you to come by." He listened then said, "It's extremely important… No, not over the phone. Trust me. You'll understand when you get here. Bye."

"She'll be here in about thirty minutes. Have you guys eaten?"

It was forty-five minutes before they heard a car door slam. Seconds later the front door opened and Lisa Bowers walked in.

"Sorry it took me so long, Daddy, had to go by the post office and…" She looked at the two people sitting on the sofa. "CJ Washburn?" She looked at her father. "What's going on?"

"Lisa, this is CJ's companion, Stella."

"I know who she is, Daddy. Their faces are plastered everywhere. I should be placing them both under arrest."

"I understand. I'm asking that you just sit down and listen for a bit."

"Listen? Damn it, Dad, you're placing me in a bad situation here. How about if I place them in handcuffs and read them their rights. Then, maybe, I'll listen."

"You don't really believe he committed these murders, do you?"

"It's not for me to decide and you know that."

"Lisa," CJ said, holding up his hands, "I'll make you a promise. We'll turn ourselves into you, give you the honor of the collar, if you feel after listening to us that that would be the best route to take."

Still not convinced, Lisa's head swiveled between CJ and her father.

"Please, Lisa," Stella said. "We were prepared to turn ourselves in this morning until we thought of you and your dad. You're our last hope. We're begging you. Please, give us a chance to share our thoughts with you first."

"I'll probably take you in no matter what you tell me, even if I totally believe you. I'm a sworn police office. If you're innocent, let the system work it out."

"Do you think the system would have found me innocent if CJ hadn't uncovered the truth six years ago?" her dad said.

Lisa glared at him.

"Do you know who the lead investigator is on this case right now?" CJ asked her.

"I know it's not Payne."

"It's Bunko," CJ said.

"Bunko! You've got to be kidding me." She looked at her dad. "Really?"

Dave nodded.

"Fine." She sat down in what CJ assumed was her mother's chair. "I'm listening. But, no promises."

Chapter 30

One more time CJ and Stella went over everything, from the very first two murders, although Lisa knew more about them than did they, all the way to sitting in her father's house, including the belief that the killer was a cop.

At the end Stella said, "I have been with Clint around the clock since noon on Wednesday, during which time the last two murders took place."

Lisa looked at CJ. "So you're thinking that this guy, this cop, is doing this just to frame you?"

CJ had been sitting forward, his forearms on his knees. The question from Lisa sent him back against the sofa again. "I can't say I've ever thought of it that way. That's certainly true now, but..." He thought about it for a time while everyone waited on him. Finally he said, "No, not initially. There would have been no way he could have known I'd wind up close to the case. I'm just a PI now. It was a fluke that I showed up at the scene of the old woman, who ended up being a copycat and then a pure coincidence that I found the fourth one because I couldn't sleep. It was from that one, the perp's third, that he had to have come up with the idea to divert the heat toward me and so planted a body in the trunk of my car. Then, when he discovered that I had gone to Idaho, he followed me and did another kill up there."

"Trying to drive the final nail into your coffin, I'd say," Dave said.

"Most likely; however, if he'd left well enough alone I'd still be suspect number one to everyone."

"You still are," Lisa said.

CJ looked at her. "I'd like to think I've got you all on my side."

Dave and Stella gave their over-whelming confirmation, but CJ was still waiting for Lisa's nod. When she finally gave it, though obviously with reluctance, he said, "Add Detective Payne and that's four. If not for these last two kills when I had iron clad alibis, I'd probably have zero."

"I'd still be with you," Stella said.

"Out of loyalty, but, understandably, you'd carry a certain amount of reservation."

Stella started to open her mouth to argue, then closed it and looked down at her hands. "I rescued you, remember, before the Idaho murder. I was with you from the onset." She turned her head up to look directly into his eyes. "I never once, for a second, lost belief in you."

After a short silence Lisa held up her hands. "Okay. You've got me, but I still feel very uncomfortable."

"Well understood," CJ said.

"What do you think I can do for you?"

"I don't really know. Your dad seemed to think you might have some connections." CJ looked at Dave. "What were you thinking, Dave?"

"Yeah, what were you thinking, Dad?" Lisa said.

"Who's the friend you have in Personnel? Krystal something."

"Krystal Kramer."

"Officer Kramer. Right. She would know who has taken time off. Think you could talk to her?"

"First of all I don't believe vacation schedules are her area. Second, how could I possibly do something like that? It's one thing to agree with you all here in the safety of my father's home; it's quite another to go asking fellow officers for help. I could lose my badge."

"We know you can't reveal why you're asking," CJ said. "You could say something like you're investigating a situation and just wanted to know if there was anyone who had taken sudden time off August 1st and 2nd for sickness, family emergency, anything. It may not be her area but she likely has access to the data."

"Maybe, but she couldn't give me names, privacy crap and all that."

"Probably not and it'd likely make her uncomfortable for you to even ask; however, she could confirm whether there were any such requests made, and she'd likely not even think twice about it, especially if you imply that there is an official twist to the request?"

"Twist is certainly a good word for it. It would make more sense to her if the request was coming from internal affairs, which I certainly am not."

Silence prevailed for a time, then her father said, "Call for a girls' happy hour tonight, a little girly gossip time. Give her the old what-if… like, what if this was a cop doing it, not CJ Washburn? Put a spin on it that makes it her idea to go looking at vacation schedules."

"Who do you think I am, Dad? For one, I don't do girls night out, didn't even when I was unattached. It would not only be weird to Krystal, but I'd have to answer to Jerry."

"Who's Jerry?" CJ said.

"My husband."

"Tell him the truth," Dave said, "or as much of it that he'd accept. You're doing a quiet investigation into a situation that you can't talk to him about and you need to enlist Krystal's help."

Lisa considered it for a time and then pulled out her phone. She stood as she poked the phone and disappeared into another room with it pressed to her ear. "Hey. It's Lisa," she said before her voice faded away.

"Every serial killer eventually makes a mistake," CJ said, "and trying to purposely divert the suspicions toward me might be this guy's mistake. He revealed a card in his hand which said, 'cop.'"

"And he doesn't yet know it," Dave said.

"Makes him vulnerable until he does."

"How so?" Stella asked.

"He's leaving tracks galore," CJ said. "The first three of his murders were almost exactly one month apart. That's typical of a serial killer to kill on a schedule, usually the same time of month, week or day. I don't know the CSI details, but I'd be willing to bet those three were within an hour of each other, 2:00 a.m. for example. When he suddenly decided to use me, he stepped completely out of his box."

"And it's got to be getting harder for him to find victims, because it's all over the news." Dave said. "University sororities are engaging male body guards. Prostitutes are working together, eye balling or sneaking pictures of each other's clients in case one of them should wind up dead. Parents of teenage girls are putting the brakes on dating. Women, in general, are not going anywhere alone. He started out with prostitutes and then diverged to young women in general, it seems." He looked at CJ. "Did you know that the one in Idaho wasn't a prostitute, or anything even close to that definition? She wasn't even a college student. She was a young mother of a 2-year-old, picked up while walking between her parent's house and her apartment where she lived with her husband and son, a two block distance."

Stella's hands went to her mouth. "Oh my god!"

CJ dropped his head while the impact of that settled in. When he finally looked up he said, "I've got to turn myself in. He's gone berserk. Once I'm in custody he'll stop."

He looked at Stella. Tears where flowing so freely that he grabbed her and pulled her to him. "It's okay. It'll be okay."

"He's destroying people," she blabbered. "He's destroying families. That baby's mother is gone." And the tears just kept coming. "It's never going to be okay for that family."

While she was crying Dave had gotten up and left. He returned with a kitchen towel and handed it to her. She took deep breaths and wiped at her face. When the sobbing had subsided and she had herself under control, she said, "I don't want you in jail."

"But…" CJ started to say.

She put her finger to his mouth. "I know. I don't think you have any choice."

They all went silent for a time; the only sound that of Lisa's voice coming from her phone conversation in the kitchen. When finally her phone call ended and she stepped back into the living room, everyone was staring at her.

"What?"

"What do you know about this morning's victim?" Stella asked. "Was she a prostitute?"

"I don't know. Having the day off, I haven't been keeping up with things."

"She was a college student," Dave said, "according to the news. Top of her class, well respected by her peers. Didn't say much more."

CJ and Stella looked at each other. When Stella nodded CJ stood and turned to Lisa. "I'm surrendering to you, turning myself in."

Stella stood, once again tears flowing like the tap was stuck open. "Me, too."

"No!" CJ said. "You don't need to."

She ran the towel across her face. "If I don't they're going to continue looking for me. This way I'll probably be out fairly soon and then I can freely move about and try to help figure out who this guy is."

"I don't like it."

"It's the way it's going to be. If you go, I go." She looked at Lisa. "Did you get a meeting with your friend?"

"Tonight at *Risky Business*, a sports bar on Tanque Verde. If you two go ahead with this, it'll help justify my questions to her. It'll look like I'm part of the case whether I am or not."

"We're going ahead with it," CJ said. "How do you want to handle it?"

Chapter 31

Lisa had refused to put handcuffs on them even though CJ insisted she do so. When they arrived at the station, however, he prevailed, saying it would look better for her. They compromised on just him, but not Stella. Now he sat in an interrogation room, handcuffed to the table as though he might suddenly go crazy and kill everyone within reach, who, in this case, consisted of two FBI agents, Stratton and Crane, and Detective Bunko, a shit-eating grin on his face. If CJ was to go crazy, he decided that Bunko would be his first target. He grinned at him and winked.

Agent Stratton looked between CJ and the detective. "What's that mean?"

"Nothing," CJ said. "Just glad to see Ralph on the team." CJ had no idea why he said that; maybe to keep Bunko off guard. If there was a way to wipe away that grin, CJ would find it. "We were pretty good buddies back in the day."

The grin disappeared; the mouth opened, then shut.

The agent looked down at his paperwork. "Clinton Joshua Washburn. We've got you on one count of murder, transporting said body across state lines and eluding state and federal officers."

"CJ."

The agent looked up. "What?"

"You can call me CJ. I'd rather be accused of murder, which I didn't do by the way, than be associated with a president who happened to have my name."

The agent folded his hands on the table in front of him, providing no more than a hint of a smirk at the comment. "A woman's body was found in the trunk of your car, Mister Washburn, after you drove her from Arizona, through Nevada, all the way into Idaho. Did you kill her before you left Tucson, after you arrived in Idaho or somewhere along the way?"

"I did not kill her. Sometime during the night before I left, the real killer took her life and placed her in the trunk of my car."

"You're saying you drove all the way to Moscow, Idaho with a dead woman and didn't know it?"

"That's exactly what I'm saying."

"So you admit to transporting her body across state lines."

"Don't try twisting the facts. I had no knowledge of the fact she was in my car. He jimmied the lock on the trunk so that it would open with neither the trunk release nor the fob. If your forensic team is doing their job then they should already know that."

"Who is this *he* that you're referring to?"

"The perp. The person who is actually doing the killing."

The agent nodded and looked down at his notes. "You checked into the Palouse Inn in Moscow, Idaho the evening of July 31st, this past Tuesday. Somehow you became aware that using your credit card sent a red flag to law enforcement, and so you managed to evade capture. If, as you say, you didn't do this, why didn't you turn yourself in right then?"

"I'm not sure. I panicked, didn't at first know what was going on with a slew of cops converging on my car. When I saw them pull a quilt-wrapped body out of my trunk, I knew I had been set up, that I was in trouble."

Agent Stratton tapped his pencil against the table for a bit and then turned to the other agent. "Make a note to get any video footage from that night. I want to go through it." He returned to CJ. "If I'm correct, there is no vantage point from which you could have viewed what was removed from the trunk of your car, outside of the motel itself, and we know you weren't there. You already knew in what she was wrapped because you're the one who put her there."

"I was in the one place the officers didn't look. I was in a tree between the motel and *McDonald's* parking lots, at least twenty feet above the ground, looking right down at the scene. I was returning with my dinner when Moscow's finest came roaring into the motel parking lot, so I climbed the tree and watched the horror show."

"What do you have against prostitutes?"

CJ blinked for a few seconds at the sudden change in topic. "I don't have anything against prostitutes."

"Then you like them."

"I didn't say that."

"Then you don't like them."

"I didn't say that either. You're trying to make me say something incriminating."

"I'm not trying to make you say anything, Mister Washburn. Where did you go after you left the tree?"

"I found a pilot who would fly me back to Arizona."

"Who was that?"

"I'd rather not say."

The agent tapped with his pencil again for a half minute and then said, "With every law enforcement agency and dog catcher within a hundred miles on high alert for you, you managed to evade them all and locate someone with a plane fueled and ready who would be willing to fly you all the way to Southern Arizona. Is that what you're saying?"

Although he flew to New Mexico, CJ was fairly certain it wasn't smart to divulge even that little detail. "Yes."

"Are you aware that there was another murder that next night just like all the others, and you are the prime suspect?"

"Yes."

"This individual who you say flew you back to Arizona could be your alibi."

"I don't want to get him involved. Since I didn't commit that murder, or any of the murders for that matter, you're not going to find any forensic evidence or witnesses that place me at any of those scenes. I therefore see no reason to give up that name."

"Actually, Mister Washburn, Clinton, we have forensics from three of the murders that point directly at you. Too early to tell on this last one from this morning but I'm guessing there'll be something. That'll be number four."

CJ's mouth went dry. He sucked up some fluid and said, "That's impossible."

"One," Agent Stratton said, holding up one finger, "Rebecca Cling. She's the victim who you claimed to have discovered early in the morning of July 28th. She was covered with your blood, hair and alcohol laced saliva."

"I had to climb in the dumpster to determine if there was a body and if she was still alive. I fell on her. What do you expect?"

Stratton held up two fingers. "Two, Ashley Johnson. Discovered in the trunk of your car in Moscow, Idaho the evening of July 31st. Found your hair."

CJ started to hold up his hands but came to the end of the handcuff on one. "My trunk," he said. "Probably loaded with my forensics. Means nothing."

"Three, Maria Rodston, found dead the morning of August 2nd, thirty-two hours after you arrived in Moscow. Your hair, confirmed with DNA match, was found on her."

"That's impossible!" CJ jerked against the handcuffs again.

Stratton held up a hand. "Easy, Mister Washburn. You might hurt yourself." When CJ settled Stratton folded the thumb down, leaving four fingers. "Four, Sherri Cural. She was discovered this morning, August 3rd, here in Tucson, in another dumpster, wrapped in an old quilt. Hair samples that obviously didn't belong to her were taken and are now, as we speak, being analyzed. We will know something within the hour. I have my suspicions."

CJ opened his mouth and then closed it. He put his one free hand to the back of his neck in an unconscious attempt to massage away the growing pain. Stratton, he knew, was waiting for a response. He didn't have one. He snatched the bottle of water provided for him, the one he'd initially refused to touch because it was Detective Bunko who brought it in, unscrewed the lid with the assist of his handcuffed hand and took a mouth washing gulp.

CJ knew three law firms that he could trust, firms for whom he'd regularly done work. Only one of them specialized in criminal defense. He pointed at Stratton's notes. "Write this down; Gianna Onassis." He spelled the name for him.

"Who is Gianna Onassis?" Stratton said.

"My attorney," CJ said. "The Onassis Law Firm." He then put his head on the table and closed his eyes.

Chapter 32

It was after 5:00 before Gianna showed up. The first thing she did was insist that the handcuffs be removed. Stratton argued.

"He's an ex-cop who turned himself in for God's sake," she said. "You're treating him like a damned terrorist."

"It's procedure, counselor."

"Fine. You've gotten your procedure all afternoon. Now I get mine. Even the most hardened criminal is not stupid enough to do something crazy in front of his attorney. Remove the cuffs."

They stared at each other as the seconds ticked by. CJ wasn't certain Gianna would prevail, though he'd only seen her back down from court judges, but even then, not as a rule.

When Stratton broke eye contact CJ held up the cuffed arm and raised his eyebrows. When his arm was free he stood and stretched.

"Can we continue with our questioning now?" Stratton asked.

"No," Gianna said. "I want time to get the facts from my client. You know the drill, Agent Stratton. Listening devices and video equipment turned off."

"How much time do you need?"

"As much as it takes." She made the shooing away motion, not unlike a woman shooing her pesky kids outside to play. When the door was closed she sat down. "Sit. I've been on my feet all day and I don't want to look up at you."

CJ sat.

"How are you doing, CJ?"

"Certainly could be better. I really appreciate you taking this on. It's turning into a big mess."

"Not a problem. I hear that Stella is being held as well. Do you want me to step in for her?"

"Please. I don't know how we can afford you, though."

"Don't worry. We'll figure that out later. How is she fitting into all this? What are they charging her with?"

"I don't think they're charging her with anything at this point. Accessory or some such thing I imagine is what they're thinking."

Gianna rose and knocked on the door. When it opened she said to someone CJ couldn't see, "I'll be talking to Stella Summers next. I hope to hell you don't have cuffs on her, too. I'm also going to expect a good reason to hold her all night."

She returned to her seat, pulled out a mini recorder and said, "Okay. Let's get started."

It took an hour and a half for CJ to recount his story, leaving out nothing. Even though he didn't want to reveal Stella's sister and her husband, he knew he had to give Gianna everything. He had seen attorneys get blindsided with surprise information so he probably went overboard. Better too much than not enough.

"I really want Bill and Sara's names left out of it, if at all possible."

"I understand, CJ, but they may be your best alibi. If we can prove that you were in New Mexico at the time the girl was killed in Idaho, it'll throw doubt on all the rest. It'll show that the hair, your hair, found on her body was planted, adding validity to your claim of being framed, and tainting all the rest of the evidence they have against you. By the way, I was advised on the way in here that the hair found on this morning's victim was in fact yours."

CJ sat back and looked up at the ceiling, then put his hands on his head and closed his eyes. "Who the hell is this guy?" He looked back at Gianna. "What about Stella's testimony of being with me last night?"

"As your girlfriend, Stella doesn't carry much weight. And please don't get your hopes up with Bill and Sara either. If they're as anti-authority as you say they are, a good prosecutor could turn it against you."

"Another good reason not to bring them up," CJ said.

"The hard question, then, is going to be, who flew you out of Idaho? If you refuse to answer, at best, a judge could find you in contempt of court. At worst the prosecutor could use it to turn a jury against you."

"I'm damned if I do, damned if I don't."

"Either way is a gamble."

"Then we can't go to court. We have to find evidence that forces them to drop the charges, that clears me of all suspicion."

"I'd send my best investigator out on it, but it seems that he is in jail." She tilted her head and raised her eyebrows at him. "Do you have anyone else you'd recommend?"

CJ considered the question for a few seconds and then said, "Dave McDermott."

"Never heard of him. Is he a licensed PI?"

"No." Then CJ remembered Lisa's comment when he'd seen her at the crime scene where he was first arrested, where he'd been drunk. She mentioned her father was thinking of becoming a PI, that maybe it was too late to advise him against it. Did he file his paperwork already? "Actually I don't know. I think he's been considering heading into the private sector. He's an ex-cop like me. Everything I just told you, I told him this morning, so he's fully up to speed. It was at his house where I turned myself in to his daughter by the way. Is it a problem if he isn't a licensed PI?"

"Somewhat, though maybe I can work around it. Give me his number and I'll give him a call."

"Any chance of getting me out on bail?"

"Highly doubtful, but not impossible. We have to wait for all the charges to be filed and then for the preliminary hearing."

There came a knock and then the door opened. Agent Stratton poked his head in and motioned to Gianna. She rose and went to him. CJ watched Stratton's lips and tried to pick up some of his words. All he got was Moscow.

Gianna returned and sat down. "He wanted me to pass this information on to you, as a courtesy, he says."

"What else could there possibly be? They're already trying to hang me on four murders. Has there been another?"

She shook her head. "No. It seems that Maria Rodston, the Moscow, Idaho victim, resided in a basement apartment directly across the street from where your daughter lives."

CJ just stared at his attorney, hardly breathing, his mind reeling, searching for the implication that the information delivered. What are they thinking? He leaned back in his chair and put his arms out. "What are they going to do with that? Are they going to say that I went to visit my daughter but saw this other woman first and decided to kill her instead, evidence, thus guilt, by proximity?"

And then the real truth of it occurred to him. His eyes got big and his mouth dropped open. Why hadn't he already seen it? "Holy shit! I need Stratton back in here, now!"

Chapter 33

When Agent Stratton arrived at Gianna's request, Agent Crane on his heel, CJ was pacing back and forth. Stratton didn't appear too happy to have been summoned by his suspect. Before he could even open his mouth, CJ rushed at them.

"You've got to put protection around Patricia," was all CJ got out before the two agents had him in a double arm lock, pressed against the wall. "He's going to kill her!" he all but screamed as they pushed him back to his chair and handcuffed him to the table. All Gianna could do was stumble aside, out of the way.

"So, what are you so excited about Mister Washburn?" Stratton said. "Who's going to kill who?"

"Don't say anything, CJ," Gianna interrupted as CJ started to open his mouth again, jerking against the restraint. She pulled a chair around next him, sat down and glared at the two agents. They backed up to the door. She learned toward CJ. "From now on you don't talk to them until you've talked to me first? Is that clear?"

CJ nodded his head, rocking to and fro like an autistic child. Gianna placed a hand on his bicep.

"I need you to settle." She waited a few seconds. "Now, CJ."

He looked at her and then at her hand. He nodded. "Sorry."

"Good. Now take a deep breath, relax and tell me what's going on in your head."

CJ took the deep breath. It stopped the rocking but he still felt like there was an anvil sitting on his chest. He turned again to talk directly to Gianna, trying his best to keep his voice low. "That was no coincidence that the victim in Moscow lived across the street from my daughter." He tried taking another deep breath; the anvil still didn't go away. "That was a warning from the perp to me. He's saying Trish could have been a victim, will be if I don't confess."

Gianna nodded. "I understand. Did you see your daughter at all while you were there, or communicate with her?"

"No. I was going to surprise her, never got past checking in to the motel. The only time I talked to her was the next day, as I told you, while flying out. Stella had set that up."

She sat back and motioned to the agents. "I think this is worth listening to. Go ahead, CJ."

Stratton sat down while Crane remained standing, as though blocking the direct line to the door. "I ask again, Mister Washburn, what has gotten you so excited?"

"It's obvious what's going on here. Not only is this guy planting evidence but he's trying to use my daughter as a threat. He wants me to know just how close to her he can get."

"You think your perp knows enough about you that he was able to locate your daughter, find someone who lived near her who sort of fit his MO and then catch her alone so he could grab her and kill her without being seen?"

"Exactly."

"And you want us to put police protection around your daughter; is that right?"

"Yes! I'm glad you understand."

"What I understand here, Mister Washburn, is that the murder of Maria Rodston was planned out by you just in case of this very situation."

"What?"

"You figured we'd take your story more seriously if we bought this little 'threatening you with your daughter' scenario."

"No!"

"After evading the authorities for twenty-four hours you found your way to your daughter's residence and then remained hidden until a neighbor woman showed up, who you then killed."

"No no no no no!" CJ slammed his hands on the table. "I have killed no one!" he shouted, shaking off Gianna's hands.

"She wasn't even a prostitute," Stratton continued, seeming pleased with CJ's outburst. "She had a husband and a two-year-old son. Becoming desperate, you broke away from your MO and got sloppy, started leaving clues behind."

By this time CJ was on his feet, waving his free arm in the air. "No! You've got it all wrong."

Gianna jumped to her feet and held her arm, palm out to the agents who were moving toward him. "This interview is over." She snagged CJ's arm. "Clinton Joshua Washburn!" The strident use of his full name brought him around to look at her. "Sit down and shut up," she said with a controlled, even voice.

He blinked a couple of times and then sat, dropping his chin to his chest and closing his eyes. He resumed his rocking.

Gianna turned to the Agents. "Out."

"We're not removing the cuffs this time, counselor."

"Fine. Just go."

After they'd left CJ said, "I'm sorry."

"Nothing to be sorry about, CJ. They were goading you. You didn't say anything I wouldn't have said, so everything is fine."

"Do you believe me?"

"It's not my job to believe you. It's my job to defend you."

He looked at her. "I know that, but do you believe me? Doesn't it help to defend someone if you actually believe they're innocent?"

"I'll say this once, CJ. I believe you. I'm only saying it once because I cannot get emotionally involved with your plight. I don't believe I can adequately defend you if my judgment becomes clouded by the emotion of it all. When we get in court it is only the facts that will weigh for or against you. Do you understand where I'm coming from?"

He put his hand on hers. "Thank you. Yes, I understand. But do you understand that I can't *not* get emotionally involved? This is my child and she's in danger because of me."

She considered him for a moment. "What would you want me to do?"

"Talk to Stratton and his goons. Convince them that they have it all wrong. Talk to…" CJ leaned back and put his free hand to his forehead. "Oh, Christ. What's happened to Dan?"

"Detective Payne?" Gianna asked.

"Yes. Do you know? The last time I saw him he was racing across the desert with a helicopter in pursuit."

"I don't know anything about him, but I'll try to find out."

"He may need an attorney as well." He stared up at the ceiling for a time and then said, "I guess there isn't much else you can do. Help Stella get released. Help Dan if he needs counsel. Turn Dave McDermott loose on the case if he's able and willing. I'll sit here on ice and hope to hell someone figures it all out."

Chapter 34

It was forty-five minutes before Agent Stratton gave in to CJ's request to call his daughter, by which time CJ's blood pressure and agitation had dropped. He was in fact able to ease the stress and tension by convincing himself that as long as he was in jail, Trish was safe. The perp would have no need to go after her.

Crane escorted him to a room with a phone, handcuffed him to the table and left him alone. He dialed and waited, reversed the charges and waited some more until finally he heard her voice.

"Daddy?"

"Hi, Gumdrop."

"Is everything okay now? Where are you?"

"I'm in Tucson. Don't say anything about how I got here, okay? I'm sure this phone is being monitored."

"Monitored? Where are you?"

"I turned myself in this morning. I'm in FBI and police custody."

"Oh."

The sound in her voice nearly broke CJ's heart.

"But you didn't do any of it," she said. "Why did you give up?"

"It's very complicated, but basically the last three women he killed were because of me. He was trying to frame me." CJ had decided he wasn't going to say anything about the perp's reason for killing one of Trish's neighbors. He didn't want to frighten her.

"So you're thinking he'll stop while you're in jail?"

"Yes."

There was a long silence and then Trish said, "Maria Rodston lived across the street from me. Did you know that?"

CJ looked up at the ceiling. "Yes. I just found that out."

"I knew her, Daddy. I babysat her little boy, Billy, a couple of times."

"I'm so sorry, Trish."

"And that's not the worst of it." Her voice went up an octave. "Well, maybe that is the worst of it because Maria is dead and Billy is without a mother. The other worst part is that the word is out that I'm the daughter of the *Dumpster Killer!*" The last two words had CJ pulling the phone away from his year. And then she yelled, "I'm like a leper now!"

CJ didn't know what to say.

"I'm sorry I yelled, Dad, but this morning someone broke a jar of red paint on my car. I'm surprised it didn't crack the windshield."

"Oh God."

"Oh God is right! How did you get involved in this? How did you let this happen?"

CJ couldn't think of a thing to say.

"You still there, Dad?"

"Yes," he said. His mouth felt like he'd fallen face-first in the Southern Arizona desert.

"Then tell me. What the hell did you do that this guy is trying to frame you?"

"Wrong place at the wrong time. Then you do believe that I didn't do any of it?"

"Of course I believe you. I know where you were when Maria was killed. What I'm still trying to figure out is how not to blame you."

All CJ could do was shake his head. "I'm sorry."

"I'm sorry too, Dad. Do the police believe that you did it?"

"It appears so. The thing is…"

"What?"

"As long as I'm in jail he likely won't kill again."

"That'll just make it look like you're guilty."

"I know. I've thought of that. I just couldn't bear hearing of another woman being found in a dumpster. This was the only way I could stop it."

CJ heard a sigh and then some noise in the background. "Are you by yourself?"

"Dillon is here."

"Good."

"I hope so."

"What do you mean you hope so?"

"Well…"

"Is he not being supportive?"

"You could say that."

"I'm really sorry."

"At this point I'm not."

"I don't think you should be alone. Is there anyone you could stay with, girlfriend, neighbor, or someone who could stay with you?"

"I would have thought there was until the paint started flying, but not anymore."

The door opened and Agent Crane stuck his head in. "Time's up."

"I've got to go," CJ said to his daughter. "Whatever you have to do make sure you're not alone tonight."

"I'll be fine, Dad. I'm just pissed off is all. Nobody died from being pissed off."

"Still, please find someone."

"I will. Oh! How is Stella doing?"

"I don't know. We both turned ourselves in. I haven't seen her since."

"Oh. What do they think she's done?"

"Aiding and abetting or some such thing. They really don't have anything to hold her on so I expect she should be out before long. I've hired a good lawyer for both of us. You probably remember Gianna Onassis."

"Yeah, sort of. I never paid much attention to what you did."

"I should have a report from her before long that Stella has been released."

The door opened again and Crane stepped in.

"My phone time is up. I've got to go."

"Okay, Daddy. I love you."

"I love you too, Gumdrop."

Chapter 35

It was still dark when CJ awoke with a jerk. At least it seemed like it was still dark with the subdued lights. He was sweating worse than the other half dozen times he had jerked awake from one nightmare after another. The memory of them faded fast but he was sure they all had something to do with Trish and the killer. He sat up on the edge of the cot and thought about the one dark image he was still able to hold onto this time, a killer all in black with a face he couldn't see.

He stood, stretched and began pacing.

And then it suddenly came to him that not only was it a cop but it had to be one who not only knew him, but knew him well. How else could he get to Trish so fast? The suspect list could be narrowed very quickly. It had to be someone he had either worked with at one time or crossed paths with a number of times. Either that or this guy had a ready source of personal information about ex-police officers. It had been eight years since CJ had been on the force so any personal information would be old. Who could get a hold of Trish's current address? What source could be tapped on a moment's notice to find that kind of information? Trish had moved out of the dorm into that apartment less than a year ago. What CJ needed was a roster of all the past and present police officers and sheriff deputies from which he could check off names he recognized to create a new list of suspects. Bounce that against the vacation and time-off schedule, then add the FBI's profile, which they certainly should have up and running by now, and the suspect list could be whittled down to just a handful, if that many.

But of course they wouldn't have a profile. They think they've got their man in one CJ Washburn. They're probably getting ready to go home, satisfied to turn him over to the legal system to be tried and prosecuted.

He sat down on the bunk and put his head in his hands. He had no clue where his life was going to end up. When they dumped him in the holding cell for the night he was told he would be fetched at 9:45 in the morning for his Initial Appearance before a judge. He knew that was strictly a formality, that the Preliminary Hearing before a Grand Jury would come a few days later followed by the Arraignment before the Superior Court. The latter could be a month out and then another three months until the trial, and during all this time he'd be sitting in jail, stressed and depressed, unable to do anything to help himself.

And they hadn't released Stella yet. Although he fell into another depression when he was told, Gianna assured him that she would be released after the Initial Appearance. He really wished she hadn't turned herself in.

He lay back down on the cot and closed his eyes. There would be no more sleep, however.

CJ opened his eyes sometime later to the sound of footsteps outside his door. "Breakfast!" a voice said. With that came the sound of the pass-through opening from the jailer's side and then closing. "Get it while it's hot," the voice said and then clip-clopped away.

CJ stood and opened his side of the pass-through, pulled out the box and carried it to the cot. Scrambled eggs, bacon, toast and juice; a spoon made of cardboard. No coffee. He considered putting it back but realized it did no one any good if he didn't keep his strength up. After one bite of the egg which tasted like ground up recycled wood pulp with yellow food dye, he ate only the bacon and toast and drank the juice.

He wondered what time it was.

While he sat and waited, his stomach growled. No way was he eating the egg.

CJ was still on the cot, leaning against the wall, when the cell door opened.

"Time to go," a uniformed officer said. Another stood just outside. Together they looked like a pair of refrigerators, one black, one white. "Standup, turn around and present your wrists."

CJ did as he was told so that the handcuffs could be applied. With that the two officers escorted him out, a big, beefy hand on each arm.

In the courtroom there were only a half dozen people plus the judge. CJ sat at the opposite end of a table from Stella, Gianna between them. All he and Stella managed to say to each other was, "Hi," along with an exchange of assurances that each was okay.

"You don't say anything unless asked directly by the judge," Gianna said to him, "which he likely won't. If he does, I'll speak for you."

They all stood and the judge entered, she, not he. She sat and then everyone in the room sat, except for the two officers who never took their eyes off of CJ.

"Give me a minute to read the points that have been given me," she said. After a few minutes she looked down at the individuals seated across the aisle from Gianna and her charges. "Detective Bunko?"

Bunko stood. "Yes, Your Honor."

"Do you have anything to add to this, Detective?"

"No, ma'am."

"There is nothing here as to why Ms. Summers is being held."

"We felt that she assisted Mr. Washburn in his evasion from law enforcement, state and federal."

"Is that all you have, Detective; a feeling? You have no evidence?"

Bunko looked around nervously, then back at the judge. "No, ma'am."

"Detective Bunko, when we are out in public, say bowling or playing badminton for example, I'll call you Bunko and you can call me, ma'am. In this courtroom you call me, Your Honor. Is that clear, Detective?"

Bunko's face turned red. "Yes, Your Honor."

The judge looked at Stella. "It says here that you surrendered to the police along with Mister Washburn. What compelled you to do that?"

Gianna put her hand on Stella's arm and then stood. "Your Honor. Gianna Onassis, counsel for Ms. Summers and Mister Washburn. Ms. Summers had become aware that there was a bolo out on her and her car as part of the efforts by law enforcement to locate and bring into custody Clinton Washburn. He is her boss after all. It was partly through her efforts that Mister Washburn made the decision to turn himself in. Because of the bolo she felt she needed to surrender as well."

The judge appraised Stella for a time and then said, "Cut her loose, Detective. As for Mister Washburn have him here 10:00 Monday morning for the Preliminary Hearing. No discussion."

"Certainly, Your Honor."

Everyone rose as the judge left the chamber. Before CJ had a chance to get words in with Stella, the beefy refrigerators had him by the arms. As they left the chamber there was a small swarm of people with microphones and cameras suddenly shouting his name, followed by a barrage of questions. CJ was very appreciative of the two massive officers mowing people to the side. Just as they reached the door where the reporters couldn't go, CJ twisted to look over his shoulder. Between heads and cameras he was able to see Gianna and Stella attempting to make their escape out the other end of the hall. Surprising the two officers he held his ground for a few seconds, attempting to turn as if to make a statement.

Just as the two ladies disappeared from view, the officers gave him a hard jerk. "Don't go and do something stupid, Washburn," the white one said.

"Have a nice day," CJ called to the crowd and for a second lost contact with the floor. The door slammed closed behind them and he regained his feet. "Thank you."

"For what?"

"Just thank you. You guys are doing a great job. When I start my own police force I expect to see your resumes."

"Why do we always get the comedians?" the black one said and then all went silent.

Chapter 36

The weekend was the longest in CJ's entire life. He was allowed a phone call twice and in both cases was not able to raise anybody, not Stella, not Trish, not Gianna, not even his ex-wife. Why he thought to call her he had no idea; maybe to ensure himself that Trish was okay, that maybe Pat had talked to her.

Sunday night, an hour or so after the box of crap they called food came and went, CJ was in the middle of a tattered Clive Cussler novel when two officers, not the beefy refrigerator types, fetched him to an interrogation room. They left him alone, as before, handcuffed to the table. After a half hour of waiting CJ began wishing he'd brought the novel with him. He was halfway through a Dirk Pitt adventure for the second time, liking it even less than the first time. He wondered if Cussler actually made a living writing the stuff. At least it helped the time pass, though.

He had just laid his head on the table when both FBI agents came in. Stratton sat while Crane remained standing. Crane looked nervous. Stratton clasped his hands together and cleared his throat.

"What?" CJ asked, more of a demand than a question.

"It seems that we have lost your daughter."

CJ came straight up in his chair, blinked a couple times and said, "Trish? What do you mean you lost her?"

"We had the city police keeping an eye on her, just in case your claims were right. She disappeared."

"Just in case my claims were right!" He burst to his feet. The chair slammed over backwards as he jerked to the end of the handcuffs, knocking him off balance. He caught himself on the edge of the table and leaned forward into Stratton's face. "Damn straight my claims were right and I asked you to protect her. Seems like a simple thing, don't you think?"

Stratton hadn't moved. He put out his hand. "Settle down Mister Washburn. She knew they were keeping an eye on her and she likely just gave them the slip, figuring they were invading her privacy. She's just a kid after all. Probably doesn't know the seriousness of the situation."

"She's not a damn kid!" He gripped the edge of the table, knuckles white. "She 21 years old and there's a damn killer out there who wouldn't blink an eye at killing her. And she knows the situation because I talked to her Friday night. She was angry and scared."

"Sit down," Stratton said, a firm edge to his voice.

CJ glared at him and then wrestled the chair upright with his free hand and sat, still breathing hard.

"If you're correct, Mister Washburn, this guy won't touch her as long as you're in jail and he thinks we think you're the killer. We're almost certain your daughter slipped away on her own. We've got a witness who thought she saw her and another woman cross between the houses behind her residence."

CJ leaned back in his chair and considered what the agent had just said. "A woman."

"Exactly."

"No idea who the woman was?"

"The witness had never seen her before."

"What about her car?"

"Hasn't moved an inch. Doubt it would go very far until the paint is scraped off the windshield."

"What time?"

"The witness was just getting home from church; about 11:30 this morning."

CJ pressed his forehead into his hands. "I tried calling her this afternoon. I couldn't get her."

"We haven't been able to raise her either. We also haven't been able to track her cell phone. That means she's turned it off."

"Or someone else has turned it off," CJ added, a mixture of anger and fear in his voice. "There's been plenty of time between Thursday night and this morning for him to get back up to Idaho. This may be him adding an exclamation point to his earlier warning."

"The profile on this guy tells us he is highly intelligent. He would already know that such a move would take the heat off of you. We truly believe that your daughter has gone off with a friend, probably going into hiding on her own. Let's face it. If the police can't find her then neither can the perp. My impression is that she would be smart enough to know that. Am I right?"

CJ nodded. "She may have had another reason to get out of there. She's being called the daughter of a murderer, thus the paint thrown on her car. I told her I didn't want her there alone, to find a friend to stay with. That's probably what she did."

"Do you know who her friends are?" Agent Crane asked.

"No, other than her boyfriend, Dillon. Don't know his last name."

"Dillon Jones. He's been looked into," Stratton said. "Apparently the two of them had a fight Friday night. He hasn't seen her since."

CJ shook his head. "Trish saw it as his not wanting to be seen with an accused killer's daughter, which pissed her off. I think they were on the edge of the fight when I talked to her. Good riddance is all I can say."

CJ looked at the blood oozing from a tear in his skin from when he jerked against the handcuffs. He shook his head and looked back up at Stratton. "My gut feeling is she's okay, that she's taken action to take care of herself. I actually feel better about that than her being watched by the police. He can't find her now."

"I assume you've put a lot of thought into who this perp can be," Stratton said.

"Then you believe me."

"Let's just say your claims have some merit. Who do you think this guy is?"

"He's a cop."

"Why do you say that?"

CJ looked up at Crane and then at Stratton. Neither had an expression of surprise. "You two are already thinking that, aren't you? That's why Bunko isn't in here. You're trying to keep this on the down low because you don't know who to trust. For FBI ears only."

"We have no reason not to trust Detective Bunko."

"Except that he's an idiot with a mouth. Anything you tell him will probably be known by every patrol officer within an hour."

Again there was no change in expression from the two agents. CJ extended the handcuffed arm. "If you believe me why do I have to wear this?"

Stratton looked over CJ's head for a few seconds before turning to Agent Crane. "What do you think?"

"You've already cracked the egg. Might as well fry the bacon."

Stratton snorted, shook his head and turned back to CJ. "You're right. This is on the down low. Video and audio is off so this is just between you and us and our report to the chief of police and the county sheriff. We're certain it's a cop. It's not all that unusual, though it generally doesn't involve a killing spree. A cop gone vigilante usually keeps it quiet and often with several other like-minded individuals."

"This guy isn't just vigilante," CJ said. "He's gone rogue. He started out targeting prostitutes; now he's killed two who were anything but."

"For some reason he saw an opportunity to direct the heat at you when you stumbled, figuratively and literally, onto one of his victims."

CJ started to say he wasn't drunk and then remembered the report of his alcohol level. "I admit that I should have handled that different."

"Probably would have if you hadn't been inebriated. Once a cop, however, always a cop. Most people would run away from the crime and dial 911. A cop will run toward the crime first. We checked your background. You were a good cop. The key word here is were. You're a PI now and a PI is not the same as a cop, therefore you don't run at a crime anymore. You dial 911. You work for your client, not the city and not the state. If we figure out a way to cut you free you have to stay away from this investigation."

CJ shook his head. "Put me on the street and this guy will find another woman to kill and dump on my doorstep. I'll be back in here and another woman will be dead."

"Our thoughts exactly. Thus you can never be alone and the spin we put on it has to be just that."

"What kind of spin? Tell the media you don't think I did it and then let them know I'll always have a police or FBI shadow? A bit of a mixed message, wouldn't you say?"

"Maybe, but it'll let this guy know he can't kill again and we can focus on the existing evidence and through a detailed process of elimination will be able to drill down to his badge number."

"What if he's not a cop, say a secretary or janitor, hell possibly even a vendor who's been able to worm his way into the inside?"

Stratton held up his hand again. "Don't worry. We're covering all the possibilities. We appreciate your suggestions. What you really need to do is stay out of the way."

CJ sat back and thought about it. "I'll try to stay out of it, but I don't need one of your guys shadowing me all the time. How about Dave McDermott? He's an ex-cop. I'll promise to be his best buddy until you catch this guy. You can say you've assigned a team to stay with me 24/7."

"McDermott isn't a team."

"His daughter's a cop. Her coming on board would give it an official spin."

"You think she would?"

"Maybe. Add in Stella. That makes a team."

Stratton drummed his fingers on the table for a time and then said, "I could probably get you house arrest, wear an ankle monitor to make sure you don't go anywhere."

"Certainly be better than the accommodations here. The food alone should fall under the category of police brutality."

"Very funny. Tell it to the judge at the Preliminary Hearing tomorrow when we present our argument. Until then, hang loose."

Chapter 37

The night went as bad if not worse than the previous two. Twice CJ awoke in a cold sweat. The first he couldn't remember the dream, but the second was so vivid that he was afraid to go back to sleep. He sat on the edge of the bunk with his head in his hands, thinking about the images of that last nightmare. He'd been reliving the scene in the tree when the police officers pulled the woman out of the trunk of his car, only this time the woman was Trish and she'd turned an accusatory stare directly at him. He shook his head then stood and paced, wanting nothing more than to call her to ensure that she was okay. He considered banging on the door, but knew that would be useless, so he just kept pacing. She likely still had her phone turned off anyway.

After a time he sat back down on the bunk and leaned against the wall. Before long he stretched out and fell into a dreamless sleep. The next thing he knew someone had his arm and was shaking him and for a few seconds he had no idea where he was.

"Washburn! Wake up!"

As the last two days flooded back at him, he turned his head and cracked an eye. One of the refrigerators peered down at him.

"Time for the hearing already?" CJ asked.

The refrigerator dropped a pile of clothes on him. "Hearing's been cancelled. Put your clothes back on. You're getting out of here."

CJ swung his feet to the floor. "Out? Am I wearing an ankle monitor?"

"Above my pay grade. You've got five minutes to pretty yourself up." With that the officer left, leaving the cell door open.

It was just 6:30 when CJ finished signing for his personal effects, thoroughly confused by the sudden turn in affairs. When he turned around Agent Crane was approaching him.

"What the hell's going on? Did you catch the guy?" CJ demanded.

"Follow me," Crane said. "I'll answer your questions as soon as we are out of the building."

Crane led him through parts of the Westside Police Service Center in which CJ had never been. Actually, he'd never been in most of it as it had been built after he'd left the force. They stopped outside a room where Crane told CJ to wait and then went in. When the agent came out he handed CJ a jacket, ball cap and sunglasses. "Put these on."

CJ raised his eyebrows at the huge FBI letters on the back of the jacket and on the front of the ball cap. "I'm going out incognito so the press doesn't see me?"

"You're a quick study, Washburn."

"It's probably a hundred degrees out there already. This may draw some attention."

"It's all we had on short notice. We really don't expect any problems at 6:30 in the morning, but thought it'd still be better than nothing. You won't be in it very long; no more than a couple of minutes, and it's only about eighty degrees."

"Do I get a badge, too?" CJ said, pushing his arms into the jacket.

Crane ignored the question as he opened the door. He looked about and then they stepped out into the morning sunshine.

The gate at the entrance of the official parking lot swung open and they exited out onto Flowing Wells Road. Crane pointed the vehicle north.

"The down and dirty," the agent said, "is that Judge Delgado couldn't sleep with your high-profile case looming over her, so at oh five-hundred this morning she called a meeting with Stratton, Bunko, your attorney and myself. She wanted to see the evidence and get the FBI take on it before the hearing. She wanted no surprises. When Stratton informed her that he'd intended to put you out with an ankle monitor she said, 'Screw that.' Basically, she didn't want the press and any other hotheaded interested parties storming her courtroom when she ordered your release. She was being proactive."

"I don't get it," CJ said. "With the evidence you've gathered, I'd hold me as well."

"First of all the evidence was so obviously planted, a boy scout… hell, a cub scout could have figured it out. The night Maria Rodston was killed in Idaho, we know for a fact you were in New Mexico."

"Oh."

"We don't know where exactly, but we tracked you from when you were picked up on a county road east of Moscow to a stop for gas in Utah, then to a small airfield outside Albuquerque."

Crane stopped at a light and looked at CJ. "Would you care to fill in the blanks, tell us who your Good Samaritan was?"

CJ just smiled at him.

"We'll figure it out, though you'd be saving us some FBI time on the taxpayer's back."

"You certainly have a way of making us regular folk feel guilty. I'll pass, let you do the work, if you think you can."

"We understand that Stella has relations, sister's family actually, who live in the Albuquerque area. When I was in grade school I learned how to add two and two. Most of us FBI types had the same training."

"Shouldn't you be using that training to zero in on the individual on a killing spree?"

"We are, Mister Washburn. It's just that the Albuquerque field office hasn't much to do right now. Federal crime is a little slow at the moment in northern New Mexico so finding your Good Samaritan is a little something to keep them busy."

CJ looked out at the passing scenery for a time, trying to read between the agent's words. "Where're we going?"

"A short meet-up where you're being turned over to your team."

"My team?"

"Don't you remember your conversation with Agent Stratton last night?"

"Yeah, right."

"He passed the idea on to Judge Delgado. She liked it so much that she's made it a court order. Your team consists of Stella Summers, Dave McDermott and Officer Lisa Bowers. You are always to have someone with you, no exceptions. There's a press release going out in about an hour stating that you're in around-the-clock protective custody, that the perp has been targeting you for these murders. We believe he won't go after anyone just for the sake of framing you once he knows we know, and as long as you're in protective custody."

"How long is this going to last," CJ asked.

"Until he's caught."

"What if he's never caught?"

"Hopefully we'll never come to that bridge. With the mistakes he's made trying to frame you, we're very confident we'll get him."

They'd turned east onto Wetmore Road and CJ considered what Crane had said about the Albuquerque office. "So what exactly are you wanting from me?" he asked.

Crane glanced over at him. "You mean in lieu of doing further investigation into your New Mexico connection?"

CJ grunted.

"Full cooperation. Stay out of the case, out of the investigation unless we ask you a question. Keep your head low and stay with your team. Do everything they tell you to do. That's not coming only from us. It's also a directive from Judge Delgado."

Crane swung the black SUV into the left turn lane, waited for traffic to clear and then accelerated across the westbound lanes into the Tucson Mall entrance, turning left onto The Loop. A few seconds later he broke off into the nearly empty JCPenny's parking lot. CJ immediately spotted Dan Payne's silver Tahoe, Dan leaning against the hood in jeans and a University of Arizona Wildcats T-shirt. It told CJ two things: First, Dan wasn't dressed for work on this Monday morning; second he wasn't carrying an off duty piece, unless it was in the truck. They pulled alongside, passenger door to passenger door.

"Oh, yeah," Crane said. "I forgot to mention your team leader."

CJ climbed out and grabbed Dan's outstretched hand.

"Damned good to see you, CJ," Dan said. "Had mixed thoughts about you turning yourself in. Looks like it may work itself out."

"Certainly hope so," CJ replied. "You taking a day off or are you looking for a job?"

"Suspended. You didn't know?"

"Nobody tells me anything, though I suspected."

"I'll tell you all about it on the way to the house." He turned to shake Crane's hand as the agent came around the SUV.

"Get him out of here," Crane said. "We don't want to see him again until this thing is over."

"That's the plan," Dan said. He slapped CJ on the shoulder and started walking to the driver's side of his Tahoe. "Get in. We've got people to see."

CJ shed the FBI jacket and hat, threw them in Crane's vehicle and climbed in with Dan. He kept the sunglasses.

Dan took Oracle south until it turned into Main and then intersected with Speedway, where he turned west in order to pick up I-10 East. During the entire time he was explaining to CJ how he'd managed to get out of the desert after their little meeting. "When I hit a split in the dirt road," he said, "I threw the bug one way and went the other. I was really glad I'd installed the master switch for my brake lights when I bought the truck. Between that, the head start I had and then throwing the bug, they had no idea where I went. By the time the helicopter flew over where they thought I'd gone I was parked under a carport in Branding Iron Park, the owners of which, fortunately, weren't home. I remained there until morning commuter traffic started up and then melded in."

"But you're on suspension," CJ said.

"Did I say that? You shouldn't believe everything you hear. Sure the Feds were waiting for me when I showed up at work. They couldn't prove anything but they could certainly add up the numbers. I'm actually on a forced paid leave of absence until all the dust settles. Chief Rague is just covering his ass. I'll be back to work before you know it.'

"So you're leading up this team that's babysitting me?"

"That's the way it's rigged up. A couple of washed up detectives, a green cop and a PI secretary slash squeeze." He looked over at CJ and grinned.

"I actually feel rather honored," CJ said. He watched as Dan took the off-ramp onto I-19. "Where're we going?"

"It seems that after McDermott retired he invested in a property in Sahuarita, thinking to take advantage of the housing slump. He set it up as a rental figuring that he and his wife might move into it one day. It's in that new master plan community, Rancho Sahuarita, the one with the lake, and it just happens to be between renters. For the duration it'll be your safe house. With three bedrooms you and Stella will live there and the rest of us will rotate in and out on shifts. No one else knows the location except the two FBI agents."

"How about Ralph Bunko?"

"Nope, and he doesn't much like it. Doesn't break my heart one iota."

After Dan exited I-19 onto Sahuarita Road, he spent the next ten minutes seeming to meander through a complex housing development, a mixture of one and two-story family dwellings, some inside gated communities. CJ tried to memorize the turns and then gave up. Dan finally pulled into a driveway to park behind Dave McDermott's truck. A car, which CJ didn't recognize, was sitting on the street. A second car, Stella's, was parked next to Dave's truck and sent a rush of relief washing over him. He was quickly out of the truck and on a lighter step. Dan said Stella would be here but CJ wasn't going to believe it until he saw her.

Dan pulled the front door open and CJ stepped in, fully expecting to find Stella running into his arms. What he got instead he hadn't even had the thought to guess.

"Daddy!"

Before CJ could even breathe Trish was in his arms. And then there was Stella and for the first time in a long time everything was right with the world.

Chapter 38

All six chairs around the dining room table were occupied. CJ sat next to Stella and directly across from Trish. Next to Trish sat Lisa Bowers. Presiding at the two ends of the table were Dan and Dave. They all sat back with mugs of hot coffee, remnants of eggs, bacon and pancakes littering their plates.

"So, what's the plan?" CJ asked after taking a sip from his mug.

"Lay low until this guy is caught," Dan said. "Let the FBI work the numbers."

"Does anyone here think that's really possible?" CJ asked. "Are two ex-detectives, an almost ex-detective and a Tucson police officer going to be able to patiently lay low?"

"We don't have much choice in it, CJ," Dave said. "The judge's order also said that we were not to get involved in the investigation."

"Really, Dave?" Dan said from the length of the table. "Did the order actually say that or did the judge simply imply it?"

"If we get involved and she gets wind of it, you know which way that split hair is going to fall. Your leave of absence could become a suspension or permanent, not to mention what it could do to my daughter's career."

"Probably no more than a slap on the wrist, Dad," Lisa said. "And my helping break this case can mean a commendation."

"Stick your gold star commendation on a glowing note from your lieutenant and your mother can paste it to the refrigerator where she used to paste mine," Dave said to her. "Your chain of command won't remember all the good stuff you've done. They'll focus only on the one screw up, even if it wasn't your screw up. You'll become a scapegoat like your old man."

"Things have changed since you left, Dad."

Dave lifted his eyebrows and smiled at his naive daughter. "We've had this conversation before."

She glared back at him.

CJ broke in, an attempt to break the father-daughter tension. "Agent Crane said that the perp has made a lot of mistakes. Is there anything I don't already know?"

"Not really. The fact that he followed you to Idaho was probably his biggest mistake."

CJ looked at Lisa. "Did anything come out of your meeting with Officer Kramer Friday night?"

Lisa shook her head. "Not yet. I should hear from her this morning. She expected to be able to get into the office sometime over the weekend. If not, then early this morning."

"Who's Officer Kramer? I don't know that name," Dan asked.

"Krystal Kramer," Lisa said. "She's strictly a desk rider, works in Personnel. I asked her to poke around a little, see if there were any officers who took unscheduled or emergency time off last week."

"She's a friend?"

"Very good friend."

"Whatever you find, share it only with this group. I'm still not sure of your dad's assessment of Judge Delgado's order; however, there's no point in taking chances. If there's anything you find out that might be viable, let me be the one to share it with Agent Stratton. Anything you do to help break this case, I promise you'll get credit when the time is right. I'm already in the shits so let me take the heat from the judge if there's any heat to be doled out."

Lisa nodded, but didn't look happy.

"Has the FBI developed a profile yet?" Stella asked.

"Yes and no," Dan said. "The basic profile is easy, a restating of average statistics. They're figuring he is a black or white male, 25 to 40..."

"Wait a minute." Stella held up her hand. "I thought most serial killers were white male."

"That was quite true last century. Since 2000 it's done an almost total reversal. In the nineties it was roughly 60% and 30%, white versus black. In the first ten years of this century it was more like 60% and 40%, this time black versus white. Hispanic, Asian, etcetera, almost negligible."

"So the FBI is thinking he's African American?" Lisa said.

"Not necessarily. I'm guessing they're simply keeping all the options open. I believe they lean toward white but can't overlook the statistics. I personally think he is white, if for no other reason than all his victims have been white."

"What else are they saying?" Dave said.

"He likely comes from a broken or very dysfunctional home, a victim of mental and/or physical abuse from one or both parents. He may be the oldest or only child with an average to above average IQ."

"Aren't all serial killers above average IQ?" Stella said.

"Another fallacy let loose on us via Hollywood. Script writers put in what draws the viewers, and the viewers don't want their serial killers to be average. In actuality the medium IQ of said killers is close to 100. People often bring up Ted Kaczynski as an example, who was in the 165 range, or Bundy in the 130s. They don't know or have forgotten about Watts at 75 or Pirela at 57. The IQs run the gambit. All that said, however, my belief is that this particular killer is, in fact, on the intelligent side. He has to be to pull off something like this. He's calculating and fast on his feet."

"His big mistake was going after me," CJ said. "If he'd left well enough alone we'd be looking anywhere but at someone in uniform."

"You mean the FBI would be looking," Stella said. "If he'd left well enough alone we would not be sitting here, hiding away like a bunch of frightened rabbits."

CJ put his hand on hers.

"Sorry," she said.

"It's okay."

Dan lifted his mug to his lips and found it empty. "I'm getting a refill. Anyone else?" No one followed him to the kitchen so he returned with the pot, poured where the desire was indicated and sat back down. "So, the way I see it he had more than just a motive of opportunity."

"What do you mean?" Trish asked.

"I don't believe this individual would have taken such a risk to only direct suspicions at someone else. Let's face it, we had no leads whatsoever. What would be the return for the risk?"

Trish looked at her dad and then back at Dan, shrugging her shoulders.

"I suspect that means you can't think of one. Well, I can't think of one either. Every action a killer makes has a motive and this guy's motive to target your father has to be personal, so personal that he's willing to take additional risks."

"Therefore, he knows me," CJ said, "thus, I know him."

"Either you know him, know of him, or have crossed his path in some way in the past. Whatever it is, he may feel he has a vendetta against you. It could be as simple as you writing him a traffic ticket back when you were a cop, or entering his home on a domestic disturbance call, or maybe his brother's home. Whatever it is he's carried that anger all these years and then you pop up on his kill. Not only would that further piss him off, but he would see it as an opportunity that he could not pass up. Because it was so spontaneous, he had no time to plan, to think it through, thus the mistakes. He may be good at not leaving evidence, but purposely leaving false evidence may have been beyond his experience."

"If he's a cop," CJ said, "then likely the scenario examples you just presented didn't happen. I don't recall ever having official dealings with another cop or his family in all the time I served on the force."

"You never pulled over a cop on his off duty time for anything?"

"Nope. I know others who had but I was never so privileged. I did pull over the mayor once but he talked his way out of it."

"Really?"

"I was green and he was real nice about it. What can I say?"

"Well, I'd given him a ticket just for being a politician," Dave said.

Everyone laughed and then the table went quiet. After a time Dave said, "What about after you went into the private sector, CJ. Ever piss someone off in your PI duties?"

"There are a few husbands, but the only one who comes to mind who's a cop is Ralph Bunko. What do you think?"

Dave grinned. "Boy, would that be a gas." He then shook his head and became serious. "We're looking for an intelligent cop. Bunko would be the first one I'd cross off the list."

The table went quiet again. After a time CJ looked at Lisa and said, "Maybe you ought to call Officer Kramer. That's the biggest thing we need to know right now. Who took time off?"

Lisa shook her head. "I'd rather not call her at work when I've no idea who she might be with. Don't want to get her in trouble. She promised she'd call as soon as she found something. If she found nothing she'd call no later than this morning." She looked at her watch. "It's just after nine now. If she doesn't call before ten, I'll call her, how's that?"

"Fair enough." CJ looked around the table. "So, what do we do if she turns up anyone worth taking a closer look at?"

"Pass the names over to Stratton and his goons," Dan said. "Tell him we have reason to believe they took sudden time off during the Idaho mess. Let them investigate for more details, such as use of a credit card to make an airline reservation. That's the kind of thing they're good at."

"What if Stratton wants to know how we got the names?" Lisa asked.

"I'll give him the friend of a friend dance," Dan said. "Like I said, Lisa, let me take the heat."

Stella stood. "Well, I can't just sit here." She started stacking plates. Trish joined her and then before long everyone was crowded into the little kitchen.

"Men! Out!"

As the three men backed out of the kitchen a cell phone went off. Like Larry, Moe and Curley, they stuck their heads back in. It was

Lisa's phone but upon looking at it she shook her head at them and said, "Husband."

They went into the living room and sat down.

"What are you guys going to do?" CJ said.

"What do you mean?" Dan asked.

"Shifts. Do you have a schedule as to who's with me when?"

"To be truthful, with Stella and your daughter we might be overmanned. The two of them have flat out stated that they have no intentions of leaving your side. We may be able to release Lisa after she receives the call. Let's face it; she has a regular job to report to. The rest of us don't."

"I don't think she's going to like that," Dave said. "She's fully engaged with this now. Told me she was ready to take personal time."

"She wants to be in on the collar," Dan said.

"Wouldn't you if you were a rookie?"

"Damn right! But I'd think she'd be closer to being part of that if she was on regular duty rather than being stuck down here in friendly family neighborhood la-la land."

"You don't like this neighborhood?"

"It's nice, sure, but I've gotten lost both times I came here. Wouldn't want to live where I'd have to light off my GPS in order to find my way home."

"There's a club house, fitness center, water park, lake stocked with fish, miles of hiking and biking trails."

"You sound like a damn realtor. You getting a commission?"

There came the distant tone of Lisa's cell phone again and they went silent, heads turned toward the kitchen entryway. After a few seconds Lisa appeared, heading for the dining table, one hand pressing the phone to her ear, the other digging for her notebook and pen.

She sat and opened the notebook. "Okay, go ahead… Greg Wilston. Right." She wrote for a time, adding a line of bulleted points. "Okay, next… Santo Montez." Again she wrote then said, "Okay... Tommy Clark."

CJ rose from his seat and walked over to her.

"Days they took off?" she said into the phone. "Okay. Anything else?"

CJ said into her ear, "Ages."

Lisa held up her hand, nearly poking CJ in the eye with her pen. "Yeah. I'll keep you updated. Let me know if you hear anything else. Thanks."

When she put the phone down she looked up at CJ. "Don't worry. I've got it covered. I'm not the rookie you guys seem to think I am."

"My daughter's never been a rookie," Dave said as he and Dan each took a chair at the table. To Lisa he said, "So, what have you got?"

She looked up a CJ again. "As soon as you are all seated I'll tell you."

Like an obedient puppy, CJ sat.

Stella and Trish appeared and took the remaining chairs.

"First of all, Krystal says that the FBI has already been going through everything, but she has no idea what they've found. They're being very closed mouthed. She came up with three names on her own, however. Greg Wilston, Santo Montez and Tommy Clark, ages 28, 39 and 26 respectively."

"I know Montez and Clark," Dan said. "Can't say I know the name Wilston."

"Do you know them well?" CJ said. "I don't know any of them."

"Fairly well on Montez, not so much on Clark. It's more like I know of Clark because I've seen him around. I think he's friends with Bunko. Other than that, I know nothing about him. Montez is solid: Family man, teenage daughter and son, twins I believe."

"That and he's Hispanic knocks him out of the profile," CJ said then turned to Lisa. "Why did Krystal flag him?"

"He took emergency time off at the same time you were in Idaho. His wife's mother had a serious car accident in El Paso, didn't think she was going to live."

"Definitely out. That leaves Clark and Wilston. What did she give you on them?"

"Wilston is married, but in the middle of a divorce. No children. Wife moved to Phoenix."

"Could be the trigger that set him off to start this killing spree to begin with," Dan said.

Lisa continued. "He took sudden time off Wednesday through the end of the week to go up to Phoenix to try and save their marriage. He doesn't want the divorce. Works the day shift."

"Doesn't fit, if you ask me," CJ said. "Next."

"Tommy Clark. He's the only one I actually know. He and I started as rookies a couple of months apart. Worked a few scenes together. A bit intense if you ask me. He's not married. Took time off Wednesday, August 1st, due to sickness, said he'd gotten food poisoning. He works days. His regular days off are Thursday and Friday. He reported to work as usual on Saturday."

"Did he see a doctor?" CJ asked.

"Krystal said there was no indication in his file that he visited a doctor or an urgent care."

CJ sat back. "Food poisoning is an easy excuse when someone wants time off for some other reason. He'd have been able to fly to Idaho on Wednesday, kill Maria Rodston, then fly back on Thursday. When he found out I was back in Tucson he'd have had plenty of time to kill the last victim Thursday night or Friday morning. Since he works days he easily qualifies for all the other murders."

"And he's friends with Ralph Bunko," Dave said. "I already like him for this."

Dan held up his hand. "Let's not go racing down the Tommy Clark track just yet. All the right timing in the world doesn't tie him to any murder scene, and knowing Bunko means nothing. Bunko's not a bad detective, he just made a mistake and his damned pride got the best of him."

"At my expense," Dave inserted. "Maybe he's not a bad detective, but he's not a good one either."

"In any case," Dan continued, "it doesn't mean that everyone he's associated with is in his league. Officer Clark might be one fine cop."

"How do we take a closer look at him?" CJ said.

"Like I said, we pass him to the FBI."

"From the sound of it they likely already have his name, are probably doing a check of his credit cards to find out if he's spent anything on travel to Idaho. If he's smart, though, he'd have used cash."

"He'd still have had to give his name and present a driver's license," Dave said. "There'd be a trail."

"Exactly," Dan said. "It's a fairly easy check when you have access to all the airlines' databases."

CJ nodded. "Okay. Let's do it then. Check with Stratton and see if they're already investigating these guys, especially Tommy Clark."

"I'm still really liking Clark, too," Dave said. "Any way we can put a tail on him, attach a GPS to his vehicle maybe?"

"We can't do anything," Dan reminded him. "If they need to watch him closer, the FBI has sophisticated surveillance techniques. We have to trust them."

"Have you been drinking, Dan?" CJ said. "Since when have you started saying trust and FBI in the same sentence?"

"Since they came to their senses about you. Stratton and Crane both seem to be a cut above the rest."

"Well, damn. My best friend has gone over to the dark side. Next thing you know he's going to become one of them. Probably already has a job offer, a half a dozen bureau approved dark suits hanging in his closet."

"You're very funny, CJ. I'm just recognizing where the strengths of our assets are."

"Or is it without them you'd still be sitting in the nosebleed section, suspended until the cows come home."

Trish laughed. "Nice mix of metaphors, Dad."

"Just saying it the way I see it." He looked at Dan. "Make the call to Stratton. Let's get this ball rolling, or at least give it a little push."

Chapter 39

"Have you checked in with your mother?" CJ and Trish sat alone in the living room. Stella was taking a nap and Dave was in the dining room poring through a newspaper. Dan had gone off to meet with Stratton and Crane while Lisa took off for parts unknown. It was just shy of 11:00 a.m.

"Not yet," Trish said.

"She's going to be worried about you."

"All this crap going on and I haven't heard from her once; not even a voice mail or text. That doesn't sound like worry to me."

"I thought the two of you talked all the time."

She shook her head. "She calls me once a month. As a matter of fact I can set my watch by it. On the 25th of every month at 6:38 a.m. I can pick up my phone and wait for it to ring."

CJ just looked at her with his "I don't get it," face.

"6:38 is the time I was born, Dad. January 25th."

"Oh."

"I can see her calling me at that time on my birthday, but why every month?"

"I've no idea."

"When she first started doing it I thought it was cute, but now, after two years, it's rather old, a bit immature if you ask me."

"She does love you."

"I know that, Dad. But why couldn't I have a normal mother?"

"Or a normal dad," CJ added.

"You are normal, except for the cop part."

"I'm not a cop."

"You know what I mean. Once a cop always a cop."

CJ laughed.

"And I'm staying in this house surrounded by cops. What a nightmare."

"Stella's not a cop."

"She appears to be turning into one being a cop's secretary and girlfriend."

"Oh."

"I really like her by the way," she said.

"Me too."

"You planning on marrying her?"

CJ smiled, surprised by the question. "That's not outside the realm of possibility."

"If you do I want to be there. A regular wedding, no justice of the peace thing. She's never had a wedding, right? Never been married?"

"No."

"Then it has to be a real wedding with the dress, bridesmaids, the works."

CJ thought about his proposal to run off to Las Vegas and realized he'd have to rethink that entire scenario. Why couldn't it just be simple? Why couldn't anything with a woman be simple?

"Okay," he said. "I'll keep your advice in mind."

She took his arm and propped her head on his shoulder. "Good. It'd be weird, though, having a step-mother."

"You have a step-dad."

"That started out weird, but now he's just Mom's husband. And his children..." She made like sticking a finger down her throat. "I'm not claiming any relation to them, no way, shape or form."

"I understand," he said, nodding his head.

"Do you think Josh would come?" she said after a long silence.

"To what?"

"The wedding."

"Oh. I've no idea where your brother is," CJ said.

"I do."

There was a stretch of dead space while CJ digested the meaning of those two words. Trish must have sensed the sudden tension in his body. She straightened up, but held onto his hand.

"I'm sorry. I shouldn't have told you that."

"Why not?"

"Josh asked me not to tell you where he was, both you and Mom."

"Oh."

"I've always known where he was."

"You have?" CJ didn't know whether to be angry or pleased. As he thought about it, he realized he shouldn't be surprised. The two of them were always close. "Is he okay?"

She nodded. "Yes. He's fine."

"When did you last talk to him?"

She thought about that for a few seconds. "In May, I think. Right at the end of the semester. He likes to check up on me to make sure his little sister is staying out of trouble."

CJ considered whether or not he wanted to know the answer to his next question before finally coming out and asking it. "Is he still angry?"

"Of course he's still angry, Dad." She let loose of his hand and her voice went up an octave. "Hell, I'm still angry. You and Mom getting divorced wasn't part of the big plan. We were a happy family and then we weren't. It was like you guys flipped a switch without consulting us first. It came completely out of the blue. Sure, Mom was a bit weird but as long as she was our mom that was okay. Now she's not only more weird, or weirder, if that's a word, but she's also someone else's mom, and we have step-siblings who demand her immediate attention more than we ever did. And you started becoming weird, too, with quitting the police force and trying to start your own private eye business. You got obsessed with that and then the divorce happened and your children fell by the wayside. I sort of adapted, but Josh did not. That's why he took off. He couldn't deal with it anymore."

"So, where is he now? Does he have a good job? Is he married? What?"

"Technically, as long as I don't tell you where he is, I haven't broken the promise. He has a very good job and no, he's not married. He does have a girlfriend but I've never had the impression it was very serious."

"What kind of job?"

"All I'll say is, you'll approve, despite what…"

"What?"

"Never mind. I think you'll approve."

"Despite what? Is there something he's doing I might not like?"

"Forget it Dad. I've said more than I should have and none of your police interrogation techniques are going to get anything more out of me."

"Even prying out your fingernails one by one?"

She held out both hands so all the nails showed. "They're in rather bad shape, so there'd be no loss."

He laughed and hugged her. She got up to go to the bathroom and he sat back thinking about all that he had just learned. As he thought, his gaze fell onto her cell phone on the coffee table. He looked up to where she'd disappeared and then snapped up the phone and searched for her address book. He scrolled to "W" but found no Washburn. He scrolled up to "J" and there it was, Josh, simple as that. He touched the name and the phone number displayed with a 303 area code. He turned his face away to avoid seeing the entire number long enough to memorized it, immediately feeling guilty for snooping. He cleared the phone to the home screen and put it back on the table. What would he do with Josh's phone number, anyway?

He went in to lie down next to Stella. She didn't even stir.

He stared at the ceiling thinking about the 303 area code; wondered what city it served.

Chapter 40

Stella awoke just before 1:30 p.m. announcing she wanted to run to her apartment for clothes. CJ put down the newspaper under which he was attempting to fall asleep. When he'd tried sleeping next to Stella, all he could do was think. Wasn't much better with the newspaper. The previous three days and accompanying lousy nights were playing havoc on his body. He desperately needed to be doing something and running out with Stella sounded real good.

"I could use some fresh clothes, too," he said. "We could go by my place at the same time."

"You're in a safe house for a reason," Dave said. "To be safe. This guy could be just waiting for you to pop up."

"If he's after anybody, it's Trish. You stay here with her. Stella and I will go."

Trish turned off the TV soap that nobody was watching and dropped the remote on the coffee table. "You're not going anywhere without me, Dad."

"Judge's orders state that you're to stay put," Dave reminded CJ.

"These are the same clothes I was wearing Friday at your house, Dave. You should be begging me to find something clean."

"There's a washer and a dryer," Dave said. "You can wash them."

"You've got clothes at my place," Stella said. "I can grab everything that's yours."

"We don't want you going out alone, Stella," Dave said.

CJ had to agree with that.

"Then you go with me," she said to Dave. "Trish can stay here. What time did Dan say he'd be back?"

"He didn't."

"I only need one person with me," CJ said.

"And that would be me," Trish reiterated.

CJ opened his palm in agreement. "All I need is a witness that I don't go out and dump a body in a dumpster. It's not like the perp's going to come after me. His purpose has been foiled. I'm beginning to not see the point in all this."

"The point is public perception for one," Dave said, "and letting the perp know that you always have an escort in case he's too stupid to realize his framing plan has been foiled. We don't want him killing someone else in your name."

"I think we've already determined that this guy isn't stupid," CJ said. "I'd be willing to bet he knew what was going on before the press release."

"The bottom line is he has to be caught before he kills someone else, whether to frame you or otherwise. Prior to you climbing into the dumpster to check the pulse on his third victim, his kills were a month apart. When he got the grand idea to set you up, he killed three in under a week. As long as he knows you can no longer be framed, he'll likely return to his previous schedule, giving us at least three weeks, if I'm figuring it right."

"What were the dates?" Stella asked.

"Yeah, I'd like to know that, too," Trish said.

Dave stood, snatched the mess of newspaper under which CJ had been trying to snooze, and sat back down. "This morning's paper summarized it all." He sorted and restacked the pages until he found what he was looking for, scanned the article for a few seconds and then read the names out loud. "Brenda Radcliff, May 26; Mandi Frond, June 30; Rebecca Cling, July 28."

"Right at the end of each month," CJ said. "There must be something significant about that."

"What it means is that we've got until August 25th, less than three weeks," Trish said, staring at the calendar on her phone.

"On what days of the week do they fall?" CJ asked her.

"They were all on Saturdays."

"The last Saturday of every month. Our prime suspect, Tommy Clark, is off Thursdays and Fridays. Not very telling, but certainly possible. He spends those two days picking out and watching his victims. He kills her Friday night, dumps her body two or three in the morning, then goes home to put on his uniform and get ready for work. Maybe he likes to be part of the police force working the case that same morning, his way of returning to the scene."

"Great theories, but not enough for an arrest or a warrant. Not even enough to bring him in for questioning."

"I know," CJ said. "We need a smoking gun with his fingerprints on it."

"I thought they were all strangled," Trish said.

Stella rolled her eyes. "Another of your dad's metaphors. Yes, they were all strangled."

Trish went silent as though embarrassed by her confusion. And then she started crying, pulling a tissue from her jeans pocket.

Stella slid over next to her and put an arm around her shoulder. "What's the matter?"

"I was just thinking—" She sniffled and blew her nose. "I got this picture in my head of Maria Rodston—" She closed her eyes and took a deep breath. "—being strangled. She was only a year older than me, and my friend. Her poor baby; such a sweet little boy." She looked up at her dad, blinked back more tears. "There was a memorial for her this morning. I should have been there."

There was nothing CJ could say to her. To Dave he said, "So, all we still know is that Clark could have done it."

"And so could have half the cops in Tucson," Dave added, "as well as half the sheriff deputies in the county. Then there's highway patrol and border patrol not to mention surrounding small community police departments. There's also any civilian geek out there who knows how to hack into police servers and listen to radio traffic. What I'm trying to say is let's not hang Clark just because he's convenient and sort of fits the profile."

"You were the one who liked him for the killings when Lisa first came up with the names this morning."

"Yeah, and I got to thinking how I was hung by the media, the public and fellow blues based on testimony that contained nothing but fiction."

"What we've pulled up on Clark so far has been all fact."

"And all purely coincidental. Yes, I liked him for it, but for all the wrong reasons, primary of which was that he is friends with Ralph Bunko. I should be ashamed of myself. To avoid reusing your metaphor, what we need is the strangulation device with the killer's DNA on it."

"That's something I've never heard in the news," Stella said. "What did he use to kill the women?"

"At this point all the media has said is that they were strangled. I haven't heard whether the weapon was left behind at the dump sites, or if the perp took it with him. I'm not even sure if the police investigators, that is Dan or now Bunko, or the FBI, have determined what was used. We'll pose that question to Dan when he returns."

"Speaking of Dan returning, when might that be?" CJ asked.

"No idea. Tried calling him about a half hour ago, went to voicemail."

CJ drummed his fingers on the table for a time and then said, "Why don't you go ahead and take Stella for some clothes; give Trish and me some father-daughter time."

Dave considered it for some time before finally agreeing. "My gut doesn't like it, but my head can't come up with a reason why. You're probably right that he knows he's been foiled and has likely taken you off his radar; however, I want to remain in constant communications. I'll call when we get to Stella's and then again right after we leave. We might stop for groceries on the way back as there isn't much here for dinner."

"Get some fish," CJ said.

"Fish. You mean like fish sticks, what?"

"Chipotle," Stella said. "I know what he wants." She looked at Trish. "How about you, anything special?"

Trish shrugged. "Fish is okay, I guess. Wouldn't mind some peanut butter, strawberry jam and bread. How about some beer?"

Trish caught CJ looking at her. "I'm old enough, Dad, so don't give me that look."

He laughed. "I just never envisioned drinking beer with my daughter while eating peanut butter and jelly sandwiches."

"There are probably a lot of things about me you might not have envisioned."

CJ opened his mouth and then looked up at Stella.

"Don't look at me. I could probably use a sandwich and beer myself, and whatever."

CJ blushed and the women slapped hands like they were on some kind of team together. Inside, though, he was pleased to see that they were bonding, even if at his expense.

Chapter 41

After Dave and Stella left, CJ laid down in an attempt to return to his earlier failed nap while Trish returned to the afternoon soaps. After a time he gave up because his mind wouldn't shut off. The drone of the television in the next room didn't help either.

He plopped down on the sofa next to Trish.

"How about we go out for a walk?" he said. "I don't think that lake is very far away and this is our father-daughter time."

"I'd like to, but you aren't supposed to leave the house."

"I don't believe going out in the neighborhood really counts. It's mainly staying away from places around Tucson where I might be spotted. If the perp is looking for me, it'll be around my apartment, or my office, or where I shop for groceries. He's not going to be near here because he doesn't know where here is. As a matter of fact there's nobody on the streets. This is very non-public for being a residential area."

She looked at him, considering his words.

"I can't sleep and just sitting around waiting is driving me crazy," he added.

"You do know it's 2:20 in the afternoon and close to 110 degrees out there, don't you, Dad? That's why there's nobody out. They're smart and staying inside."

"It's only about a tenth of a mile to the lake and then it's a small lake. Can't be all that bad."

She turned off the TV and stood. "Fine. We need to talk anyway."

They had a map of the neighborhood, which Dave had left on the kitchen counter. They peered at it and found a paved trail that meandered along behind rows of homes and that would take them to the lake. They stepped out, immediately spotting the trail entrance from the front door. CJ looked up and down the street, more as an automatic procedure than to actually look for something or someone suspicious. The streets were deserted, no more than a half dozen vehicles within sight. If he hadn't been so exhausted he likely would have considered each of them before moving on and then, upon analyzing one, would have had second thoughts, would have pulled them both back inside, locked the doors, made phone calls. Instead, his brain registered the absolute lack of people, exactly as he'd expected, and concluded that all was well.

They set out.

It was more like a quarter mile to the lake and by the time they got there CJ realized it was, in fact, too hot, but he was enjoying his time with Trish. What she wanted to talk about was her boyfriend, or ex-boyfriend, the one who bailed when the press got wind that her father was suspected of being a serial killer.

"We were actually talking about doing something more permanent," she said.

"Like marriage?" CJ said, trying to keep the shock out of his voice.

"No, Dad. Not that permanent. We were considering living together, though we had discussed maybe doing the big M once we graduated."

"Ah. The big M."

"But now—"

"But now he's a scumbag, not the person you thought he was. He abandoned you."

"I like the word scumbag," she said. "I like scumbag a lot."

"Do you still care about him?"

"Oh hell no, Dad. The scumbag abandoned me. That boat has sailed, as they say. No second chances with me."

He gave her a one-arm hug. "Good for you."

"What I want to know is, how do you know when you've found the right one? I don't want to make this mistake again."

CJ nodded his head and stepped aside for a big kid on a small bicycle, a towel around his neck. "That's a damn good question."

"How did you and Mom know?"

"We're divorced now; maybe we didn't know and thought we did."

"Oh! I never thought of that." She contemplated it for a few seconds and then said, "Did you think you loved each other and then found out later, after raising two kids, that you actually didn't?"

They walked on for a half minute before CJ answered the question. "As I think about it I have to say that we did know it was right. We loved each other; still do as far as that goes, but now it's in a different way. How can I not love the mother of my children? We simply lost compatibility after a dozen years, though we did try to hold on for a while after that, tried to work on it."

"But how did you know at first? I know you lived together for a while. How long?"

"About eight months."

"Were you engaged before or after you started living together?"

"After." CJ had to think a minute to remember more precisely. "We were six months into it before I popped the question."

"So you had six months to determine whether you were suited for each other."

"Exactly."

"We didn't even get to that point before...."

"Before his scumbag colors showed."

"Exactly."

"When you started talking about moving in together," CJ said, "did you have any doubts?"

"Yeah. Loads of doubts."

"There's the difference. If he was the right one, you'd have had no doubts."

"Oh." They stopped and looked at the water park next to the clubhouse, kids splashing and laughing and then continued on. "Did you and Mom have doubts?"

"I had no doubts, and I'm fairly certain your mom would say the same thing."

"Do you have doubts about Stella?"

CJ smiled. "None."

"Good. She said the same thing about you. She also told me you asked her to run away to Las Vegas with you. Do I need to talk to you again about a proper wedding, Dad?"

CJ chuckled. "No, dear daughter. I got it the first time. I'm taking your advice to heart." As they continued their walk, making the turn around the south end of the lake before heading back, CJ began to wonder about the true purpose of Trish needing to talk. Was it about her and her recent failed relationship or about him and Stella? Did she start this entire conversation about her looking for the right guy just to let him know that Stella had no doubts and was ready? He was suddenly filled with pride at realizing the woman his daughter was becoming.

When they completed the loop around the lake, CJ was ready to jump in just to cool down and there was still a quarter mile to go. He chided himself for not taking water. Trish didn't seem to be bothered by the heat, striding along as though it was a mild spring morning. They turned away from the lake and followed a short street for about fifty yards to the entrance to the trail that'd take them back to the house. They followed that for four or five minutes; CJ was more and more starting to fade from the heat and wished, again, that he'd brought water. As they rounded the last bend where they would step onto the street upon which David's rental house waited within view some hundred yards away, CJ's head was down, his gaze focused in front of his feet, his worry upon whether he'd make this last stretch before passing out from heat stroke. He was starting to seriously regret having made this suggestion to go for a walk. They could have talked in the cool of the living room.

It was in those last few yards of the trail where he sensed something in his peripheral. He didn't register a concern, however, or enough energy to turn his head for a closer look. Instead he kept his head down until suddenly there was a vehicle in the way and Trish was pulling him to a stop. He brought his eyes up to discover a black van with dark shaded windows, the side door open six or seven inches. For a couple of seconds something about this van was bothersome.

"Are you okay, Daddy?" Trish said as she tried guiding him around the obstacle.

It was then that it came to him, cutting through the broiling fog clogging his brain. This was the van he'd seen the night he climbed into the dumpster, the same one he'd noticed amongst the half dozen vehicles when they stepped out to begin the walk. There came an adrenaline rush and he turned to reach for Trish when the dark form that seconds before had shown in his peripheral, loomed larger.

"Daddy!"

"Run!" CJ screamed and then suddenly the entire world ignited; every muscle seemed to spasm, then go limp and he found himself being shoved forward into the van, unable to control his decent to the carpeted floor, landing half on his back with one arm underneath him. In police training he'd been hit with stun guns several dozen times, but for some reason this was different. He should have had muscle control almost immediately, but it seemed like he was stuck in mud, his mouth dry and his head spinning. Suddenly Trish was lying next to him and the guy was sitting on top of her. CJ got his hands underneath him and started to push up to drive the guy off of her when the stun gun hit him again. Anger and fear surged through CJ as he jerked up to his knees and then was knocked back down with a third jolt. As he struggled to rise once more he heard the gun go off another time and understood immediately that it was Trish taking the shock. For an unimaginable period of time this cycle continued until finally the guy stepped out and the van door closed. A few seconds later the vehicle was moving.

Chapter 42

CJ turned his head and saw the frightened look on Trish's face. They were on their stomachs, hands handcuffed behind their backs, duct tape across their mouths, several wraps around their ankles. He'd lost count of the number of times he'd been hit, the number of jolts sent through his body, and hoped Trish had not gotten so many. He closed his eyes and wished that he'd not insisted on going for the walk. But would it have made any difference? This guy knew where they were and was determined.

After a few minutes, when CJ sensed that they'd gotten onto the interstate, he rolled away from Trish and maneuvered enough to be able to see between the front seats. For the most part, however, all that came into view was the blue sky. He couldn't tell if they were moving north or south. A road sign whipped by, but from his angle all he caught of it was the corner.

Another whipped by a few seconds later with the same result. As he started to struggle to get into a better position, he glanced back at Trish and was shocked to find her sitting on her butt, her handcuffed hands in front of her, peeling back the duct tape around her ankles. By the time he got over to her, her legs were free and she was peeling the tape from her mouth.

He shook his head at her. She pulled the tape from his mouth.

"Lay down," he whispered.

She did so and he moved up close to her and looked back over his shoulder. He couldn't see the guy's eyes in the rearview mirror which meant he didn't have it adjusted to see them.

Close to her ear he said, "Are you okay?"

She nodded though appeared ready to burst into tears, on the edge of hysteria.

He whispered, "If he should move his rearview mirror we've got to look like we're still as he left us."

She nodded.

"There's no way I can do what you did without dislocating something. Once he's off the interstate he's going to have to stop at a light or stop sign. When he does you hit that door and run like hell."

She shook her head and stuck her lips up to his ear. "I'll get your tape off. We'll both run."

"You'd be faster without me. I can distract him, jump into his lap if I have to. If there's traffic around you yell, 'call 911.' Attract as many witnesses as you can. If you can get a license plate number, more the better."

She continued shaking her head, her tears breaking free. "You go with me."

He looked at her for a long time, his little girl, considering the chances of success. If he was able to keep the guy occupied she most certainly could get away. If they both tried to escape, chances were he'd manage to recapture at least one of them and the odds were it'd be Trish. That wasn't a chance CJ was willing to take. But if his legs were free he certainly could be more affective at keeping the guy occupied while she escaped.

"Okay," he said. "But I don't know if you can get my tape off without him noticing."

She glanced down at his ankles and then back up at him. She didn't have the where-with-all to come up with a suggestion.

"I'll roll away from you and bend my legs. If he looks, he shouldn't be able to see us doing anything."

He waited a long time for her nod then rolled away and bent his legs until his heels touched his butt. While she worked on the tape he watched the rearview mirror. Not once did it appear that the guy had any thought about paying mind to his captive passengers. It was likely that his attention was completely on traffic, maybe too over-confident that he'd left them well secured. However, once he *did* stop for a light, his focus very well could shift to what was taking place in the cargo area. CJ began running all the possible scenarios through his mind. What if the guy became aware of what they were doing and was able to get to the door before Trish could get it open? He'd most likely have the stun gun, or worse yet, a real gun. What would he possibly do with witnesses on the street?

The guy's insane. He'd likely do anything.

A road sign flashed by and he caught only the first few letters, "Vale..." That had to be Valencia, so they were heading north. In a few minutes, unless the guy took that exit or one of the following two, they'd be merging onto I-10. Would he go east or west? CJ pulled his thoughts back to the possible scenarios.

Instead of coming around to the door, the guy could come back between the seats and zap them both back into submission. No witnesses; just pissed off drivers who'd see no more than a stalled van. CJ would have to be proactive, then. As soon as the van begins to slow he'd rush the guy, keep him occupied while Trish jumps out and runs away. He'd take another zap if necessary. Maybe he could force him to have an accident. That would certainly create a scene and witnesses. But what if the door is locked or Trish just simply can't find a way to get it open?

Was there an alternative?

Not one that CJ could think of, but anything was better than waiting until the perp got to his intended destination.

The letters on a blue sign, "Irvi..." flashed by and CJ's legs suddenly came free. He straightened them out and rolled back to face Trish.

"What now?" she said.

"We're coming to the Irvington exit. Whichever exit he takes we wait until he's slowing for his second stop."

She scrunched her face in confusion.

"The first is going to be right after taking an exit. There may be few or no witnesses there and no place to go. The second most likely will be a light. That'll be our best bet."

"Okay."

"As soon as I get up, you go for the door. I'm going to rush him, distract him."

"But…"

"When I know you have the door open and you're out, I'm coming out right after you. Remember to yell at the top of your lungs."

She seemed to consider the plan for a time, maybe preparing her argument. "What if I can't get the door open? What if it's got a child safety lock or something?"

"If you can't get out the door, kick out a window; anything to attract attention. Remember those kickboxing lessons you took?"

She nodded.

"It's time to put that to good use." He grinned at her, but all she did was nod again. "I'm going for his head to try and knock him unconscious."

She looked so scared that all he wanted to do was take her in his arms and say that everything was going to be all right, but that would certainly be a huge lie.

The van started slowing. CJ rolled to his back to be able to see. When he was certain, he turned back to Trish. "He's getting off onto Ajo. Be ready."

Trish nodded.

CJ rolled to his back again and watched. They turned onto Ajo Way, west-bound, went through an immediate green light and then another a minute later. Holiday Boulevard, he thought to himself. Mission Road would be next, a busy intersection; lots of witnesses if he catches a red light. After that it'd be La Cholla and then something he couldn't remember and then Kinney. Beyond that there was nothing but open desert highway all the way to Three Points, nearly twenty miles. If he never catches a red light and doesn't turn before passing Kinney, they'd be out in the Sonoran Desert with absolutely no hope.

The van started to slow and then CJ saw a green light. It took him a few seconds to realize the perp was moving into the left turn lane. He'd have to stop and wait for his opportunity to go. CJ tried to remember if this was a leading or following left turn green and decided it didn't make any difference.

He turned his head to Trish, gave her a smile, nodded and then rolled to his knees and onto his feet. An immediate wave of dizziness dropped him to one knee. He waited for it to pass, briefly wondering if it was a result of the multiple shocks or dehydration. Probably both. It cleared and then he pushed back to his feet. Bent at the waist, hands still behind him, he rushed forward and threw himself between the seats, aiming his head toward the perp's head. He heard the side door slam open and then a screech of tires and Trish screaming. Almost at the same time the perp's elbow hit him in the sternum and the stun gun discharged on his cheek. Then the engine roared and CJ flew back against the rear doors of the van. A searing pain shot through his shoulder.

He shook off the pain and struggled up enough to get a look out the back window. Trish was lying in the street in front of a car and people where running to her. With no more than a two-second look, enough to make CJ sick to his stomach, the perp slammed on the brakes. CJ tumbled forward against the seats and the side door slammed closed. There came another jolt from the stun gun followed by a second roar from the engine and CJ was once more thrown against the rear door, this time slamming into it headfirst. He struggled to one knee, momentarily unaware of where he was, white flashes filling his inner vision, a strange music off in the distance. The van swerved and he fell from one side of the van to the other, cracked a side window with his head and then felt nothing.

Chapter 43

CJ awoke shivering. He had no idea where he was and for the first few seconds couldn't even think of his own name. What he was aware of was that his head hurt like hell, his face felt as though he'd been branded and he was lying on the floor in a semi-dark room. Drunk? he wondered. Hung-over? He started to push up and was struck back down from what felt like a hot spike being hammered into his shoulder. He waited for the pain to subside and then, very carefully, rolled onto his back. *A bar fight?*

His mouth and throat dry, he tried sucking up some saliva.

Nothing.

He looked around for water and found a room with which he was not familiar, maybe a motel room.

Where the hell am I?

He settled back, took a couple deep breaths and began trying to remember what led up to his being wherever he was. He recalled being in jail after surrendering to… it took him a few seconds to recall who that was. Lisa. He surrendered to Dave's daughter, Officer Lisa Bowers. He was in jail through the weekend until Agent Crane pulled him out and turned him over to Dan Monday morning.

In a rush the rest of Monday flooded back at him culminating with the stun gun hits and Trish jumping from the van, her scream, her lying in the street, the van speeding away. And then he closed his eyes and wept.

It was many minutes before CJ opened his eyes and attempted to sit up. Day was breaking and the light that was finding its way past the gaps in the drapes revealed what he suspected, a cheap motel room. The air-conditioning unit under the window was on and blowing frigid air. The bed appeared not to have been disturbed. Nothing was making sense. Why would the perp kidnap him and then leave him in a motel room?

There was a phone on the nightstand. With great care he struggled to his knees and then, using the bed, carefully rose to his feet. Dizziness washed over him and he had all he could do just to sit on the bed without completely passing out. After a half minute, when his head had cleared enough that he could think, he scooted over to the phone and picked it up. There was no dial tone. He put the phone down and looked at the tag above the keypad. *Smoky's Rest Motel*, it read. There was a phone number, but no address. He didn't recognize the name, so he still had no idea where he was.

He got to his feet, waited a few seconds to be sure he was stable and then staggered into the bathroom.

The battered and bloodied face in the mirror left CJ's mouth agape. He looked like he'd been struck on one side of the face with a hot poker and on the other side with a brick. Dried blood caked his mangled hair and the side of his face, partially covering a black eye. More blood had splattered onto his already badly soiled shirt. After making use of the toilet he considered standing in a hot shower for a time, but the persistent vision of Trish lying in the street had him turning away and heading for the door.

In his rush to open the door, while still a tad off balance, CJ stumbled and struck the doorjamb with his injured shoulder. The searing pain nearly dropped him to his knees. When it finally eased, he stepped out only to be blinded by the sun just breaking over a desert full of saguaros and ocotillos. He shielded his eyes and looked left then right. With the number of cars in the small parking lot it appeared that less than half the rooms were occupied. Then his attention was drawn to the car directly in front of him. He blinked several times while continuing to push away the glare of the sun and then once again started replaying all the events of the afternoon before. At no time, other than the black van into which he was forced, had he gotten into any other vehicle.

However, in front of the motel room, in which he had mysteriously awakened, sat Stella's car. He walked around it to be certain, spotted the familiar scratch on the rear bumper, peered in at the empty interior and then returned to the motel room door to check inside for anything that might be lying around that would help solve the mystery.

The door was locked.

He checked his pockets. What came out in his hand was not the key to the room, but the key and remote to Stella's car. He turned around and looked again at the little blue Hyundai. Had she found him and in the few minutes before he woke up decided to run out for breakfast, first shoving the key into his pocket? He looked up and down the road passing in front of the motel. There were no eating establishments within view, thus within reasonable walking distance. Why did she not take the car? Why would she have left him on the floor? Why did he have her keys?

He searched again in his pockets but found no room key. Noting the room number, 114, he approached the office at the end of the building. The office door was locked; a key drop-box to the side. A sign on the door indicated it opened at 6:30. He looked at his watch. It was 6:07. He walked back to Stella's car, trying to decide what to do.

Get to a phone, was the only thing that came to mind. He had to find out about Trish. He unlocked the car and got in. He'd drive along this road until he found a phone. In the meantime he'd hopefully figure out where he was.

His shoulder injury made it difficult to get the key in the ignition. Once he did so and got the car started, he twisted a little further in his seat in order to reach across to put the gear selector in reverse, only to wrench his shoulder. He dropped the seat back, closed his eyes and waited for the searing pain to settle. Just as he started to bring himself upright the inside of the car started spinning, and he became nauseous, something acidy rising in his throat, the taste of bile in his mouth. He tried to suck up saliva and wished again that he had water, that he'd at least drawn some from the bathroom tap when he was in there.

He remained in the semi-prone position until the nausea faded away and the inside of the car appeared normal again. Suddenly there came the sound of a roaring engine followed by a car skidding to a stop and then another. He pulled himself up far enough to look out the driver's side window. Legs spread, service revolver pointed directly at CJ, stood a sheriff's deputy.

"Turn off your vehicle and put your hands on the dash," the deputy ordered.

CJ complied as best he could and then pressed his head against the steering wheel. In a way it was a relief because he could get all his questions answered, though he had no idea why he was being arrested again. Over the next few minutes, as he was extracted from Stella's car and subjected to more mind-numbing pain as they handcuffed him and pushed him into the patrol car, CJ was able to conclude that he was once again setup by the perp. There was likely another body. Whose body was it? Another hooker? How did the perp get Stella's car? Where was Stella? What about Trish?

The deputies, tight-mouthed against his questions, only read him his rights and reported their prize catch on their shoulder mikes.

Chapter 44

"The key to the motel in front of which you were parked was found at the most recent crime scene, next to the body of a young U of A coed. Again, not a hooker, Mister Washburn. You've apparently scared them all off the street so you had to grab the first young female you saw. Didn't even take the time to put her in the dumpster this time, just dumped her in the weeds next to it. You were in such a hurry you dropped your motel key, thus the reason the deputies found you asleep in the car instead of in the motel room. You're getting sloppy."

CJ wanted to reach across and punch Agent Crane in the nose and then stomp up and down on the smirk on Detective Bunko's face. The relief he felt, however, with knowing that Stella was not the victim was enough to settle him. Ignoring the agent's opening statement, CJ asked, "Where's my daughter, Patricia? What's happened to her?"

"Your daughter is in intensive care. She's being taken care of. If you're lucky, she'll live and you won't be charged with manslaughter on top of all the first degree murders."

"Man slaughter!" CJ was incredulous. "You think I had something to do with…." He couldn't believe his ears. "We were both kidnapped, zapped with a stun gun, handcuffed. She jumped from the van trying to escape while I distracted the perp. There were people around, witnesses."

"What the witnesses saw, Mister Washburn, was your daughter jumping or being thrown out of a black van and then the van speeding away."

"She wasn't thrown out!" CJ realized he was yelling, tried to relax, remain calm. "We talked about what to do. At the first red light where he had to stop, I'd distract him while she escaped." He sat back and his chin dropped to his chest. "It didn't work. She got hit by a car and I got zapped a couple more times and thrown around inside the van."

"So you say."

"I'm not talking any more until my attorney gets here."

"I'd say that's the only smart thing you've said all morning. She's on her way."

"And I want to see my daughter."

"That's not going to happen."

Five minutes after Gianna Onassis arrived she was in Agent Stratton's face and pointing at CJ. "You need to get him to an ER. His shoulder is either dislocated or broken, he has a black eye and it looks like he's been struck in the face with a baseball bat. I'd be willing to bet that he has a concussion."

"You a doctor, Ms. Onassis?"

"Do you want the heat if I'm correct and you never did anything about it? My client has the right to medical care, Agent Stratton, and you know that."

Stratton scowled. "I'll get it arranged."

When the agent had left, Gianna sat down next to CJ. "I checked on Patricia for you. She's pretty much out of danger but she's still in a medically induced coma until the swelling goes down. She's lucky. The car that hit her had almost made it to a stop."

"How bad were her injuries?"

"A broken ankle. The issue is the swelling on her brain, I'm told. She hit the pavement rather hard."

CJ gulped back another bit of bile that now seemed to have taken up permanent residence in his throat and looked up at the ceiling.

"Tell me what happened," Gianna said. "They believe you were driving."

CJ shook his head. "We were abducted, subdued with a stun gun, or several stun guns. The way they kept coming he may have had two. Look at my cheek, my neck. I've got at least a half dozen burn marks all over my body. So does Trish. It's lucky neither of us are dead with all the shocks he hit us with. When she jumped out I was trying to distract the perp. He had my hands cuffed behind my back so when he took off I was thrown around like a rag doll." He held up his right arm even though the pain was excruciating. "See the contusions around my wrist. That's from the handcuffs."

Gianna took his hand and carefully turned it this way and that. "Start from the beginning. Walk me though the entire series of events until the deputies found you this morning."

CJ sat back. "I could use some aspirin."

"Not until we get you checked out. Tell me what happened."

He adjusted the position of his arm to gain a little less discomfort and then started with the two of them heading out for a walk the previous afternoon.

Not long after Gianna had departed, giving CJ the order not to talk to anyone, two uniformed officers showed up to escort him to Northwest Medical Center where he was taken in through a side entrance. He didn't want publicity any more than did they so he'd agreed to wearing a floppy hat, though it hurt his head and he doubted anyone would have recognized him if he looked as bad as he felt. After the shoulder X-rays he was sitting on an exam room table while a nurse cut away hair and washed the two areas on his head where he'd been bleeding. She hadn't quite finished when a doctor walked in. She stepped aside and he took a close look at the contusions.

"Have you vomited?" he asked.

"I don't think so," CJ said, noticing the name, Gordon Blask, on his name badge. "I have had some feelings of nausea this morning, some dizziness. Before I woke up, though, I think I was unconscious for fourteen or fifteen hours."

"Really?" The doctor pulled over a stool and sat. "Look directly at me," he said, then shined a light in CJ's eyes. "So this happened yesterday afternoon, I'm to assume."

"Yes."

The exam room door opened and closed, but because CJ's back was to the door he didn't see who had entered. He assumed it was another nurse. One officer was already inside. Maybe the other one came in.

"Have you taken any drugs, pain killers?"

"No, but I could sure use something for my shoulder."

"I'll write a prescription for that. Meanwhile I suggest you take nothing more than acetaminophen. You can get it over-the-counter. No aspirin or ibuprofen or any other anti-inflammatory drugs."

CJ glanced over at the officer who was keeping an eye on the procedure, maybe making sure the doctor didn't slip him a file. "I doubt a stop at Walgreens is in the orders."

"That will be taken care of." The voice came from the individual behind CJ who had just entered. The voice, so familiar, though he hadn't heard it in years, paused CJ's breathing and sent his heart rate up a few beats, followed by a wave of nausea. He clenched his jaw and tried to will it down.

The voice belonged to…. CJ wanted to turn to look, but didn't want to be disappointed, didn't want to face him like this if it was. What would he be doing right here, right now anyway? Anyone could have a similar voice pattern, so it was obviously someone else. He looked at the police officer standing guard and saw no concern on his face, thus total acceptance to the individual who'd walked in. Another cop or FBI agent most likely, CJ surmised. He certainly had to be mistaken as to who he initially thought the voice belonged.

His stomach suddenly felt like someone had stuck it with a cork screw and was twisting it. He gritted his teeth, took a breath and held it; grunted.

"What's the matter?" Dr. Blask said.

CJ forced away the bile rising up his throat, suddenly feeling a chill. "Urts... Naus-us," he said. "Co…." Then he broke out in a sweat. He knew his words were slurred, but he couldn't get them to come out correct. "Eel afy."

The doctor took CJ's wrist and looked at his wristwatch. "Pulse is 120," he said then shined his light in CJ's eyes again. "Look at me."

CJ tried to look at him but the room was swimming.

"Squeeze my hand."

CJ didn't understand what the doctor was asking. He raised his hand and tried to push him away, push the light out of his eyes, out of his face. "Moof," he said. "Urts. Wha…?"

And then suddenly, it all stopped; his focus snapped back, the nausea and the pain ceased, his heart rate settled. He looked at the nurse, over to the officer who appeared to be ready to jump in if CJ had gotten violent and then at the doctor. "What just happened?"

The doctor shined the light again and started moving it back and forth. "Follow the light."

CJ did so.

"Squeeze my hand."

Again CJ followed the command.

The doctor took CJ's left arm and appeared to study it for a short time. He let it go. "It appears Mister Washburn that you just suffered a seizure."

"A seizure?" CJ was flabbergasted. "From my head injuries?"

Doctor Blask stood. "That was my initial thought, but I see you've had a recent injection in your arm. Does that mean anything to you?"

CJ looked down at his arm, saw the tiny red area to which the doctor was referring. "No. I haven't had anything since a flu shot last year."

"It's possible the seizure was from the injuries; however,, if I were a betting man, which I am not so I'll wait on the tox-screens to confirm, I'd say you've been drugged."

"Drugged? With what?"

"My best guess—again the tox-screen will confirm—is flunitrazepam, the most common brand being Rohypnol."

"Rohypnol. I've never heard of it."

"I'm sure you have," said the voice behind him. "It goes by several street names. You'd be more familiar with *roofie*."

"The date-rape drug?"

Dr. Blask nodded. "That is quite correct. Haven't seen too much of it around here, however."

"It's prevalent in Texas and Florida," said the voice. "Doesn't usually get this far west."

"Have you been unusually irritable or restless?" Dr. Blask asked.

CJ looked at the doctor. "I'd have to say both, but then I do have a situation going on here that's a tad on the stressful side."

The doctor held out his hand. "Squeeze my hand again."

CJ did so.

"Do you sense any loss of strength?"

"No."

He looked at CJ's eyes again. "How long did you say you were unconscious?"

CJ thought about what time they'd gone for the walk. "Roughly fourteen hours."

"Are you sure you didn't take anything to knock you out, something to help you sleep?"

"Yes, I'm sure. I hate drugs. I put off taking aspirin until I have to and right now I'd be grateful for something extra strong."

"Hmm," the doctor said.

"Do you know anything about my daughter, Patricia? Is she at this hospital? What is her condition?"

The doctor looked over CJ's shoulder as though getting an okay from the mystery individual. When his eyes returned to CJ he said, "She's still in intensive care, Mister Washburn, but only because she needs to be watched closely while in an induced coma. I expect a day or two before she'll be awakened. After that, barring any unforeseen complications, a full recovery, though she may have a slight limp for the remainder of her life, or maybe not."

"Thank you."

"I'm going to order up an X-ray of your cranium and a CT scan just to make sure the bases are covered." He looked at the nurse. "You can go ahead and finish up." With that, Dr. Blask left.

There was complete silence while she did her work. When she was finished she said, "Someone will be by to get you for your X-ray and CT scan," and then was gone, followed by the police officer.

But CJ wasn't alone. He could still sense the individual behind him, the one who had entered and said he'd take care of the prescription, the one whose voice sent a shock through CJ's system. He slid off the table as carefully as he could without jarring his shoulder and then turned around.

Standing before him was a physical attitude in a government prescribed suit that stood out like the shiny badge on a rookie cop, and it screamed FBI agent. Also standing before him was the man CJ hadn't seen in over six years, but whose voice he'd have known if it had been sixty. The emotions that rose up in him seemed to rip out his vocal cords and he was immediately tossed between having to sit down and wanting to step across the room and give the man a hug. All he managed to do was remain rooted in place and force out the name he and his mother had given him nearly twenty-five years before.

"Josh."

Chapter 45

"It's been a long time, Dad."

Suddenly CJ felt dizzy and had to reach out for the edge of the exam table. Before he could think much beyond that, Josh had a chair pulled over and was guiding his father into it.

When he was settled and his thoughts had cleared, CJ said, "Looks like you've done well for yourself. How long have you been an agent?"

Josh sat back against the exam table and crossed his arms. "About a year."

"Where?"

"Denver."

CJ nodded, but didn't know what else to say. After a time he said, "You must have gone to school."

"Boston University, criminal justice."

"How did you manage that without my finding out about it?"

"It wasn't easy."

There was another stretch of silence.

"Have you checked on your sister?"

"Of course. She's the reason I'm here."

"But you thought you ought to stop in and say hi to your old man, the accused serial killer."

"Something like that."

"How long you staying?"

"Until Trish is awake and out of intensive care, maybe even out of the hospital. I'm here on personal time so it all depends."

CJ bowed his head. "I'm sorry she got involved in this."

Josh pushed to his feet. "Me, too." He stepped to the door then turned back to his father. "Like I said, I'll make sure your prescriptions are filled." And then he was gone.

The officer came back in and CJ remained seated, staring at his feet.

By the time CJ had gotten his X-ray and CT scan, the word had apparently gotten out that he was there. As they stepped out the side-door through which they had entered, CJ's hands again handcuffed in front of him despite his shoulder being bound, the floppy hat covering his face, they were met by two teams of reporters with tiny little recording devices pointed at his nose.

"Mister Washburn, is it true that you kidnapped your own daughter with the intent to murder her and throw her into a dumpster just like the rest of your victims?"

CJ lunged toward the woman, but was snapped back by the two officers. The resultant pain surge dropped him to his knees. One officer drew him up by his good arm then guided him, or more like pushed him, through the reporters to the waiting van. Inside, CJ settled and closed his eyes for the twenty minute trip back to his holding cell, the bile in his mouth a constant presence.

On his bunk, he laid, staring up at the ceiling, wishing for sleep, knowing it wasn't going to come easy. He also wondered if Josh was actually going to fill the prescription, or would he just leave his old man hanging, in pain? He probably deserved it if he did.

Chapter 46

On Wednesday, about noon, CJ was taken to an interview room by two of Tucson's finest, handcuffed to a table and then left alone. Except for his shoulder, he was feeling much better. The prescribed pain killer, which magically showed up early Tuesday evening, deadened the pain to a tolerable level and helped him sleep. As far as why he was summoned from his cell, he wasn't told and he didn't ask. At this point he didn't much care unless it was to give him good news about Trish. He doubted that was the case because it seemed as though no one gave a damn about him, or about how he felt. Out of sight, out of mind. He hadn't even heard from Stella. She was probably pissed at him because now her car had been impounded. Apparently, according to Stratton, it had been used in the commission of the last murder. Trace evidence of the victim, one Jasmine Stone, had been found in the trunk. CJ was certain that the samples they took from his clothes, his hair, and under his fingernails would also, thanks to the ingenuity of the perp, reveal little bits of Ms. Stone. Add to it that they arrested him while sitting in the car and they might as well just put the needle in him now and save the tax payers a lot of money.

The perp may have been sloppy in the past in his attempts to get the finger pointed at CJ, but this time he made up for it in volume. CJ could see no possibility of talking his way out of it any longer. And maybe that's as it should be. There would be no reason to go after Trish again, or Stella, as long as CJ was in jail. Maybe, for a time anyway, all the murders would stop.

But that's the wrinkle, isn't it? CJ thought. The murders won't stop, not forever anyway. A serial killer has an obsession to do what he does. His reason, his need, doesn't go away just because someone else gets his lethal injection. He will kill again, if not in Tucson, somewhere else. Tucson may not even be his first.

The door opened and in came Agent Stratton and Detective Payne. CJ sat up a little straighter in anticipation of learning why Dan was there. Did they allow him to come in just to deliver bad news? Had Trish made a turn for the worse?

They both sat down and looked at him across the table.

"What?" CJ demanded.

"The number one person of interest, we just wanted you to know," said Stratton, "is not you. We're telling you this because we have to keep this information just between the four of us. No leaks."

"Four of us?" CJ said. He sat up even straighter.

"Well, five, if you count Chief Rague. Myself, Agent Crane, Detective Payne here and you. I've made a request for two more agents. We have to tell you because we don't want you spilling to anybody who we're investigating, not even your attorney."

CJ let out a breath he didn't know he was holding. "Tommy Clark."

"Yes."

"That's why Bunko isn't on this little task force. He's friends with Clark."

"Yes. However, we don't believe he has anything to do with the murders. He's just too close to the suspect."

"The agents and I were meeting with Chief Rague Monday afternoon," said Dan, "presenting our suspicions concerning Clark, when this thing with you and Trish went down. The chief, at the time, was a little leery to start suspecting one of our own. When you were picked up yesterday morning, the whole theory pretty much got squashed in light of the evidence against you. This morning, however, he's changing his tune. He's congratulated Bunko on a job well-done and reassigned him to a series of home invasions up in the north area. Bunko didn't even blink at how unprecedented the reassignment was. He took it and ran."

"What happened this morning?"

"Nothing in particular, if you're thinking another body. What happened is we met with the chief again to present additional evidence. Although Officer Clark was on duty Monday, he took the afternoon off, supposedly to meet with a realtor about buying a house. That was enough to turn the chief a few degrees. He assigned a task force to work with the two FBI agents to quietly investigate Officer Clark."

"Have you been able to determine if that's what Tommy was actually doing?"

Stratton shook his head. "Not yet. We're working on it but what we don't want to do is spook him. We want him believing that all our focus is on you."

CJ nodded his head. "I understand." For just a few seconds there, his hopes had been up. Now, for the good of the investigation, he'd be stuck in jail.

"I'm sorry. Can't even remove the cuffs. Have to put on the full pretense."

"I've given a recommendation to Chief Rague that I bring one other person in on this," Dan said. "I need someone on the ground who can keep her mouth shut, and who already knows what's going on."

"Stella?" She was the first person who came to CJ's mind.

"Oh, hell no, CJ. There's no way I could pry her away from Trish's bedside, nor would I want to. Besides, she's civilian. By the way, Trish was taken out of coma this morning."

The relief on CJ's face must have been visible.

"I'm sorry, CJ. Should have told you right off. Things are looking much better with Trish. Stella and Pat are right there with her, along with her brother."

Pat! CJ had totally forgotten about his ex-wife, thinking that Trish was all alone. Stella and Pat and Josh. "That's good," he said, more to himself than the two men. Then something else occurred to him. "Trish was able to tell you what happened. Right? That's the main reason why the chief changed his mind and you two are here right now."

"Well, yes. There's that, and the fact that your blood test came back with a massive dose of Rohypnol." Stratton said. "It appears that

Dr. Blask was right; you were injected with a *roofie*, enough that you're lucky you're alive. He believes that there'd have been no way for you to have driven during that time, let alone commit a murder. As far as your daughter, she wasn't as coherent as we'd have liked, but she did say enough to confirm about half of what you've told us, making the rest of it, if not believable, at least conceivable. By the way, Mister Washburn, when were you planning on telling us about your son, Agent Joshua Washburn?"

"Yeah, CJ," Dan said. "I knew the two of you were estranged, but you never said anything about him going the bureau route."

"We were estranged because I had no idea where he was," CJ said. "As far as I knew, he was living on the streets. He was an angry young man when he walked away over six years ago. I never heard from him until yesterday, figured he was gone forever. Believe me; no one was more shocked than was I."

"What was he angry about?" Stratton asked, "if you don't mind my asking."

"His parents getting divorced. Trish took it pretty well, but he never did."

"So now he's talking to you, I gather."

"His mouth was moving and words were coming out, so, yeah, I guess you could say he's talking to me."

"I have a daughter who won't stop talking," Stratton said.

"How old is she?"

"Five."

Dan and CJ both smiled in understanding. "It'll change when she becomes a teenager," CJ said. "Then she'll talk to everyone but you unless she needs money."

"I keep hearing teenage daughter stories and am starting to get a little worried."

"As you should," Dan said. "Back to what I was saying. I'm proposing bringing in Officer Bowers, and maybe even her friend in admin. She's familiar with the case already and has proven her discretion."

"Meanwhile I'm stuck right here. The world needs to believe you all have your man."

"And as long as the world believes that," Stratton said, "Officer Clark, or whoever this perp is, will likely ease back on his killing spree, at least for a while. Give us some time to sort through the evidence."

"What about the van in which we were kidnapped? What kind of vehicle did the witnesses see and what does Clark drive?"

"That's just it. The only thing consistent from the witnesses was black and van. Make and model is everything from GMC to Toyota and even Mercedes Benz, from smoked glass windows to blacked out windows to paneled with anything but Arizona plates. One individual insisted it had New York plates. Another swears that it was Nevada. Clark drives a ten-year-old Ford Galaxy, light gray, not black, registered in Arizona. It's the only thing in his name."

"I can testify that the windows were smoked glass," CJ confirmed, "as I could see out of them, but I doubt very much anyone could see in. Never saw plates. The fact that Clark has only a gray Ford Galaxy doesn't mean he can't have something stolen that he keeps hidden away somewhere."

"We're hoping that's the case, otherwise we may be barking up the wrong suspect tree and there's someone else we haven't even considered."

"Could he have a partner?" CJ asked.

"The chances of that for a serial killer are so nil," said Stratton, "we haven't even taken it into consideration."

"But let's look at this. He abducts us with the van and then dumps me into a motel. He then goes back for Stella's car."

"He didn't check you into the motel until almost 10:00 that night."

"When did he steal Stella's car?"

"Dave and Stella got back to the house about 4:30," Stratton said. "Her car was gone then. She thought at first that you and Trish had taken off somewhere with it so until Dave got the call from me telling them about Trish getting hit by a car, they were more angry with you than concerned. By the way, they said that when they returned, the house was unlocked."

"When we went out for a walk, we didn't have a house key, so we left the back door unlocked."

"The perp just walked in and found Stella's car keys. You guys played right into his hand. He couldn't have stacked the deck any better."

"Here's the rub, though. What did he do with the van, with me in it, while he was stealing Stella's car?"

They all silently considered that question.

"What time did Trish get hit?" CJ asked.

"The first 911 call came in at 3:25," Stratton said.

"Stella found her car gone at 4:30. That's only an hour. It seems to me it'd be rather risky to try to go back for it. How would he know when anyone would return? How would he coordinate two vehicles by himself? When he dumped the body yesterday morning, he purposely left the motel key next to it. I don't think he fully thought that through. How was I supposed to get into the motel room without the key? There wasn't a second key found, was there?"

Stratton shook his head. "I see where you're going. In order to leave the car key in your pocket he'd have had to have dropped the car there first because after leaving the motel key at the crime scene he couldn't have gotten back into the motel room to leave you and the car keys."

"The chicken and egg thing," Dan said, "unless there was a second motel key and the perp took it with him. We need to check with the desk clerk to determine if he gave out one or two keys."

"Speaking of the desk clerk," CJ said, "did he have a description of the individual who checked in?"

"The guy had the memory of a nat. No surveillance system. Nada. The perp checked in under your name using your credit card."

"That means he accessed my wallet. Have my wallet and credit cards been dusted for prints that aren't mine?"

Dan and Stratton looked at each other.

"I can't imagine he'd be that stupid," Dan said.

"Consider the bank robber who wrote his demands for money on the back of instructions from his parole officer," CJ said. "We all have our stupid moments."

"Which I'm sure you can attest to in the last few weeks," Dan said.

CJ nodded his head. "No argument there."

"Okay," Stratton said. "We're going to talk to the motel clerk again and run your wallet for prints."

"I think you need to seriously be considering if there are two individuals here," CJ said. "I fail to see how it could have all been done otherwise. He couldn't have accomplished it by himself without using a taxi service, and that would leave a trail."

"True, but we have to check it anyway. A lot of stuff to do with such a small team."

"I'd say forget the taxi for the time being," CJ said. "Here's how I think it went down. The perps were parked down the street watching the house, discussing how they were going to get to us. Then, much to their surprise and pleasure, we stepped out and headed off for a walk. We entered the trail and they guessed, correctly by the way, that we'd return by that trail, so they parked the van in such a way that we'd walk right into it. Perp number one stayed with the van while perp number two entered the house, discovered the car keys and thus began formulating the new plan, which was to kill Trish, use the car to dispose of her body and then put me in it."

CJ put his fingers to his forehead and closed his eyes. "Hold on a minute. Let me think through the abduction again."

Dan and the agent looked at CJ. After thirty seconds, Dan said, "What are you thinking?"

"I was tired, dehydrated, hot, thus my senses, my awareness as to threats around us extremely compromised. There was something or someone moving to my right as we came to where the trail stopped at the street. Lurking would be my afterthought, but it didn't come to me at the time. Then I looked up and saw the van parked in our path. The side door was open six or seven inches, maybe a foot. In the bright sun I couldn't see anything or anyone in the dark interior. I remember suddenly realizing the van was similar to the one I saw at the third crime scene, where you got me arrested the first time, Dan, but it was too late. I was hit with the stun gun from behind and the next thing I knew I was falling or being pushed into the van. How could he have hit me from behind and then opened the van door and shoved me in, while at the same time subduing Trish?"

"You're thinking prep number two was in the van, ready to open the door and receive you?"

"Exactly. I was hit so many times with the stun gun, I remember thinking there were two guns. How can one person handle two stun guns while handcuffing and taping up two individuals? He only has so many hands. With the shocks hitting me one after the other, I wasn't cognizant enough to be aware of how many people there were, one or a dozen."

"One guy was handling the stun guns while the other was doing the honors with the tape and cuffs," said Stratton.

CJ closed his eyes again.

"What else are you thinking?" Dan said.

"It's what I'm remembering. In the van, just as I was blacking out from being thrown around after Trish jumped out, I heard music. There had been no music or radio prior to that and I doubt the perp would have chosen that particular moment, in his rush to get away from the accident scene, to put on some merry tunes."

"You're thinking it was an incoming call on his cell phone?"

CJ pointed a finger at Dan. "Yes. They would have had to stay in communications with each other. After grabbing us, perp number two followed perp number one out of the subdivision in Stella's car which means he would have been right behind us when Trish jumped out."

"He'd have witnessed it," Dan said. "And the first thing he'd have done was call perp number one to find out what the hell happened."

"Bingo," CJ said. "Do you think there's any chance that one of the other witnesses thought to try videotaping the event with the hopes of getting some YouTube footage?"

"Thus possibly capturing Stella's car with perp number two driving, trying to get around the accident?" said Dan.

Agent Stratton sat back, an astonished look on his face. "You two guys should be partners."

"We used to be back when we wore the blue uniform," Dan said, "then CJ here bailed."

"Too bad," Stratton said. "So, we need to start checking cell phone records for our suspect and find out if any witnesses turned on the video cameras on their Smartphones. I have to admit that it all makes more sense than anything else we've come up with, though I still think it's a long shot. A pair of serial killers? It'd be one for the books."

"It's already one for the books," Dan said. "Cops and ex-cops, multiple states, at least seven bodies."

"There's one other thing you need to be looking at," CJ said.

"What's that?"

"How did the perp, or perps, figure out where we were? There were only a handful of people who knew we were using Dave's rental. How did it leak, who leaked it, and to whom did it get leaked? I really hate to say this, but is there any chance the second perp could be Ralph Bunko? He's got a big beef against me."

"Oh, no, CJ!" Dan pushed back in his chair. "Ralph may be a lot of things, maybe even out to get you, but serial killer, no way."

"What's the story with Detective Bunko, anyway?" Stratton asked.

Dan and CJ told him about the attempted rape charge against Dave McDermott and how CJ was hired to investigate it and found out it was all a hoax, making Bunko, the lead detective on the case, look like a clown.

"Barney Fife of Tucson," Dan said. "That's what CJ called him to his face in the squad room."

CJ held up his hand as far as his taped up shoulder would allow. "I admit that it was probably not the best thing to say about him at the time. Doesn't mean I was wrong. Dan's right, though. Bunko may be a lousy detective, but he's not a killer. Is there any way he could have found out about the safe-house location and without realizing what he did, tipped off Tommy Clark? That's the kind of thing I believe he's capable of doing."

Stratton stood and pulled out his phone. "Officer Bowers was returned to her regular duties this morning. I'll call the chief and second Detective Payne's recommendation that she be reassigned to us. I'll ask for Officer Kramer, too. We're going to need the manpower." While he waited for the connection to be made he added, "You need to be back on the force as a detective, CJ. Your talent is wasted as a PI. If Josh is anything like you, he's going to make one fine FBI agent."

Stratton stepped away to talk with the chief and CJ drifted off, thinking about Joshua and hoping it was time for his meds.

Chapter 47

"If you're not arraigning him and not charging him, why in the hell are you holding my client, Agent Stratton?"

It was right after Dan left to meet up with Officer Bowers, following Stratton's call to Chief Rague, that Agent Crane came in with Gianna Onassis. She didn't look very pleased.

CJ put his hand on his attorney's arm. "It's okay, Gianna."

"The hell it is, CJ. This is the third time you've been arrested in less than two weeks. There's been no charges filed, no hearings, nothing. What the hell is going on, and how much have you been talking to them without me present?"

"There was an arraignment," CJ said.

She tilted her head at him. "Well, whoopee-do. Whose side are you on? It was right after that when Judge Delgado cancelled the hearing, the one she scheduled and then set you free. Now here you are back and no one seems to be all that excited about it, except the press. I had to run the media gauntlet to get in here."

CJ looked over at the two FBI agents, lifting his eyebrows. He knew there was no way they were going to be able to keep Gianna out of it. She wasn't considered one of the best criminal attorneys in Southern Arizona for nothing. When he looked back at her she was glaring at him.

"There's something fishy going on here, CJ, and if you don't tell me I'm going to fire my favorite client and walk out of here."

CJ nodded at Stratton who returned it.

"I think she needs to be on the team," CJ said. "If she walks, the press is going to make a big deal out of it and the perps might get suspicious."

"Perps?" Gianna said, looking between CJ and the agents.

"Counselor," Stratton said. "Your client hasn't been charged because the only thing he's guilty of is stupidity and if that's a crime we'd all be in jail by now."

"Then why is he still handcuffed to the table?"

"Pretense."

"Pretense! Pretense for who?"

"We believe the killer is getting inside information, that most likely, he's a cop."

"And so you're keeping my client locked up?"

"For a reason we have yet to be able to determine, Gianna," CJ said, "this guy is targeting me to take the fall for his killings. As long as I'm in custody, or appear to be in custody, he can't kill again."

Gianna sat back and just blinked at him.

"The last woman he went after was my daughter. I'm okay with being shackled and on bread and water, if that's what it takes, as long as I know she is no longer in danger."

"And you didn't want to tell me… why?"

"Ms. Onassis," Stratton said. "When we released CJ Monday morning there were only a handful of people who knew the location of the safe-house, yet the perp was able to discover it that same day and then abduct CJ and his daughter. There's a leak."

"And you think I—"

"No." Stratton held up his hand. "No. We're not thinking of anyone in particular for the leak at this point, and certainly not you. It might be that someone wrote the address down and then the perp walked by and saw it. We need to keep those in the know to as few as possible and all of us have to be extra vigilant in what we say, to whom we say it, and what we do."

Gianna sat in silence for a time, considering the agent's words. "Well, if it's any help, I never knew the location, so it couldn't have been me who made the mistake."

“We already knew that, thus eliminated you. It eliminates the two of us as well,” he indicated himself and Agent Crane, “as we also did not know the location. This is a very touchy investigation,” he said. “We’re wading in blue water trying to find a poisonous fish among a giant school of fish that all look alike.”

“And they all carry guns,” CJ added, “and have a passion to cover each other’s back.”

“So, now that you’re letting me in, you want me to put on the pretense that CJ is still an active client and is the sole suspect in all the murders.”

“Yes,” Stratton said. “Avoid the press if you can, but if you can’t, as his attorney you can say that you believe your client is innocent, an injustice has been done, yada yada yada; the kind of verbiage I’m sure you’re good at in front of the camera.”

“You don’t really know me, do you Agent Stratton?”

“No. But I do know attorneys. The good ones know how to wrangle the press. Are you saying you’re not one of those, Ms. Onassis?”

She laughed. “I like you Agent Stratton. You should have gone to law school.”

“I did, then I decided to put the guilty away instead of defend them.”

“Or was it easier to get a job with the FBI than a law firm?”

CJ looked between Stratton and Gianna, semi-smiles on their faces, and couldn’t tell if they were a couple of jungle cats about to jump into a fight or if they were just sniffing each other’s butts, coming to some kind of unspoken truce to share the territory.

“Who else is in the know?” she asked.

“Detective Payne, Officer Lisa Bowers and of course, Chief Rague.”

She looked at CJ. “Are you planning on telling Trish and Stella why you’re still in jail, or are you going to let them go on believing you’re actually going to hang for this?”

“I’ll tell them,” Stratton said. “I’ll swing by the hospital after we breakup here.”

“Do they have protection?” she asked.

"We have an agent with them."

She looked between Stratton and Crane. "I thought you were the only two agents on this case."

"We now have five," Stratton said as he looked over at CJ. "Josh has been temporarily reassigned to us from Denver. There are also two more in route from that field office."

"You never told me that," CJ said.

"I only just found out. Received the text while on the phone with Chief Rague."

"Did you ask Josh before you made the request?" CJ asked.

"I never made the request. I'm assuming Josh did. I just asked for a couple of more agents."

"Who's Josh?" Gianna asked.

"CJ's son, Agent Joshua Washburn."

"I thought…"

"So did I," CJ said in answer to her unfinished question.

Stratton stood. "We've a lot to do, so unless you have more to discuss with your client, counselor, we need to send him back to his abode."

"No, I'm good. I just need to have a little time to prepare for the barrage of mini-recorders and cameras."

"Thank you." Stratton opened the door and said to the officer standing outside. "Take this piece of crap back to his cell."

Agent Crane winked at CJ and stood. "Thanks for the help," he whispered.

The pretense appeared to be working. As CJ was escorted back to his cell uniformed officers had to step to the side to let them pass, several of whom CJ knew. CJ caught the eye of one, but the return look was anything but friendly. Overall, there was a lot of glaring going on. Another officer, who CJ didn't even get a clear look at, elbow-jabbed him in the back. CJ stumbled and the two escorts pulled him up straight, sending his shoulder into another spasm.

"Knock it off," one escort said to the assailant, but his words carried so little conviction, CJ expected another jab, maybe from the escort himself.

There were no more, but he could feel icy and acid-filled stares at the back of his head, even after they turned a corner and were alone.

By the time they got him back into his cell, the spasm had settled to the customary dull ache. He stretched out on his bunk and for a time watched the ceiling swim. A small piece of his brain made note that there was something wrong, but before long he didn't care and fell into, not sleep, but total unconsciousness.

Chapter 48

Twice CJ surfaced long enough to become confused as to where he was and to welcome the return to darkness. The third time he came fully awake to discover something was covering his mouth. He tried to reach up to remove it, only to find he had hardly any strength. He shook his head to dislodge the thing while struggling to get his hand up to his face, not fully understanding why he was so weak, why his left arm felt like jelly, why he couldn't move his right arm at all, why it was trapped against his body. He remembered the abduction and a new level of panic began rising in him. But he was in jail. How? Why? Was it happening again?

He tried yelling but the thing on his face muffled his cries.

"Clint! It's okay."

A hand touched his arm, clasped his hand; a face loomed over him.

"Hush," the face said.

Stella.

CJ's panic subsided.

"It's okay," she said. "You're in the hospital."

Hospital? He reached again to try and dislodge what he finally understood was an oxygen mask, but Stella grabbed his arm.

"No. Wait. I've called for the nurse."

He nodded, though knowing the panic hovered close by, that if the thing wasn't removed soon he'd lose control. He looked in her eyes, pleading for her to tell him what happened, aware that he was breathing too fast.

"They found you unconscious in your cell, couldn't rouse you. On the way to emergency you stopped breathing." Tears filled her eyes and she appeared to have to gulp something back. "I think you died."

I died? He wanted out of the bed, NOW! He tried to get up but couldn't fight against Stella's iron grip. "Let me go!" he yelled but the mask converted the words to something he was sure was unintelligible, making him sound like a mad man. "Let me go!" he yelled again.

"Mr. Washburn, knock it off!"

It wasn't Stella. It was a nurse and she went straight to removing the mask. CJ just stared at her.

"Is that better?" she asked.

CJ nodded and dropped his head back. "Water," he said, his voice raspy, his throat dry. A bottle with a straw appeared in front of his face. He sucked at it until he couldn't anymore, then rested. "Thank you."

It was thirty minutes before CJ felt somewhat human again, though extremely exhausted. The bed had been raised and the oxygen mask staged close by. There remained an intravenous tube in his arm. Stella never left him once, though she remained out of the way while the nurses worked. A doctor came in and poked at him, asking questions similar to those posed by Dr. Blask the day before.

When the doctor left and the nurses stopped fussing, Stella took his hand. "You scared the hell out of me. Between you and Trish, I've been going crazy."

"Thank you for being there for her." He took a little more water, couldn't seem to get enough. "How is she?"

"Much better. They plan to move her out of intensive care into a regular room sometime today."

"Is she nearby?"

"Yes." Stella pointed. "Just down the way."

"Wish I could see her."

"Eventually. She sends her love."

"Me too."

In the silence that followed, CJ could tell that Stella wanted to say something else. She was on the verge of tears again. He squeezed her hand. "What?"

She wiped at her eyes and sniffled. "They think you overdosed on your pain medication, that you tried to commit suicide. I told them you wouldn't do that." She opened her mouth to say something else, then closed it.

Overdose? CJ tried to remember when he took his last dose, but there was still too much fuzz in his brain. Did he at anytime consider ending it all? He shook his head at her. "I didn't…" *Suicide?* "…at least I don't think so."

"You're not sure?" That seemed to upset her even more.

"I can't remember the last time I asked for the pain killer," he said.

"Asked for? You had to ask for the pills?"

He blinked at her for a time, considering her question, suddenly understanding her question. "Yes!" He rose up from his pillow and immediately had to wait out a wave of dizziness. When, finally, it cleared, he said, "I had to ask for them."

"The prescription bottle was found in your cell, almost empty," she said.

"That'd be impossible. There's no way they'd put someone in a cell with even a bottle of aspirin."

"Oh."

CJ had to cut through his mental fog in order to come up with why it was impossible. "All dispensing of medicine to prisoners…." He fell back against his pillow. "It's controlled; suicidal reasons."

"My God!" Stella said. "That means he got to you."

"Yes." He listened to his own raspy breathing for a time, considering the implications. "If he can get to me in jail, he can get to me anywhere. Any doubt about being a cop… gone." He looked toward where the nurses flitted about, just outside his curtains. "Who's guarding me? Who's guarding Trish?"

"Josh is with Trish right now. She's never been left alone. Either Josh, me or Pat have been with her around the clock. It was against the rules but Josh flashed his badge and talked to someone. He stayed with her all night.

"Also," she said, looking toward the nurses, "you have a police officer just outside."

CJ looked closer and saw the edge of a uniform, realizing, not for the first time since he'd awoken, that he was not restrained. There were no handcuffs. "Who?" he asked, at first thinking that there were no uniformed officers on the team. Who did they put on him? How did they know who they can trust?

"Officer Bowers right now," Stella said. "Dave's daughter, Lisa. You remember?"

"Of course I remember. I'm not an invalid."

"Sorry. She and Officer Kramer are going to be taking turns with you, though I haven't seen Kramer yet. So far it's only been Lisa or one of the Denver agents."

CJ took a breath and relaxed. Stratton had talked about getting Officer Kramer reassigned to the task force.

"You said that Trish would be downgraded from critical this morning," he said.

"Yes."

"That means… What day is this?"

"It's Thursday. This happened to you yesterday afternoon. The Denver agents flew in last night."

He'd lost most of another day. He thought about the fourteen hours he lost after he was abducted and then drugged, waking up in the motel room, confused, feeling the same as he felt in the previous hour. Exactly the same, as a matter of fact, it suddenly occurred to him. It was the same drug, the date-rape drug, the official name of which he could not remember. The street name was Roofie. But how could the perp have gotten into the cell and injected him without his remembering it? No one came in to see him after he returned from the meeting with Stratton and Dan, and Gianna. Two cops escorted him back. Could one of them have poked him with a syringe without his realizing it? If one of the officers had squeezed his arm until it hurt, then CJ would not even have felt the needle.

And then he remembered the elbow jab to his back.

"Where's Stratton?" CJ blurted, sitting up again.

The suddenness of his question made Stella jump. "I don't know. Why?"

"There's no way they could have forced a bunch of pills down my throat. I'd remember that. I think I know when he got to me. It wasn't an overdose. The prescription bottle was staged."

Her eyes went wide. "Are you sure?"

"There's no other explanation. Find Stratton and get him here. Have him bring in the doctor, preferably Doctor Blask from the other day."

Stella went to talk to Officer Bowers while CJ laid his head back. The burst of excitement had him suddenly feeling very tired and cold, and the room was spinning. He pulled the flimsy blanket up to his neck, wishing he had another. He closed his eyes.

Chapter 49

"Clint."

This time when CJ awoke, he had enough of his mental facilities to realize he was wearing the oxygen mask again, and it was Stella talking to him. He started to reach up to remove the mask, but she beat him to it.

"The nurse thought it would be better that you have the mask when you're sleeping," she said. "Agent Stratton is here now." She moved aside, taking the mask with her, and Stratton stepped into view.

"How are you doing, CJ?"

"Feel like I've been dragged through the cow pasture, twice. Other than that, quite peachy."

"Stella told me what you said about being drugged again. That's exactly what happened. Your tox screen didn't indicate an overdose of the pain meds as was initially assumed. What was found was that you received another huge dose of Roofie. She says you know when it happened?"

"Yeah." He pointed to the water, and Stella retrieved it for him. Once he'd managed a good sip he continued, although it still felt like his tongue wanted to stick to the roof of his mouth. "When I was being escorted back to my cell, after meeting with you and Gianna, someone jabbed me in the back. It had to have been a uniformed officer because I don't remember noticing anyone in civilian clothes. At the time I thought the jab was an elbow."

He sucked up more water.

"As I'm sure you're aware, I'm not very well thought of around the police department, so it didn't surprise me at the time. Now, to think back on it, I'd be willing to bet there was a hypodermic needle involved. That's why I asked for Dr. Blask. He'd be able to find the injection point and know for sure."

"We're still trying to find him. Did you see the person who jabbed you?"

"No. I went down to my knees and my escorts had to pull me back up; hurt my shoulder like hell. They should remember the incident and may have noticed who it was."

"We'll pull them in, put them on the hot seat. Anything else?"

"The prescription bottle."

"What about it?"

"It was planted, so you need to dust it for prints. Someone who has access to that and the holding area threw it into my cell. Did you get prints off my wallet and credit card?"

"There was no wallet," Stratton said. "Do you remember having one when you gave up your personal effects?"

CJ closed his eyes and tried to recall. Between the aftereffects of the first drug and then being hit with it again, his brain kept slipping in and out of fog. "I don't know." He closed his eyes.

"CJ! You still with us?"

"Yeah. Trying to remember. I was handcuffed, my hands in front. I couldn't have reached into my back pockets. At some point they removed the handcuffs and I was told to strip and put on the lovely jail ensemble."

"Glad to see you still have your sense of humor."

"I was being serious."

Stella snorted.

Stratton said, "So, your clothes were taken away without emptying pockets."

"Yes." He looked at Stratton. "Was it listed in the inventory?"

"No."

"That was stupid on the perp's part. It's another piece of coincidental evidence that points to someone besides me. He should have wiped the wallet and credit card and put them back in my pocket."

"Apparently this guy is not as smart as we've been thinking he is," Stratton said.

"Or he doesn't think we're smart enough to catch the little things." CJ emptied the water bottle while thinking. "With the hookers, he was very careful. The only evidence was one he couldn't have foreseen, my eye-witnessing his vehicle on number three. I think that was a trigger that started him obsessing on me. He became sloppy, started making mistakes. It's as though he knows I'll eventually be exonerated but gets off on seeing how long he can string me out there, confident that even with that, there'll be a black cloud hanging over my head for years afterwards."

"Because you saw him that night?" Stratton asked.

"No. There's something else. I think he has a personal beef against me that's been simmering for some time, probably years. My discovering his third kill put the beef directly on the burner." After a few seconds he grinned. "Pun intended."

Stella snorted again.

Stratton shook his head. "I've got one of the two agents from Denver digging into everything they can find on Tommy Clark, from the time he sucked his momma's…" he looked over at Stella, "ah, cried in his crib."

Stella rolled her eyes. "Would you like me to leave so you guys can talk your man talk?"

CJ reached for her hand. "Don't want you to ever leave, but…"

"But what?"

He let loose of her and handed her the water bottle. "Could you find some more of this, and maybe a Big Mac with extra cheese?"

She snatched the bottle. "Water and no Big Mac, and I'm only serving you because you're in a hospital bed."

"What would you do if I was in a regular bed?"

She grinned and blushed, then turned and walked away.

"Not easy to get her to blush," CJ said.

"I can imagine," Stratton said.

"I'm worried that these guys are going to try for her. I'm protected and Trish is protected. Who's protecting Stella?"

"I know what you're saying, CJ. We just don't have enough man-power."

"Take Bowers off of me; put her with Stella."

"Can't do it. You're technically still in police custody. Have to keep an officer on you."

"Do you think he hasn't figured it out by now, that I'm no longer a suspect?"

"We think the chances are very low that he's found out. Give us a day or two, enough time to do a deep background check on him. For right now instead of in jail, where apparently he could get to you, you're here." Stratton glanced out to where a nurse was talking with another nurse. "Much better view, moderately better food."

"Arguable on the food. Would rather see the inside of my apartment. What about Officer Kramer? You did bring her onboard, right?"

Stratton nodded. "She's been fully briefed and is now our eyes on Clark. Worked with Chief Rague to get her quietly transferred from admin to Tommy Clark's division. Ideally we'd like her assigned as Clark's partner, but not sure if we're ready to go there."

"Awfully risky."

"No doubt. As far as Stella, she has yet to leave the hospital. She's always either with you or your daughter."

"Eventually she is going to have to go home, if for no other reason than to get clean clothes."

"We'll work it out," Stratton assured him. "With five agents and two officers, one of us should be able to cover a trip to her apartment."

"Thank you."

After Stratton left, Stella went to look in on Trish. CJ sipped the water she'd fetched for him, took a deep breath and closed his eyes. He didn't want to fall asleep; instead, he wanted to revisit everything that happened from the time he was first hit with the stun gun to when he woke up in the motel room. All he could see in his inner eye, however, was Trish lying in the street and getting farther away. And then CJ slipped off into a nightmare in which he found Trish and Stella lying next to each other in a dumpster.

"Clinton."

CJ's eyes snapped open to find the one person he didn't expect to see. He started to say something, but found his mouth dry again. He lifted the water bottle for a sip then said, "How are you, Pat?"

"I'm fine, but I'm not here to talk about me. We're divorced because of you and now Patricia was almost killed because of you."

"I didn't do any of this."

"I know that. Agent Stratton has filled me in on the secret. Don't worry, I'll keep the secret until they catch this lunatic. Just because you didn't kill all these women doesn't mean you aren't responsible for putting your daughter, our daughter, in the hospital. What in the hell were you thinking getting her involved in this? Why in the hell did you think you could go off to visit her in Idaho when this lunatic was after you?"

"I…."

"And when were you planning on telling me about Joshua following in your footsteps?"

"I didn't know."

"I'll bet you didn't. Had to do his dad one better. I feel sorry for the woman he marries."

CJ started to open his mouth to say something, then, noticing Stella standing in the doorway, closed it.

"I've said my piece," Pat added, then turned around. As she left, she said to Stella, "You could do better."

Stella looked after her for a few seconds and then looked at CJ.

"Sorry you had to hear all that," he said.

Stella shrugged her shoulders. "She's a mother concerned for her children. Can't fault her for that. She is wrong about one thing for sure, though."

"And what's that?"

"I don't think I could do better. You're not going to get rid of me as easily as you got rid of her."

"I…"

She put her finger on his lips. "Hush. Also, none of this is your fault, and you should be proud of your son." Then she kissed him.

Chapter 50

By day's end both CJ and Trish had been downgraded from critical, first her in the morning and then him around 3:00 in the afternoon. He'd hoped they'd share a room but was told that wasn't possible. They did allow him to visit her in route to his new digs, however. It was a wonderful, but too short, fifteen minutes. He was pleased to learn that Stella could sleep in the room with him and Josh was going to do the same with Trish. Pat was there when he rolled in. She gave him a bit less than the time of day, told Trish she'd return in the morning and promptly departed.

Once CJ was settled, Officer Bowers went home, saying she'd be back at midnight, and one of the Denver FBI agents, Janet Crosby, took over. Josh stopped in a bit later to check on him. The conversation was just as stilted as before, CJ trying to pry out information about Josh becoming an agent, about his love life, about anything, Josh giving up little.

At 9:00 he was wiped out. Just before falling asleep Stella kissed him and then curled up on the cot the nurses provided and opened a book. His eyes fell closed.

CJ awoke just after 1:00 am in a sweat, wide awake and clear headed. He figured it was a nightmare that woke him but it faded so fast he was unable to think about it. He was sure, however, that it had to do with Pat's comments and then Stella's. He couldn't argue with his ex-wife in her belief that he was at fault. Stella was wrong in saying that he wasn't. There was no doubt he'd made some very stupid decisions.

Suddenly it occurred to him that it wasn't a nightmare that woke him. It was something else. He looked over at where Stella should have been sleeping, but she was gone. Did he sense her getting up? Where did she go? Bathroom? Something didn't feel right.

He sat up and swung his feet over the edge of the bed, expecting a wave of dizziness, surprised that there was nothing. He eased off the bed until his feet were in full contact with the floor, then pushed away. He was steady and confident. After considering the IV rack he pulled the IV from his arm and started around the bed.

"No need to go anywhere, Mister Washburn."

CJ looked up from his feet, over to the door that was open a crack, light slicing into the otherwise darkened room. Just inside the door stood a person, the light from the hall illuminating just enough to tell it was a uniformed police officer, face too dark to see features. The voice was male.

"Who are you?"

"If you were Batman, I'd be The Joker."

"Why?"

"Your sweetheart is with your daughter. Your guard, well, she's getting what her father deserved. For right now the rest of your ladies are accounted for, except your ex, of course, but then she isn't your lady anymore, is she? But what about that fine looking attorney. Is she one of your ladies, too?"

"Why are you doing this? What did I do to you?"

"Nothing… to me." He looked out into the hall then turned back to CJ. "When you stopped being a cop, you should have stopped meddling in cop business."

CJ glanced down to see if there was anything in his path. When his eyes came up, the guy was gone. CJ ran to the door and looked out. The back end of a blue uniform disappeared through a door marked by an exit sign with a stairs symbol. CJ sprinted to the same door, burst through, ran up one flight and exploded into another hall. As he had come at it from a different direction in the wheelchair six hours before, he wasn't positive which room belonged to Trish, but one door was fully open, and there were voices.

He sprinted the distance and rushed through the doorway, nearly crashing into a table.

"Dad?"

CJ steadied himself and looked at his daughter and the people around her. "Are you all right?" he sputtered.

"I'm fine. What's wrong? Why…?"

"I just… had a nightmare." He steadied himself again as Stella came to him, and josh grabbed his arm.

"Sit down," Stella said.

"I'm okay." He pulled Josh's fingers from his arm. "Really. I'm okay." He looked around. "Where's Officer Bowers? Wasn't she supposed to come in at midnight?"

"She did," Stella said. "She was with you when I left about thirty minutes ago. I couldn't sleep so I came up to check on Trish. She and Josh weren't sleeping either so I joined them for a bit."

"She's not there now."

"Probably in the bathroom," Josh said, but he was moving toward the door. "Stay here."

Ignoring Josh's order, CJ followed him into the hall, catching him by the arm. "Josh," he said, keeping his voice low. Josh stopped and looked at him. "He was in my room."

"He? He who?"

"The perp. He said that Officer Bowers got what her father deserved."

Josh pushed his dad back toward Trish's room. "Go! Stay with them." With that he took off on a run for the stairs.

"Wait!"

Josh stopped.

"He's a cop." CJ considered that for a moment. "Or else he's dressed as one. I never saw his face."

Josh nodded and took off; CJ returned to Trish and Stella.

"What the hell is going on?" Stella demanded.

CJ suddenly felt exhausted. He pulled over a chair, only then realizing he was wearing the hospital gown and was probably exposing something to someone. He tightened the gown up, sat and then told them about waking up to find the perp in his room, and everything the perp said.

"Oh my God," Trish said and then looked up to a nurse coming in.

All eyes turned toward the nurse who must have seen the look on their faces. "Is everything okay?" she said as she turned her attention directly at Trish. "You having problems?"

Trish opened her mouth and looked at her dad.

"Are you aware of anything happening on the next floor down?" CJ said.

The nurse looked between CJ and Trish. "No. I got a call to check on Patricia, but no details. You're her father, is that right?"

"Yes."

"I'm not so sure you should be up here right now. You should be in your room, resting."

CJ shook his head. "I don't think so."

Trish shook her head. "I don't think so either."

Stella smiled. "I think you're out-voted."

"Aren't you supposed to be under guard, or something?" The nurse said to CJ.

CJ was wondering how to respond, if at all, when another nurse rushed in, male this time. He recognized him from when he come into his room earlier. His name was Michael.

"Carol," Michael said. "We need you right now."

Without questioning him, Carol turned and walked out into the hall, Michael closing the door behind them. CJ, Trish and Stella just looked at each other, all realizing there was nothing to do but wait.

Chapter 51

The next time the door opened, about 45 minutes later, Trish was asleep, Stella was pacing and CJ was wanting to do laps up and down the hall. His shoulder was killing him and his head wasn't doing much better. The worst was the worry about Lisa Bowers.

Dan walked in.

CJ jumped up and Trish woke up. All heads turned to Dan.

"Did you find Lisa?" Stella asked.

Dan held up his hand. "Yes. She's fine, or as fine as can be expected. She was in bed in an unoccupied room not far from yours, CJ, in only her underwear. Her clothes, her weapon, even her shoes, are gone. She's not coherent at this point because it appears she was hit with the same date-rape drug you were hit with and, like you, she was first subdued with a laser gun."

"She was careful," CJ said. "How did he get the drop on her?"

"Because he was in uniform?" Stella asked.

Dan shook his head. "She knew the score and exactly who was on the team. She would have immediately been suspicious of Tommy Clark or any other officer."

"This wasn't Clark," CJ said. "This guy I saw was five-seven, maybe eight. Clark, from what I understand, is closer to six-two."

"Josh didn't tell me the details," Dan said. "Tell me what you saw, what he said."

CJ recounted everything.

"You sure about the height?"

"Very certain," CJ said. "You're six foot, right?"

"Give or take a quarter inch."

"Go stand by the door, turn off the lights."

Dan did so.

"Now, open the door about ten inches."

Dan complied and then stood to the side as CJ had described.

"There's no doubt. He was at least four inches shorter than you, and he was wearing an officer's hat."

Dan started to move and CJ said, "Wait! Step back and inch over closer to the door."

"Like this?" Dan said.

"Yeah. Now move your hand like you're getting ready to grab the edge of the door and step out." Dan did so and CJ said, "Stop! There!"

"What?" Dan said, his hand on the door.

"When the perp reached for the door I noticed something odd. Backlit by the hall light I could see the silhouette of his hand. It's one of those things that sometimes a detective notices but doesn't register until later."

"Fine," Dan said with a bit of impatience. "What did you notice, thou great and honorable Detective Columbo?"

"He only had four digits on his right hand, a thumb and three fingers. He was missing the little finger."

"Maybe he had one curled up and you didn't see it."

"Try curling up your little finger while reaching out. First, it's not easy. Second, why would you? I'm 95% certain this guy was missing his little finger, and…" He pointed in the air as though coming up with another idea, "…he touched the door."

"Well, that's certainly something. Anything else you noted about him?"

CJ shook his head. "He was otherwise in the shadows. I was going to rush him, but had to glance down to be sure there was nothing in my path. When I looked up, he was gone. The next look I got was a brief view of his back side as he was going through the door to the stairs. I can only assume he went down from there. I came straight up to here."

"Did you notice any nurses, wandering patients, witnesses?"

"No one."

Dan pulled out his phone and punched a number. He pressed the phone to his ear and after a few seconds said, "Dan here. We need to put an officer, or someone on Washburn's hospital room; lock it down as a crime scene. We need to get people on the door, dusting for fingerprints near the door edge, knee high to shoulder high." He looked up at the ceiling while he listened. "Yeah, I know. Cat's outa the bag so I don't see much point anymore. We need to find out who's been opening the damn bag."

When he hung up CJ said, "Cat's outa the bag?"

"This guy seems to know our every move. The pretense that you're the prime suspect isn't working. There's no point in keeping you in custody any longer, and it's taking too many resources. I think we need to come up with another safe house where we can keep you all together and under protection."

"What about Gianna Onassis?" CJ asked. "He as good as threatened her, and Pat, too."

"I'll get someone to check on both of them. Meanwhile, I'll make sure Josh or someone is here with you all until we can get you broke out of here. No later than a few hours, I hope." He looked between Trish and CJ. "If you all still need medical attention, they'll have to come to you."

"I'm for that," CJ said.

Trish nodded. "Me, too."

"Whoever you bring in has to be fully vetted," CJ said. "This leak has to stop."

"Let me do my job, CJ."

"The way I see it, everybody's been doing their jobs," CJ said, his voice taking on an irritated edge. "This guy is getting the information anyway."

"We're working on it."

"Well, you'd better work harder!" CJ yelled.

Stella put her hand on his arm. He took a breath and calmed himself. "I've lost count of the number of women he's killed, and now he's threatening every woman even remotely close to me. You're lucky the guy left Lisa alive."

They stared at each other for a few seconds before Dan responded. "Have you finished venting?"

CJ didn't say anything.

"One question is," Dan said, "why did he leave Lisa alive?"

"Maybe because he's a cop and he can't kill another cop."

"We're not so sure he's a cop, now," Dan said.

"What do you mean? I saw him, saw the uniform?"

"We believe he was wearing Lisa's uniform. She was left in the bed, just two doors down from your room, by the way, in only her underwear. Her uniform was gone. He left behind, though, the garb of a hospital nurse."

"That's how he got close to her," Stella said. "She thought he was a nurse."

"Right. After changing into her uniform, he visited CJ and then left the hospital. We actually have a witness who saw him go out shortly after that. Didn't get a much better view of him, unfortunately."

"That certainly confirms it wasn't Clark. He couldn't have gotten into Lisa's uniform, but the man I saw could have."

"Right."

"What about the guards who were with me when I was hit with the drug?" CJ said. "Stratton was going to interview them. Do you know anything about that?"

"Yeah. Both guards remember the incident; neither can recall who the individual was, more concerned with their charge, that being you. We also tried to figure out who else might have been a witness to it, but no luck there."

"The blue code of honor," CJ said.

"What's that?" Trish said.

"No officer will rat out a fellow officer," CJ said.

"That's stupid."

"It's a constant debate across the country, very heated at times; however, it may be that code that saved Lisa's life," CJ said.

"I thought you just determined that it wasn't a cop," Stella said. "He stole her uniform and he's too short to be Tommy Clark."

"Still doesn't mean that he wasn't a cop, just not Tommy. One thing he told me was to stay out of cop business. 'Stop meddling,' were his exact words."

Dan nodded. "Only a cop would say that."

"Or the partner of a cop," CJ said.

Everybody looked at CJ.

"What are you saying?" Stella said. "You think the partner of a gay cop is doing this because somewhere along the line you wronged his partner?"

"I don't know. The notion only just now came to me. I've been thinking for a while that there are two people, that the perp has a partner. It just never occurred to me that they might be life partners."

"A husband, husband team?" Dan said. "It's certainly an angle that can't be ignored."

"Do we know if Tommy Clark is gay?" CJ asked.

"We know very little about Clark. Sexual persuasion is not something that's noted on personnel files."

"Was Lisa sexually violated?" CJ asked.

Dan shook his head. "No. It doesn't appear so, but we haven't received the final report as yet. The fact that he left her underwear on tells me sex wasn't his intent. He only wanted the uniform."

"And to show how close he could get to me," CJ added. "He wanted to show how close he could get to anybody."

Silence filled the room for a time as everyone digested what had been said.

"Officer Kramer!" CJ blurted. "Is there a chance he knows about her? Has anyone checked on her?"

Dan pulled out his phone again, found the name in the contact list and hit Call.

After a long interim when it didn't seem like she was going to answer, CJ said, "Is she married, live alone? Do you know?"

Josh walked in just as Dan held up a finger. "Officer Kramer, this is Detective Payne. Is everything all right there?" He listened and then held his hand out, thumb up.

CJ, Stella and Trish all relaxed. Josh pulled up a chair and sat.

"The perp made a run on Officer Bowers tonight," Dan continued and then went on to detail what took place.

"No," he said. "We don't want you breaking cover. Bowers will be okay once the drug wears off." He then explained that it wasn't Tommy Clark and the theory that it may still be him with a partner, possibly gay. "We still need your eyes and ears in there, but be very careful. See if you can learn from others in his division as to his sexual leanings, cop to cop chit-chat kind of thing. It's strictly a theory, a weak one at that, so tread lightly. The Feds are still digging into his background. Am hoping to learn something later this morning."

He went on to assure her again that Lisa Bowers was going to be fine, and to call him in the noon hour and they'd exchange updates.

When he hung up, Stella said, "She's not alone, is she?"

Dan shook his head. "I know she's not married but I heard a male voice ask who it was, so she must have a boyfriend." To Josh he said, "How are things going down there?"

"They're sealing off Dad's room. Waiting on the forensics team to finish up with the room in which Officer Bowers was found. Agent Platt is keeping an eye on it all."

"Good. You're going to stay with these guys, is that right?"

"For the duration."

Chapter 52

At 6:00 Agent Stratton walked in. Nurses had already been in and out preparing for getting rid of their charges.

"You're both being taken out of here in thirty minutes."

"Is the hospital okay with that?" Stella asked.

"They're thrilled. They want the police disruption gone, so the sooner for them, the happier they'll be. For you all, we need something with which we can have better control. This is just too wide open. We've secured a safe house west of the city, about twenty minutes away. We're working with Chief Rague to put together a team of officers to maintain around the clock surveillance in six hour shifts. Each one is being closely vetted."

"Do you know if Clark has any idea he's being looked at?" CJ asked.

"We believe he's still in the dark; however, our focus is no longer on him. Other than the time he's taken off, nothing else has pointed to him."

"What about the background check?" Stella asked.

"I'll have that this morning, have had New York people working on it, but I think it's a dead end."

"New York?"

"That's where he grew up," Stratton said, "and where he lived until he joined the academy and later took the job on the Tucson Police Force."

"You'll find something," CJ said. "I'm certain of it."

"I know you want Clark for this, CJ, but there's just not enough there. We need to put our efforts into figuring out who it is, not wasting it on who it probably isn't. Just so that you know, I had a set of eyes on his apartment building last night from the time he got home from work until this guy showed up in your room. Clark never left the apartment. I pulled the surveillance fifteen minutes ago. Like I said, it's a dead end. Once I have the report, I'm certain that line of investigation will be history."

"Does Dan know you're quitting on Clark?"

"We just talked about it. He's pulling Officer Kramer out. Would rather use her on the safe house detail."

CJ wasn't pleased, but he refrained from making any more comments. He liked Clark even more as the serial killer and was convinced that the partner; however, the term partner was defined, was the perpetrator who took down Lisa Bowers. He looked over at Josh who'd provided no input into the conversation. He held no expression as to whether he agreed or disagreed with the senior agent. Of course he'd agree. He was too junior as yet to have his own mind. He was just a body the bureau utilized to meet their missions as they came about. He also realized that although he'd been officially loaned from Denver, Josh had done nothing but guard his family. Was Stratton being nice when he made the request to Denver or was it a means of keeping him in the loop but out of the way because he was too close to the players and too junior to be of a benefit. He'd certainly want the best senior agents he could get playing this game. And Josh probably didn't mind because his number one priority was his sister; let everyone else run around Tucson chasing a serial killer.

Stratton's phone chirped. "Stratton," he said into it. "Thanks."

To the group in the hospital room, he said, "Your chariot is in-route. Am told your clothes have been picked up, CJ, so you don't have to wear the prom dress out of here."

"Thanks." CJ hadn't even thought about the hospital gown.

"How's the shoulder doing?"

"Either it's getting better or the pain killer has been improved. I feel that I could actually use it except that they've got it so strapped down. How is Lisa doing?"

"She's semi-wake. As with you, they administered Romazicon."

"What is that?" Trish asked.

"They call it a benzodiazepine antagonist. A big term for a drug that will counteract the Rohypnol."

Stratton's phone chirped again. After he answered it he left, saying he'd be right back.

Josh got up and went to his sister, asked how she was feeling. CJ watched them as they interacted, proud of them both, glad that Josh had come, wishing that it'd been under different circumstances, wondering if there was anything he could do to counteract Josh's anger. Maybe I need an anger antagonist, CJ thought.

It was actually closer to an hour before they were rolled into the elevator. When they came out of the elevator CJ realized they were being taken out through the morgue. "Are there still press outside?" he asked of Stratton.

"You have no idea. They're lined up around the parking lot as though the president was having a Mideast summit in here. We're not even sure this is going to work, though we have agents standing by to intercept and block if it appears there's going to be a chase."

The van door was open, the wheelchair lift down. CJ was wheeled in first, against his demand that he could walk just fine.

"You stay in this chair or we leave you to the vultures," Stratton said, pointing out to a couple of satellite trucks visible in the near distance.

CJ remained seated as the lift rose. Someone grabbed his chair from behind and pulled him into the van. "I'm Joseph Foronda," said the guy as he navigated him into place. "I'll be you all's constant companion nurse for the next thirty hours or so."

When Trish was in, along with Stella and Stratton–Josh left them to follow in his car–and the van was moving, Joseph continued his introduction. "You all can call me Joe. Although the hospital was real glad to discharge you, the administrators thought it prudent to maintain your medical care through tomorrow morning, just to be sure there are no unforeseen medical complications."

"They just want to be sure we don't make off with the wheelchairs," CJ said.

Joe grinned. "Well, yeah, there's that too, along with concerns over liability should you all have relapses, fall out of the chairs, or exert yourselves playing bingo."

"Where're you taking us, to an old folk's home?" CJ asked.

Joe laughed. "Sorry for the bingo reference. I'm also an on-call nurse for several senior care facilities. Little inside joke. I should be a little more politically sensitive. Not the first time my mouth has gotten me in trouble."

CJ decided this guy wasn't going to be so bad. "You're not in trouble as long as you let me out of this wheelchair when we get wherever we're going."

"Not a problem. You get dizzy and fall down, you're back in it. We straight on that?"

CJ nodded and grinned at him. "Straight as a reformed alcoholic in a twelve-step program."

"You know a bit about that?"

"No! no. A joke I picked up from a client one time."

"I hope it's a joke cause if I catch you with alcohol, you'll be back in the chair. It doesn't mix with the crap you have in your system."

CJ nodded. "Gotcha." A couple fingers of Jack Daniels sure would have hit the spot.

Chapter 53

The safe house was a ranch style on ten acres of desert cactus at the base of Gates Pass, west of the city. "The owners, or past owners in this case," Stratton said as they pulled up a long, dirt drive, "were an elderly couple who passed away, one right after the other, back in November. The kids live in the Seattle area and have pretty much ignored the property until this last month when they hired someone to clean it out and prepare it for placing on the market. The state it is currently in, I'm told, is almost perfect for us. Four bedrooms and a big kitchen. We won't have provisions until later in the morning."

"Any idea how long we'll be here," CJ asked.

"Wish I could answer that. This guy doesn't let the moss grow around his feet, nor around yours. Speaking of that, I've had a fresh set of eyes poring through your case files and records since and before you left the force, looking for anyone who could be holding a grudge against you. He's Agent DeBonski of Phoenix. Sometime today he's going to come here and sit with you and Stella. He's going to bring what he's learned from the files and start picking your memories."

Good, CJ thought. Maybe something will come to light that proves Tommy Clark is the one. In response to Stratton he only nodded his head.

Stella said, "I think before your agent talks to us we need to get some sleep. It's been a long night."

"I'll tell him not to come before 3:00."

As they pulled in CJ recognized Dan's Tahoe. An older, non-descript car was parked next to it. Agent Crosby, Janet Crosby was how she was introduced, stopped the van at the bottom of a convenient wheelchair ramp.

"We got lucky," Stratton said. "The husband half of the couple was wheelchair bound for the last ten years, so the house is wheelchair friendly."

Dan came out and down the ramp, followed by a female police officer. "Is that Officer Kramer?" CJ asked.

"Good guess."

Two more government-looking cars pulled in as CJ and Trish were being pushed up the ramp. CJ recognized Agent Crane but not the other in an obvious fed suit. Another car pulled in and parked facing out, not government issue. Josh got out.

"Looks like you got away clean," Crane said, after everyone was in the house and gathered in the living area.

Stratton introduced the new face, Agent Brown, from Phoenix. One more Phoenix agent was on his way, plus a small team from Washington, DC would arrive in the afternoon.

"This case has been elevated to the highest level," Stratton said. "As a result all the stops have been pulled. Expense accounts are wide open. We have to get this guy and we have to get him fast."

Joe returned from inspecting the bedrooms. "We've got linens but I still need to make up the beds. Patricia gets the master bedroom because the bed is suited for someone disabled." He looked at Trish. "That's where you're heading right now, with a light sedative."

"I can't wait," Trish said, her head bobbing with exhaustion. "I don't think I need the sedative."

"Never-the-less," Joe said. "You two," pointing to CJ and Stella, "I'm assuming you'll be together."

Stella nodded.

"Bedroom two, right next door. I'll let you make up your own bed." Joe swung Trish's chair around. "Let's get to it. Bodies don't heal without rest."

CJ didn't think he'd be able to sleep.

CJ's eyes popped open. He listened while looking around the darkened room. A muffled exchange of voices from beyond the closed bedroom door, along with Stella's light snore next to him, reminded him where he was. He relaxed and rolled his head to see the bedside clock. 1:42. He eased to the edge of the bed and swung his feet to the floor, pleased that there was no dizziness, only minor pain in his shoulder, none around the bandages on his head.

After doing his business in the bathroom, including removing the bandages binding his arm and then splashing water on his face, he joined the agents in the dining room where they'd set up an office with laptop computers, large monitors and a printer. Stratton was on one laptop, another new FBI face on the other. The new face glanced up, nodded, and returned to his task.

"You're looking better," Stratton said.

"Feeling better."

"Sit down," Joe ordered, appearing as if by magic. "Let me take your vitals. How's the shoulder feeling?"

"Great," CJ said as he sat down.

To Stratton CJ said, "What did you find out from New York?"

"Like I expected, dead-end. No police record, not even a sealed one. Went to academy, graduated in '09 and joined the Tucson force. Squeaky clean." He rose from his chair and headed toward the kitchen, dropping the report in front of CJ along the way. "You're welcome to read it. There are sandwich makings, so help yourself."

"Sit still while I get your blood pressure," Joe said.

CJ slowly paged through the report until Joe was done.

"You're looking normal," Joe said. "Normal is good. Let me see your eyes." When CJ turned his head, Joe looked from one eye to the other, back and forth a couple of times, then shined a light and did it again. "Much better than this morning. Still, no bar fights and no pulling your gun and shooting people."

"Police confiscated my gun. Not much chance."

"I hate it when they do that. Is Stella awake?"

"No."

"Good. I swear she looked worse than you. She's not one of my charges but I'll give her a once over when she's up."

"How is Trish?"

"Sleeping like a baby. Her brother has been checking on her more often than I have."

"Is he with her now?"

"No. I just came from there when I heard you get up. Are you sure you're okay without the shoulder wrap?"

CJ did a slow windmill with his arm. "A little sore, but I think I'm okay."

"Josh is out walking the perimeter with Officer Kramer," Stratton said from the kitchen. "The next six hour shift starts at 4:00 when Kramer's relief shows up. My agents are supplementing. Been rotating them in and out regularly. It's too hot to stay out there very long."

"Have Gianna Onassis and my ex been advised?"

Stratton walked back in with a soda and a sandwich on a plate. "Crane made the visit to your ex this morning. Her husband has taken the next few days off. Crane tells me she blames you for everything."

"Of course she does. Really can't blame her."

"She was a bit pissed when Crane wouldn't tell her where her daughter had been taken."

"I'll bet."

"As far as Ms. Onassis, she told Crane that she's a big girl and can take care of herself. Her purse is armed and licensed, by the way."

"Really? I had no idea."

"She impresses me as a woman who knows how to use it, too." With that Stratton sat down at his computer and took a bite of the sandwich.

CJ remembered the sparring that took place between the two of them in the interview room and wondered if the tenor in Stratton's voice indicated something more than official interest in Gianna Onassis. Stratton was single, CJ was sure, so....

CJ stood and went into the living room, found a comfortable chair and sat. He continued to go through the report. It appeared that

Tommy Clark and his brother, Kevin, were raised by a single mom. An "A" student with a "B" sprinkled here and there. Chicken pox and tonsillitis, no hospital stays. CJ wondered if Clark was his father's name or if his mother was ever married. He paged through looking for any information on the father, but found nothing. As a matter of fact the only thing on the mother was that she was deceased, died in January, just seven months ago.

He put the report aside. Stratton was right; there was nothing.

In the kitchen he made a sandwich and with that and a bottle of water, returned to the chair. He ate the sandwich, staring at where he'd dropped the report on the coffee table, until Josh and Officer Kramer came in. Josh fetched a bottle of water, went down to check on his sister and then returned to sit on the sofa.

"How're you feeling, Dad?"

CJ felt something jump inside of him. His son, who he hadn't heard from for seven years, who in the last few days hadn't said more than a handful of words unbidden, actually inquired as to his father's well being.

"Not too bad actually, Josh, and I haven't taken a pain killer yet today." CJ stressed for a dozen heartbeats over what to say to keep the exchange going without making it look like he was prying into his life. "I assume you've read that," he said, pointing to the report on the coffee table."

"Yes."

"Not much there."

"No."

"I still want to like him for it," CJ said. "What do you think?"

"Not my call."

"Ah." CJ smiled. "You haven't earned your thinking badge."

"What do you mean by that?"

"You can't earn the right to think and express your thoughts on a case until you're a more seasoned agent; you haven't earned your thinking badge."

After ten seconds of feeling the glare from his son, CJ wanted to retract all those words. If he wanted a relationship with him he shouldn't be giving him a hard time about being a rookie."

He softened his voice. "Is this your first case, your first time in the field?"

Josh's jaw tightened. "Yes. I have a lot of office duties and responsibilities."

CJ looked toward the dining room and then rose from his seat and went over to sit next to Josh. Keeping his voice low he said, "I know you've come for Trish, but while we're here, in this house, and Joe is keeping an eye on her, you have an opportunity to show your stuff. If you want in the field you have to show them it's worth their while to put you in the field."

Josh considered his dad's words for a time and then said, "What do you think I should be doing?"

"Walking the perimeter is important, no doubt about that, but what gets attention is contributing to solving the case, actively involved in figuring out who this guy is. Even if what you discover isn't what breaks it, at least they can see you digging… thinking."

Josh nodded. "Okay."

"Like I said, I still want to like Tommy Clark for this. What do you think?"

"I'm kind of the same way. What you've said about there being partners makes a lot of sense to me."

"So, you and I have both been through this report and agree that it is pretty empty."

"Right."

"I think it's in there. We're just overlooking it. What are we both missing?"

Josh reached for the report, enclosed in a clear plastic report cover, and opened it. CJ leaned closer to look at it with him. They went through page-by-page and then put it aside again.

"He has the intelligence, as per the profile some of us put together."

"Who's that?"

“Detective Payne and Dave McDermott, Lisa’s father. He’s a retired police sergeant. Trish and Stella were there, as well as Lisa.”

“Krystal told me it was she and Lisa who dug up Tommy Clark’s name.”

“He and two others, yes. We eliminated the other two right off, but Tommy Clark fit the bill until the guy showed in my hospital room last night a half foot too short. I’d already been thinking partners because I don’t know how one person could have abducted Trish and me by himself.”

The two of them sat back, one a younger version of the other, neither realizing how much resemblance they shared.

“What about the brother?” Josh said.

CJ considered that for a moment. “The report said younger brother but didn’t mention age. I’d certainly like to know where he is right now.” He picked up the report again and opened it. “Mom died in January. It might be worth finding out how she died. I don’t think this report is complete until those details are filled in.”

Josh took the report from CJ’s hand and stood. When he disappeared through the dining room door, CJ sat back and smiled. The chances that the answers to those questions would lead to anything were likely remote, but the conversation he just had with his son filled something inside of him that had been empty for a very long time.

Chapter 54

The kitchen had a table barely big enough for four people to eat a modest breakfast. CJ and Stella shared it with Agent DeBonski. They were poring through his notes which included photocopies of two cases in which CJ was involved the year before he left the force. DeBonski also had notes on cases CJ had worked since becoming a PI. CJ had a hard time not taking offense that his office was now free FBI property.

"I remember this one," Stella said, one of the reports open in front of them. "It was right after I started working for Clint." She pointed to a note on one page for the agent's benefit. "That's my handwriting. After a nasty divorce in which the wife was rewarded the winter property..."

"Winter property?" the agent broke in.

"They were snowbirds; spent half of the year here and the other half in Illinois, Chicago area. She got the home here, which was mortgage-free. He got the Chicago home which was mortgage-maxed. She got alimony and the dog."

"And he got pissed."

"Exactly. She left for a ten-day cruise in January of '08 and came back to a vandalized house, spray-painted slur on every wall inside, broken furniture, power breaker smashed, food spoiled; even broken roof tiles. He lobbed big rocks from the cactus garden onto the roof and cracked more than a dozen tiles. You name it, he did it.

"One of the neighbors who'd heard the rocks hitting the tiles, looked out. It was middle of the night and all he saw was a person, couldn't tell age or gender, throwing rocks. He called 911 but by the time a patrol car got there, the person was gone. The damage wasn't discovered until the wife returned. When she accused her ex-husband, he claimed he'd been in Chicago the entire time. Since his office was his home, no employees or coworkers to verify his whereabouts, it was his word against hers. She had no proof."

"So she hired you to find proof," DeBonski said to CJ.

"Yes, and I would have never found it if not for her. Utilizing some contacts I had and calling in favors I'd built up from my time on the force, I managed to obtain passenger lists of flights to and from Tucson for the days before and after the night in question. His name wasn't on them. When I mentioned that to my client she said, 'What about his alias?' Apparently, his business wasn't all that above board. He had another name with a driver's license and credit card based on a second Social Security number. Anyway, the alias was in fact on the passenger lists, coming in the day before, leaving the next morning. Put that together with his fingerprints left on items she'd purchased after the divorce was final, she had him by the you know whats. Then he faced federal charges with using a social security number that belonged to a baby who'd died the same year he was born. The guy went down hard and was pissed more than ever."

"So it's possible he's back and is wreaking revenge," the agent said.

"The threats he made were more at my client than at me, but you never know. I'd contact her to be sure she hasn't heard from him. As far as I know, however, he might still be incarcerated in Illinois."

CJ sat back for a moment, thinking about it and then pointed at the case files the agent had laid out. "To be truthful with you, incarcerated or not, this guy isn't a murderer. If he was he'd go after his ex-wife, not random women. Neither are any of these others you've dug up. This seems like a big waste of time."

The agent leaned forward, elbows on the table. "The person we're looking for is a psychopath disguised as someone you know or someone you've done business with in the last few months, or years."

"Right, but what you also appear to be looking for is someone who's entire goal in life is to get back at me. That's not what's going on here. If I was his prime target, he wouldn't have started killing women in hopes that I'd show up at one of his crime scenes. He would have come at me head-on. Instead, I showed up in the middle of his..." he waved his hands in the air, "whatever you call it, psychopathic game, and he saw an opportunity to divert the focus onto someone else for a while, a fun little side game, you might say, in his psychopathic world. Not only has he had the opportunity to make a run at me, but he also has had an inside track to always be able to know where I am and who I'm with." He pushed from the table, rattling it and the agents nearly full coffee mug. "I'm a mouse he's having fun playing with."

Realizing he was shouting and noticing DeBonski's sudden reach for his coffee, CJ said, "Sorry."

Stella jumped up and got a paper towel to hand to the agent.

"Our perp *has* to be a cop," CJ continued. "Looking anywhere else is a waste of time."

Agent Stratton, who obviously had heard CJ's rant from the operation center in the dining room, walked in.

"We hear what you're saying, CJ, but all ground has to be covered. We can't not look left just because we think he's somewhere to the right. We're being thorough."

Josh suddenly appeared in the doorway from the living room, where, CJ knew, he'd been on the phone with the field office in New York. Although Stratton had not thought it worthwhile pursuing further study into Clark, he did see the necessity to continue to be "thorough" and so told Josh to do the follow up on Clark's mother and brother. CJ was certain that all Stratton was doing was pushing Josh out of the way, keeping him busy on the lower odds side of the investigation.

"We might have something," Josh said.

Everyone turned and looked at him.

"Actually it might be three things," Josh added.

"Okay, Kid," Stratton said. "Spit it out."

"This is stuff that should have been in the first report."

"Fine. What is it?"

CJ winked at Josh and nodded for him to continue.

Josh grinned at his father and then turned his attention to Stratton.

"Tommy Clark's 18-year-old little brother, Kevin, relocated here to Tucson after their mother died in January."

"So he's living with or near his brother. That's not much help. What else you got?"

"When Mom died Kevin inherited her vehicle, a 2010 GMC Savana Van, color black."

"Not bad but still coincidental. What's the third?"

"Their mother was murdered, strangled, her body discovered in a dumpster, wrapped in an old quilt. Case is still open, no leads."

Stratton's mouth fell open. "Why wasn't this in the report?"

"No idea. I think they're busy pointing fingers at each other."

"The same fingers that were probably busy scratching their asses when they should have been getting it all in there the first time." He started heading back to the dining room. "This changes our entire focus. I'll get on the line with Chief Rague and then we'll rig up and bring this psychopath in."

Just as Stratton hit the door, Josh said, "You don't want the fourth?"

Stratton stopped and turned, his hand still on the swinging door. "I thought you said there were three?"

"I miss-counted. Sometimes I do that."

Stratton looked at CJ who just grinned back at him.

"Fine! What's the fourth?"

"Mom was a mobile prostitute, her van a rolling bedroom."

Chapter 55

"What the hell do you mean, you're waiting?" CJ couldn't believe his ears. "You've got everything you need to take him down. Motive, means, everything. No judge is going to deny the warrant. What happened to rigging up and bringing this psychopath in? Did you talk to the chief?"

"Actually, CJ, I did. Where do you think I've been for the last three hours?"

"Then what are you waiting for?"

"After we got past the knee-jerk reaction, we realized that we haven't enough to even print off a warrant, let alone get a judge to sign it. What we have is the mother murdered in the same fashion; however, we cannot put the boys anywhere near her at the time. Tommy was here in Tucson. Although off duty and unaccounted for during those two days, there are no records that he flew to New York, or even left Arizona, not even any out of state credit card transactions for that time period. There is record that he flew to New York the day after she died, though there is no record of a return flight. It's believed he returned with Kevin in their mother's van. As for Kevin, he was in the hospital after an accident in his apartment building. Not only can't we place either of them at the scene of their mother's death, we can't put them even close to any of the crime scenes here. As far as motive, nada for killing off Mom."

"So what are we waiting for, another woman to turn up in a dumpster?"

"The New York office is doing more digging into the mother's murder, and your son is doing a damn good job of staying on top of that. We've now got eyes on Tommy around the clock."

"Does Tommy know he's being considered for this, that he's being watched,?" Stella asked.

"We don't think so. I'm using only agents for that. In the Tucson Police Department, only Chief Rague and Detective Payne know about it."

"What about Kevin and the van," CJ said. "Is there an APB out on the van?"

"An APB would go out everywhere and even though Tommy is off duty, he may have a scanner and could know about it immediately."

"But since you have eyes on him, they'd be able to see his reaction. If he tries to disappear, you'd know for sure he's the perp and could grab him. If he comes in saying, 'Hey, that's my brother's van, what the hell guys?' we'll have reason to believe he's not the perp."

"Just because someone appears to act guilty, doesn't provide meat for a warrant. What we're more afraid of is if he is the perp, upon hearing the APB broadcast he'll have reason to suspect that there are eyes on him. Once he identifies who the eyes are, which wouldn't be too hard once he knows they're there, he'll more easily slip away. And then we'd lose both of them until bodies start turning up in some other part of the country."

"So, like I said, you're waiting for another woman to turn up in a dumpster with the hopes that this time there'd be connecting evidence?"

"We're waiting for a break, CJ. No, that's wrong. We're digging for a break; we just haven't found it yet. Yes, we'd like to get him before he kills again. We could bring Tommy in, and question him as to his whereabouts during all of the murders, but if he doesn't confess or we don't find something that can tie him, we'd have to release him and then what? You've been a cop. You know how it works."

Josh came in, pushing his phone into his belt holster. He sat down. "We may have motive."

"You've been on the phone with New York, right?" CJ said.

"Yes, and they're scrambling. It seems that this is not the first time little brother has been in the hospital or has been seen at the emergency clinic. This is the third time he's had an accident in his apartment building, or," Josh made a pair of quote signs with his fingers, "*fallen* down the stairs. He has been seen in emergency a total of eight times in the last six years."

"Mom's a bit aggressive in her discipline?" Stratton said.

"The previous time, March of 2011, he'd fallen down the stairs and fractured a leg. Hospital records show that it was Tommy Clark who checked him out."

"Child welfare was never called in?" CJ said.

"Actually they've been called twice, per the records," Josh said, taking a seat. "Both times Kevin claimed he was clumsy."

"Okay, so we have a maybe motive," Stratton said. "We still can't put either of the boys close enough to even have an opportunity of killing her, which puts us nowhere. We can have all the motive in the world, but if there is no way they could have physically been there, they couldn't have done it. We have absolutely no other suspects, whether a single perp or a partnership."

The room went quiet for a long time, each man, and woman in the case of Stella, deep into their own thoughts. CJ was so sure it was Tommy Clark or his brother, or both, but he had to admit that Stratton was right. It wasn't like they knew they did it and just couldn't find enough hard evidence to get the warrant. That would be one thing. Now it appeared that they couldn't have done it, despite a reasonable motive.

"The brothers make too much sense to give up on this easy," Josh said. "I still believe they did it. We're just overlooking something."

"And what may that be?" Stratton said, the tone in his voice obviously humoring the junior agent, expecting a junior agent kind of answer.

"We need to get into their shoes and then, like them, become psychotic."

"Expound, please, Mister Washburn," Stratton said.

Not taken back by the tone in the senior agent's voice, Josh continued. "Let's look at the family. The boys are very different. Tommy is six-two, two-twenty-five. All muscle. Is that right?"

Stratton nodded. "That's what his personnel file says."

"Kevin is five-seven, one-forty-two according to his latest hospital records, a runt compared to his brother. Tommy was in high school football and wrestling, got good grades. Kevin, on the other hand, did not participate in sports and was mediocre at best as far as academics. Mom may have been happy with Tommy as a child, thus didn't find it necessary to be physical with him, or if she did, he was big enough to stand up against her and take it without serious injury, and maybe dish some back."

"I'd be willing to bet it was the latter," CJ broke in. "And with a strong abusive mother, the boys probably had a very close bond, Tommy being very protective of Kevin."

Josh nodded. "Looking back at the span of Kevin's urgent care visits, they all occurred after Tommy left home."

"Tommy was no longer there to protect Kevin," CJ said. "Mom had full access to her runt and disappointment of a son, so she kept beating him up, sometimes throwing him down the stairs."

"So," Josh continued, "Kevin lands in the hospital on Thursday, January 26th, a broken arm and concussions. Tommy finds out that night and on Friday, flies to New York, kills his mother and then returns on Saturday. He receives the call after getting home that afternoon, that his mother is dead, so he takes bereavement and flies to New York on Sunday. He buries his mom then packs Kevin into his mother's prostitution van and brings him back to Tucson."

CJ picked up the narrative. "The thing is, he is not fully satisfied with killing his mother. He is angry at all prostitutes in general and after a few months, he starts grabbing them off the street and killing them. In some twisted logic way, he is ridding the world of a few cockroaches."

"Cockroaches?" Stella said.

"Just trying to be in their heads, think like they're probably thinking."

"So for four months they do nothing except start a new life for Kevin here," Stratton said. "Why did they start killing all of a sudden, do you think, Josh? What are they teaching you in the academy nowadays?"

"What they taught us was how to think beyond the obvious; how to think like the criminal."

"So why did they start up?"

"First, Tommy may have gotten a rush from killing Mom, maybe a greater sense of power than anything he has ever felt. He may have become a cop for all the right reasons, to catch and put away the bad guys. After a time most cops get disillusioned with the legal system. Of those, most stick it out with the confidences that they are doing the best they can. Of the rest, most walk away, but a few start taking things into their own hands, become judge, jury and executioner."

"In this case, police, judge, jury and executioner," CJ said.

"Exactly," Josh said. "After four months the warm glow from Mom's kill wore off and he started looking for a new glow."

"Or," CJ said, "something triggered it again. As a cop could he have been involved in a case having to do with a prostitute and abuse? Maybe he saw something in her that reminded him of his mother. Has that ever been looked at, whether Tommy was involved in an official capacity with the first victim before she was murdered?"

"Good point," Stratton said. "I'll get Dan to pursue that line of investigation." He looked over at Josh. "Okay, Junior Washburn." He shifted his gaze over to CJ. "Senior Washburn. The theory is great, I have to admit. We still have a problem. How did Tommy get to New York and back in two days without leaving a trail?"

Josh, who was sitting in one of the kitchen's swivel chairs, swung around to face Stella. "The same way the husband got from Chicago to Tucson to ransack his ex-wife's home."

"False identification!" Stella said.

CJ held out his hand to Josh, open palm up. "An alias! Of course."

Stratton considered that for a few seconds. "That shouldn't be too hard to confirm now that we know what we're looking for."

"A single individual who flew to New York on Friday and returned on Saturday. If there's more than one, there won't be many," Josh said.

"You could also bounce that name against passengers flying to Idaho and back," CJ said. "You get a match, we've got him for sure."

"No, we don't. We'd still have to tie the name to him."

"There will be video monitors you FBI guys can tap into."

Stratton stood. "It's not that easy."

"Don't you guys have facial recognition software or something?" Stella said.

"You watch too much TV. Yes, it exists; however, it has a very questionable reliability factor. I still trust trained eyes looking at every face. Takes time but if he's in the crowd, they'll see him. First thing we have to do is find the name that's common to flights out of either Tucson or Phoenix on the dates in question, and into New York and Spokane, Washington. Spokane is the closest major airport to Moscow, Idaho. Once we have that then it's just a matter of matching the security ticket scans with video. If it's him we should have enough to take to the judge to get a warrant for his arrest."

Stratton turned toward the operational center in the dining room. "You guys hang loose. I've got to get everything rolling."

Sometime later CJ, Stella and Josh puttered together around the kitchen, cleaning up after plowing through four large take out pizzas. Agents had come and gone; now only Agents Stratton and Crane remained in the house, sequestered in the dining room. Agent Crosby and Officer Kramer were out walking the perimeter as daylight faded. Silence prevailed in the kitchen until the leftovers were in the refrigerator and the dishwasher was loaded. Josh grabbed a wet cloth and started wiping the table and counter. Stella followed with a dry dish towel.

"The killing of Mom was premeditated," Josh said.

"Of course it was premeditated if he flew to New York under an alias to carry it out," CJ said.

"No, I mean premeditated in the sense that he obtained the alias months back, just for this purpose."

"You're saying it wasn't spontaneous in the sense that he got angry when Kevin landed in the hospital again?" Stella said.

Josh threw the cloth into the sink and sat down. "That's what I'm saying. We know that when Kevin broke his leg March of last year,

Tommy went to him. Would your brother come visit you from clean across the country if you broke your leg?"

Stella and CJ sat down at the table with Josh.

"I only have a sister and I'm sure she wouldn't. I doubt she'd even come from Albuquerque, and we're pretty close."

"Here's what I think. Mom knocked Kevin down the stairs last year, which according to the records may have been the second time. Tommy, who was very protective of his little brother, went to New York to deliver a promise to his mother, that being, if it ever happened again, he'd kill her. He may have actually wanted to kill her at that time, but was smart enough to know he'd probably not get away with it. Not all that optimistic that his mother would listen, or certain that she wouldn't, Tommy came home and started making plans. Police officers know how to find people who create false identifications, especially in a community this close to the border. He found one such dealer who could also provide a usable social security number and had false identification made and then, just like the husband in Chicago, applied for a credit card under that name. The next time Mom got physical with Kevin, in January of this year, Tommy was ready, and he didn't hesitate. A promise was a promise."

"And it worked so well, he couldn't resist pulling it out again to follow me to Idaho."

"Exactly. That may be his undoing."

"We can certainly hope so."

Chapter 56

CJ rolled out of bed just after 7:00. Stella was already gone. He brushed his teeth, threw water on his face and opened the bedroom door in time to find Joe Foronda walking by.

"Mornin'" Joe said.

CJ returned the greeting and then walked in the opposite direction, out to the kitchen where he found Stella, Trish and Lisa at the table drinking coffee and chatting. Trish was in her wheelchair. Lisa was not in uniform.

"Good morning," he said to everyone. "Are you back on duty, Officer Bowers?"

"Not officially. I'm fully recovered but they want me to take an extra day. I asked to remain on the team, even if I have to do it on my own time."

"You're not feeling guilty because you let this guy get past you, I hope."

"Oh hell, I'm past guilt. I'm pissed. I want to be in on it when this guy is taken down. No one puts a needle in me and takes my piece and gets away with it."

"That's another thing," CJ said. "The department doesn't take kindly to an officer losing her weapon."

"Yeah, there's that, too. Thanks for reminding me. Fortunately, since I'm not suspended yet, I'm allowed to carry my backup."

Josh and Agent Frank Platt from Denver came through the door.

"We've got a bit of a problem," Platt said. "There're press parked at the front entrance."

"How did they find us out?" CJ said.

"We've got enough agents on this now to field a baseball team. All it takes is for one of us to slip up and unknowingly pick up a shadow."

"I thought you guys were trained for this kind of operation," CJ said.

Neither Platt or Josh responded to CJ's comment.

"They're like ants," CJ added. "The entire colony will be here before you know it."

"That means the safe house cover is blown," Lisa said.

"Where's Stratton?" CJ asked.

"Should be coming in the door any second," Platt said. "He was having words with someone with a microphone in her hand at the bottom of the gate as we were coming in. He's going to be pissed."

With that Agent Stratton came through the door. "Who in the hell led the press here?"

Joe strolled in from the hall, stethoscope draped around his neck, blood-pressure cuff in his hand. He stopped as everyone turned to look at him. "What?"

"Did you go out this morning?" Stratton asked him.

He nodded slowly, the look of *'What the hell did I do?'* on his face. "Went home and then by the hospital. Why?"

"How did you go? Did someone pick you up?"

"My wife. I took my car from the hospital."

"What time did you get back?"

"About fifteen minutes ago."

Stratton looked down at the floor for a time and then over to those gathered in the kitchen area. "We've had other developments during the night."

"Another body?" Stella asked.

"No report of that yet, so let's hope not. Tommy Clark went unaccounted for between maybe 11:00 last night and about an hour ago."

"Unaccounted for?" Platt said.

"You know how it goes, Frank. Subject gets by the surveillance without the team knowing. They think he is tucked sweetly into his bed until they see him return hours later. In this case, Tommy was last seen at 10:47 last night. The next time they spotted him he was jogging up the street to his apartment building at 6:32 this morning."

"Jogging," CJ said.

"Yes, jogging. His car never moved."

"Do you think he's made us?" Josh asked.

"Couldn't be determined. He may have just gone out for a morning run before work."

"And on the way out he just happened to pass by two sharp-eyed FBI agents without being noticed," CJ said. "What was he wearing?"

"Jogging suit."

"What color?" Josh asked.

"Navy blue."

"Jogging suit, not shorts," CJ said. "Long sleeved?"

Stratton tilted his head at CJ, then pulled out his phone. When his call connected he said, "On that jogging suit, was it long sleeved as well as full length pants?" He waited a few seconds. "Thanks. When he leaves for work, report back here."

When he hung up he said, "Long all the way; matching ball cap."

"It's already eighty degrees out," CJ said, "so that begs the question, why?"

"Certainly does, doesn't it?" Stratton walked over to lean against the kitchen counter which separated the cooking area from the eat-in area. He crossed his arms. "What really puzzles me is why we haven't gotten wind of the brother. We know that his forwarding address through the New York post office was to Tommy's address. We have no record of any activity by Kevin Clark since he left New York; no application for an Arizona driver's license, no change of vehicle registration, no employment, at least nothing above the table."

"Does he have his own place, but lets his mail come to Tommy?" CJ said.

"That's what we're assuming. What is he living off of, then?"

"As you said, there's no above the table employment. With the illegal Mexican traffic through here, there are plenty of under-the-table opportunities, many who would pay extra for someone who speaks fluid English. He gets paid in cash and then buys his groceries, gas, whatever in cash. If where he lives provides electricity and water, he'd have no record. Basically, the kid could be totally off the grid, either purposefully or as a result of dire conditions."

"I don't think it's dire," Josh said. "When Mom died she not only left the van, paid off, she also left a considerable wad of savings; a bit over $80,000."

"A New York prostitute does fairly well, it seems," CJ said. "Kevin could survive off-grid a long time on $80,000. So, if we can assume that Tommy was with his brother all night, that puts Kevin within walking or jogging distance, unless...."

"Unless what?" Stella said.

"Unless we've been made and Kevin dropped Tommy off two blocks away so that the van wouldn't be spotted," Stratton said.

"Which means...." CJ and Stratton looked at each other and then CJ added, "Have you heard from Dan this morning?"

"Called him when I got the news from the surveillance team."

"So what does all this mean?" Trish asked. "You think they were off killing again and you're just waiting for a report of someone finding a body?"

"That's what it means."

"Holy crap!"

All heads turned to Joe who was still standing where he'd stopped when Stratton questioned him.

"Sorry. It's just that this is like a real life Criminal Minds."

"That's exactly what it is, Joe. And you and I need to talk. Please step into my office." Stratton walked into the dining room. Joe followed, a worried look on his face.

CJ turned to his daughter. "I think we're losing our nurse a few hours early."

The sound of Stratton's phone going off spilled into the kitchen and all heads turned toward the dining room entryway. Seconds ticked by and just when they thought all was well, Stratton stepped into the doorway.

"We have a body."

Chapter 57

"Josh. Call Brown and DeBonski. Find out if they still have eyes on Clark. Tell them to stand by, I'll have Tucson police units on the way. If he tries to leave, for work or whatever, they're to detain him until the units arrive. Platt, get a hold of Crosby. You two get over to the crime scene. Call Detective Payne for the address. He's on his way there."

As Josh and Agent Platt pulled out their phones, Stratton made a call of his own. "Chief Rague. Agent Stratton here. I recommend we take Clark in. Here's what we have...." He disappeared into the dining room.

Several seconds later Joe came hustling out as though he'd been kicked in the pants, looking a tad white. He saw CJ and Trish staring at him. "Did I cause all this?"

Lisa moved away, her phone pressed to her ear. Josh stepped off toward the dining room as he explained the situation to the one of the agents watching Tommy Clark. Agent Platt went out the door while waiting for his call to connect.

"No, CJ said in response to Joe's question. All you did was bring the press and expose our hiding place. It's all rather moot now as it's all about to blow sky high." He beckoned to Stella and Trish. "Let's all go into the living room and stay out of the way."

Joe scrambled to get behind Trish's wheelchair, as though moving from the kitchen to the living room would get him further from the craziness beginning to erupt. Stella followed. CJ detoured into the dining room.

"No, we haven't anything new other than losing track of him for nearly eight hours," Stratton said into his cell phone.

"He just came out, in uniform, heading for his car," Josh said, holding his cell phone away from his ear. "Do you still want him detained?"

Stratton held up his hand to Josh. "No." Into the phone he said, "If we can get into his apartment I'm sure we can find evidence." To Josh he said, "Maintain surveillance only. Get a hold of Lacrowski. He and Nash have been working on the passenger lists. Find out if they've come up with anything. And find Crane. Tell him he needs to get control of the media, to get a statement written."

Stratton's attention returned to the phone. "Right chief. He belongs to you so we'll follow your lead for right now. However...." He looked up at the ceiling. CJ knew Chief Rague was chewing on his ear, that he wasn't going to take kindly to being run over by a bunch of Federal boys in fancy suits. "I don't care if he's a cop or a street sweeper. He's still our prime suspect and the stack of coincidences is getting to the point that I'll have no problem getting a signature on a search warrant, maybe even an arrest warrant as well."

CJ could also tell that this wasn't the first time Agent Stratton had to dance around the top dog of a city police department.

"Fine. I'll keep you informed." Stratton hung up and looked at Josh. "I hope to hell you've got something?"

Josh held up a finger for a few seconds, said into the phone, "Thanks. Call as soon as you have something else." To Stratton he said, "They've got one name on flights to and from New York the days around Clark's mother's death. John Dorne. They're checking that name against flights from Tucson or Phoenix during the Idaho thing."

"Good," Stratton said. "Have you found Crane?"

"Not yet."

"I'll find him. You run with John Dorne. Find out if there is such a person living in the Tucson area. If so, do a face-to-face." He punched a button on his phone and put it to his ear.

As Josh swung his chair around to a computer, his phone chirped.

"Washburn," he said. He listened for a time and then said, "Thanks. That may be the golden spike."

When he looked up after holstering his phone, his dad said, "Don't keep us in suspense. What's the golden spike?"

"I had a hunch this morning while walking the perimeter so I called New York to have someone take another look at Kevin's medical record. What I wanted to know was how many fingers he had. The call I just received was my callback."

CJ's eyebrows went up.

"He's missing the little finger on his right hand, a kitchen accident seven years back."

"Hold on," Stratton said into his phone and then turned to Josh. "What did you just say?"

Josh repeated it.

"I can't believe it," Stratton said and then returned to his call.

CJ returned to the living room where Lisa had just rejoined the group. He filled them in on the new developments.

"I just talked to Krystal," Lisa said. "She's on her way to the crime scene with Detective Payne."

"And you want to be there."

"Hell yeah, I want to be there, but I'm not on duty. Captain doesn't like it when his officers show up at a scene when off duty."

"But you've been reassigned to this task force. You don't answer to the captain now. You answer to Detective Payne, or Agent Stratton."

She stood up. "That's true."

"But be careful what you ask for. You may wind up ordered to remain right here, guarding us anyway."

She looked around, realizing everyone else was off on other tasks. She sat back down, dropping into silent contemplation.

"So, what do we do?" Trish said.

CJ looked toward the door to the dining room. "We've got enough now. It's all about figuring out where they are, so we wait."

The minutes ticked by to an hour, then an hour and a half. CJ drifted into a nap in the easy chair. Trish and Stella were attempting to get involved in magazines. After Joe had done all the blood pressure and eye scanning procedures he could do, he'd settled back with a book, something about therapeutic procedures with the elderly. Lisa sat for a time and then got up and paced. Occasionally she did a walkabout of the property and then returned to pace some more.

"CJ."

CJ's eyes popped open.

With a slight movement of his head, Stratton beckoned him into the dining room.

CJ pushed off the chair, curious as to what was up, why Stratton was suddenly so quiet, so calm. CJ sat down in the nearest chair to Stratton's work area and looked him in the face. "What?"

The agent pushed his fingers through his hair. "We've got an ID on this morning's victim."

CJ could already tell from the, 'I'm about to tell you some bad news' look, that it was going to be someone he knew. The only women in his life besides those currently under the same roof as him were his ex-wife and his attorney, both of whom the perp had spoke of in the hospital. CJ closed his eyes, waited for the shiver to course up his spine and then slowly opened them again.

"Who?"

"Alexandria Rothbower."

CJ had to think a minute to remember who Alexandria was. He remembered Gianna talking about her, the niece from Indiana who was living with her aunt while attending the University of Arizona, the beautiful young woman who Gianna loved like the daughter she was never able to have.

"Gianna's niece." CJ's chin dropped to his chest. "You have got to get him. He's completely out of control."

"I issued the order to bring Clark in; however, it seems that between his apartment and the precinct, the agents lost him. He never reported in for duty so we're assuming the worst."

"He's in the wind?"

"He's in the wind. A search warrant is being issued on his apartment. Chief Rague is preparing to address everyone from his bureau chiefs down to his captains, and a new statement for the press is being drafted. An all points for Clark's car and his brother's van is being issued. This is turning into an all-hands-on-deck man-hunt involving everyone from animal control to border patrol. If he's still in the county there's a fair chance we'll get him."

"You could have taken him when he walked out his door."

"Yes, we could have. Chief Rague wanted to wait because there just wasn't any hard evidence. Even still we don't have anything except that he shook the tail and didn't report for work. And we don't know if he purposely shook the tail or if my agents just got sloppy. He could show up and say that he stopped to buy a birthday card for his grandma or there was a long line at Starbucks."

"Sure, and pigs fly."

"An officer has been dispatched to your ex-wife's work place, as well as to her home to check on her step-children."

CJ looked over at Josh. "You should probably go to her, you think?"

"Considered it, Dad. Seeing as there's an officer with her and she is pissed at both of us, I thought it better to keep my distance. I did call her, so she's aware."

"What's she pissed at you about?"

"Not telling her where I've been. Joining the FBI. I'm better off right here doing my part to get this guy."

CJ nodded his understanding and then said to Stratton, "What about Gianna?"

"Two officers just delivered the news to her at her office. They'll stay with her."

CJ sat in silence for a time staring at the wall, then started to get up to deliver the news to the others, when Josh popped up with, "I've got an address for John Dorne."

"Thought you said there was no listing in the Tucson area," Stratton said.

"I went back through the credit card used to book the airline reservation, and...." Josh bent closer over his computer, clicking and scrolling. "Bingo! We've got him."

"What?" Stratton and CJ said at the same time.

"There have been only four charges made on that card since its inception a year ago. In addition to the flight to New York and back, there's a rental car in New York, then a flight to Spokane, Washington and back on the correct dates and a rental car associated with that."

"Okay, so John Dorne is our man. Now we've got to match him to a face."

"Tommy Clark's face," CJ said.

"I certainly hope so, otherwise we don't know who the hell we're looking for. Josh, tell DeBonski and Nash to visit the address. I expect it's going to be an empty lot, or an abandoned house."

"Why don't I go?" Josh said. "I grew up in Tucson, know my way around the streets. Tracking down airport security video is right up Nash's alley, I understand."

"I can't have you going there alone and I don't have anyone else. I'm heading over to the meeting with Chief Rague and his honchos."

"I'll go with him," CJ said.

Stratton actually looked at CJ for a bit, as though seriously considering the proposal. "No."

"This guy has taken a piece out of every part of my life."

"And that puts you too close to it."

"Chances are it's an empty lot, anyway, or an abandoned building, or John Dorne is an eighty-year-old who just happened to travel on the same days as our killer."

"You trying to make pigs fly, too?" With that Stratton stood, picked up his suit jacket and headed to the door. "You know where I'll be. Keep me informed."

After the front door closed behind Stratton, CJ and Josh looked at each other.

"He didn't say no the second time," CJ said.

"No, he didn't."

"You okay with me riding shotgun?"

Josh considered it for a long time. "I have to agree with the boss."

"That I shouldn't go, that I'm too close to it?"

"Well, yes, there's that. More importantly, I shouldn't be going into something like this without a backup. Technically I should wait until another agent frees up. Also, I don't want to leave Trish alone."

"Officer Bowers is here. She's a good cop. And Joe is here as well, at least for a few more hours. It won't take us more than two to check this out and get back here."

"Are you armed?"

CJ shook his head. "No. They took my Glock away from me when I was first arrested."

"The scene at which you showed up intoxicated?"

CJ grimaced. "Yeah, that one."

Josh pushed his chair back so he could reach into an oversized briefcase. He came out with a gun in a compact belt holster, and two clips. He pushed them across to his dad. "That's my backup. If you're going to have my back I don't want you resorting to throwing rocks."

CJ grinned as he pulled the weapon from its holster. "Glock 27. Same as mine, which was my BUG when I was on the force."

"BUG?"

"Backup gun."

"In the bureau BUG has a totally different connotation."

"Ah."

"A Glock 27 is what you taught me to shoot with."

CJ dropped the clip, knew by its weight that it was full, then pulled back the slide to eject the chambered 40 mm round. Next, he removed the slide entirely, followed by the spring and barrel. After a quick inspection he put it all back together, pushed in the clip and let the slide slam closed. Knowing that chambered a new round, he dropped the clip to reload the round he ejected before taking it apart. The entire procedure took him forty seconds. "Nice piece." He stood and started putting the gun on his belt.

"What are you doing?"

Both CJ and Josh were startled by Stella's sudden appearance. CJ was already thinking they shouldn't tell the women where they were going, that as soon as he had the gun on he would pull out his shirt to cover it.

"Ah... Josh and I are running out. We won't be too long."

She gave CJ a long stare and then looked over at Josh. "You guys do know what you're doing, don't you?"

"Yes," Josh said. "We do."

"Does Agent Stratton know about it?"

"Yes."

"Does he approve?"

Josh didn't respond so CJ jumped in. "Not in those exact words, but...."

She snorted. "I don't like it." She was looking at the Glock that CJ was trying to get secured on his hip.

"You've never had a problem with it before," he said.

"That's when I was only your secretary. In the beginning I was more concerned that if something happened to you I'd lose my job. Now I'll lose my job and my boyfriend."

"Oh. Kind of like losing your boss with benefits," CJ said.

Stella blushed. "You just come back with no additional holes." With that she kissed him, then without pause, returned to the living room.

Several seconds later, Lisa appeared. "What's going on?"

Josh explained about John Dorne and the address from the credit card.

"I should be the one going with you, but..." she looked between the father and son, "I get it. Be careful."

Out at Josh's car CJ said, "I figured you had a rental."

"Hate the paperwork necessary to fly with weapons and body armor. It was just a twelve hour drive."

"It's more than twelve hours."

"Not for me." Josh pulled a vest from the trunk. "Try this on."

"I don't need...."

"You don't have my back if you don't have armor."

Not having an argument against that, CJ slipped on the vest. "You travel with all this just to come down to check up on your sister?"

"You never know. You taught me to always be prepared."

"How to shoot and to be prepared. What else did I teach you?"

Something flashed across Josh's eyes. "That's about it, I guess." He loaded the address into his dash-mounted GPS. "Let's go."

Chapter 58

Most of the press were gone, likely chasing after Stratton when he left, or Agent Platt before him. They may have also received notification of the pending statement to the press. Whatever the case, only two SUVs remained, one of which fell in behind them when they rolled out. Josh seemed to pay it no mind until he turned east onto Ina Road. He slowed to let a car coming in from a side-road pull out in front of him, then, after judging the oncoming traffic, accelerated around the car, leaving the follow vehicle suddenly trapped.

"That should take care of them," Josh said.

By the time they merged onto I-10 five minutes later, CJ could see no sign of the SUV.

Heading eastbound, Josh moved in and out of the left lane, running close to 75 when he could, until taking the Valencia exit. At the bottom of the exit he turned west onto Valencia.

"I think we were supposed to go the other way here," CJ said.

"When we shook the press, they apparently had another stationed near the interstate. That one picked us up. He's not making any pretense now. He's right on our tail."

Suddenly, without so much as a signal, Josh slipped between two cars in the left lane and then immediately into the turn lane, did a fast 180 and then accelerated back the way they had come. The new follow vehicle came to a fast stop on the shoulder, throwing up enough dust to slow traffic, causing him even more delay in getting turned around.

"We should be clear now," Josh said.

"I'm impressed."

CJ turned forward and checked the GPS. "Six minutes."

They made a turn off of Valencia, then two more, the last being onto a dirt road. Josh pulled the car to the side and stopped. They studied their destination, which the GPS indicated was 300 feet on the left, an old ranch house with a barn and one out-building.

"Doesn't look like it's been occupied for decades," CJ said.

"Either our perp is only using this address for his John Dorne creation and we'll find nothing here but snakes and pack rats or...."

"Or he is actually living here and we'll find the van hidden in the barn," CJ continued. "Drive by and let's study it a bit more."

Josh put the car in drive and started it moving.

"Not too slow. Don't want to attract attention."

"I know what I'm doing."

"Yeah, I know you do. Just saying."

After passing the drive and checking the beat up and weathered mailbox to ascertain that they had the correct address, Josh drove on for a quarter mile before finding a convenient place to turn around. Once parked and facing back toward the old ranch house, Josh said, "There's been activity there. I could make out two different treads, one wider than the other. There may have been more, but I doubt it."

"I didn't see any signs of a dog. Did you?" CJ said.

"No. In this heat he'd be in the shade or in the barn. He'd have to have a source of water."

"Likely in the barn."

"I don't think there's a dog."

"Me neither."

"I loaned my binoculars to Janet a few weeks back. Never got them back."

"Janet?"

"Agent Crosby."

"Oh." CJ remembered what Trish had told him about Josh being in a relationship. "You got something going with her?"

"No. That would be unprofessional."

"Doesn't mean it doesn't happen."

"She has issues. No thanks."

"You're in law enforcement. Everybody has issues."

"Very true. One doesn't get involved with a woman who has an ex who hasn't yet let go, and who is also in law enforcement and thus carries a gun."

"Oh."

"Besides, she's a lot more senior than me."

"That's a problem."

"Yes."

CJ started to open his mouth to ask about an actual current girlfriend when something moved at one side of the house. From a quarter mile away it was hard to tell what, but it was too tall to be a dog or a javelina.

"Deer," Josh said.

CJ watched for a time until a young doe darted out into the yard. "Young eyes, I guess," he said and then the doe jumped and sprang away, lost from view in the desert growth.

"When we drove by, did you see anything in the barn?" Josh said.

"Nothing, but with the bright sun and the angle, a Mac truck could be in there and I'd not be able to see it. Do another drive-by. Something bothers me but I can't put my finger on it."

Josh started the car moving forward again until it was up to 25 mph.

Already concluding that there was no way to see anything in the barn, CJ watched the windows of the house and the area on both sides. When they got to the end of the dirt road, they turned around and stopped again. "Still not seeing anything suspicious."

"Same here. Tire tracks still bother me, though. I'm with you. Something still seems off."

"Sometimes bad feelings mean nothing more than nerves," CJ said.

"True." They watched the house for another minute. "This seemed like such a good idea at the time. Now I wish we had a swat team in play."

"Maybe you should call Stratton and get his take."

Josh grunted and then put the car in gear. "Let's get done what we came here for."

They passed through what used to be a wooden swing-gate, now pushed to the side, broken and blocked open by a complex growth of Indian Fig Cactus, which told CJ it had been a long time since the gate had been closed. As they got closer to the house he could see that some of the vehicle tracks led into the barn; however, he still could not see if anything was parked inside. With the barn's shape and size a van, car or both could be parked out of immediate sight.

"These tracks were made in the last 72 hours," Josh said.

"How do you know?"

"We had rain Wednesday afternoon."

"I don't remember that."

"It was after you blacked out in jail and they transported you to the hospital. It was one of the afternoon monsoons. Any tracks before that would have been obliterated." Josh brought the car to a stop, slightly angled to the house so that when they opened the car doors they still had some protection, yet would not have to backup to make a fast exit.

"I'll approach the door," Josh said. "You hang back and keep an eye on the windows."

They got out and stood at the car doors for a half minute, studying the front. Nothing moved anywhere. Leaving the doors open they approached. CJ stopped after only ten feet and remained rooted, letting Josh pass by him. They both had a hand on their weapon, though had not yet drawn. Josh took the two steps onto the covered porch and then moved to the door.

He knocked on the screen door, setting off an irritating rattle. When there came no response, he knocked again. "Mister Dorne!" he called. "John Dorne! We're with the FBI. We just need to ask you a few questions."

CJ watched and listened, then shook his head at Josh when he glanced back over his shoulder.

Suddenly there was a crack, like a pistol shot, and Josh went down to his knees. Without even thinking CJ had the Glock in his hand, first trained on the front door, then scanning back and forth. There was nothing. He ran up the two steps and dropped down next to Josh, out of the line of fire should it be coming through the door.

"Josh!" he said without looking at him, first studying the door and realizing that the shot had not come from inside. He swung his head back and forth from one end of the house to the other and then out into the yard expecting a second shot any moment. "Where you hit?"

"I'm fine," Josh said.

"What?" CJ looked at his son. One leg was knee-deep in the porch floor.

"I broke through the floor, damn it. Help me up before I get snake bit."

After taking a deep breath of relief, CJ offered a hand and Josh pulled himself out. The two of them then backed off the porch, each careful of additional weak spots in the boards. CJ didn't holster his gun until he was getting back in the car.

"That got my adrenaline running a bit," CJ said.

"No kidding."

What CJ didn't want to mention was that his adrenaline rush was primarily his fear that he would lose his son after only days of getting him back, that he'd wished he'd approached the door himself, had taken the bullet he thought he'd heard.

"I'm going to pull around so that I can back between the house and the barn until we can see inside."

"Sounds like a plan." CJ didn't understand how Josh could be so calm and then realized it was only he, CJ, who'd thought he heard a shot. Josh knew all along he'd only broken through the porch floor. CJ wiped at the sweat beading on his forehead and then dried his hands on his pants. Sweaty fingers made for mishandling one's gun.

After bringing the car around and then getting it lined up, Josh put it in reverse and said, "You keep an eye on the barn. I'll watch the house."

"Hold on," CJ said. "I just realized what's been bothering me."

"What's that?"

"The deer. What spooked it? It didn't just wander away. A noise aroused it from where it'd been laid down, then all of a sudden it took off like a bullet."

"Someone stepped out of the house?"

"Maybe."

"He or they watched us go by and then turn around and park down the way. We wouldn't have been able to see them if they'd gone from the house to the barn."

"Exactly," CJ said. "They could be sitting in their van right now, ready to make their escape if we should wander in to investigate."

"Then the plan still holds. We need to get a look in the barn and I'd rather do it from the car and not on foot."

CJ nodded. "Let's go."

Josh took his foot off the brake and started the car rolling back, watching the house over his left shoulder, CJ watching the barn over his right.

As they started coming abreast of the open, yawning barn door, CJ was able to make out the shape of the backend of a light-colored car, not enough for a license number or any other detail. He reached up to cover his eyes, to block out the bright of day when suddenly the backup lights came on. It took less than a second for CJ to understand what he was seeing, but another second, as the car started coming toward them, before he fully realized what it meant.

"GUN IT!" he yelled, but by the time Josh whipped his head around to take in the approaching threat, it was too late.

Josh slammed his foot down on the gas pedal in time to save a direct hit against the passenger door. Instead, the car slammed into the area from the door hinge, forward. Josh's car spun on its axis better than 90 degrees, coming to rest perpendicular to the car that struck them. In the time it took CJ to release his seatbelt, Josh was already out of the car. CJ tried to open his door but nothing happened. He twisted in his seat in time to see a black van exiting the barn, Josh in a shooting stance, his gun trained on the windshield of the van. CJ turned to make another try at the door in time to see the driver of the car coming around the front of his vehicle, gun in his hand, aiming.

"Josh!" CJ screamed. "On your left!"

CJ dove across the console and rolled out the driver's door. When he came up on one knee he had the Glock in hand. The van had turned right, ready to make a run for it, but had stopped. Josh was no longer trained on the van, but had turned to face the driver of the car. There came two shots, a split second apart, and Josh spun and fell. CJ jumped to his feet in time to see the guy run around the front of the van. He fired once, too late, then leveled the Glock on the driver's side window. He fired just as the wheels started grabbing dirt. The bullet struck the frame just back of the driver's left shoulder. He ran toward Josh, knelt, then emptied the Glock on the retreating van, his only intent by this time to strike a tire.

The van sideswiped the gate, fishtailed onto the road and kept on going.

The gun holstered, CJ put his hand on Josh, looking for where he'd been shot, finding only a dent in the armor, dead center of the chest. Josh stirred and opened his eyes.

"You all right?" Josh asked.

"Am I all right? I'm not the one who took a bullet. I heard two shots. You hit anyplace else?"

Josh struggled to sit up. "No. The other shot was mine. Missed him altogether." He felt the indentation in the armor. "Damn, that hurt. Like being punched with a hammer, a big hammer. Knocked the damn air out of me. The guy could have just walked up and put one in my head."

Josh pulled out his cell phone. When he stared at it one second too long, CJ snatched it from him and dialed 911. When the 911 operator answered, CJ said, "Clinton Washburn here with FBI Special Agent Josh Washburn. Shots have been exchanged with perps in the serial murder case." Josh rattled off the address and CJ repeated it. "Black van, same New York plate as in the all points, last seen fleeing in the direction of the interstate." CJ looked at Josh, noted the pain he was still experiencing. "Agent needs medical attention."

"No!" Josh said, but CJ had rung off.

"What's Stratton's number?"

"Hold eight."

CJ did and Josh snatched it from him. As Josh gave his report, CJ stood and walked around the two cars, not so much to inspect the damage, but to allow his tensed muscles to relax, his fears to subside. Twice in less than ten minutes he'd thought he'd lost his son. He didn't know if he could survive a third.

Chapter 59

Detective Payne walked out of the barn, squinted at the bright light and put his sunglasses on. He spoke to a uniformed officer and then walked over to where CJ and Josh were leaning against the back of the EMS vehicle.

"No doubt who we're dealing with now," Dan said. "You say you didn't actually see Tommy Clark?"

Josh shook his head. "Could see a silhouette through the windshield, but couldn't make out features. The driver of the car and the one who shot me was Kevin for sure. And that is Tommy's car."

Dan pointed to the Glock holstered on CJ's hip. "You emptied an entire clip, you say. Did you hit anything besides maybe some neighbors?"

CJ looked out across the desert, seeing nothing but cactus and desert shrubs in the line of fire. "I'm sure the van's carrying a few more ounces of lead." When Dan didn't make further comment, CJ said, "Any sightings of them yet?"

"They could have gone anywhere, could have hit the interstate and be halfway to New Mexico by now."

"Or all the way into Mexico, for that matter," CJ said.

"Border patrol has been alerted. Doubt very much they could make it across or be stupid enough to go where there might be border patrol checkpoints. I think Alexandria Rothbower was their departing shot. The first report I got from Tommy's apartment is that it appeared he had been packing, preparing to travel."

"Have you been through the house here yet?" Josh said.

"No. Heading in there now. Want to join me?"

The two Washburns pushed away from the EMS vehicle together and fell in next to Detective Payne as he headed up the front steps. The screen and front door were open, uniformed officers having already walked through to ensure it was clear.

"I'd say they had an escape plan and they're now carrying it out," CJ said as he passed into the darkened interior.

Dan made no response as he slowly walked through the small living room consisting of a broken down sofa and a recliner chair stuck in the recline position. There was no TV, only a bookshelf stuffed with yellowed and tattered paperback books. A coffee table looked like something cowboys had used for a footrest, with their spurs on. An unmatched pair of lamps stood on end tables, one without a lampshade.

Dan continued into the kitchen while CJ remained where he was, staring down at a notepad on the coffee table, the top sheet blank. It wasn't completely blank, however. There was an indent were someone had written on the previous sheet and had pressed so hard they'd scored a crease in the next sheet. Although he couldn't read it all, a set of numbers seemed to rise to the surface, maybe a trick of light and shadow. The numbers were 6892.

He picked it up and studied it, a tingle at the back of his neck telling him it was important, but he couldn't put his finger on why. He tried to make out what was after it, but the indentation was too slight. He looked around then joined Josh and Dan in the kitchen. He started opening drawers.

"What are you doing, CJ?" Dan said. "You know better than to touch anything."

"I'm looking for a pencil. Here!" From the silverware drawer where most of the utensils were anything but silver, he found a pencil, the lead broken away. He looked in the drawer again and found a paring knife with which he started sharpening the pencil. Josh and Dan just stared at him, baffled by what he was doing.

When he had enough lead exposed, he dropped the knife back into the drawer and started applying the soft lead to the notepad until the indentations began appearing. When he was done, he turned it so that Dan could see it. It read 6892 W Cactus Wren Rd.

"What's that?" CJ said, already knowing the answer.

"Holy crap! That's the safe house."

"Yeah, and every damn cop or agent on this case is either here or on the way here. No one's with Stella and Trish except Lisa Bowers?"

"They wouldn't," Dan said, but was already out the door, heading for his car, Josh and CJ right with him.

"They're crazy; they certainly would," CJ said. "One officer against these two guys, and she doesn't even know they're coming. Damn it to fuck! They could park out in the desert and walk in from the back. They're probably there right now."

As they pulled out onto the road, dash lights flashing, blue grill lights strobing, Dan handed CJ his cell phone and said, "Call them."

"I' m already on it," Josh said from the backseat. I'm not getting an answer from Trish.

Dan said into his mike, "Dispatch, David 218. This is a Code 2, this is a Code 2. Require emergency dispatch of units to the vicinity of 6892 West Cactus Wren Road, possible location of the Clark brothers. I repeat, emergency dispatch of units to the vicinity of West Cactus Wren Road and all points surrounding."

"Roger David 218."

"What about Officer Bowers?" CJ asked, staring at the phone, hardly able to breathe. "Do you have her number?"

"In the directory under Bowers."

"Where?" CJ poked at a couple of buttons. "I don't see...."

Josh snapped the phone out of his hand from the back seat, punched something, then something else and then held the phone to his ear.

"No answer," he said after nearly a half minute. By this time Dan was entering the interstate, cars moving to the side out of his way, some slower than others. He ignited his siren when one didn't appear to be paying attention at all, then left it on as his car roared on past.

Josh handed the phone back to his dad, who tried calling Stella. When he got no answer, he said, "Anyone know Joe's number?"

No one did.

Josh called Stratton, explained what they'd found. Stratton had been with the chief when Dan's call to Dispatch came through the chief's scanner, and had every special agent available in route.

"Can't you go any faster than this?" CJ demanded.

"I'm already punching through 80. Public safety, remember? And if we get tied up in an accident we won't get there at all."

They came upon a truck that said, "Fine Home Furniture" in large script on the back door. Dan looked right, saw no opportunity, then hit the left shoulder and blew on past. When they came off the Ina Road exit, they had two city police patrol cars with them. A quarter mile yet to the light at Ina, another west-bound patrol car came to a stop in the middle of the intersection, stopping traffic in all directions.

CJ held on as Dan turned hard onto Ina. Traffic was scrambling to get out of the way as they roared west, three patrol units behind them.

Josh's cell phone went off. "Washburn," he said. He listened, then said, "Roger that. We're a minute out." He closed the phone. "Police chopper is getting ready to lift off; Stratton on board. We'll have eyes in the sky in fifteen minutes."

"Officer down!" suddenly came across the radio. "We have an officer down at 6892 Cactus Wren Road!"

Dan picked up his mike. "This is David 218. Is that Officer Bowers? Is there anyone else present?"

"David 218. Confirmation on Bowers. One civilian 10-20, a Joe Foronda. Standby 218." There was a long pause and then the officer returned. "David 218."

"Go ahead," Dan said as he slowed to take a turn.

The officer said, "Foronda states that the two women, Stella and Patricia were abducted."

CJ slammed his hand against the dash. "Shit!"

"Roger," Dan said and dropped the mike. "Damn!" He slowed again for the left turn onto Cactus Wren. Twenty seconds later he turned onto the property and came to a sliding stop next to a patrol unit. As they poured out of the car Dan started yelling orders to the units who came in behind them. "Lock down this entire area in a three mile radius; all the way out Picture Rocks Road and Twin Peaks Road and all spokes in all directions." His phone rang. "Payne," he snapped into it.

CJ and Josh didn't wait around to hear anything else. They ran through the door to find one uniformed officer on his knees next to Lisa Bowers. He was applying direct pressure to a shoulder wound.

"How bad?" CJ said.

"Lost a lot of blood. We need the wagon here now!"

"On the way," CJ said. "Stay with her." He followed after Josh who was already sitting next to Joe Foronda. Joe's head was in his hands.

"How long ago?" Josh demanded.

Joe shook his head. "It seems like it just happened, minutes ago, but I don't think... I don't know." He considered it for a few seconds. "Five minutes maybe, or maybe fifteen."

"How did they come in? Front door or back?"

"I... I don't know. They were... they were just there."

Josh seemed to lose patience with him. "You're a nurse!" He pointed at the officer attempting to arrest Lisa's bleeding. "You should be over there helping save her life. Free up the cop so he can help get these bastards and maybe save yours."

With that Josh stood, disgusted.

"Josh."

CJ and Josh both turned to Lisa's voice, weak, slow. Her eyes were open, very tired looking.

"They came in the back... I heard them... Not fast enough... Tommy... Kevin... Sorry."

"It's okay, officer. We shouldn't have left you alone."

"Two shots," she said. "Got off two."

"Did you hit either of them?" Josh asked.

"Don't know. Maybe. Tommy shooter." She closed her eyes.

Suddenly Joe was by her side next to the officer. "Yes," he said. "She hit the one with the gun." To the officer applying pressure he said, "I've got this. There's a first-aid kit in my car, blue Toyota, backseat.

Please get it for me." When the officer rushed out, he said. "I'm sorry. I... I don't know what came over me."

When neither CJ nor Josh said anything, he added, "They went out the back. I know she hit one because he was the one who grabbed me and threw me against the wall. His right arm was useless, bleeding a lot. He hit me with his left."

"Hit you?"

"Threw me against the wall and then gut punched me, twice, knocked me to the floor. Strong as hell. From where I was I could see them leave through the kitchen. The ladies, Stella and Trish, were in handcuffs."

CJ and Josh rushed into the kitchen, noted a bloody mess around the sink, the sliding glass door out the back, open and streaked with blood. Josh went out first followed by CJ, guns raised, pointing. Across the patio they ran and out into the yard, noting a uniformed officer coming around from one side and then another from the other. Josh waved them over.

Keeping his voice low, he said, "Tommy Clark and his brother Kevin. At least one of them is armed, maybe both. They have two hostages, women, one of whom is in an ankle cast. Officer Bowers was able to shoot one of them, right arm. We believe it was Tommy. Bleeding badly." He pointed down and out toward the fence that separated the property from the desert. There were drag marks in the decorative white stone pebbles that took the place of grass. Several splashes of blood stood out against the white stones.

"They're going to be moving slow," CJ said. "No idea how far away they had to park. There are road accesses all over the surrounding desert."

"There will be a chopper in the air shortly, but if they get out of the desert before then, we may lose them."

"They may already be out," one of the officers said.

"Let's hope not," Dan said, just joining them. "What's the plan?"

"Spreading out fifty feet apart and driving through on foot," Josh said.

"Then let's do it."

With that the officers went right and left while Josh and Dan broke slightly away leaving CJ to follow the main trail.

At the fence line, made up of three strands of barbed wire, CJ tried to imagine how they got over, through or under with Trish and Stella in tow and handcuffed. Several shreds of material the size of a little finger hung on the barbs. CJ separated the wires and stepped through, catching a piece of his own clothing. With Glock in hand, pointed up, he began working his way between prickly pear cactus, saguaros and giant palo verde trees and came upon what appeared to have been a scuffle around a grouping of cholla. On the ground, caught up in pieces of broken off cholla, lay a bloody towel that CJ recognized as being from the kitchen. Scores of cholla spines can penetrate the skin instantly. One of them must have had a painful run-in and sacrificed the towel to extract them. CJ hoped it was one of the Clark brothers and not Stella or Trish. After one such run-in of his own some ten years before, CJ's comment to Pat was that he'd have been better off falling into a pit of rattlesnakes or wrestling with a porcupine.

CJ stepped across the towel and pieces of cholla lying about and picked up his pace. Although the wail of sirens seemed to be coming from everywhere, in the desert they could all be a mile or two away. CJ welcomed them because he was sure he was making too much noise.

And then he saw it, through a small space beneath a palo verde tree, the black van, side door open, legs moving about, Trish sitting on the ground, head bowed... still. He skirted around the tree and several huge prickly pear cactus until he was clear and within thirty feet.

Tommy had Stella by the arm, trying to force her into the van, his right arm hanging by his side, dripping blood. Kevin had Trish by the arm, trying to lift her to her feet. In his right hand he was holding what looked to be a Glock similar to the one CJ was pointing at him. Trish wasn't cooperating, appearing to play the part of a rag doll.

"It's all over, boys," came Dan's voice from CJ's left.

"Put it down, Kevin," said Josh from CJ's right.

Kevin stiffened for a split second then dropped to his knees behind Trish and put the gun to her head. In the same second Tommy spun around, bringing Stella with him, his arm tight around her neck. Although there was a gun in his holster, he would not be able to get to it without letting Stella go; however, it was obvious with his size that he could break her neck as fast as Kevin could pull the trigger on Trish.

Certain that Dan and Josh had their sights on Kevin, CJ leveled his Glock on Tommy's head and stepped slowly forward.

"Let them go and let's end this quietly, right now," CJ said. "You're a cop, Tommy. You know you can't get away. Tell your brother to put the gun down and then both of you step away."

"Don't listen to him, Tommy," Kevin said.

"The women you killed didn't do anything to you, Tommy," CJ said. "It's your mother who you should be angry with, and you took care of her already, isn't that right?"

Kevin looked up at his brother. "What's he saying, Tommy?"

"Nothing, Kevin. Shut up."

CJ considered Kevin's question for a second. "You never told Kevin that you flew to New York for the sole purpose of punishing your mother the last time she beat him and knocked him down the stairs? You promised her that's what you'd do if she ever touched him again, and a promise is a promise, isn't that right?"

"You think you're so smart, Mister Ex-cop," Tommy said. "Had to get your PI license and then show off by making Ralph Bunko look bad. You think you're such a badass. He's full of bullshit, Kevin, just like he's always been. Clinton Joshua Washburn. A bullshit name. And see that guy behind you Kevin. That's his little boy. Joshua James Washburn, Special Agent for the FBI. Another bullshit name. Can you believe that? Fuckin' with the Tucson police force wasn't enough. Now he's brought in his FBI son to fuck with us, too."

Kevin looked over his shoulder, at Josh, at CJ and then brought his gaze back around to Detective Payne who'd closed the distance to less than twenty feet. After several seconds Kevin looked up at his brother again.

"Did you kill Mom, Tommy?"

"She hurt you one too many times."

"I didn't ask you to kill her. I thought..."

"You thought what, Kevin? That she put herself in that dumpster? You were always so damned innocent, so damned forgiving."

"It was my fault that she got mad at me."

CJ chanced a look down at Trish. She was sitting with her casted leg straight out, the other turned under. What was most noticeable were three fist-sized chunks of cholla stuck to one arm, from the wrist to elbow, like three massive pin cushion balls, only in this case the pins pointed out and were a lot more deadly.

"Your fault!" Tommy said. "It was never your fault, Kevin. I can't believe you said that, that you thought that."

CJ moved to his left to come around where he could see Trish's face. He knelt down ten feet from her.

"Don't even think about it," Kevin said, pressing the barrel of the gun tighter against Trish's head.

"I'm not thinking anything, Kevin. I just want to see that Trish is all right. Looks like she came in contact with some cactus."

"Stupid bitch," Tommy said. "Ran me into it, too. Think she did it on purpose. Should have killed her right on the spot is what I should have done."

"Trish. You okay?" CJ said.

Trish slowly raised her head. She locked eyes with her father, raised her arms and smiled.

"Standup and back away," Tommy said.

CJ looked at her, trying to understand what she was attempting to tell him, because he was certain she was trying to pass a message. Again she raised her arms and with it her head ever so slightly, shifting her eyes toward Kevin at the same time.

"I'm okay Dad," she said. "Just give me ten."

"You hear her?" Tommy said. "Says she's okay. Now step away."

"Okay," he said, though still confused. He stood and stepped a few steps to the side, keeping the Glock leveled on Tommy's head. At the same time, from the corner of his eye, he noticed Trish's damaged foot start to twitch and then he got it.

One, he thought to himself.

Two.

"What were you doing?" Tommy said.

Three.

"Checking that my daughter was fine."

Four.

"Not real happy the way you've been treating her," CJ said.

Five.

"Who the fuck cares?" Tommy said.

Six.

"She's a fuck'n bitch."

Seven.

"All bitches are worthless; just like this one who's neck I'm going to snap if you don't back off."

Eight.

Stella no longer struggled, appeared to have faded into unconsciousness. "That why you killed all those women, Tommy?"

Nine.

"Yes."

Ten.

Trish twisted and then slammed her cholla filled arm back into Kevin's face. As they both erupted in screams CJ fired a single round straight through Tommy's left eye.

Before Kevin could accidently shoot Trish or himself, Josh rushed in and snatched the gun out of his hand. Kevin grabbed for the cholla and within seconds both of his hands were stuck to the cactus pin-cushions and he was screaming louder than Trish and thrashing out of control. Josh ejected the clip and the chambered round from Kevin's gun, then used the gun to slam him alongside the head until he stopped thrashing and screaming. Then he dropped down next to Trish, pushing his dad out of the way.

"I'll take care of her," Josh said. "Go to Stella." He placed his hand on Trish's face and said, "Hush sweet girl. Lie still. It's over."

Stella and Tommy had fallen in opposite directions and Dan had caught her just before she hit the ground. CJ slid in next to him.

"She's breathing," Dan said. "She's breathing. He didn't break anything, just cut off her air."

"I had to shoot him," CJ said. "He'd have killed her if I hadn't."

"I'm with you on this, CJ."

CJ touched Stella's face. "Stella." When she didn't respond he pushed her hair back and called her name again.

She opened her eyes, closed them and then opened them again. She looked between Dan and CJ. "Is he...?" The words came out as a whisper.

"Don't try to talk," Dan said. "We'll get you water. It's over, Stella."

"Trish," she said.

"She'll be okay," CJ said. "You're both okay."

"I heard her... screaming."

"And now she's crying, yes. Cactus is all. She's okay. Josh is with her."

The police helicopter appeared overhead, blowing sand and making talk impossible until it set down in an open area about fifty yards to the north. Five minutes later an EMS vehicle arrived, followed shortly by another. Within minutes the EMS techs had sedated Trish and cut away all the cactus joining her to Kevin Clark, leaving only the barbs. The hospital, under sterile conditions, would do the rest. Tommy Clark lay right where he had fallen backwards into the van. Techs covered his body and face with a white sheet.

It seemed forever before the EMS vehicle carrying Kevin Clark departed, an escort of two uniformed officers aboard along with vehicle escorts front and back.

Ignoring Stella's protest that she was fine, the EMS techs forced her into the vehicle with Trish. The techs would only allow one family member to ride with them. CJ and Josh stood next to each other, staring in at the two women, Stella holding Trish's hand.

I'm okay, Clint," Stella said. "Let Josh come and be with his sister."

CJ looked between Trish, who was already out of it thanks to the pain killer, and Stella and then at Josh. He slapped Josh on the shoulder and said, "Take care of them both. I'll be along as soon as I can."

"That may be a while," Detective Payne said as he walked up. "Got a shooting here. Have to make sure we have all the facts down before we cut him free."

"You know it was a good shoot, Dan," CJ said.

"No doubt in my mind, but you know the drill. A firearm was discharged and a life was taken. Has to be investigated. You had four witnesses, all law enforcement, which means by the book all the way. I don't think there'll be any problems."

"He also confessed to the murders," CJ said, "and threatened to kill Stella."

"That he did, and we all heard it. The question will be, what if you had missed?"

"He wouldn't have missed," Josh said. "In all my FBI training and all my time on the range with other agents, I've never seen anyone who could shoot like my father."

With that, Josh stepped into the EMS vehicle.

"Josh," CJ said.

Josh turned to look out at him. "Yeah, Dad?"

"I'm really glad you came."

Josh nodded. "Me too."

Chapter 60

CJ watched out the second floor office window overlooking Tuesday morning traffic on Broadway Boulevard. The killings were finally over but there'd been so much damage that could never be repaired, damage to parents, siblings, grandparents, aunts and uncles, friends; damage to the security and independence of all young women; damage to the Tucson community. The national media was only beginning to slow down their reporting on the horrific drama that had been played out over the previous few weeks. One of what was thought to be the city's finest had taken the lives of so many Tucson daughters. Little had been said, however, about Maria Rodston, the young woman Tommy had killed in Moscow, Idaho. The only details about Tommy's death that had been released was that he died in a police shootout. That was just fine with CJ. He wanted no credit, nor blame.

He thought about the special he watched on TV the night before by local television news personalities, Reuwben Chavez and Candice Reed. It was entitled, "The Tucson Blues... Can the Cops be Trusted?" Another was running tonight, entitled, "The Tucson Blues... Fathers, Keep an Eye on Your Daughters," as though Tommy Clark had spread his insanity to all other young men. CJ wondered if there were going to be more "Tucson Blues," a month long series or some such thing. How long would they drag it out, continuing to whip up the anger of a mourning community? How long would it be before a single young woman, or anyone for that matter, would be able to trust a male cop at the same level as before? Or would they simply shrug and move on, a little bit more guarded, a little less trusting?

How long before the local media, or community, started asking the question, "Who fired the killing shot?"

CJ had been led in by Eleanor Mann and asked to sit. "Ms. Onassis will be along momentarily," she'd said. Eleanor Mann had been with Gianna for as long as CJ could remember.

CJ was too nervous to sit, so he had stood near the window and gazed out.

Eight women dead. It would have been nine if not for Officer Berk and Joe Foronda who kept Lisa Bowers alive until EMS arrived. Trish was alive because of pure luck. CJ had no idea what he was thinking when he told her to jump from the van. He didn't consider that she might land in the middle of traffic. Was there another alternative at the time? Waiting it out to see what happened, even now, seemed not to be a viable option. As a result, though, another woman died in Trish's place. CJ felt selfish for that and glad at the same time.

Stella suggested this morning that he should see a shrink.

And then in the desert when Trish slammed her cactus needle-laden arm into Kevin Clark's face, so much could have gone wrong with his finger on the trigger of a gun to her head. And CJ saw her plan and condoned it, went with it. Luck was with them that day... again.

He really didn't want to see a shrink.

Trish was released from the hospital into CJ and Stella's care Sunday afternoon. Pat got out of sorts about the arrangement, trying to play the custody card in front of the hospital and the nurse who wheeled Trish out. Trish reminded her mother that she was an adult and could make her own decisions, that custody no longer had any part to play. As in the past CJ made a point of not getting between Trish and her mother, and so stood just out of the way. Pat tried to act okay about it, giving Trish a kiss on the cheek just before glaring at Stella and walking away with the *I am pissed* slant to her back that CJ knew all too well. After Trish was settled into CJ's rental car, the nurse gave him a look of pity, just before turning away with the wheelchair.

CJ watched an EMS vehicle race by on Broadway, lights strobing, siren blaring, and wondered how much longer Gianna would be. He wiped his hands on his pants and thought about the conversation he'd had with Detective Bunko. He had been spending a few hours this Tuesday morning at the office by himself, responding to calls from two new clients who had seen him on the news, making additional calls and setting up his investigative approaches. He really wasn't ready to go back to work, but as an independent PI, he couldn't afford to start turning down clients. He'd also gone too long without an income.

He'd just finished his last call and was coming to his feet to go meet with Gianna when Ralph Bunko knocked and walked in. CJ was so surprised, he was almost speechless.

"Do you have a few minutes, CJ?" Bunko said.

"Maybe five, Ralph. I have another appointment." CJ pointed to a chair just before sitting back down in his own.

Bunko sat and then leaned forward with his elbows on his knees, appearing rather embarrassed, overly nervous. "I just wanted you to know that I had no idea what Tommy Clark was up to."

"I never had a thought that you did."

"He used me to get information about what you and Dan Payne and the FBI were doing. It was just by accident that I saw the addresses to your safe houses and then I opened my big mouth. I didn't even know that he had a brother, let alone that he had brought him to Tucson from New York."

"Did you know about his mother?"

"That she died, yeah. That was it. When I asked him how she'd died he'd told me breast cancer. How was I to know otherwise? Didn't have any reason to doubt him."

"Tommy had a rough childhood," CJ said, "thus he kept everything about his personal life a secret."

"That, he certainly did," Ralph said. "But he was a good cop. I took him under my wing and he learned fast, respected me. I...."

"You had no reason to suspect that he was anything but a good cop," CJ said. "I know how it goes. The two of you got together, knocked back a few brews, spouted off about past run-ins with other detectives and PIs, made more about it than it deserved and Tommy took it to heart. You may have been the first true friend he'd ever had so he became your self-appointed bodyguard, maybe figured he'd right some wrongs that he thought were done to you. It was by accident, or fate, that I stumbled upon one of his murders the way that I did. From that he saw an opportunity and ran with it until burying me became his driving obsession. No way could you have known."

Ralph shook his head. "No way could I have known. You probably know that I've been placed on temporary suspension."

"Sorry to hear that," CJ said, even though he wasn't. "I'm sure it's just a formality until the investigation is completed." CJ actually hoped that he'd be forced to resign.

Ralph stood. "I just wanted to say, I'm sorry."

CJ just looked at him for a long time, wondering if he had ever thought to say he was sorry to the families of the dead women. "Thank you for that." There was nothing more to say.

Without another word, Ralph Bunko turned and walked out.

Still staring out Gianna's office window, CJ wondered, not for the first time, if he should give up his PI license, find a job doing something normal or go back to school and finish up his law degree. He turned his head to look at Gianna's framed diploma hanging on the wall. He was maybe five years older than her. Was it too late in life to start over?

The door opened and he turned around to find Gianna Onassis standing before him. She looked worn and haggard, dressed in black.

She took his hand. "Thank you for coming to see me, CJ," she said. "You look like hell."

CJ touched the scabs covering one side of his face. "Nothing permanent. Should have seen the black eye a few days ago."

"I did, remember? Have to admit, you looked worse then. How's the shoulder?"

"Not bad. I've got ninety percent of the mobility back."

"I understand it didn't affect your aim."

"No," was all CJ could say. He didn't know if she approved of what he did or not.

"I haven't much time as I leave within the hour to escort Alexandria's body back to Indiana."

Whatever words CJ had planned for this moment when he faced Gianna were suddenly lost. There simply were no appropriate words. I'm sorry for your loss seemed lacking on so many levels. "I'm so sorry, Gianna," he said. "I...."

She held up her hand. "I can only take so many *so sorrys* in a day, CJ, and from you I don't need to hear it." She moved toward the sofa on one side of her office and sat. CJ sat next to her.

"I can see it all over your face, as bad as if you'd lost Trish," she continued. "I admit that I was angry with you; however, it was because you were convenient. Tommy Clark killed her because of you, because of some twisted thing he had against you that was absolutely no fault of your own. As a matter of fact it was because of something you did right, because you were a good private investigator trying to right a wrong. I can't fault you for that, nor can I blame you. I am still angry, no doubt, and will be for a long time, but I've learned to redirect my anger to where it belongs, on Tommy Clark."

She stood and walked over to the window. "I'm a criminal attorney, CJ, sworn to defend the innocent and the guilty without prejudice. I've always believed in the phrase, innocent until proven guilty." She turned around and looked directly at CJ. "Tommy Clark was deserving of death. I'm glad that you killed him. My only wish is that I could have had the opportunity to pull the trigger myself." With that she turned back to the window.

"You and my sister are the only people who will ever hear those words come out of my mouth."

CJ nodded to her back. "I understand."

"I hope you do, because I will forever deny that I ever said them."

She pulled a Kleenex out of a fancy box on her desk, dabbed at her eyes and returned to where she'd been sitting. "I'm running out of time so let's talk business. I came to your aid pro-bono when you were in jail. Now I ask the same courtesy from you."

"Name it."

"Alexandria's father walked out of their lives five years ago, at least that's what I think he did. Alexandria's mother, my sister, thinks otherwise, that something happened to him."

"Why would she think that?" CJ asked.

"He gambled; got in over his head. She thinks someone killed him and buried his body somewhere."

"If he owed money, what would be the advantage in killing him?" CJ said.

"Exactly."

"Has she ever been contacted by anyone wanting her to make payment on his debt?"

"Not that I know of." She reached across her desk and picked up a white envelope. As she handed it to him she said, "This is the information you'll need. My sister's number, friends, business associates, etcetera."

"I'll do everything I can."

"When I say pro-bono, I'm referring to your time only. If you have expenses, such as travel to Indiana, or anywhere for that matter, I expect to be billed. Is that clear?"

"Certainly."

"No stone unturned."

"You want him found no matter what."

"Exactly. There's no rush, though. Alexandria's funeral is in two days. If he walked out, he doesn't deserve to be there. If he's dead it won't make any difference. Take the time you need to be with your family. Get started when you're ready. Give my sister a couple of weeks, though, to get through all this."

"Thank you, Gianna. I'll get started toward the end of the month."

"Is Trish going to go back to school?" she asked.

"She says no, but I'm pushing her to transfer down here. The death of her friend and then how she was treated has left a bad taste in her mouth. Stella and I are going to fly up and gather her belongings and then either bring her car back or sell it. That'll depend on whether the locals will release my car or not."

"The University of Arizona will be good for her, especially with family around," Gianna said.

"She'll have to deal with her mother, though."

"Things will work out as they should."

"Maybe."

"I understand there might be something brewing between you and Stella," Gianna said, her voice taking on a happier note. "There may be a wedding in the future?"

CJ's jaw dropped open. "Where did you hear that?"

"Sorry, I cannot divulge my sources."

"We're kicking around the notion, but no plans have been set."

"Whatever. I expect to be on the guest list."

CJ stepped out of the office complex and breathed in the humid air, a somewhat foreign concept in Tucson. A series of Southern Arizona monsoons had rumbled through Pima County during the night and the morning air had that fresh, clean feel.

CJ took another deep breath and returned to the thoughts he'd been having while waiting for Gianna, that of giving up the PI practice, surrendering his license. For right now he'd put the notion aside and do this thing for Gianna. Meanwhile he had to eat, and so did Stella. He really didn't want to tap into the inheritance money anymore. In addition to the two new clients, Stella had told him that there were a couple of inquires on his answering machine. He had yet to listen to those. He'd also have to get back to city hall to ensure Desert Investigative Services was still on the subpoena call list. He'd need to get his gun back from police custody. He wondered what kind of paperwork nightmare that'd be. Josh was returning to Denver in a few days and CJ still had his Glock. He felt under his shirt to where it rode comfortably on his hip. Maybe Josh would let his dad keep it for a while. In the past CJ only carried his weapon when he was serving subpoenas or thought he could possibly enter a dangerous situation. Now he found he couldn't go out the door without it.

Stella had watched him put it on as he was dressing, before going to the office and then meeting with Gianna. She didn't say anything about the gun, but she did make the comment about the shrink. He knew it wasn't rational to have the need to carry it.

He touched it again.

It was time to get back to work.

Maybe he'd go see that shrink.

Or maybe he wouldn't.

Gianna had it right. Tommy Clark was deserving of death.

****

Thank You...

...for reading *Deserving of Death*. If you enjoyed this book, please consider the next book in the CJ Washburn, PI series, *Sailing into Death*. Alexandria's father walked out of her and her mother's lives five years ago. Now Alexandria has been murdered. Her killer is dead; case closed. Her father deserves to be told, but first, he must be found. Leave no stone unturned, CJ is told. Find him no matter what. From Tucson, Arizona to Fishers, Indiana to St. Petersburg, Florida, he follows the leads only to find himself handcuffed to a table in a St. Petersburg Police Department interview room in front of Detective Parker DuPont. The charge: Murder. In fly Special Agent Joshua Washburn, CJ's son, and Stella Summers, his fiancé and partner. With the FBI, HLS, Interpol and who knows what else involved, can CJ and Stella figure out what it all has to do with Alexandria's father being born in the middle of the Battle of the Bogside in Derry, Northern Ireland in 1969? And what's the United Irish Republican Army doing in Florida?

And now, the first two chapters of *Sailing into Death...*

Chapter 1

Clinton Joshua Washburn–CJ to his friends, Clint to his fiancée, Clinton only to his mother–stared at the man standing before him. *Sales Associate* the badge read. Roger Miller it also read. CJ considered commenting on the name, whether he'd ever heard of "King of the Road" or "Dang Me" or "You Can't Roller Skate in a Buffalo Herd." He then wondered if Sales Associate Miller even knew who the King of the Road was, likely a toddler when the

Nashville singer, Roger Miller, died. Of course, CJ knew better than to make fun of someone's name. It'd been nearly two decades since he'd dropped his use of Clinton in favor of CJ to keep the hecklers off his back.

"How may I help you, sir?" Miller said, smoothly turning about so as to come alongside CJ. "Looking for a gift for your wife or girlfriend? You've come to the right place. You or she, or both, must have great taste as these are the most popular lingerie ensembles in the store, the entire mall for that matter, maybe all of Tampa."

CJ turned his head away from the sales associate as though admiring a sexily clad mannequin and rolled his eyes.

"Any woman would *die* for the opportunity to slide into bed in one of these," Miller said, stroking the fabric on the mannequin, "especially if she was sliding in next to her man."

"How much?" CJ asked, if for no other reason than to deflect the man's spiel before he got more personal.

"We've got this little piece priced special for the weekend at only $219.99. Can I gift wrap that for you?"

CJ exited the mall empty-handed. When he'd picked up the rental at the airport he'd decided to make the gift selection his first project because he knew that once he started focusing on the investigation, he'd forget, or he wouldn't remember until he was in route back to Tucson, having to pick up something from the Atlanta Airport mall. No matter how nice it would be, she'd somehow know. There was no way he was going to get Stella an airport gift. No way!

He started the car and thought about what brought him to the west coast of Florida on a job that was paying nothing but expenses. Contrary to what he would have suspected, business had been good since the serial killer fiasco four weeks back. Maybe it had to do with his name and picture in the news as being the individual who was, first, the prime suspect and then who later shot and killed the cop who turned out to be the killer of eight young women. CJ didn't have much choice at the time. The cop, one Tommy Clark, confessed his crimes while squeezing the life out of Stella with a deadly chokehold, his brother pressing a gun to CJ's daughter's temple. CJ didn't flinch when the opportunity presented itself. He put a bullet through Tommy's eye. The resulting publicity had clients coming out of the woodwork to the point that CJ had to turn people away, some of whom seemed as crazy as Tommy Clark.

It was all because of a vendetta that Clark had against prostitutes and then women in general and then CJ. The Clark brothers were insane, no doubt about it, the result of dysfunctional and abusive childhoods, according the slew of criminal psychologists that popped up on every news network.

But that was all over, an ugly chapter closed and gone; at least it would be gone if everyone would just leave him alone about it. Stella and Trish continued to suggest that he seek counseling. The more they picked at him the more he dug in his heels. They attended counseling themselves, sometimes together. He understood that. Hell, his daughter was kidnapped twice and then watched her father kill her kidnapper. Trish was still a kid, only 21-years-old. His little girl. It probably screwed her head up good. And it was hell on Stella, too. The two of them had been through a lot and the counseling seemed to be helping them.

But he was fine. Tommy Clark deserved to die and CJ just happened to be in the position to pull the trigger. Not one person that he talked to disagreed. What should he need counseling for? He did the right thing.

As the air conditioner pulled the temperature down in the rental, CJ paged through the folder he had on Douglas Rothbower, the brother-in-law of Gianna Onassis, CJ's attorney and biggest client. CJ was her number one private eye. While in the throes of the Tommy Clark fiasco CJ had landed in jail three times. Gianna came to his aid for two of those, pro-bono, only to have Tommy target and kill her niece, Alexandria Rothbower. It was the day that they found her body that CJ put the bullet in Tommy's head. The death of many of the women

Tommy killed weighed heavy on CJ, but none more so than Alexandria. Tommy went after her only because of CJ, and Gianna knew that, but she didn't blame him... much.

CJ still carried a heavy burden of guilt.

He thought about the meeting he'd had with her two days after her niece was murdered. She was dressed in black, her meeting with CJ her last stop before departing to escort her niece's body home to Indiana.

"I'm running out of time so let's talk business," she'd said. "I came to your aid pro-bono when you were in jail. Now I ask the same courtesy from you."

"Name it."

"Alexandria's father walked out of their lives five years ago, at least that's what I think. Alexandria's mother, my sister, thinks otherwise, that something happened to him."

"Why would she think that?" CJ asked.

"He gambled; got in over his head. She thinks someone killed him and buried his body somewhere."

"If he owed money, what would be the advantage in killing him?" CJ asked.

"Exactly."

"Has she ever been contacted by anyone wanting her to make payment on his debt?"

"Not that I know of. Reason her theory seems off to me." She reached across her desk and picked up a white envelope. As she handed it to him she said, "This is the information you'll need. My sister's number, friends, business associates, etcetera."

"I'll do everything I can."

"When I say pro-bono, I'm referring to your time only. If you have expenses, such as travel to Indiana, or anywhere for that matter, I expect to be billed. Is that clear?"

"Certainly."

"No stone unturned."

"You want him found no matter what."

"Exactly."

And so now here CJ was, following a lead to Florida, the only viable lead he'd come up with during his trip to Indiana the week before.

Three weeks after Alexandria's funeral, CJ had visited Gianna's sister, Kassandra, in her Indiana home, the home deserted, voluntarily or otherwise, by her husband and then hollowed out with the tragic loss of her daughter. When he called on her he found a wife alone and broken, a mother forever in mourning. CJ stood before her, wanting to be anywhere but there, looking at a woman in desperate need of help. Aged beyond her years,

Kassandra thanked CJ for coming, offered him coffee or water, obviously out of gracious habit, for she appeared to fear that he would accept. He thanked her and declined, asked questions, got no answers and a flood of tears. She said she'd wished Gianna hadn't sent him, that it was a waste of his time.

"Your sister says that you think he might have met foul play; that he might be dead."

Kassandra had sighed, wiped at her tears and then apologized. "I was angry back then, said some things I probably shouldn't have said, like I hoped he'd gotten himself killed. I may have thought or may have even wished that he did, but I really had no reason to believe it to be true."

"Then you do think he is alive," CJ had said to her.

"I assume he is."

When he left her home CJ doubted that much would come of the two names and phone numbers he was able to force out of her, but one must investigate everything, follow every lead as though it would be the case breaker. Although it didn't break the case, one name did lead CJ in the direction suspected by Gianna and sort of confirmed by Kassandra, that Douglas Rothbower simply walked away from his family and his job. Reason... unknown or unwilling to say. The source was Douglas' best friend, Paddy McLane. CJ found him at *Paddy's Irish Pub* in Indiana.

"I couldn't o' asked for a better friend," Paddy had told him in a thick Irish brogue.

"Why did he leave?" CJ asked.

Paddy shrugged. "Can't really say."

"Don't know or won't say?"

"You have any Irish blood in you, Mister Washburn?"

"Can't say that I do," CJ admitted.

"Then you shant know of the thick blood of Irish friendship, now do you? It's as thick as our brogue, you see; thick enough to stand a fork on a hot, windy day."

"That's pretty thick," said CJ.

"You got a friend like that, someone who, as you police type like to say, has your back?"

CJ thought about Detective Dan Payne, his best friend in Tucson. "Yes, I do."

"Well, with us, we have each other's back, front and sides. A man, you see Mister Washburn, with an Irish heart takes care of his friends..." he paused for a long time and then added, "and his family."

CJ just looked at him, trying to read the deeper meaning in his words. "Are you saying that Douglas Rothbower was Irish?"

"You don't know?"

CJ leaned in closer. "Know what?"

"Doug was pure Irish. Don't let the name fool you."

CJ sat back. "Rothbower?"

Paddy held up his hand. "No. That is German. Doug was born of an Irish mother in Ireland and was presented with the name Douglas O'Reilly. She supposedly died when he was three days old."

"Supposedly?"

"Aye. Can't say for sure... word of mouth you see. Anyway, the father could not be found. So the baby, in some underhanded, under-the-table deal, was adopted by a couple of wealthy Americans by the name of Rothbower and brought to Chicago. The rest, as they say here in your country, is history."

"The rest may be history, Paddy, but there are some interesting questions. Did Doug know any of this? When did he find out?"

"Can I buy you a pint o' Guinness, my friend?" Paddy said, looking down at the half consumed soda in front of CJ.

CJ's gut response was to decline, however, he had to remind himself that he was a private investigator, not an on-duty officer of the law. He also had a hunch that Paddy was not finished talking, had additional info to provide. He just needed a little more time and maybe a little more lubrication.

"Thank you, Paddy. I'd like that."

Paddy held up two fingers to the barmaid and said, "A couple o' pints of the black stuff." In just over a half minute they had two foaming mugs of dark beer.

CJ pointed to his mug. "Black stuff?"

"The finest Guinness that'll ever pass your lips." Paddy drank down a quarter of his and then said, "Have you ever been to Florida, Mister Washburn?"

"We be Guinness-drinking buddies now, Paddy. You can call me CJ."

Paddy slapped him on the shoulder. "CJ! A fine name. What does the C stand for?"

CJ looked at him for a long time and then admitted, "Clinton."

Paddy threw back his head and laughed. "No wonder you go by CJ." He took another swig of his beer. "Again I ask, have you ever been to Florida?"

"I can't say that I have," CJ said.

"Well, if you ever get down in the area of Tampa, you need to visit St. Petersburg. You'll find a couple o' Irish pubs worth looking up. One is much like this one here in which you be enjoying a fine Irish lager."

"St. Petersburg?" CJ said.

"Aye. St. Petersburg. That's all I have to say about that. Now don't let that Guinness go flat on ya, CJ."

CJ took a swig.

"By the way," Paddy said, "Doug knew all along he'd been adopted. He didn't learn of the sordid details until five or six years ago."

After checking out the other name and phone number given to him by Kassandra, which led him to poking around Douglas' old work place, to no avail, CJ returned to Tucson. With Stella's help he typed 'Irish Pubs St. Petersburg Florida' into Google. St. Petersburg had several, one of which was called *Paddy McGee's Irish Pub*. Its website banner displayed the same slogan in the same Irish-like font that CJ had seen hanging over the bar in *Paddy's Irish Pub* in Indiana.

WHERE YOUR FRIENDS ARE OURS, AND OUR FRIENDS ARE YOURS

"...one much like this one here..." Paddy McLane had said when he recommended the Irish pub in St. Petersburg. CJ didn't believe in coincidences.

Chapter 2

CJ drove along Bay Shore Drive, finding it hard to keep his eye on traffic while stealing glances at the single and double masted sailing yachts moored on both sides of one pier after another. There must have been hundreds of them of all different sizes. He'd never seen anything like it.

He turned east onto 1st Avenue–what appeared to take him to where he could view the yachts closer–noted *St. Petersburg Sailing Center* on the right and then St. Petersburg Marina to the left. Choosing neither, he went straight into *Demens Landing Park* where he parked and got out. For the next hour he walked, gazing upon the yachts with mast after mast pointing to a cloudless sky. He watched people coming and going with coolers and packs, many dressed in sailing attire, others in well worn shorts and T-shirts, smiles on their faces, laughter in the air. He looked across the harbor where more yachts came and went, feeling like a kid in his first candy store, but with no means to try a sample. He wondered what it would take to learn to sail.

After a time he exhaled a lungful of air and turned away. He was a landlocked landlubber, always had been, always would be. He knew nothing about this life, suspected in any case that it was too rich for his blood. He started the car and looked once more out at the masts jutting into the air and thought about Stella, wondered if she'd enjoy sailing. Maybe, when they got married, they'd go sailing for their honeymoon.

After another sigh he entered the address to the Irish pub into the GPS and headed out.

Paddy McGee's Irish Pub was little more than a half dozen blocks from where CJ had been admiring the sailboats. A few cars littered the parking lot just shy of 4:00 in the afternoon. CJ stepped through the entryway and stopped. As he waited for his eyes to adjust to the dark interior, a young woman breezed by.

"*Céad míle fáilte!*" she said. "Welcome to Paddy McGee's; have a seat anywhere and I shall be right with you," she added and then was gone. CJ approached the bar and sat. He looked at the menu and drink specials until the young woman appeared in front of him. "What can we do for you today, me friend?"

"Kade meal... whatever you said. What does it mean?"

"*Céad míle fáilte*. It means, 100,000 welcomes."

"Ah." CJ pointed at a board that read *Daily Specials* and said, "What's a *Car Bomb*?"

"Tis a bit early for that, I should think."

"I don't necessarily *want* one, just curious."

"We give you a pub glass o' Guinness stout, half full, and a shot glass o' Irish Whiskey and Irish Cream. You then carefully drop the shot glass into the stout and in the blink of an leprechaun eye, drink it all down before the cream curdles."

CJ noted her grin, wondered if the brogue was real. "Sounds a bit out of my league." He pointed to the specials board again. "I'll have the $7 Angus burger and Guinness draught."

"Aye. Fine choice me friend." A minute later when she presented him with the draught, she said, "Burger in five. Obviously you're new to Paddy McGee's. What brings ya to our fine establishment?"

"For one, I'm hungry. Been a long day flying."

"Arms must be tired."

He chuckled. "You also were recommended by Paddy McLane in Fisher's, Indiana."

"*Paddy's Irish Pub.* Paddy's cousin Paddy. You a regular of Irish pubs? A reviewer of fine Irish pub grub maybe? If so I'll tell Paddy to spice your burger up a bit, throw in some chips on the house."

"Sorry. Not a food critic. Is that Paddy McGee himself doing the cooking?" CJ nodded toward a middle aged guy working over a grill down at the end of the bar.

"Aye, tis he."

"I'd appreciate a chat with him when he has an opportunity."

"And who shall I say tis beggin' for his attention?"

CJ pulled a card from his pocket and handed it to her. "CJ Washburn."

She looked at the card. "Private eye, aye, Mister Washburn? Haven't had one in here before, least not one who'd admit it. Arizona? Indiana? Now Florida? Must be important."

"Every case I pursue is important to someone."

"Aye. Very true." With that she walked back to the grill and handed the card to Paddy McGee. He glanced toward CJ, said something to the girl and pocketed the card. When she returned she said, "Why don't you make yourself comfy in one of the booths? Paddy will join you with your burger in short order. I'll make sure he throws in an order of chips even though you're not a critic."

"You just never know. I might want to moonlight as one if I can be bribed with food." CJ picked up his Guinness, thanked her with a wink and then made his way to a booth well away from other patrons.

CJ sipped at his Guinness and thought about Stella. He visualized the two of them on a yacht in white boat shoes, white shirts and shorts, hair blowing in the breeze, his hand on the helm, sails and shirt sleeves billowing as they tacked along the surface of a mildly choppy sea. He had to admit, though, that he wasn't sure what it meant to tack. He was more and more wanting to find out.

"Mister Washburn."

CJ looked up as his burger and chips were placed before him. The man stuck out his hand and CJ took it. "CJ, please."

"CJ. I'm Paddy McGee. Welcome." He slid into the booth across from CJ. "I understand my cousin sent you me way."

"In a way, yes," CJ said. "During a chat I had with him a week back he mentioned that if I ever got down this way I ought to look you up."

"Me cousin tis like that. Always trying to send business me way. I often try to do the same by him. Only a week ago, is that so? I spoke with Paddy about a week ago as well and it seems to me he might have mentioned you."

"Then you know why I'm here."

"Aye, I do. Something about searching for Douglas Rothbower. Don't know how I can be o' much help. I don't know o' Douglas being around here. You may have wasted your time... and your money. Me cousin was just being kind to recommend me establishment. You maybe became a bit confused when he mentioned St. Petersburg in the same conversation as was mentioned Mister Rothbower."

"Tis odd," CJ said, "that you and your cousin should discuss Douglas Rothbower when, apparently, the name holds no importance to you."

"I didn't say that the name doesn't hold importance, Mister

Washburn. We are a close family. Me cousin and I talk frequently. When I last spoke with him he mentioned that a PI had been to see him, looking for his best friend who went missing five years ago. I knew Douglas, met him many years back when visiting up in Fishers so it was not that unusual for Paddy to mention your visit, that after five years there was someone looking for him." He took a swig from a bottle of water he had brought over with him. "Me cousin cares about his friend and, therefore, so do I. That's the importance to me, Mister Washburn, but I know nothing of his whereabouts."

"Did your cousin by chance mention why I'm looking for him?"

"No, can't say that he did. You and Douglas were mentioned just in passing. It must be mighty important to have someone like yourself chasing about the country. Wife suddenly desperate to find her husband I gather?"

A memory of CJ's meeting with Kassandra Rothbower flashed through his mind. She'd looked broken, but how much of that was losing her daughter? Did he just assume she was still mourning her husband's disappearance?

"In addition to the wife, Douglas had a daughter, Alexandria," CJ said. "She was killed about a month ago. The family felt it important to find Douglas. He has a right to know."

Paddy sat back, the shock evident on his face. "That is awful. How did it happen?"

"She was murdered."

He shook his head. "Most dreadful. As a father myself..." he looked away for a brief few seconds and then back at CJ, "I understand. However, I'm afraid I cannot help you. I do not know o' Doug's whereabouts."

CJ had followed Paddy's eyes to the barmaid and now sat back and considered the man, the typical image of the owner of an Irish pub; round face, red hair, rosy cheeks, a tad robust with a bit of a potbelly. Instead of a bottle of water he just needed a beer mug and a pipe to make the picture complete. The barmaid was his daughter, CJ concluded. This was a family business.

"Well," CJ said, "to avoid wasting a trip I may just indulge myself with a little tourist time. I've never been sailing. You have any recommendations along that line?"

"Sailing?"

CJ sensed that Paddy was relieved by the change in topic.

Paddy snorted. "Never been myself, never even considered it. Prefer something with a motor. I'd never trust the wind."

"But they do have motors from what I can tell, in order to get in and out of the harbor, and as backup I imagine," CJ said.

"Aye, they do, and that makes for an interesting point. Why all the trouble to install and put up and down the sails if ya have to put a motor on it anyways?"

"Save on fuel?"

"From what I can see, those who can afford to keep one of those yachts, can afford the fuel for a real boat."

CJ laughed.

"Look up *Bay Shore Charters and Sailing School.* They might be able to answer your questions about lessons and all that. Go straight east from here until you hit the water. You can't miss them."

CJ wrote it down. "Thanks."

"Well, I'll leave you to your fine Angus burger. I've got more cookin' a waitin'."

CJ pulled out a another business card and pushed it across the table. "I'll be in town until Saturday. Give me a call if you think of anything."

"Where are you staying?"

"The Hilton over on 1st."

"Hilton Bayfront. I know of it. Nice place." Paddy pushed the card back at CJ. "I have your card already." He shook CJ's hand. "Nice meeting you, CJ. The luck 'o the Irish be with you."

CJ took a bite from his burger and then turned to be able to gain a better view of the establishment. Another waitress had apparently arrived, an older woman. Paddy's wife maybe or an employee clocking in before *Happy Hour* starts up, he surmised. He watched her for a bit, noted how she seemed to be in charge of the younger girl. He considered the resemblance between the two. *Mom*, he concluded and then glanced over at Paddy. He was scraping the grill with one hand, the other pressing a phone to his ear.

Curious, CJ thought. When Paddy had referred to Douglas Rothbower as Doug, CJ wondered if it was a slip. There also seemed to be a lot more shock than CJ had expected when he mentioned that Alexandria had been murdered. Maybe Paddy knows Douglas better than he lets on.

Paddy put his phone away, glanced at CJ and then bent over his kitchen tasks.

* * * *

About the author

James Paddock is the author of numerous mystery and suspense novels, an inspirational novella and an anthology of thirteen of his best short stories. Born and raised in the Big Sky Country of Montana, he now resides in West-Central Florida with his wife, Penny. Readers may learn more about him and his work, visit his blog or correspond with him on his website at www.JamesPaddockNovels.com.

Made in the USA
Columbia, SC
08 November 2021

48462173R00186